THE RESISTANCE GIRL

JINA BACARR

Boldwood

First published in Great Britain in 2020 by Boldwood Books Ltd.

A CIP catalogue record for this book is available from the British Library.

Paperback ISBN 978-1-83889-376-7

Large Print ISBN 978-1-83889-796-3

Ebook ISBN 978-1-83889-378-1

Kindle ISBN 978-1-83889-377-4

Audio CD ISBN 978-1-83889-374-3

MP3 CD ISBN 978-1-83889-793-2

Digital audio download ISBN 978-1-83889-375-0

Boldwood Books Ltd
23 Bowerdean Street
London SW6 3TN
www.boldwoodbooks.com

To all the brave and daring women of the Resistance... may their stars shine bright in the annals of history.

SYLVIE

A DAY IN THE LIFE OF A FRENCH FILM STAR

Paris

1943

I slide out of the shiny, black Mercedes-Benz with two miniature swastika flags waving in the breeze. I feel a tug at my heart when I'm back here in the old neighborhood in the IIe *arrondissement* filled with age-old *ateliers*, workshops devoted to the art of making beautiful things. A creative spirit lives on here from the days when workers crafted exquisite décor for the aristocracy. Golden doorknobs, Chinese silk wallpaper, gilded wood paneling.

I inhale the smell of freedom born here in the Faubourg Saint-Antoine during the Revolution. Now the Germans occupy Paris and it remains bottled up.

Waiting to uncork.

The tension in the air makes me tighten my gut as I take in the familiar sights of the narrow passageway. The vine-covered walls, cobblestones polished with the patina of footsteps from the past, curious faces sneering at me through multi-paned windows, telling me I'm not welcome.

I feel like a crushed rose in a bouquet.

Still, I can't help but relive the days when I was young and innocent to the ways of politics.

It's not something I'm proud of, but I can't ignore being chosen as one of Goebbels' select few in French cinema.

Not if I want to survive.

Before I can take a breath, the Nazi staff car is surrounded by an unruly crowd. I wasn't expecting a welcoming committee.

Or *not* so welcoming.

Banging dented pots. Waving a dead fish. Holding their noses. I feel a rising frustration, not to mention a great hurt, at their indignation, but I can't let anything sway my mission. Or do anything that looks suspicious. I have a message to deliver right under the nose of the SS officer breathing down my neck. Besides, you never know who's watching you.

I smile big, put my game face on. Play to the crowd. After all, I *am* an actress.

'Bonsoir, mes amis, je suis Sylvie Martone...'

'We know who you are,' I hear from the crowd.

'We don't want you here.'

The mood gets ugly when someone spits on the toe of my elegant black pump.

I grit my teeth and ignore it, knowing my leather-soled shoe is another reminder of the hated German occupiers and the pain and sacrifice forced upon Parisians. I'm well aware they don't have enough to eat, they're obligated to observe curfews, and they patch the soles of their shoes with varnished wood.

Unlike me.

I dine at the Hôtel Ritz, move about the city freely, and sport haute couture high heels courtesy of the studio wardrobe department. New leather shoes are impossible to come by since the Germans requisitioned millions of pairs from the shops and boutiques to send to the *Vaterland*, a phrase I hear often from my handsome escort.

Captain Karl Lunzer. An SS officer from Berlin, decorated hero to hear *him* tell *it*, avid sportsman, and trusted aide to a top Nazi

Wehrmacht commander stationed here in Paris. He wears his status well as an officer in a finely pressed, grey-green uniform along with a Luger pistol in his belt, and black leather gloves. A tall, lean man with his bright blond hair cut so short on the sides it bristles. He has a fetish for carrying a polo whip with a brown leather handle, which he is quick to use at the slightest provocation.

He's glued to my side like a postage stamp I can't get rid of. I pretend not to notice the spontaneous gesture of defiance on my poor shoe. Karl is not so forgiving.

'Get back in the motorcar, Sylvie. It's not safe for you here.'

'Don't be ridiculous, Karl,' I toss back at him, then grab a tied bunch of yellow daffodils from the leather seat of the luxury motorcar parked near the carriage gate. I keep my smile big but my voice low so only he can hear me. 'These are my fans.'

'I must *insist, Liebling…*'

I pat his arm and then wet my lips. 'I'm not going anywhere.'

It takes every ounce of self-restraint I have left to keep smiling, not lash out at my old neighbors for putting my mission in jeopardy. The bigger I smile, the more tension I feel, my body vibrating with a familiar anxiety, similar to what comes over me when someone forgets their lines and I have to improvise. And do it fast.

But this is no movie set.

The fools. Don't they know the whole lot of them could be shot?

I quiet my breathing, sway my shoulders to catch Karl's eye, knowing that although he exhibits meticulous manners around me, he's an SS officer known for inflicting justice on anyone who challenges his authority. I cringe, remembering earlier today when we rushed out of *Aux Deux Magots* café after raising a toast to the premiere later of my new film, *Le Masque de Velours de Versailles* (The Velvet Mask of Versailles), his Nazi cohorts downing beer after beer. I couldn't ignore the note slipped under my plate at the café demanding my immediate attention.

The flower of the day is yellow daffodils.

I froze. The color of danger.

A change of plans. I couldn't let my fear show, alert Karl anything was amiss. The late afternoon sun cast the perfect light on my skin, my black Fedora cocked at a right angle as I smiled and asked the dashing lieutenant sitting across from me to film us with my home movie camera. A spontaneous whim on my part to allay suspicion from my actions and keep up my act in front of my German admirers.

. That only attracted *more* attention.

I couldn't escape the press eager to photograph France's '*beloved actress Sylvie Martone with her new Nazi friends*'. As a newsman snapped a photo of us posing in front of the silver Mercedes, all I could think about was, *Emil will love all this publicity.*

Then we raced off, headed to the private screening, but not before the SS officer harassed a poor soul crossing the street who failed to get out of the way, forcing the staff car to hit the curb. Without a backward glance, Karl bolted out of the car and struck the man's face with his whip, drawing blood. My adrenaline spiked, my sense of decency pushing me forward to help him, but the deprecating look on Karl's face stopped me. I did nothing. And for that I'm ashamed.

When Karl got back into the motorcar, he chatted about his last post in Warsaw as if nothing had happened. How ugly the city is now, in ruins from the fighting, and how grateful he is Hitler spared Paris and she retained her beauty. *Like you, Fräulein,* he was quick to add, kissing my hand and glaring at my breasts straining through the silk. I answered him with a wide smile, playing my part as his companion.

I didn't dare show any indication of the unpleasant sensation that hit me when he touched me. No wrinkling of my brow or teary eyes, only a forced smile. A difficult moment. He'd take any show of unpleasantness as a sign of my distaste for der Fuehrer, something I wasn't careful enough in the past to disavow. It took me a while to convince the captain I find being in his presence most attractive. I can't afford to let anything get in the way of that... even the natural changes my body is experiencing as a new life grows within me. A secret I must keep from Karl, my fans. I never expected this at thirty-three... quite an inappropriate time for it to happen to me, but I feel blessed.

I talked Karl into stopping at a flower market along the way so I could greet fans and boost awareness of my first film opening since the Occupation, then pass by my old apartment in the Faubourg Saint-Antoine before heading to *Le Grand Rex*. He seemed to genuinely enjoy mingling with the curious onlookers smiling and nodding at us. He took a daffodil from the bunch I bought and handed it to the elderly madame selling the blooms, telling her in decent French she reminded him of his *grand-mère*. I regarded him with a wistful sigh. For a moment, he seemed almost human. I soon wiped that attribute from his slate.

He is and always will be a Boche. A not-so-flattering term for the German occupiers.

Now, wary of jeopardizing my mission, my body shakes with uncertainty at how to deal with this spitting incident. My nerves are getting to me. My stomach plummets and I swallow down a bout of nausea. I have only myself to blame. I knew suggesting we come by here might put me in a heartbreaking dilemma.

I swallow hard, hoping Karl doesn't grasp the intensity of my toothy smile. Even when I don't feel it, I act the part, never forgetting how hard I worked to get here.

It's important to me to show the people of Paris I'm still their Ninette. That doesn't stop me from feeling like an imposter. Tears sting my eyes as I wonder what happened to the memorable character I created in silent film serials back in the late 1920s. I keep asking myself, how did I, Ninette, end up holding on to the arm of an SS officer? Nuzzling up to the Nazi swine like a she-hound in heat, the foul smell of his deeds rubbing off me and staining my soul?

These Parisians staring at me were once my neighbors when I was starting out in pictures. I lived here back then, at number 23, a three-story, white stone building with ivy climbing up the walls and a hand-carved blue door. They helped make me a star, drank rich espresso with me on cool mornings while they acted out their favorite scenes from my early films. Before I became box office gold, according to Emil, the director who discovered me as a teen.

Now they hate me.

Ten or fifteen hearty souls gather around me, staring, waiting for something dreadful to happen. I let my gaze wander over the motley group, knowing their foibles. Like the baker's wife with the big laugh, or the wizened cabinet maker, or the aging soubrette. And the teenage girl with freckles and glasses, her mother using her broom to sweep her daughter inside whenever a lad smiled at her. All waiting for the deadly reprisal of the SS, the smirk, the arrogance, followed by a keen shot from a Luger or a public beating. I feel the intensity of their foreboding, believing someone will be singled out to pay for the rash deed of spitting on my shoe. No one runs. That would define them as the guilty one.

Instead they wait.

Their angst hangs heavy in the air as I step forward, my arms filled with daffodils tightly bound with coarse string. I ignore the shiny spittle on my expensive shoe as I look up and down the cloistered passageway. The inhabitants of the Faubourg Saint-Antoine do their best to keep out the distasteful flags of the Third Reich, for whatever happens outside, German soldiers have no reason to wander in here. No brothels, no *tabac* shops. The street seems untouched by the Occupation, its secret passageways revealed behind black iron doors you only have to swing open... if you know the secret and, thank God, the soldiers in grey-green and black hobnailed boots don't.

'Shall I arrest them all, Sylvie?'

Karl brandishes his whip, cracking it against the stone wall washed clean of the blood of the revolutionaries. The sound is as chilling as if he were striking bare flesh. I abhor his show of power, like he's a bully on a school ground. The younger ones clap their hands over their ears, the women make the sign of the cross. The men shield them with their bodies.

I draw the line here.

'No, Karl,' I say in a clear voice, laying my hand on his arm. 'These are my fans... whatever happened is merely a mistake, *n'est-ce pas?*' I scan each face, my eyes pleading for them not to make things worse.

'We're not your fans anymore,' comes a daring speech from a woman with a baby on her hip, her blue apron soiled and dirty.

'I still like your movies,' spouts a girl of about fifteen. Her eyes sparkle with admiration for a moment, then she holds her nose and furrows her brows. 'I don't like *him*.' She points to Karl, who steps forward, forcing the girl to jump back into the crowd, who form a protective barrier around her.

'That girl needs to be taught a lesson.'

'She doesn't understand, Karl, how hard you and Herr Goebbels are working to keep the French culture alive.' There's no one more hated in Paris than Goebbels, the Minister of Propaganda for the Reich. Holding the bouquet with my black suede gloved hand, I continue. 'That's why we're here... to invite them to see my new film.'

'What's the name of your film?' The fifteen-year-old dares to peek her head out. I grin. Ah, the audacity of youth. I remember it well.

'*Le Masque de Velours de Versailles*,' I answer with an eagerness that lightens the mood. I project my voice to the crowd so everyone can hear me, keeping my tone upbeat, a bit sugary not squeaky. Like I'm doing a voiceover to promote my films. 'It's the story of a milkmaid in the Sun King's court who becomes a spy when she catches Louis' eye and then saves her little sister from a nasty sultan's harem.' Wild escapades of a heroine rising up against authority, exactly what movie-goers want these days. 'I hope you'll come to see it when it opens next week at the Gaumont.' Undaunted by the tension in the air, I dig into my jacket pocket, grab some tickets and wave them above my head.

'Oh, yes, please!' The perky girl with the glasses and freckles holds her hand out, but her mother grabs her by the arm and pulls her back.

'You ain't taking nothing from that woman,' she spews in a husky voice. Her square face is flushed, grey hair escaping from the plaid scarf wound tight around her head. 'She ain't the Sylvie Martone we used to know.' Her words are harsh, but her eyes betray disappointment and that hurts me the most. I've always prided myself on being an actress who can make an audience cry and bellow with laughter, who can incite intense anger as they stare at me up on the silver screen. But never disappointment in my performance... never walk away shaking their head. Now it's because of my acting ability they turn against me and therein lies the hurt.

I can't tell her the truth...

I leave the movie tickets sitting on a nearby wrought iron table, knowing full well the children will grab them after I'm gone. Behind me I hear—

Whispering. I know what they're thinking as I walk up to number 23 and knock on the weathered wood. Then again. No one answers. I turn. 'Where is Fantine?'

A rhetorical question. Only I know *why* Fantine won't answer the door.

'She's too ashamed to show her face, *mademoiselle...*' says the woman, leaning on her broom, 'with the likes of *him* stinking up the street.' Her proud, lined face sets into a sneer, her short, pudgy nose wrinkling with distaste.

I hear Karl snarl like a hungry tomcat.

My arms filled with yellow daffodils. I step forward when I see him reach for his Luger.

Not so fast.

If I have to play this part, I may as well use it to my advantage. These are *my* people even if they hate me. I'll not let him make them any more miserable than they already are.

'Please tell Fantine I brought these yellow daffodils to cheer her up.' My whole body is tingling though fatigued. I find it harder to keep up the pace I'm used to. I pray my hormones adjust and I don't make a fool out of myself. Though I'm thrilled with the changes within my body, it's got to remain my secret... I have to act the movie star, deal with the insolence of the crowd. They don't want me hanging around their neighborhood even if I own the apartment and hired a woman to take care of it.

A woman they adore. Fantine is a charitable ex-baroness, twice widowed with a raspy voice, a kind-hearted soul with a limp, giving them cheese she commandeers from the black market, watching their babies when they have to queue up for bread, always ready with a cheerful tune to lift their spirits.

No wonder she doesn't want to come out when her employer is hated so much, they say to themselves.

I fight to keep smiling, knowing why Fantine can't show her face, but they'll never know my secret.

'I'll place the daffodils outside for her.' I lay them on the neatly kept stoop. 'It's important she gets the flowers.'

'You may leave them, *mademoiselle*,' says the woman with the broom, 'only because they're for Fantine.'

'*Merci.*' I nod. I feel confident the blooms will remain undisturbed until a pair of large, steady hands removes them, the message received. A life depends on it. The locals would never reveal what happens here after curfew, thanks to the pride instilled in them since so many who fight against the Nazis call here home.

I grin, mission accomplished. I slip my arm through Karl's.

'Come, Karl, we'll be late for the premiere.'

Cheers at our departure, then more jibes tossed at me. By heckling me, my old neighbors in the working class district perform their parts well.

For that, I'm grateful. Or lives will be lost. Including the man I love.

As the big, silver Mercedes races through the winding streets on the Right Bank, I break into a sweat. I lean forward and hold onto the door handle as the touring car enters the traffic circle, then makes a sharp right onto the Boulevard Voltaire. My stomach turns... but I can't reveal to the handsome SS officer sitting next to me *why* I feel faint...

All that matters is, in his eyes I'm *Sylvie Martone, film star – and Nazi collaborator.*

I can never let him believe otherwise.

JULIANA

A ROAD NOT TRAVELED... TILL NOW

Los Angeles
Present Day

Rain splatters against the bay window echo my heavy pencil strokes.

I grip the number 5B drawing pencil so tight, the point breaks off.

I heave out a deep sigh that's got me so coiled up inside. I can't shake this unbearable loneliness that's swept over me, like I'm alone in the world without her. *Maman*. She was my whole world these past two years, my life taking a detour to care for her. The end came all too quickly, and I'd give anything to have more precious time with her, but I can't. I have to pick up the pieces and pretend I'm fine when I'm not.

She never judged; she was always there for me.

Now she isn't.

And it hurts. I was her round-the-clock caregiver but at the end when she looked into my eyes, she didn't know I was her daughter. She told the nurse before she died, 'She's the pretty lady who takes care of me.'

I denied the subtle changes in her personality for months. *Maman* (I always call her that since she was born in France) started showing signs two years ago, but I never expected the downward slide to happen so fast. I watched my kind, intelligent mother lose control of who she was, the blankness in her eyes, the unsteadiness in her walk. That was coupled with times of complete lucidity, brilliance almost, a portal in her mind opening for the briefest time to give me hope... then see it dashed when the door slammed in my face. Finally, my mother fell into a calm sleep... taking in oxygen through a tube from an ugly green tank I grew to hate because it was taking her from me... breathing slower... then slower... as if she knew the end was near.

Maman, how I miss you...

I want to tell her my news about my new job and I'm angry she's not here. No wonder my mind is wandering this morning like a spool of thread come undone. I feel like a lost chord without a song.

Sketching is my haven. A place I can call home, an anchor to find the road forward again.

Which is why I've spent the past hour fidgeting with this retro costume for an upcoming sixties TV drama, *Wings over Manhattan,* working on the design for the blue and white flight attendant uniform. I spend a long time thinking about a design before I pick up my pencil then sketch it quickly, the curves and lines appearing almost magically like an animated film clip.

My meet-up with the producer isn't for another two weeks. Yet I've got it into my head that I *have* to finish the sketch right away. A penance, I suppose, when I should be trying to move on.

I jam the pencil into the automatic sharpener, the eerie whir jarring my nerves. I could venture out into the rain to the art store and buy another one, but the idea of sloshing through LA streets that see rain twice a year isn't inviting.

Yet the longer I stare at the sketch, the more I need to share my feelings. I'm not into grief groups and I'm not close with the people from *Maman's* life before she retired to move in with me. I walked through her funeral last week like a puppet on strings, picking up one foot then the next but feeling numb inside. I have no family and few friends I can count on in my crazy world designing costumes for TV.

Apart from Ridge McCall who never left my side.

I can't help but smile, remembering how we met our first week of college when we bumped heads in the darkroom in photography class. I couldn't believe this incredible guy with the gorgeous smile noticed me when the lights were *on*. He had a hot reputation since he'd already racked up movie credits as a stuntman and had every girl in class drooling over his muscular bod. Imagine my shock when he went out of his way to sit next to *me* in class, and then when he picked me for his partner for field trips, saying I had a good 'eye' for color and style and I should follow my dream to be a costume designer. (He caught me doodling costume sketches in class.)

And then when he asked, would I mind riding on the back of his motorcycle?

I liked him right away and we ended up getting amazing shots on film from the beach to the desert and cutting up doing it. We became great pals, pulling pranks on each other, like hiding canisters of film or shooting goofy poses to loosen up our creativity. I was so busy working and drawing and studying, I never thought about *dating* him. We had too much fun together to screw it up. He'd listen to me talk about my crushes, I'd comment on the long list of girls impressed by the stuntman in the stonewashed jeans and tight tee with James Dean eyes. Somewhere along the way, we eased into being a comfy twosome.

We don't talk about our dating lives anymore.

I don't have one, not since I started taking care of *Maman*. No regrets there.

Ridge... I don't know. Maybe he's got a girl. If so, he doesn't talk about it. Either way, I'm lucky to have him for a best friend.

Maman always smiled when the handsome stuntman brought her fresh flowers and kept her mind busy extoling his exploits on film as a dashing swordsman or crashing a tank through a wall. I know she wondered about us, but I told her we decided long ago not to ruin a beautiful friendship by getting involved.

I pick up my cell to text him, pour out my heart to him like I've done for years when I need a strong shoulder to lean on, then put it down. *He's already done so much, walking me through the steps of* taking care of her affairs and sitting with me for a long while when we came back to the bungalow after the funeral so I wouldn't have to be alone.

I can't bug him. He's knee-deep working on a big archival assignment for a stock footage company with over a hundred years of film in its vaults, a gig he's worked long and hard to get. I respect that.

That doesn't help this bout of loneliness I can't shake.

If only I had family here... someone who knew *Maman*. Someone who'd laugh with me about how she'd let her glasses slide down her nose when she was happily surprised, or how she insisted on having a box of chocolate nonpareils on her birthday every year since the sweets reminded her of idyllic days growing up in a French convent outside Paris.

I've never been to France, always had a job since high school, including working as a tour guide at a major movie studio. I was born in California, but grew up speaking both English and French. I'm thirty-six and I know zilch about my Gallic roots.

I never thought about it till now.

Which brings me to the matter of *Maman's* possessions.

My study is like most parlor rooms in these 1930s-style Spanish bungalows on the West side. Built in a time when hanging multi-colored beads separated it from the main house, it's become a convenient storage room since I work on my laptop on the veranda on sunny days, or sit on the love seat under the bay window, steadying the old artist's wooden board I've had since college on bent knees.

My work habits make it easy for me to avoid this room. And what's in it: anything and everything that belonged to *Maman*, sealed up like holiday presents with perfectly aligned tape and shipped over from my mother's apartment in Santa Clara. Boxes that have sat here untouched, which saddens me.

When she first came to live with me, we talked about going through her things, but I could see she didn't want to, as if by opening these boxes she'd have to come face to face with the reality she was no longer that person. Worse yet, she may not have any memory of what she saw, and she'd feel empty inside. Even if memories are rose-colored, we cling to them because they give us pleasure as well as the courage to go forward in hard times.

If she couldn't remember, she'd have neither.

So I abided by her wishes to wait for the day when she felt strong enough to accept whatever she found. Waited for a day that never came.

I didn't have the heart to go through the boxes without her. I kept avoiding it, telling myself I was too busy with the day-in, day-out routine taking care of *Maman* with a strong mind but a lonely heart. As if by going through her things, I'd have to relive watching her fade away all over again. I know what her last wishes were regarding her personal things and I admit I've been remiss in carrying them out – something Ridge and I talked about yesterday over lattes at the gym not far from the studio.

'I worry about you since your mom died, Juliana,' Ridge said when I found him throwing quick jabs at a heavy punching bag. Tall, dark, gorgeous, engaging his entire body as he hit the bag like he was hell-bent on turning it into a pile of sawdust. Yet he was a man who sang lonesome cowboy songs off key, could lift twice his bodyweight, but also had a tender place for me in his heart I sometimes took for granted.

I felt guilty bugging him, but I needed to talk.

'I'm good, Ridge... sort of.' I straddled the black leather bench and put down the steaming mocha lattes I'd picked up while checking out the amazing abs on this man who works out every day at 6 a.m. like clockwork. 'I'm... well, confused.'

'Join the club. You're going through a big transition. Like me.' He punched the bag and the sweat rolled down his face and made his bare chest shine bronze and gold under the hot lights. I'm not immune to his appeal. I just don't go there in my mind. I don't want to be another groupie.

Ridge is a legend in the world of stunt work and the recipient of numerous awards for his contributions to the industry and high-risk stunts. He doesn't talk about himself, but it pains me to see how he's struggling to accept the fact that at forty, time is catching up with him. I've watched him perform on the set and the man is a warrior-god in action. When it's time to go to work, his head is in the game and he never gives up.

Last year he cut back on his stunt work to focus on his future (he's been in the business since he was sixteen). He's quick to admit you can only get set on fire or die by the sword so many times.

I couldn't believe it when he told me he had a new gig as a film archivist. It's been his dream for a long time to ensure the films high-lighting the greatest stunts from the early silents to the present aren't lost, but preserved for the next generation of stunt performers.

I've been so wrapped up in my problems with *Maman*, I didn't realize I'd gone into a strange shell of my own.

Which was why I'd showed up this morning. I needed a pep talk.

'For years, I ignored my fears,' Ridge continued, 'let the adrenaline override everything else. Pushed forward and got the job done.' He punched the bag so hard the sweat on his face spurted into the air. 'Then I got hurt and reality hit me like a steel drum. It took me a while to come to terms with my vulnerabilities.

'I'm not afraid to jump out of a plane or leap onto a moving train. I am afraid of letting down my team... and that means you, Juliana. You're always there for me when I do something stupid, or how you make me talk about something that happened on a shoot I don't want to talk about.

'I won't let you down now. You talked about how you've been avoiding letting go of the past, moving on. Don't run from your past, embrace it. The hardest part about doing a stunt is that moment before you make the jump. If you think too much about it, you'll make a mistake. If you get nervous, that's when you get hurt. Just do it... make your decision and go with it.'

My talk with Ridge about finding the courage to move on has fueled my energy in a new direction. I've put this off too long. So why not start on a rainy afternoon? I'm working on the designs for a show that takes place around the time *Maman* was a teenager. Maybe I'll get some inspiration from her for the uniform for my friendly skies attendant. I smile. I like that idea. As if she's helping me move on.

I push down the deep ache in my chest, heave out a big, cleansing breath. Then I put down my coffee cup and get to work.

It's time, *Maman*.

* * *

My mother, Madelaine Chastain, was just a baby when Paris was liberated in 1944, but the demure Frenchwoman always put off talking about her family when I asked her, waving her hand about like she was signaling someone unseen to go away lest they spill the beans. A ghost, perhaps. To my knowledge, *Maman's* family were all killed in the war. That didn't excuse her lack of *une famille* in my eyes. When I asked the faculty staff who came down for the funeral if she ever mentioned any relatives in France, they shook their heads. I admit I was too distraught over her death and exhausted from the toll caregiving took on me to go searching any further. I wonder if I should have. She must have *someone* I can write to, talk with about my mother's last few years, her downward spiral into a deep depression that made her believe she was a burden to me. She once said something I tucked away in my mind.

That I'd have enough to bear if I ever found out about 'her'.

Who she was talking about, I never figured out.

Maman never spoke about my grandparents, insisting they died in the war. As a teenager, I spent hours conjuring up a fantastic tale of them being Resistance fighters, brave partisans fighting the Nazis but making sure their daughter was safe with the nuns since they'd most likely be killed before their country was free again. I'd come up with various 'looks', but my favorite was a sketch of my grandmother outfitted in partisan chic – pencil skirt, silky cream blouse, knee-high, brown suede boots, and a bomber jacket cinched in at her waist. A deep navy beret pulled down over one eye, her lips bright with a sizzling red lipstick.

So unlike my mother. I often tried to get *Maman* to add a necklace or earrings to her ensemble, but she always pooh-pooed the idea, saying she was a convent girl at heart. After all, glam is my business. Giving actresses the right cut on a dress, the fit of a pair of jeans, the angle of a hat. The retired art history professor never deviated from her black suit, crisp white blouse, low pumps, and square glasses.

These memories of *Maman* and fantasies of my grandmother are all I have to cling to. I realize now I avoided a *lot* of things in my life because I was too busy following my dream of making it in Hollywood. In college, I was picked as the model for the movie studio tour ads, though I never saw myself as an actress or beautiful. The only thing I can lay claim to as anything interesting about my face is the deep dimple on my left cheek.

Ever since I was a kid I've loved to draw... stick figures in my mother's textbooks, making clothes for my Barbie, working on costumes for school plays. I do visual storytelling, designing costumes specific to that character and give it the cinematic flair to work on the silver screen.

Maman didn't understand my love for design or the movies. She loved her history books and her students and rarely talked about anything else. I never pressed her about where we came from and she seemed happy I didn't. My mother was such a private person, so careful with saying and doing the right thing, even her handwriting was precision perfect. I never wanted to look behind the curtain and see otherwise. No wonder I feel empty inside when it comes to knowing my roots. I suck in a sharp breath and take the plunge to find out.

Let the unpacking begin.

I take my time and rearrange the boxes I've kept stored here in my study. I do the smaller ones first, blowing off the dust coating the brown cardboard. Cutting the tape with scissors with a reverence that doesn't surprise me. Taking my time with each packed box as if *Maman* is watching me, nodding her head in approval.

I go through her possessions with a careful eye, my heart pounding, looking for clues about my roots in each box. Nothing yet... no wild revelations, but with every box I open, every memory I find helps me cope with her loss. Still, my curiosity tugs at me to find out more about her, to fill in the gap of where I came from. I'm delighted when I find a sealed box of letters written by my parents – I never knew it existed.

Maman told me years ago my father was American, but my parents never married. How they had this long-distance love affair that culminated when my mother came to America to have her baby. Me. After skimming several letters, I wipe away a tear, feeling the deep love between them, but there's no hint of my mother's family, like she was born without a past.

I find photos of me as a baby, then from my childhood since I grew up in a time before everything went digital. First communion, dressing up for Halloween, teenage angst years where I shied away from the camera. I love handling these glossy four-by-six prints, the color as vibrant as a scene out of Oz. Then I find old movie camera tapes I gave her of my trips to San Francisco and New York for location shoots, cities *Maman* loved to visit with me. Nothing here that says anything about her life before she settled in California except for a few letters in French. Letters from the convent where my mother lived until she met my father, signed by a nun named Sister Rose-Celine.

I put the letters aside, looking for something about my mother as a young girl. She was forty when I was born, she must have had a life before me, relatives somewhere... but nothing. Even her finances were straightforward: bills, savings, retirement checks every month. I admit I was pleasantly surprised when I discovered *Maman* left me a generous stipend which I'll save for a rainy day. Or that vacation I never went on. While my mind is flirting with the idea of tropical breezes and white, sandy beaches, I'm attracted to a square box that's different from the others. Elegant wrapping and neatly tied string with an elaborate knot. The box is inside a bigger box hidden under out-of-date clothes. A convent uniform. Grey, linen jumper, white blouse with a Peter Pan collar and short sleeves, light blue sweater. The scent of a lovely French perfume wafting from the closed-up box makes me sigh with delight. *Rose... then plum, is it? And raspberry...*

and a spice I can't identify. A provocative scent in stark contrast to the uniform.

Under the clothes, I find a thin box from *Aux Trois Quartiers* department store in Paris. *Ooh...* how very French. The old tape is yellow and crumbles between my fingers as I look inside. There, wrapped in an ivory lace veil woven with the most delicate design, I find a slim, burgundy velvet jewelry box. My hands tremble as I open it – my mother never wore jewelry.

Who does it belong to?

I open the jewelry box and discover a gorgeous, heart-shaped, diamond pin. With an arrow through it. And something else.

A photo of a striking platinum blonde that takes my breath away.

The startling moment makes me queasy. I have a queer feeling I'm looking at something I shouldn't, but I can't look away. The woman looks like a star from the era of classic films. An actress or model? The staging, pose, hair and makeup are very theatrical, as opposed to the look of high society. My gut – and experience – tell me this is a publicity still used in a press kit. I stare at the black and white photo. A woman bigger than life, a woman hypnotizing anyone under her spell. Gorgeous, wavy hair falling over a bare shoulder, a low-cut, slinky gown hugging her body, smoldering eyes that burn with a passion that speaks of forbidden nights... and unspoken desires.

I swear the woman is wearing the same diamond heart pin with an arrow through it I hold in my hand.

A coincidence? A funny itch crawls up my spine, making me tingle. *Or is it?*

I look through the box, but find no other photos. Who is this beautiful woman? I pride myself on my knowledge of stars of classic film, but I don't recognize her.

Why did *Maman* save the picture?

The imprint on the lower right corner indicates the photo was taken in Paris, most likely before the war and before my mother was born. Also, written in white ink is a number – most likely the photographer's index code since it's too long to be an address.

I turn it over and see an inscription on the back of the photo written in French:

To my sweet daughter, Madeleine. Someday you will know the truth.

I go into complete shock, hand shaking, heart pounding as I stare at the photo.

This gorgeous blonde with the seductive smile is my grandmother?

It can't be true. *Can it?*

I look again. Under the inscription she wrote *Ville Canfort-Terre, France* and the year 1949. *After* Paris was liberated. *After* my mother said her parents were killed.

Who is she? I realize I've stumbled across a secret I was never meant to find. That I had a glamorous grandmother who survived the war. What happened to her? And even more upsettingly...

Why did my mother lie to me?

3

SYLVIE

A STAR IS BORN

Ville Canfort-Terre, France
1926

A loud, roaring crescendo coming from the old church organ draws me
to sneak inside the stuffy movie theater. I'm missing the best part of the
film. The heroine is tied to the railroad tracks and is about to get run
over by a train... or a rogue sea captain is holding her tight in his arms
and proclaiming his undying love.

I slide my fingers over the lever at the backdoor entrance... and
giggle. It's unlocked. I pull down the lever when—

'Your ticket, madame,' a man grumbles behind me. Insistent,
coughing.

I turn, smile big, showing him my teeth smudged with burnt ash.
'It's me, *Monsieur* Durand... Sylvie.'

'Ah, but of course, my Sylvie...' He winks. 'I didn't recognize you,
mademoiselle.'

He's lying, but it's a game we play. '*Merci, monsieur,* what do you
think of my disguise?'

'Wonderful, Sylvie,' Claude Durand is quick to add. 'You're as good
as any actor I've seen in pictures.'

I strike a dramatic pose with my nose up in the air and wild hand gestures. He laughs. I like him. He's a good-hearted old soul who turns a blind eye to my escapades.

'Ah, you've got a fine talent for pretending, *mamselle*.' He lights up a Gauloise and draws it deep into his lungs. I frown. I wish he'd stop smoking; his cough is getting worse. 'I saw that in you the first time you snuck into my theater and tried to convince me your little sister was lost and had wandered in. You were... thirteen, *non*?'

'I was just a child then, *monsieur*.' I stick out my chest. 'Now, I'm a woman.'

His eyes turn serious. 'Even an old braggart can see you've got a real talent for mimicking those actresses up there on the screen, Sylvie. You're better than the lot of them. Be careful of those who'd take advantage of you. You're a beautiful girl and with that angel-white hair of yours hanging down your back in that long braid, you make an old man wish he were young.'

I feel my cheeks tint pink as I push back wisps of unruly hair sticking to my forehead and sling my braid over my left shoulder. 'You flatter me, *Monsieur* Durand, but I'm not interested in men of *any* age... only acting.'

He puffs on his cigarette, thinking. 'Then follow that road and don't look back, no matter where it takes you.' He exhales a perfect ring of smoke, then smiles. 'Now get on inside the theater before the picture is over. It's one of your favorites, *Mesdames en feu*.' He chuckles and opens the door of his private entrance then bows from the waist, inviting me in. 'Free of charge,' he insists, as always. I sometimes think he believes I'm his lost daughter. He's always warning me to watch out for 'bad men with pretty bedtime stories' promising me fame and fortune, but I don't mind because I know he speaks from his heart.

I can't get enough of going to the pictures. I cherish these moments sitting in the dark with the magical light coming from the projector behind me, wrapping me up in a spiritual place between dreams and reality. A place where I can be free in my thoughts. *And* my heart.

The Order of the Sisters of Benevolent Mercy took me in when I was *une petite jeune fille* of three when my mother had to give me up – a grand drama in itself, or so Sister Vincent tells me. I don't have any recollection of it and it's too late to ask my mother since she died in a fire afterward. All the records were destroyed.

I swear Sister Ursula, the Mother Superior, has been there that long.

She makes it her business to order me about; she has me working on my knees scrubbing the stone floors until they bleed, or burning my hands in hot water in the laundry. She's so crotchety and mean. I don't know why she hates me so much unless it's because my mother was an aristocrat.

She'll send me to my cell for days without food or water if she finds out I sneaked out today (I conned Sister Vincent), but the movie theater is where I come alive, acting out roles where I can lose myself. I find the challenge of becoming somebody else exhilarating, which is why I hobbled my way to the private entrance at the back of the Théâtre Durand with a hickory branch I found as a cane, the long, ivory lace veil Sister Vincent made for my Confirmation day when I was fourteen, draped over my head and shoulders (it's my favorite prop), and blueberry juice rubbed on my cheeks. Burnt chestnut leaves mixed with olive oil ring around my eyes for dramatic effect and *voilà*, I'm a *woman of an indeterminate age*, as Sister Vincent would say. I may be only sixteen, but motion pictures have taught me so much about *life*, I can play *anyone*.

Every time I say that, the sister smiles and rolls her eyes.

I love the jovial nun so much. She's kind and the reason I haven't run away from the convent – yet. She helps me slip away to the cinema, finding excuses to bring me with her when she goes into town to buy fresh lamb and apples and pears for the convent kitchen. I left her in the textile shop ordering silken and linen thread and pins to replenish the cupboards to make the beautiful handmade lace the sisters are known for.

Which gives me at least twenty minutes or so before she comes looking for me.

I rush into the darkness of the theater in my usual wild manner and bump into a large man standing off to the side near the stage. I can't help but sneak a peek at the stranger when he steps into the light streaming in from the creaking iron door. I get a good look at him. Heavyset, wearing a white Panama hat with a black satin band pulled down low over his face, a dark grey, pin-striped suit like I've seen in the gangster flicks.

The strong smell of his lit cigar makes me hold my breath.

'*Pardon, madame*,' he tips his hat, respectful. 'May I be of assistance?'

I giggle. He bought it. *Bon*. He thought I was an old lady.

Wrinkling my nose and completely in character, I say in a raspy voice, 'No harm done, young *monsieur*.'

I stifle a giggle and go about my way, limping for effect, knowing how you make an exit is just as important as your entrance. It is, I'm proud to say, a success. I'm curious why a patron would stand in the wings where he can't see the screen very well. The cozy theater holds about a hundred and fifty moviegoers and has a small stage platform in front of the screen for live acts.

I toss my braid over the *other* shoulder and forget about the stranger. I hover off to the side of the screen upstage where I'm nearly invisible in the dark. Once I see what's happening on the silver screen, I can't look away. A fancy party with beautiful people having such a lovely time flashes before my eyes. Flappers in beads and fringe and their beaux in black tuxes, smoking and flaunting champagne flutes and whooping it up at a supper club. We can't hear their laughter, but the organist loosens his collar, foot-stepping on the pedals, hands flying over the keyboard to keep up with the raucous goings-on up on the screen. His lively tune begs to be heard over the audience filled with rowdy kids, whistling and hollering.

It's too much for two elderly ladies. Shaking their heads, they get up and leave in a huff while I see a man sneaking a flask in the last row. I ignore them all. I *love* this film. I've seen it five times. I know all the parts.

I can't resist tossing down my fake cane and whipping my lace shawl around me in a saucy Spanish swirl though no one can see me in the darkness. I start tapping my black flats with the white-button straps on the wooden floor, saying the dialogue on the title cards between the frames I've memorized in a loud whisper (no one can hear me) while pushing away cigar smoke creeping into my face. I look over my shoulder and see the man in the Panama hat huddling with *Monsieur* Durand and pointing to me. I don't care. I don't care about *anything* but playing the part of the wild flapper.

I dance around the small stage in a tight circle, my derring-do shielded by the coveted black shadows hugging the screen in a cool embrace. Sweaty bodies, wild silent laughter... it's all there on the big screen... and I'm in it... yes, I'm *in* the scene. Losing control... loving it... lifting the skirt on my ugly, grey convent frock, not caring if my left garter wiggles down my leg and my tan cotton stocking with it. No one can see me in the dark... *Monsieur* Durand and the man in the Panama hat wouldn't be able make out more than my shadowy figure... and the first row of seats is far enough away I disappear in a blur... I'm dancing, acting out the lead role... filled with the exhilarating awe of being in the moment... reaching that pinnacle of complete loss of self where nothing can touch you, when you throw yourself down into the abyss and you become that character—

Till the reel of film breaks, thrusting the theater into a mesmerizing darkness.

The lights come on in a snap. Bright, insistent electric eyes beaming on everyone in the theater.

But none more insistent than on finding me. Spotlights. Hitting me in the eyes. *Me*, standing there like a puppet on stage with her strings cut. My cover of darkness blown. Holding up my skirt, revealing my bare thigh, my cotton stocking puddling around my ankle. And that ridiculous makeup I put on. I imagine my blue-red checks and the charcoal rings around my eyes glowing like the girl I saw in an old vampire film when *Monsieur* Durand ran a special showing before Lent last year. Scared me out of my drawers.

Now I'm scared out of my drawers again.

Because my secret's out. My *acting* secret.

Sure, I've seen kids snicker at me when I'm acting out scenes in the back of the theater, tossing their leftover rotten vegetables at me instead of the screen (*Monsieur* Durand forbids tossing smelly food at the stage, but everybody does it). It's one thing for me to let myself go and act in the dark when no one can see me, when no one can judge me, to fly high in my dreams. I always land back on my feet when the lights come on. But to expose myself in front of everyone like a tawdry fan dancer has set me on a new compass. That if I want to become an actress – and I do with all my heart – I can't hide anymore.

I have to face the audience. Show them what I'm made of. Do *something* to entertain them while ignoring my state of undress until *Monsieur* Durand changes the reel. So I do it. What I was born to do. I'll either make a complete fool of myself or find my footing as an actress.

I clear my throat, then go into a speech like I'm reading from a placard on the screen.

'The film will resume in a few minutes, *mesdames et messieurs...*' I begin with a booming voice and a grand gesture. 'Ladies, please remove your hats. Gents, no smoking please—'

'Ah, go home, Sylvie.'

'Yeah, go back to the convent where you belong.'

'You ain't no actress... *get out of here!*'

I bristle inside, wanting to cry at their insults, shut down and pretend none of this ever happened. I can't. It means too much to me. My soul has been crying out to act in front of an audience and though this is the most god-awful way to do it, I can't stop. I love the spotlight wrapping me up in a warm embrace, a hug that feels so good, giving me what I never get – attention just for *me*. As if I *am* somebody.

I don't back down even when I hear someone yell, '*Let'er have it!*'

I duck, but not fast enough. A big, juicy, rotten tomato hits me square on the shoulder, then another. I don't stop. I march up and down the stage dodging tomatoes, then a soggy cabbage lands at my feet. I keep going, acting out the scene in the film as

I memorized it, reciting every line on the title cards without taking a breath... giving it my all... the organist getting into the spirit and piping out a lively tune, keeping up with me, beat by beat.

Then the lights go out and the screen behind me lights up. And the film resumes.

But do I get off the stage? No, the rush of doing what I've yearned to do is too strong an addiction. A sugar high that won't quit. I blink, glancing down at my hands, my grey uniform, the flickering lights from the movie projector dancing over me, tomato juice running down my cheeks and mixing with my tears.

I don't wipe them away.

I look out at the audience, hands on my hips. In a saucy voice, I say, 'You run out of tomatoes?' I smell a mix of human sweat and moldy cabbage as I cross downstage and leer at the audience. I hear mumbling and snickering. 'Good. Now we can get back to the film *Monsieur* Durand so kindly allowed you to attend for a nominal fee.'

Moving in a slow waltz across the stage in front of the film, I become the human shadow of the actors on the screen – the flapper and the playboy – performing their jazz baby antics in a nightclub scene bigger than life behind me, toying with the act of love and seduction with their body movements, their eyes, their lips...

I mirror every gesture, every movement... I've watched the film five times and memorized the title cards so it's easy for me to recite the dialogue loud and clear like the film *does* have sound. Flapper with headband plays hard to get. Playboy offers her champagne.

Monsieur, *you are too kind.*

And you are so beautiful.

How do I know you won't take advantage of me if I drink the champagne?

You don't...

Now you intrigue me...

Mon Dieu.

'Go home, Sylvie!'

'*No*,' someone yells in a loud voice with such authority, a hush comes over the audience. 'Let her go on. She's good.'

'Thank you,' I say to my unknown benefactor, giving him a wave. I can't see who it is since the theater seats are again sheathed in darkness. 'I'm staying right here. You're all watching me, aren't you? No one's left the theater...' I pace up and down the wooden stage, keeping their eyes moving on me so they can't look away. 'You're glued to your seats because you can't *not* watch me. I make you feel something inside you... hate, pity, even envy because I've got the guts to stand here and pour out my heart doing what makes me fly to the moon. I admit I have a lot to learn about acting, but the raw truth is, I set off your emotions. To be a great actress you need to show your feelings, not let anyone stand in your way. Sure, I memorized the lines, but to be a great actress, to make *you*, the audience, feel the depth of the character's emotions, you have to suffer. To know the heartache when you cry yourself to sleep at night because it's lonely and you don't have anyone to snuggle up to, and it's so cold your toes freeze or so hot in summer the air is as stifling as a tomb. It's made me tough... and not *anyone*, not even you out there with your insults and rotten tomatoes are going to stop me.' I pick up a mushy tomato and hold it up high before tossing it down on the stage and squashing it with the toe of my shoe. 'I make this promise right now. Someday, you'll see me up there...' I gesture toward the screen with the party-goers dancing and boozing. 'And you'll have to *pay* to see Sylvie Martone on the big screen. Remember that when I'm a big star and you're still sitting in the last row.'

Dead silence.

I tap my tomato-juiced toe on the stage, giving them a moment to think about what I said – brave words, but I'm not waiting to see what happens next.

I spin around on my heel and head for the back exit, my film career lasting not even twenty-four minutes.

The length of a one-reeler.

* * *

'It took real guts to make that speech, *mademoiselle*, after those rabble-rousers kicked you around like a dead toad.'

I feel a tug on my arm and smell the cigar smoke before the man blows it in my face. I don't cough, though I want to. I recognize that voice. He yelled at the audience to let me go on. I sense it's more important I put all my attention on him, give him a pious nod for saving my butt. I look up slowly, not surprised to see the man in the white Panama hat.

'Thank you for what you did, *monsieur*, but it won't do any good. They'll do it again the next time I sneak into – I mean, come to the theater and they'll bring even more rotten vegetables.' I wrap my lace shawl over my face. 'I have to go...'

I try to be polite as Sister Vincent taught me, but the good sister is probably frantic waiting for me, saying a novena, wondering what mess I've gotten myself into. The sister often makes excuses for me, but today I dread showing her my uniform soiled with seedy tomato mush.

'You've got real acting talent.'

I stop. '*Me, monsieur?*'

'I've been watching you... Sylvie, *n'est-ce pas?*'

I nod. 'Yes.'

'At first, I was merely amused when I saw you acting out the scene in my film—'

'*Your* film?' My pulse races with a different kind of excitement than I'm used to when I'm called into Sister Ursula's office for being late to vespers.

'But that performance on stage, the way you grabbed the audience by the throat, pulled every emotion out of them and didn't let them go...' He smacks his fingers against his lips. 'You were *magnifique!*'

'Who *are* you, *monsieur?*' I beg to ask, my head aching with the downside of my exuberant high crashing then soaring upward again at hearing his praise. 'Don't make fun of me, please.'

'Allow me to introduce myself, *mademoiselle.*' He takes off his white hat and bows from the waist, his cigar dangling from his fingers and dropping ash everywhere. I catch a glimpse of *Monsieur* Durand wiping his sweaty face with his long, black cravat, but he makes no move to reprimand the man. In the next moment, I find out why. 'I'm Emil-Hugo de Ville, the esteemed and successful director of such films as...'

He rattles off a long list of motion pictures – some I know, some I don't – but what's most important is, he said he was a *film* director.

I try to get my feet to walking, but my fervor to leave the theater is gone. He proffers me a small white card, and, with sticky fingers, I take it. I hold it up to the bare lightbulb hanging from ceiling, turning it this way and that, marveling at the elegant, raised text on the pristine, white card. Under his name I make out an address in Paris on Rue de Sevis and the name of a film studio, Delacroix Films.

'Are you *really* from Paris, *Monsieur* de Ville?' I sound like a country schoolgirl because I *am* a country schoolgirl. 'I've never been to Paris... the Eiffel Tower and the Moulin Rouge...'

'Call me Emil,' he says, then continues, 'I often travel to villages and towns outside Paris to gauge how my films are doing.' He leans down closer to me and I feel oddly breathless as if I'm standing on the edge of a cliff. He tells me at first his only interest in me was that he thought me pretty enough to be a background player in his next film, but after my stage performance—

I giggle. *He* calls it a performance. I call it my moment of liberation. I never expected it to last past this afternoon.

I don't protest when he guides me out of the back of the theater toward his parked Citroën as shiny as a tart lemon. He keeps talking about how he can make me a film star if I leave everything behind and become his protégé. It will take hard work, he says, and I'm buying it. Long hours, hot lights, scripts to memorize, no time for anything but the work... and dedication. He doesn't let me get in a word. I couldn't speak if I wanted to as he opens the passenger door and ushers me inside the plush vehicle.

I should run, tell him I'm not that kind of girl, but I don't. I have no illusions about my looks. Except for my white-blonde hair, I'm ordinary-looking. Taller than most girls my age, skinny with no bosom, and a deep dimple in my left cheek Sister Vincent says means I was pinched by an angel when I was born. Now I feel more like the devil is after my hide because I want to go with him. Want it badly.

I don't protest when *Monsieur* de Ville puts the motorcar into gear and off we go.

'I see a great future for you, Sylvie... what did you say your last name was?' he asks out of curiosity.

'Martone... Sylvie Martone.'

'It has an elegant ring to it and perfect for a theater marquee. I like it.'

I grin big. '*Merci, monsieur.* My mother was a grand aristocrat who fell in love with a stable hand, a dark, handsome stranger who wooed her then mysteriously disappeared before I was born... it's his name I bear.'

'An amazing story, Sylvie.' He looks over at me like I'm making it up. I'm not. I sit quietly, my jaw clamped, determined not to budge with my story. Sister Vincent told me where I came from, though I admit her black rosary beads were tightly wound around her fingers, her lips moving in silent words afterward, but I'm sticking to it.

The big, clunky motorcar rambles over the cobblestone driveway behind the theater as I settle back in the plush white seat. I let go of my final bout of butterflies and settle in. 'Why did you pick me, *monsieur*?'

'I meet a lot of girls who want to be in pictures, but I see something different in you, Sylvie. An exquisite, platinum-blonde with fire and tenacity, as well as raw acting talent. What you need is my tutelage. I have connections in the film business everywhere and the savoir-faire to know what the public wants, and they want you.'

'What about my life here... the convent, the nuns who raised me... Sister Vincent *might* understand, but she reports to the Mother Superior...' I make an anguished sound, 'Sister Ursula will forbid it.'

He winks at me. 'Then we won't tell her. I'll drop you off near the convent, then you get your things and I'll come back for you for after I complete my business in town. I booked a call to Paris to check on the times of my film showings in another town. An hour, tops. If you don't show up, then I'll know you're not interested in being a star.'

'Oh, but I *am, monsieur.*' I roll down my window to get some air. I stopped breathing a while back and I feel lightheaded. 'Being in the films is all I ever wanted—'

I bolt up in my seat, panicked.

I see Sister Vincent waiting for me outside the theater near the box office ticket window as we round the corner. She sees me in the motorcar and drops her basket filled with wrapped packages then wipes her face shiny with sweat with her full black sleeve. The shocked look on her face will stay with me always. I've never seen her soft, kind face so taut, her pale skin pulled so tight with fear, her eyes big and wide.

She's afraid for me, but that won't stop her from throwing her rotund body in front of the car to stop it. My fear of seeing her body mangled over the front fender is real to me. I turn to *Monsieur* de Ville, the fear of the heavens opening and raining down on my plans draining my courage.

'Stop the car, please. I must talk to Sister Vincent... explain to her why I'm leaving with you.'

'We can't stop, Sylvie. Make your choice. Do you wish to stay here and spend your life praying, your heart torn, your soul in chains? Or do you want to go to Paris with me and get into pictures?'

4

SYLVIE

WHEN YOU WISH UPON A STAR... THEN IT CRASHES

Ville Canfort-Terre, France
1926

I clutch the door handle, my eyes filled with hot tears. Gut twisting, I hold my breath. *Yes*, I want to be in pictures, *yes*, I may never have another chance, but I'd never do anything to hurt Sister Vincent. Oh, no, she's approaching the car as we slow down to let children cross the road... she waits for the children to pass, then she darts out—

'What is that nun doing?' *Monsieur* de Ville yells, waving his arm out the window to get her to move out of the way. She stops, thank God, he floors the gas pedal, a loud squeal of rubber, then a wild skidding off to the side to avoid hitting her. She blesses herself as he straightens the large, bulky motorcar back onto the road and we race off away from the theater. I turn around in my seat, stretching my neck, see her head down, her shoulders slumped. I'd never forgive myself if anything happened to her because of me.

This is all wrong.

I don't know what to do. So many questions, so many emotions hitting me in the gut. I can't go. I owe her an apology... I want to see her smile again... hold my hand.

All the while these thoughts tear me apart, *Monsieur* de Ville never stops talking.

'I've never seen such a crazy sister. No wonder you want to leave that place.'

'Sister Vincent is trying to protect me... I have no family, *monsieur*.'

'*I'll* protect you, Sylvie. I'll be like a father to you, guiding you. Remember, I have your best interests at heart.'

I listen. A father... the family I never had. *Oh, God, yes!* A chance not to be laughed at, ridiculed, not stuck in a stuffy convent and forced to wear ugly hand-me-downs, never able to look in a mirror because it's considered a sin or have sweets on Sunday. I always believed I had no choice but to become a novice and take the veil – but not now... *no!*

I huddle in my seat and think. Then there's the matter of Sister Vincent.

I go over in my poor, turned-inside-out brain what to do about the one thing that would keep me here.

* * *

Monsieur de Ville drops me off at the chateau gate and I slip inside the convent grounds under a veil of twilight granting me sanctuary. I slink past the tall chestnut tree that has stood here for hundreds of years, then down the cloistered passageway toward what used to be the servants quarters back in the seventeenth century but is now the cells for the postulants and novices. My door is unlocked (only the sisters have keys) and no one is about as I light a candle with a matchstick. It burns with indecision in the tin candle holder, swaying back and forth on a nocturnal breeze, then nearly blowing out before flaring up again.

Warning me?

I pay it no attention as I pack the cloth bag I use for laundry. Sunday Missal, knickers and clean chemise, stockings, a comb. I grab a sweater then wrap my lace veil around my head, concealing my face. I have an hour. If I know Sister Vincent, she'll hightail it back here for help so I have to find her first. Then I'll beg her forgiveness... tell her what happened at the theater... tell her *Monsieur* de Ville is a famous director and then she'll see things my way. I know she will—

'Where do you think you're going, *mademoiselle*?'

I spin around and a deep cold engulfs me. Sister Ursula stands in the doorway. The reality of her stark presence unnerves me, along with her rigid posture and that dreadful stare. I can't let her stop me.

I pick up my bag, sling it over my shoulder. 'I'm leaving for Paris, Reverend Mother,' I say with confidence, chin up. 'I'm going to be in pictures.'

'You?' She laughs. A deep, penetrating laugh that speaks of her surprise. 'A skinny orphan who can't keep her promise to God for giving you sustenance and a place to bed down?'

'I'm grateful for everything you've done for me, Mother. When I'm a big star, I'll pay it all back, I promise.' I cross my heart, look upward. She doesn't believe me, but it's a truth I give to Him.

Sister Ursula dismisses my plea. 'I couldn't believe it when *Monsieur* Durand rang me up and told me what happened at the movie theater. Parading around on stage half-dressed, acting like you have talent when you have none. Have you no shame?'

I shuffle my feet. *Monsieur* Durand was worried about me so I don't blame him. The telephone service *never* works properly, why today?

'I'm sorry if I've embarrassed you and the convent, Reverend Mother, but *Monsieur* de Ville has faith in me.' I head for the door, praying she steps aside. I don't like her, but I respect her position as a member of the Church. 'Let me pass... *please*.'

She folds her arms across her chest. 'I forbid you to accept the director's outrageous proposition. Your life is here with us, serving God.'

I stand up tall, straighten my shoulders. 'If God is as all-knowing as you say He is, then He knows how much I want to be an actress, or He wouldn't have sent *Monsieur* de Ville here today to find me.'

Sister Ursula is having none of my philosophical tirades. The woman has an agenda that goes deep, a hatred for me that is mercilessly female at its core. Jealousy.

'You're a sinner like your mother, Sylvie Martone. Yet unlike her, you'll not do your penance in the next life, but in this one.' Her eyes shine. 'You'll repent for your sins now. On your knees.'

'No, you don't understand,' I say, my voice going up an octave. 'This is my chance to be somebody, a chance while I'm young to follow my dream so I don't end up like you... old and shriveled up and mean.'

I don't know why I let go with such hateful words, words I've kept inside me for so long, but I'm desperate. And they hit home. Sister Ursula's face turns purple, her smooth forehead below her wimple wrinkles up with lines so deep they appear like ugly scars.

I pull back, mumbling, trying to take back my words. I've gone too far this time.

'*You insolent girl!*' she shouts, spewing hatred. 'How *dare* you speak to me in such a manner.'

I see the rage flooding her black eyes like burning coal ash. She's not thinking of her vows now. She wants to teach me a lesson. The nun raises her arm up high, her long, black sleeve fanning through the air like a whip when she slaps me. Hard. *Oh... the pain...* like liquid fire singeing my skin. Her anger stuns me. I try to duck, but she hits me again... her insistent blows sending me reeling, splitting my lower lip and knocking my bag off my shoulder. Fighting for balance, I stagger a few steps, the hot pain slamming through me, burning like a firebrand. A dizzying motion sends a bout of nausea through me and the coppery taste of blood fills my mouth, making me gag. I land with a thud on the hard cot in my cell. My face burns, but it's my pride that hurts more.

'I was wrong to say those things, Reverend Mother,' I say with honesty. The woman is a monster, but there are times in your life when you have to bite your tongue to save your hide. 'But I'm not like the other girls here,' I sputter, spitting blood. I touch my right eye, which is starting to swell and is half-closed. 'I don't find peace in taking the white veil and adopting the holy habit of the order and changing my name. I'm Sylvie Martone and I have a right to choose my own path in life.' I pause. 'I don't know why you hate me so much. What happened to you that you've lost the joy of what it's like to be young and want something so bad it consumes you like a holy fire.'

A flicker of her eyelids tells me I've touched a nerve and for a moment I see a human side of her in those eyes. What I've said is true, but whatever horrid secret she's keeping stays under her wimple.

'Tidy up and I will send for you.' She smirks. 'Remaining locked in your room is too easy a punishment for your sin of vanity. You shall be admonished in front of the nuns and novices after evening prayers, lying prostrate on the cold stone, your arms spread wide, and beg for forgiveness. Then you shall remain locked in your cell for a *week, mademoiselle*. No food, only water, praying the Lord doesn't send you to Hell, a vile, black place where bad girls go, because I will.'

Then she slams the door behind her and locks me in.

Taking deep breaths in spite of the pain in my chest, I try to calm down. I'm still reeling over how I ignited such fierce anger in the woman that she struck me like I was a godless soul. I can't ignore the fierce heat that radiated from her eyes, the posture of her body as she rose up to her full height before she struck me. Hard. I touch my face with my fingertips and the pain makes me wince. I want to curl up and cry. Let my body heal as well as my mind till I get over the shock.

I can't. If I don't make my move now, I never will.

I put my ear to the wood, hear her breathing heavily. I imagine she's outside my door, expecting me to cry, yell, and bang on the door. I won't. There'll be time for tears later if *Monsieur* de Ville leaves without me and I miss my chance. I have to get out of here. I want so *desperately* to be an actress. I *have* to go to Paris, find a life for myself.

Relief floods my veins like holy water when I hear her footsteps echo down the hallway.

Then it's not tears I shed. A giggle escapes my bruised lips.

Sister Ursula doesn't know I have a key.

* * *

I spend several minutes on my hands and knees trying to retrieve the old, rusty key I begged off Sister Vincent a while ago. I hid it under a loose floorboard, but the board is stuck. I keep trying to pry it open in spite of the intense pain in my shoulder.

I never dreamed it would be the key to my freedom when I got into trouble for stealing milk to feed a litter of kittens and their mother that took up holy sanctuary in the chapel. I fed the family of five for a week before Sister Ursula found out, locked me in my room, and dumped the kittens and their mother out into the rain. Sister Vincent told me it was cruel to turn out the poor things, so she opened my door with a spare key and after a lot of cajoling on my part, she let me keep it so I could come and go without Sister Ursula knowing what we were about. Together we searched for the tiny creatures till we found them, the furry bundles shivering and nearly drowned, huddled under the weeping willow in the center courtyard, the tall tree keeping them safe like a majestic guardian.

Soon after Sister Vincent found the lot of them homes in the village, but when she asked me for the key back, I swore up and down I lost it. I didn't tell her I'd hidden it since Sister Ursula has a habit of locking disobedient girls in their cell... I wanted it for an emergency.

Five, ten minutes go by... I keep tugging on the board, bracing myself when I feel it budge a little, then—

Pop! I lift up the floorboard and reach around the damp earth underneath till my fingers wrap around the jagged key. I grab it, ignoring the settling heaviness in my body from the sister's hard blows, then rub off the dirt and pray to the Almighty to forgive me for lying to Sister Vincent as I turn it in the lock. *Click.* I can't hold back the excitement filling me, the sobs of joy. Never has a prayer been answered with such enthusiasm.

I'm free.

I grab my cloth bag and peek outside the door. The hallway with its dim gaslight is empty.

Head down, I take long strides, pulling my lace veil over my face and praying *Monsieur* de Ville won't notice the bloodstains on the lace from my bleeding lip. A blue indigo twilight provides cover as I tiptoe out of the novice quarters and hug the side of the building. I feel confident I can make it across the courtyard if I get past the stream of light coming from the outside lamp that lights up the pathway to the chapel. It's time for evening prayers and the nuns and novices are gathered there—

'Sylvie, *wait... please, child!*'

Startled, I spin around. There's no escape. I heave out a sigh of relief when I see Sister Vincent running toward me, holding up her black, filmy skirts and showing her slender ankles encased in black stockings. She catches up to me, out of breath, her spectacles smudged and askew on her face.

I grip my lace veil tight to shield my bruised face from her scrutiny.

'Thank God, you're here.' She hunches over, hands on her knees, and takes in deep, heavy breaths. 'I rushed back here after I saw you drive away with that stranger in the yellow Citroën. I've been so worried about you.'

'He's no stranger, Sister Vincent,' I tell her, leading her away from the light. What needs to be said is best done in shadows. 'He's a famous film director and he wants to take me to Paris and put me in pictures.'

She grabs me by the shoulders. 'No... is that true?'

'Yes.' I show her his card. Guilt floods me. 'Will you ever forgive me, Sister Vincent? I wanted to stop and tell you... but *Monsieur* de Ville said you'd talk me out of leaving with him.'

'As well I should.' She smooths down her skirts, then speaks to me with such tenderness in her voice, my heart tugs. 'I'm not surprised you attracted the gentleman's attention.' She giggles like a schoolgirl and clasps her hands across her chest. 'I saw you on stage at the cinema... I was so proud of you, Sylvie, how you stood up to those awful hecklers, but most of all, the fervent words that came straight from your heart.'

My eyes widen. 'You were there?'

'I went to find you... I'm not so blind behind these spectacles I can't see what you're up to.' She sighs. 'Ah, *ma petite*, you *do* have an uncanny talent for charming everyone you meet.'

'Not Sister Ursula. She hates me. She locked me in my cell, but I... I escaped.'

Sister Vincent shakes her head and chuckles. She'll keep my secret. 'I understand your desire to leave the cloistered life, Sylvie, but what do you know about this man?'

'*Monsieur* Durand speaks highly of him and his work in films.' I lie, then I embellish my plea with, 'He... he said I should I go with him to Paris.'

Sister Vincent isn't buying it. 'No, you must stay here at the convent until I make inquiries about this *Monsieur* de Ville and his promises. Then, if the Lord gives His blessing and the director is a good man, I will speak to Reverend Mother about sending you to Paris—'

'*No, you can't!*' I rail, my voice cracking. 'She'll *never* let me go.'

She puts her hand up to her cheek in surprise. 'Good heavens, Sylvie, we must do things in proper fashion. If we don't, Reverend Mother will have both our heads.'

'I can't do as you ask, Sister Vincent... *Monsieur* de Ville will leave for Paris without me if I'm not at the gate in time.'

I start to turn, to run, but the sister is quicker on her feet than I imagined. She cuts me off and grabs my arm, my lace veil falling off my head and revealing my bruised and battered face.

A loud gasp escapes from her throat. 'Oh, dear Lord, you didn't me tell me *that man hurt you!*'

I bow my head, ashamed. '*No*... *Monsieur* de Ville didn't touch me.'

'Then who did this horrible thing to you?' I wince when she touches my bruised cheek and soothes my swollen eyelid with her soft fingers.

'It's nothing, Sister, honest. I have to go. *Please* don't try to stop me.'

I try to brush past her, but again she blocks me. Her brows arch, her chin lifts. 'I admire your spunk, Sylvie, but your silence tells me who the culprit is. I should have known Sister Ursula would lash out at you when you gave her the opportunity. She despises any girl she can't bend to her will.' She blesses herself. 'As God is my witness, I would never disobey a direct order from the Mother Superior, but I won't stand by and remain silent. Punishing you for her lack of self-control goes against everything I believe in, everything in the Lord's teachings. I can't stand by and let her shame the veil we swore to serve.'

'Then you will help me?'

She nods. 'I can stall the Mother Superior, tell her I had difficulty getting all the supplies, and ask her to meet with me after prayers. I don't know for how long.'

Then she does something I will never forget, something I will hold dear for the rest of my life. She folds me into her arms and hugs me tight to her bosom, stroking my hair and mumbling prayers for my safe journey. '*Go*, child, before Sister Ursula gets suspicious and returns to the novice quarters to check on you. May God keep you safe.'

'I'll never forget your kindness, Sister Vincent... I promise.'

'Someday you can repay me.' She smiles. '*Au revoir, ma petite.*'

She turns and walks swiftly toward the chapel, her step lighter than before as if a great weight has been lifted from her shoulders.

I don't look back as I rush toward the gate, my heart skipping when I spot the yellow Citroën waiting for me outside near the tall chestnut tree. The man in the Panama hat pokes his head out the driver's window and waves me on when he sees me running toward him.

I don't stop. Not now or ever.

I feel deep in my bones that going to Paris is my destiny as clearly as the moment I stood on that stage and proclaimed I was an actress.

I keep running, never looking back, my hair undone, my lace veil blowing behind me. I taste freedom on my lips, washing away the blood, its coppery taste replaced by a sweetness seducing me, the elixir I've searched for but never found till now.

I'm either going to that place Sister Ursula says bad girls go to... or, God willing, I'm going to be an actress.

5

JULIANA

UNRAVELING THE FAIRY TALE

Los Angeles
Present Day

I never should have gone looking for my roots because now I'm obsessed. I take stock of what I found in the boxes I went through earlier from my mother's apartment sent by a kindly neighbor. Gold-rimmed, white Limoges dishes and demitasse teacups with pink roses. Textbooks in English and French, calendars – nothing dated before the eighties – and a box of photos from my childhood I haven't seen in years.

I put *Maman's* clothes aside for donation to the abused women's shelter run by the Sisters of the Good Shepherd as she wished. I handle each piece with care, lingering on the memories – the green wool dress she wore during the holidays, the soft, pink chenille robe she loved to get cozy in on Sunday mornings. I take longer to fold the smart, black silk box suit she wore to my college graduation, remembering how worried she was about me making a living in show business. I've had good years then dry spells. I love my work, sketching the characters and coming up with wardrobe details that define them. I've worked on numerous TV shows, first as an assistant costume designer or wardrobe stylist then designer, though for years I worked in the business 'washing out pantyhose'.

I didn't tell my mother that.

I heave out a long sigh. I don't find anything else significant that links to our family other than the photo of the glamorous woman in the slinky gown. And the heart-shaped, diamond pin with the arrow through it. I won't rest until I find out the truth about this woman, my grandmother... first, I must identify her.

I keep checking my phone as I await a call from Ridge. I left him a detailed voicemail about how I found something troubling when I went through my mother's belongings and I need to talk about it. Most likely, when I called he was holed up in a cold storage vault hoisting vintage film reel canisters. Going through *Maman's* things reminded me how Ridge and I almost got together one night when I was feeling awfully low and knew the end was coming with *Maman* and I could do nothing about it.

I heave out a sigh. God knows the man is a heartbreaker with that finely tuned body and dark, bad-boy looks. But like I told *Maman*, why mess up a good thing between us? The last thing I need is for Ridge to feel sorry for me.

The grey California day is a subtle accent to my mood, where nothing is black or white, simply a shade somewhere in between. I spend the next half hour looking through another box, find nothing important... put on a pot of coffee... look at my unfinished sketch, but I can't focus. I'm restless, waiting for my phone to vibrate, when the loud sound of a motorcycle backfiring catches my attention. A quick glance through the front window and I catch sight of a rider dressed in tight black leather from head to toe on a big motorbike screeching to a halt in my driveway, a billowing dust cloud spewing behind him.

He takes off his helmet and gives me the high sign.

'Ridge McCall, are you showing off again?' Arms folded, I give him 'that look' I do when we kid each other. It never fails to get a big grin from him.

'Is that any way to greet your knight in shining armor?' He holds up a brown paper bag. 'Especially a guy bringing sesame bagels.'

* * *

I grab two mugs of hot coffee and stack the bagels on *Maman's* fancy Limoges dishes, then we sit down on the comfy apple-red, plaid cushion on the bay window box and talk. Like we always do. No holds barred. Today is no different.

'*Maman* lied to me, Ridge. We do – *I do* – have family in France.'

'That's great news.' He takes a bite from a bagel.

'No, it's complicated. All my life I believed my mother's family died in the war. I know now *her* mother didn't. My *grand-mère*. I found an old photo of her from 1949. The strange thing is, I'm wondering if everything else she told me was a lie. About my father, how she came to America.'

I can't believe it's my voice I hear filled with excited jabbering and run-on sentences, sighs and sniffles. Bringing up my whole life history overwhelms me. To most people, talking about my roots may seem a strange way to deal with the grief of losing my mother, but I've never let it out till now, never shared my lack of a family tree with anyone. I've kept it inside, pretended it didn't matter until it did.

In 1983 my mother met my father, Dr Paul Warrick, a distinguished art history professor, when he came to the small convent where she lived outside Paris. The existence of a little-known artifact at Ville Canfort-Terre attracted my father's attention while he was researching a medieval manuscript nearly lost during the First World War when the Germans marched through and destroyed a monastery. Afterward, the manuscript was entrusted to the nuns for safekeeping and all but forgotten till my father started asking questions. He began a correspondence with the convent historian in charge of translating it... Madeleine Chastain, my mother.

I stop, take a breath, remembering how *Maman* told me she fell in love with the American professor through his letters before he arrived

in France. *Maman* had spent years helping translate the manuscript –
she was fluent in English – and the two of them spent several months
together, huddling over the ancient tome... and enjoying each other's
company.

Then, I tell Ridge with more emotion than I expected, *Maman* was
shocked when Paul returned to the States, his work done. Did he love
her, or was he flattering a lonely spinster? She was nearly forty and had
followed a quiet, semi-religious life up to that time. I don't think my
mother wanted to answer that question, but when she discovered she
was having his baby, she wrote to him, informing him.

'That must have been a difficult time for your mother, Juliana,'
Ridge says, his voice low and husky. 'And your father. I'm not making
any judgment, but from what you've told me, he provided for you
growing up.'

I notice he chooses his words carefully. I made my peace with my
father years ago when we spoke before he died.

'The letters I read indicate my father *did* love my mother,' I'm quick
to tell him, 'but he was under consideration for an important position
at the Claremont Colleges in California and couldn't return to France.'

'So your mother came here to California. Why the upheaval? Why
didn't she stay where she had a home, security?'

'*Maman* never said so, but I got the feeling she couldn't face the
shame of her indiscretion being found out in her village, so she
followed him here. Paul Warrick was a widower with two grown
daughters who, according to my mother, were aghast at the news. They
harassed her with numerous threats and letters, telling her how their
father couldn't afford a scandal when his tenure was in question, so
Maman went to him and told him she'd make it on her own. To his
credit, my father insisted on helping her with expenses for the baby
and found her a position in the French department at a nearby
women's college where she taught for years.'

'Did you see your father often?' Ridge asks, curious.

'I met with him a few times,' I say, sipping my coffee, 'but he
always seemed distant and his daughters treated me like the fairy

tale heroine but without the glass slipper.' I exhale, punch down the ache that still lingers in my heart from their snooty looks and bullying me as a teen. 'In the end, I had my mom and that was enough for me.'

'Your mother never married?'

'Yes, she tried not to show it, but *Maman* nursed a broken heart for years, never giving up hope her professor would marry her. When he died, she went into a deep depression and took early retirement from the college. I insisted she move to LA to be close to me, but it took persuading on my part. My mother never approved of me going into show business. She always clammed up when I probed her why she was so against it. After I convinced her to come live with me, we became closer than ever, having several long, lovely conversations about my mother growing up in the convent – both in French and English. I remember how she told me she made her decision to go to America under the sweeping willow tree in the garden. She'd always stop there... never spoke about her life in the convent before she met my father... never spoke about how she got there... or the woman who must have left her there... my grandmother. And it hurts, Ridge... why couldn't she share the truth with me? *Why?*'

'I have no doubt your mother was trying to protect you—'

'Protect me from what? My grandmother? That's absurd.' I raise my voice. I didn't realize how much I was hurting inside till I put it into words.

I show him the photo dated 1949 and he lets out a low whistle.

'She's stunning, Juliana. By the quality and texture of the photo paper and the photographer's style, I'd say this was taken at the start of the war... around 1940.' He snaps pictures of the photo from various angles on his phone.

'It sounds crazy,' I say, 'but could the woman in this glamor shot – *my* grandmother – be an actress?

'Whoever she is, I'm sure she's as wonderful as her granddaughter.'

'Can you identify her?'

'Can Superman fly?' He grins. 'I've got connections I can check with and software I can run the photo through. If this gorgeous blonde was ever in the French film business, I'll find her.'

* * *

I settle in at my drawing board after Ridge leaves. I continue working on the sketches for the new show, my pencil moving along in clean, striking lines. I feel refreshed... and mentally exhausted. I let go of the deep pain and self-inflicted anguish I've tormented myself with, that I didn't do enough for my mother. I know now I did. And it's time for me to move on... not completely let go, but enough so I don't get so wrapped in that grey world of living in the past and filling it with shades of regret that I miss living in the here and now.

It's late afternoon when my phone chimes. A text.

Ridge.

I do a quick read and my heart skips a beat. Then two. Oh, my God, he's identified the woman in the photo... *ma grand-mère.*

Yes, he has located the blonde in the photo, *yes*, she was a French film cinema star.

Then a short text. Very short.

Call me ASAP. Important.

Then, for some reason I can't explain, gut instinct if you will, I choke up with a new fear. Why didn't Ridge text me more info? Or a link... several links. A bio, more photos. He's keeping something from me.

One way to find out. I call him. He answers on the first ring.

'Hey, Juliana, how soon can you meet me at the studio?'

'What's up?' I ask, surprised. Why not meet him at the film company where he works?

'I have more info about the blonde in the photo.'

'Can't you tell me over the phone?'

'No.'

I flinch. That was direct. 'Can't you give me a hint?'

'No.'

I swallow hard. I have a feeling he's trying to protect me from something about to blow up in my face.

'This can't wait, Juliana. You need to see this.'

I've never known Ridge to be so insistent. He's used to facing a high level of danger and doing stunts in one take without rehearsal. Now he sounds downright panicked.

I let out a cleansing breath and try to remain calm, but inside I'm exploding with a hot fever I haven't felt since the night *Maman* passed.

'I'll be there in twenty minutes.'

6

SYLVIE

OOH, LA LA! THE GIRL GOES TO PAREE

Delacroix Studios, Paris
1928

I struggle with the thick rope, sweat streaming down my face from the hot lights, my hands tied to the back of a chair, and kick out my legs. My angel-white hair flies around my face while I fight off the mad doctor.

Why is the damn rope so tight around my wrists? The script doesn't call for my hands to go numb.

'You'll *never* make me talk.' I narrow my brows. 'I'll never tell you where I hid the orphans. They're safe from your evil deeds.' I lift my chin, flutter my long, fake lashes.

'You'll talk, Ninette, or I'll cut your throat,' sputters the mad doctor in his perfect, deep baritone pitch, hovering over me. Pierre Limone comes from the stage and is a seasoned character actor. He's a master of makeup and disguises and insists on delivering his lines with fervor. He's taught me what it means to 'become' the character you're playing on the screen. 'No one is coming to save you.'

'Save me? From *you*, Doctor Heidelberg?' I throw my head back and laugh. 'You can't fool me... *Lucifer*.'

'Your angel magic is not powerful enough to escape me. Now you shall die...'

He raises his knife, bringing it down toward my throat, cackling and laughing, his eyes bugging out... oh, God, he's overacting, milking the part... Why not? I'm still struggling with the damn rope knots. This is the part where I pull myself free and overpower the devil disguised as an evil scientist and save the two orphans.

I can't budge.

The shooting pain in my arms from the tight ropes around my wrists is making me helpless. I keep struggling and kick out my laced-up boots. I nearly get Pierre in the crotch.

He jumps back.

'Now you shall *die*...' he repeats, coming close to nicking the skin on my bare neck. The insane look in his eyes and that smirk tells me it's no coincidence I can't get loose.

He paid off the prop man to make the rope too tight. Giving him more screen time on his big scene. I can't blame him. His lines were cut so Emil can get the film out in the theaters two weeks earlier than planned while the public is still hot for my films.

Word around Paris is, talkies are in... silent two-reeler serials on their way out. *Les Orphelins Perdus* (Lost Orphans) is my final *Ninette* film. A serial about a seamstress, an angel sent to earth to do good deeds while the devil in various disguises tries to undo those deeds and get rid of her. We've made ten two-reelers and two features (four reels) in the past two years.

'I *am* going to die if someone doesn't loosen these rope knots, Emil,' I say, trying to find my director. Pierre is getting too close for comfort. Another minute and my career is over. I have to smile, reflect on this crazy life I've chosen while the prop man races to my side and works on loosening the rope knots around my wrists, never looking me in the eye when I offer to pay him twice what Pierre did if he puts ground pepper in my co-star's phony beard. It's part of the game in the world of cinema. With Pierre and me, it's innocent pranks. With others, it's survival if you want to make that next picture.

Always watch your back because no one else will.

Advice I got from Sister Vincent (she used more pious language) when I sneaked over to the convent when we were shooting on location nearby.

I strain my eyes, but I can't see through the blaze of lights or the eyelashes. Where is Emil? He's never far from my side. Not since that day I ran away from the convent.

I had no idea then what I was getting myself into.

* * *

Was it two years ago I was that dumb kid who would do anything to be an actress?

I often think about how simple getting into pictures seemed to me then. Go to Paris... do what Emil says... become a movie star.

It didn't work that way. I had a lot of bumps in the road and my endearing dream of finding a father figure in Emil... well, let's say it wasn't what I hoped.

Things moved quickly when we arrived in Paris with Emil getting me a place to live in the Faubourg Saint-Antoine, a working-class district in the suburbs of the city. I was in heaven. First floor apartment. Ivy-covered walls. My own bedroom with a sink and tub. Tall, beautifully carved wood *garderobe* I thought I'd never fill. Soft bed with a daisy quilt. Even an icebox in the tiny kitchen where I found ice slivers for my swollen eye and split lip. He wasn't pleased when he saw my bruised face, surmising a zealous nun struck me to prevent me from leaving. I didn't deny it and we never discussed it again. I healed up as good as new in a few days and the incident was forgotten.

Still, I wondered if I'd ever let go of the fear I have of not being loved, of not being good enough for someone to love me. This is why I defy the odds and abandon myself to the heat of the moment because it's then I *do* feel loved. I don't have an answer, but it's that recklessness that got me here, so I have no complaints. It's something that comes to the surface at times, though, and I wonder if it will be the end of me. I know Sister Vincent is praying for me and a warm, holy rush of faith fills me. I don't understand why the Mother Superior harbors such hatred toward me, but I left that life behind. Something Emil makes perfectly clear to me.

For the next two years he rules my life from the minute I wake up till I drop my head on the pillow late at night. Since I'm underage when the studio signs me to a seven-year contract, they insist he procure a 'guardian' for me. I should mention Emil also acts as my manager which gives him final say in everything, including hiring Miss Brimwell, an acting and dialogue coach who still looks after me today though I've turned eighteen. Emil keeps her on to work with me, telling me it's important I find the theatrical tone of my voice because he's working on a 'big secret' that will catapult my career into a new realm. He loves to keep things from me, so I have to depend on him. It's no secret this is the last year of making silent films.

Which brings me back to Miss Brimwell and her voice coaching lessons.

She can, at times, be a major nuisance, making me walk around with a book on my head to straighten my posture while rounding my 'vowels' and speaking through my 'mask' – my nose, not my throat. I'm not supposed to notice her imbibing her daily shot of green fairy absinthe from a flask she keeps hidden in her beaded bag.

She's quite a character with her swinging, chin-length hair the color of a ripe pomegranate, her pencil-thin brows and smooch-y, red lipstick. When she's not around, I mimic her cat-eyes with finely drawn, black cake eyeliner on my lids and then sashay through my apartment, pretending the pencil dangling from my lips is a long cigarette holder. I swirl my lace veil through the air, twirling and dancing free. I'm very protective of my convent keepsake and store it at the bottom of my garderobe. A reminder of where I came from, but I find Miss Brimwell's approach to life fascinating and want to be like her.

Except I'm not.

Emil insists I keep my hair down to my waist because it's how the fans want to see their Ninette. Angel-white hair that's bleached every day when I'm shooting a picture. *I* want to be more like Miss Brimwell, prancing around in slinky, fringe dresses, but 'sweet and innocent' is my brand – Emil quotes like it's a mantra.

I'm fed up with sweet and innocent. I have no social life. *Rien.* Nothing. I want to *live.* Act wild. How can I? I'm up every day at 6 a.m., cold porridge for breakfast with *lots* of coffee. Something I never drank at the convent.

Oh, how I miss Sister Vincent with her silver spectacles sliding down her nose when she's praying, her fingers moving over her black wooden rosary beads but also watching me, clearing her throat when she catches me daydreaming.

I secretly write to her as often as I can, telling her everything about my new life. I don't tell her about the long hours and no sleep. I pretend I *am* Ninette and give her the happy ending she deserves after risking her position in the convent to help me. My *Ninette* serial is so popular in the village, she wrote to me, *Monsieur* Durand holds special showings for the nuns and members of the local clergy (Sister Ursula attended a showing and never said a word afterward). My days are filled with wardrobe fittings, dialogue coaching, makeup, hair, learning my lines. And the actual work, of which I'm so proud. I love acting... even when we work long into the night. One scene today took twenty-nine takes before Emil yelled, *'Print!'*

No wonder I'm so tired and fall asleep in my dressing room with the sister's letters spread out on my lap. I pay for my lapse in judgment when Emil drops by to give me rewritten script pages for the next day. Till now I've kept her letters hidden, but I'm groggy and he grabs them before I can stop him. His face scrunches up. I know that look. He hates anything that challenges his authority over me.

'I told you, Sylvie, to cut off all contact with *everyone.*' He tears them up and tosses them back at me.

I jump to my feet, the sight of the nun's lovely, blue handwriting in shreds sending me into a panic with a rush of fear that smothers me. 'I can't let you take away Sister Vincent's letters... *I can't*,' I tell him, a long, guttural sob erupting from my throat.

'You need *only* me. Without me, you're nothing. Don't ever forget that.'

Hot tears sting my eyes as I try to piece the letters back together, but he sweeps the torn papers out of my hands and then stomps on them with his brown alligator-laced shoe.

'Remember this day, Sylvie, remember the pain you felt when I tore up your letters, the anger, fear, dread...' he says with a firm control in his voice. 'You can use it to better your skills as an actress, to bring up those emotions when a scene calls for such intense pain that it tears at your heart. The audience will know those raw emotions are real.' A smirk. 'And that, *ma chérie*, is what sells movie tickets.'

And the horrible, heartbreaking truth is... he's right.

An actress has to pull up the best and the worst of her experiences. *Bon*. So I shall. That doesn't change anything. I hate him and his fiendish need to control me, but somehow he's always right. The French director uses his power over me to keep me in line. Telling me I owe everything I am to him. And I believe him because I want to.

Because I love what I'm doing. I'm an actress...

And a star.

7

SYLVIE
NINETTE GROWS UP

Paris
1929

I cry when Emil insists it's time to cut off my long hair.

I didn't think I'd shed any tears let alone a steady flow when long strands of my platinum glory fall to the floor. A mantle of lost childhood surrounding me, silken threads like the strands the nuns use to weave their lace. A story lies behind each lace design and so it is with me. Winding my hair up in a long braid or curls and ringlets every day became my pattern of lace, something I can cling to as I find my way in this world of takes and retakes, bright lights and X marks on the floor showing me where to stand. Costumes too big for me pulled in with giant safety pins that come undone during my pratfalls and stick me in the butt. For all my talk about wanting to bob my hair like Miss Brimwell's, inside I want to remain Ninette. I thought I could go on forever playing the angel come to earth to defeat evil.

That I'd never have to grow up and face life. Face the fact that in spite of the piling up franc notes in my bank account, a *garderobe* filled with fancy clothes and satin shoes, I have no freedom. Emil controls everything.

Even cutting my hair.

I'm also aware Emil is tuned into my strengths as well as my weak-nesses, my ability to 'feel' a part and take direction from him without a word, merely a gesture like putting his finger to his cheek or raising his brows. As if I can read his mind. I shudder, knowing how strong his hold is on me, how he keeps me on a short leash. At first, I thought it was wonderful to have someone who cares for me – the truth is, I'm nothing to him but a film property bought and sold to the highest bidder at the studio.

Unlike Ninette, I didn't defeat the devil.

I sold my soul to him.

I hunch down in the barber chair in the stuffy, studio makeup room, the mirror framed with hot, bare bulbs witnessing the shedding of my hair. My shoulders slump as I try to conceal my anguish from the cheeky stylist chewing gum and chatting nonstop about how much she loves me as Ninette, but ain't it true ingénues have to grow up if you want to keep working in this business.

With the incessant snipping loud in my ears, she rambles on about a famous star she used to cut hair for, how the forty-something woman insisted on covering up her grey roots with henna and red dye though the only parts coming her way were dowager roles. Then one day she stopped coming in. Last she heard, the actress was working as a madam in the Saint-Denis district where her hair was redder than the girls who worked for her.

I chuckle as she expects me to do, but I find her story so sad. *That's never going to happen to me*, I vow. Still, it's a lesson learnt. Crying over cutting my girlish curls isn't going to get me anywhere. It's time Ninette grew up. I should be smart like the good girl I play and not complain about having no freedom, count myself lucky to have Emil watching out for me. Like Miss Brimwell says, a girl can't always get what she wants, but if she's smart she knows when to shut up and play a new angle.

So that's what I do.

I dry my tears and start reading the script Emil sent over for me to read. A film about a wicked woman. My first grown-up role. The studio is eager for me to make a talkie and when the actress hired to play the lead jumped ship to go to Hollywood, Emil convinced them to give the role to me. It's called *Bébé de jazz* (Jazz Baby) and is about a flapper who falls in love with a poor trumpet player but marries a rich, older banker. When she goes back to the trumpet player, the banker shoots her... and she dies in her lover's arms.

* * *

The film is a box office flop.

Emil insists the reason the movie-going public didn't buy me as a boozing flapper is because I'm still a virgin. *I* say it's because they didn't want to see their beloved Ninette go over to the dark side and lose the good girl image they love.

He insists I'm *not* Ninette anymore and the sooner I accept that the better off I am.

This is the first of many rows we have: some in public at his favorite table at the Hôtel Ritz, him looking across at me, arms folded, pouting while the waiter pours me another glass of sweet Anjou – my third in an hour – and others in private in my small apartment. It's always the same. I come across on the screen as a child dressing up in her mother's clothes, I don't carry myself like a woman who knows how to seduce a man (I wish Miss Brimwell had been instructive in that department). And I don't know how to kiss. He insists the way for me to make the transition from child actress to femme fatale is to lose my virginity.

I let out a screech that rips through me down to my toes and causes more than one head to turn in the famous Ritz dining salon. 'How dare you suggest I – that you—'

'Don't look at me like that, Sylvie. I may be a lot of things – and no, don't name them – but I'm not like *that* with my stable of stars.'

I furrow my brow. 'Is that what you call your clients? A *stable*? What are we... goats... dairy cows to be farmed out at your whim?' My voice sounds scratchy from my outburst. 'Why doesn't that surprise me? Everyone in Paris knows the great Emil-Hugo de Ville keeps a special apartment on the Left Bank for his party girls.'

He doesn't deny it as he signals the waiter for another bottle of brandy. 'Every one of them beautiful... *and* willing.' He straightens his bowtie and slicks back his deep ebony hair with the finesse of a bullfighter about to enter the ring. 'I've already made the arrangements for your... shall we call it, evening of pleasure. A young actor I have my eye on. Jean-Claude Remy is in need of seasoning before I sign him.'

'You mean you want to see if he'll jump through your hoops.' A simple statement, but true. '*And* keep his mouth shut afterward.'

He smiles. 'I've reserved a suite for you overlooking the Place Vendôme. You'll have caviar, champagne... and the smoothest satin sheets so as not to mar your delicate skin.'

'You're insane, Emil... mad. *I won't do it.*'

He leans closer, takes my hand – yes, I'm trembling – and holds it tight. 'In certain cultures, it's the duty of the father to choose his daughter's first lover. Have I not been like a father to you, Sylvie?'

'Yes...' I'm reluctant to admit Emil has guided my career to a place I never dreamed. My name in lights on the theater marquee like he promised, adoring fans, pretty clothes. 'But to think you'd *sell* my body so you can get your twenty-five per cent out of my hide...'

'It's for your own good, *ma chère*. Go out with Jean-Claude, go dancing at the Moulin Rouge, the theater, have fun... all expenses on me.' He tips the waiter when he brings the brandy then shoos him away. He pours himself a drink, downs it quickly, and then smacks his lips. 'From what the *mamselles* tell me, Jean-Claude is a stud in the sack.'

* * *

Jean-Claude is a drunk with sloppy lips, smelly hairy armpits, and a starfish birthmark on his right buttock I'm sure half the women in Paris have seen. The arrangement is far from memorable – I will spare you the requisite details to save us both embarrassment. He downs a bottle of champagne and it's a miracle he can perform. When the evening reaches its climax (his, not mine), I know how that mother cat Sister Vincent and I found felt after giving birth to her litter and then being tossed out into the rain.

I'm drenched. His sweat, my sweat, and a myriad of milky fluids that make me wish I had no sense of smell. I'm grateful no one in this hotel room uses the bidet to wash clothes in and I make speedy use of it afterward. I refuse to check the sheets for any physical signs of my womanhood (I rang for the maid to change the bedding as soon as Jean-Claude grabbed his trousers and took off for parts unknown) and rest in the adjoining dressing room on a gold-satin *méridienne* while she tidies up the room. Then, wrapped in a fluffy, clean-smelling white robe with a big 'R' embroidered on the back, I crawl into the white canopied bed and curl up into a ball, moaning in pain and crying.

I'll never forget how Jean-Claude looked at me with naked lust before diving into me. In spite of the heated hotel room, I shiver. I was merely a vessel to him, a vase to be broken. I prayed it would be quick.

It wasn't.

I clench my thighs together tight to protect what's left of my girl-hood... no, there's nothing left but a searing tear in my body that will heal, but will my soul? I feel lost, humiliated, used... and broken.

Like that poor, lonely vase.

* * *

I refuse to report to Emil the specifics of the evening except to deliver a dramatic Elizabethan moment with four simple words. *The deed is done.* I can't speak about it and he respects that. He does, however, reflect on the sheen on my cheeks, the glint in my eye, the sway of my hips. Things I don't notice. I hide from him what I *am* feeling, which not only surprises me, but pleases the female urges I've ignored for so long.

I shall explain...

First, I tell Emil, I need to close the door to my public life. I need to think, rest, drink tea instead of coffee to find my footing. This is the perfect time to send scripts my way. I ask for privacy and promise him he will never again be disappointed in my performance.

Then I sleep for two days, allowing my body to heal, my soul filling up with a new understanding that the pleasant tingling between my thighs that makes me tremble, my knees weak, is not something to be denied. That in spite of the pain, the anguish, the humiliation of being bought and sold like a bolt of silk, something wonderful and mysterious happened to me when Jean-Claude forced my legs apart. Before I could protest, I felt his warm breath on my face, hovering there, waiting to see if I was ready for him...

The odd yet pleasurable note is, I *wasn't* ready then... I am now.

Why is my body betraying me? My belly full and aching, a burning within me that is forbidden. This can't be happening to me, it can't!

A week, then two... I spend sleepless nights wishing I had another chance to be with a man. A good man who would kiss me, hug me... hold me... then I slow down my breathing, relax my body, and let it react in a most natural way as I close my eyes and imagine in my mind I'm with a gorgeous man as he runs his hands over my breasts, cupping my soft flesh. Not like I did with Jean-Claude. I pushed him away and told him to hurry up. Foolish words. Whatever deep desires I possess, they're getting stronger every day, a growing pleasure between my legs that won't go away. An intense hunger that becomes so deliciously painful, I can't deny it any longer. I need a release.

I rummage through my trunk for pieces of costumes I've collected from my films. Wigs, gaudy jewelry, lace-up boots, princess satin slippers. I don a fetching outfit dripping with fringe, a black wig, red satin wedge heels with tie-around straps that wind up my calves... and my lace veil.

No... not my veil.

I run my fingers over the veil. Tiny, static shocks prick my fingers as if a sacred aura clings to the only link to my past, a holiness I dare not violate. I return the lace veil to its secret place. It's not my past I wish to embrace tonight, but the moment of becoming a woman on my own terms denied to me.

No one recognizes me as Sylvie Martone when I haunt the cabarets in the Place Pigalle. I heard the makeup girl whispering to the wardrobe attendant about the decadent fun found here. This is the first chance I've had to see it up close. I brace myself when I slip through a door with etched glass, the smoked-filled building drawing me in, my feelings intensifying when I glance over the crowd of nubile girls in scanty frocks. Tough, muscular men from the underbelly of Paris's gangs crowded together in the stuffy room. An accordionist pumps out a slow, sensual rhythm that moves my soul to dance... and more.

I smile pretty when an outrageously handsome man with the rich darkness of a Moorish night sparking in his eyes slides up to me, buys me a cognac. We drink... stare... then drink again before he pulls me out onto the tiny, round dancefloor and we dance... twirling me... tossing me into the crowd... then dragging me back to him... working his jaw as his eyes haunt me... executing the sultry steps of the Apache with a graceful rhythm thumping in my blood as he picks me up and throws me over his shoulder.

He carries me down a narrow flight of stairs to a cool, dark cellar reeking of wine and sweat... and hot, sticky passion. With amazing strength in his arms, he slides me down his broad chest in a slow dance, rubbing my breasts against him, and then lays me down onto a soiled and dirty mattress. I arch my back, lift my hips, ignoring the lumpy, hard spots digging into my flesh. I reach out to him and he lowers his muscular body over me, and I wait, my breathing coming so fast, dizziness makes my head spin.

Strong hands wrap around my waist and when he enters me, this time I moan with pleasure...

8

SYLVIE

SYLVIE MARTONE TALKS!

Paris
1935

Hitler became German Chancellor two years ago, my country is in a political crisis, but the people of France love me.

My foray into talkies is an astounding success.

Emil builds a brilliant marketing campaign around my pictures that reflects the desperate decisions Parisians face every day. Not as Ninette. He showcases me as a woman struggling to make a living for herself in these hard times. I become every shop girl, every laundress, and every office matron working hard to bring home her own bacon. I make films about floozies fleecing men, good girls turning to sin, socialites on the run. That doesn't change the fact I'm still a piece of property to be exploited by Emil and the studio.

And I'd better look good doing it.

If I gain a few pounds, they give me pills to kill my appetite.

They shave my eyebrows and draw on skinny ones.

If my roots show too much – my hair darkens as I enter my twenties – the crew takes a break while I get a quick bleach touchup.

I'm whisked off to every film opening on a major publicity

campaign, always in a long, sexy gown with a fur stole slung over my shoulder or fluffy feather boa with a handsome actor or producer at my side (Emil hovers in the background, making sure the press shoots plenty of pictures with me in the forefront). *Silents are passé, yes,* I tell them, and I embrace the chance to continue my career in speaking roles. Thanks to Miss Brimwell and her strict voice lessons, I've developed a rich mezzo soprano voice which adapts well to talkies.

All this partying is in addition to my nights carousing at my secret haunts. I develop not only a taste for champagne, but the white powder offered to me by musicians and artists I meet, eager to share illicit drugs sneaked into Paris from Berlin.

Sniffing the drug off my long nails, I head out for a night with a handsome gigolo hired by the studio to escort me on a junket down to Cannes. Rich celebrities can't wait to be seen with me, drink and do drugs with me. When I do press interviews, I sober up quickly. I can't forget I started out in this business as Ninette.

I feel like I'm losing myself, what I am.

And it frightens the hell out of me.

* * *

Emil wants to control my sex life.

He's not pleased with my nocturnal jaunts, saying it's bad for my image.

I should fire the purveyor of the gossip on set – a script girl I barely know – but it's my own fault for not being more careful. A jealous *fille de joie* saw me dancing and cavorting with several men in a seedy club and told *her* friend who told the script girl. She couldn't wait to spread the story.

It didn't take long for word to reach Emil.

He insists on soliciting my partners, but I reject the men Emil chooses for me, preferring instead to find my lovers among the artists I meet in Montmartre and the university students in the Latin Quarter. Tall, muscular men with deep, sexy voices and stubble beards who aren't afraid to find a woman's secret places with their kisses, who take me in their arms and capture my soul with their fire, who don't care or don't know I'm Sylvie Martone.

Emil finds another way to make me do his bidding.

I'm dropped from a film for allegedly violating an obscure morals clause in my studio contract nobody *ever* pays attention to or there'd be no one making films. I realize if I want to stay on top, I have no choice but to acquiesce to his wishes. A sour moment in our relationship that makes me feel young and raw again – that I have no say in my own life no matter how much money I make or how many box office hits I have. No doubt Emil was the 'unknown source' making the accusation that was never proven, but it was enough to 'suspend' me. I hate how he uses his dominance over me to make me date the producers and studio moneymen who pay my salary. I'll bed them, if I must. But it's a cold bed. Not hot and passionate like the straw pallet in an artist loft in Montmartre, or the book-filled garret of the dashing young philosophy student.

Do I fall in love?

No, Sylvie Martone cannot fall in love. It's against Emil's rules.

God knows, my heart is fragile. I have no one to share everything I've worked so hard for.

On a whim, I drive out to the convent in my new, Italian, red Bugatti roadster to show Sister Vincent and ask her advice on how to nourish my wandering spirit. She blesses herself numerous times when she sees the expensive vehicle and asks if we can go for a ride with the top down. She never stops *oohing* and *aahing* the fancy car and I never get around to telling her the real reason I sneaked out of Paris. I'm lonely. I don't make friends easily – a byproduct of fame. The irony is I've built a golden cage for myself and even when I fly away, I must return to that cage alone. No man could ever understand my passion to make films, the sacrifices I've endured, that I'm not made to bear children and make a home.

The truth is, I can't bear a child.

Or so it seems. More than once I've fallen madly in love with a man and find such passion in his arms he can't stop and I don't want him to, hoping a child will be born of that passion, knowing I can give that child everything, love her, and adore her.

And pray the man of my passion will marry me.

Then I wait... and again I'm disappointed. My monthlies flow and I nurse an empty heart instead of a baby.

So I've embraced my fans as my children, my films are my legacy to them. I make sure the bouncy schoolchildren in my neighborhood behind the carriage gate of the Faubourg Saint-Antoine have shoes, the mothers have milk, and their husbands and brothers the tools they need to ply their trades.

To do so, I must work.

I have no choice but to fall in line, do what Emil wishes.

I never want to go hungry. I've seen the destitute humiliation of the people who live in the northern parts of Paris, men with their backs broken from arduous labor, children begging for sous, women selling their hair to buy bread.

That thought is on my mind a lot. The world is in a Great Depression, though France is hit later than the rest of Europe. What else can I do but act? I never learnt to make lace in the convent, I have no trade. I've gotten used to an extravagant lifestyle with an expensive haute couture wardrobe, jewels. Then Emil insists I take an expensive apartment in the Trocadéro in the *16e arrondissement* where I can entertain film industry notables.

But I'm still that girl who had the brashness to act out her dream at the Durand movie theater, except now I'm a *star*. And those kids who threw tomatoes and cabbages at me, made fun of me, have to *pay* to see me up there on the silver screen.

Just like I promised on that day... so long ago.

* * *

I have a string of big hits over the next few years. Unfortunately, I start believing my own publicity, the worst thing that can happen to an actor. I get cocky... sometimes arrogant if I don't get what I want. It's my way of lashing out at Emil for his mental abuse and demands, for his insistence I do his bidding with the men he chooses, men who can keep my career on top and his coffers full. It doesn't help I'm spoiled by my fans who follow my every move, embrace every story in *Ciné-Miroir* about my escapades and who my latest lover is... and every time I'm photographed in a new frock or fancy hat, a knockoff shows up on the racks of *Le Bon Marché* and *Aux Trois Quartiers* department stores. The public adores me and I adore them. I'm at the height of my success and I'm only twenty-five. My figure is svelte and my platinum hair glows bright and shiny under the spotlight of the public.

But there's another side to me.

My heart is dark... and the more I'm forced to do Emil's bidding to gain favors from the studio, the darker my life becomes. A life filled with alcohol and wild parties, men who love me, use me, then leave me. Then I start showing up late on set, forgetting my lines, missing my cues because I'm drinking too much.

'You're on a downward spiral, Sylvie. If you don't watch it, you'll end up like your mother,' Emil blurts out when he finds me in a drunken stupor in my Trocadéro apartment, empty bottles tossed about on the Berber carpet. 'Lying on your back for a few sous.'

I open one eye, curious. *What's he talking about?*

'Your mother wasn't an aristocrat seduced by a stable hand,' he continues, knowing I hear every word, his harsh words rattling my brain and sobering me up. 'But a prostitute who haunted the cabarets on the Butte.'

No, no, I insist, crying. *It can't be true.*

Emil goes on a rant, reminding me the public adores me and believes what he calls the phony biography put out by the studio publicity department. If the truth ever gets out, he threatens, and my fans find out I'm illegitimate, it will destroy their nostalgia for Ninette along with my *good girl trying to get a break* image the fans love.

And my career.

I calm down, slow my breathing. 'You're wrong, Emil. The fans believe in me, sending me stacks of mail every week, pouring out their stories to me, their hopes, and their dreams.' I bury my head in my hands, knowing losing them is my greatest fear. I'd die if the people of France hated me. *Just die...* they're my true family and I'd be lost without them.

Again, I'm caught in Emil's spider web, his cruel words digging in my spine like sharp claws, tearing away at my flesh.

'Think about what I said, Sylvie. And don't come back to the studio until you're sober.'

He slams the door, leaving me to stew in my vodka... or whiskey... whatever I gulped down after Marcel left... or was it Henri? It's not important. I can't forget the director's words. Is this why God is punishing me? Why I can't have a child of my own? Because I've chosen this life in pictures instead of taking the veil? Because I abandoned Him and everything Sister Vincent taught me?

I have to know if what Emil said about my mother is true because he doesn't make threats lightly. He never leaves a stone unturned when it comes to controlling me. I wouldn't put it past him to hire a detective agency to dig into my past. I always suspected there's more to the story than Sister Vincent let on, but I chose to ignore it. Not anymore.

I sleep off my binge, throw cold water on my face, then pick up my brassiere, stockings, and garters strewn about on the white carpet. I pull on panties and jump into a pair of tailored, grey-pleated trousers, white blouse, and houndstooth jacket. Then, as a misty dawn breaks over Paris, revealing blue and slate rooftops like stepping stones back to my past, I head west outside the city and cover the distance to the convent in Ville Canfort-Terre, pushing my fancy motorcar to go the limit.

I came back here soon after I had my hair bobbed and my film flopped to ask Sister Vincent for guidance, then again when I bought the car, revealing as much about my life as I had to, leaving out the compromising details. Guilt washes over me. I continue to write to her, though not as much as I should. (As long as I toe the line, Emil has given up trying to stop me.)

I have a raging hangover, my head is splitting, and confusion rules my brain. I'm so damn tired I can't keep my eyes open—

My head droops and I don't know why, but I jam my foot down on the gas pedal and accelerate through the wooded area outside the convent. The motorcar bounces over the road, hits a rock, bounces back and in an instant I'm wide awake.

My God... *where did that tree come from?*

I swerve, gripping the steering wheel hard and twisting it to the right, putting my shoulder into the awkward movement and ripping my jacket sleeve. Panting hard, I screech to a halt and, in a moment of self-deprecation, I bang my head on the steering wheel. Cursing... hurting inside. What insanity induced me to drive in this condition? I could have been killed if I'd slammed into that tall chestnut tree.

I push any idea of my mortality out of my mind. I've got bigger issues at stake.

Like, who *is* my birth mother?

* * *

I park the motorcar outside the gate and find Sister Vincent in the chapel, praying. In a pew. First row. On her knees. Her back is to me as my high heels echo on the stone floor, announcing my arrival. She continues mumbling in a voice as soft as a celestial cloud. As if she knows I'm coming and she's asking God to give her strength.

I stop.

She turns. Smiles at me. She looks as calm and serene as she always does. A vibrant joy in her grey eyes shines through the glass of her spectacles with such intensity I wonder if the lenses will crack. The fine lines around her mouth have deepened. I like to think that's because she smiles a lot, not because she worries about me.

'Sylvie, *ma petite*, I'm blessed to see you,' she says without breaking eye contact with me, which does nothing to dim my focused determination in my soul to say what's on my mind. Now. Without a fancy prelude. I can't wait any longer.

'Who was my mother, Sister Vincent?' I don't kneel down in the pew, but remain standing. 'I want the truth.'

She doesn't back away. Her eyes pierce my heart. Their greyness turns dark. Very dark.

'She was a prostitute from Paris...' she begins without making excuses, remaining on her knees as if doing penance for keeping her silence. I see her twisting her beads, gripping the wooden orbs, rubbing her sweat on them till they shine. 'A beautiful woman dying of consumption when she brought you here.'

'A tragic heroine, *n'est-ce pas*?' I snicker. 'It sounds like a scene from one of my films. How do I know *that's* the truth?' I can't stop looking at her, disbelieving what I'm hearing. I admire her courage to look me in the eye. I'm still reeling from knowing the fanciful story she told me as a child. How my mother was a wild and beautiful aristocrat who had a secret affair with a roguish stable hand. How she was forced to give me up lest harm come to me from her enemies. How she died in a suspicious fire rather than reveal my whereabouts. She made it sound so fascinating, I *wanted* to believe it.

'Because I would never tell a falsehood in front of Him.'

Her eyes drift upward toward the crucifix with Jesus Christ hanging above the altar. An eerie pause grips me, as if I expect a bolt of thunder to shake the rafters to disavow her words. A pungent scent of leftover incense mixes with the coriander of my perfume spiking from the heat of my body and fills my nostrils.

Still, I wait.

When nothing happens, the nun heaves out a sigh and rustles her black woolen skirts, then continues.

'I beg you to understand, *ma petite*. I made up the story because I didn't want to hurt you. Didn't want you to carry the stigma of being the illegitimate daughter of a prostitute upon your shoulders.' She stands and holds my hands in hers, hands with aging, wrinkled skin, veins popping, but the deep sadness in her grey eyes behind the wire rim spectacles doesn't move me.

'I can't believe you lied to me about my mother, Sister Vincent.

How you concocted a tale that would make a young girl's heart swell with such romantic notions she'd cling to them like they were sacred prayers.' I make it clear how angry I am with her, this dutiful creature who was the only good thing about my childhood and now I find that was a lie, too. She didn't trust me enough to let me handle the truth. I could have, couldn't I?

You're not doing such a good a job now, are you?

'I made a fool out of myself with that phony story all these years,' I continue, raising my voice and not caring if God disapproves. He knows what I've done and I'm living my punishment. What more can He do to me? 'Emil knows the truth and I'm more under his control than ever. I have no choice but to do his bidding if I don't want to end up in the gutter because I will *never* return here. I'm done... done with you... done with your pious teachings. Lies, *all lies*. I'll never believe in you or hold anything you say sacred again.'

'Please, *mon enfant*, I beg you to forgive me—'

'Forgive you? I don't know if I ever can.'

Bitter words that prick my brain to rethink what I've said, but I've gone too far. I've set myself up for a painful isolation from the one person in my life always there for me. *Yes*, I'm not thinking straight... I do that a lot these days. But I don't need Sister Vincent's preaching to me about my 'habits'. It's better this way.

Then, without turning back even when I hear a loud sob behind me and the swish of holy skirts slumping to the stone floor, I race back to Paris, anger and frustration pumping through me. Adrenaline surges through my veins and primes my juices like a glass of Pernod. I need to be with someone, someone to hold me, tell me what I want to hear. That I'm wanted... loved. My sensual urges are on fire, burning like an eternal flame.

There's no turning back and no one to stop me.

I head up the cobbled Rue Norvins toward a familiar apartment with red velvet walls and a big, soft four poster bed at the top of Montmartre, a place where I can forget how lonely I am. No lies... no promises. Just sex with a beautiful man who doesn't care who my mother was.

* * *

Montmartre

The heady warmth of smooth brandy quiets my fears and calms me.

I lie nude on the rich, cherry-red velvet coverlet, listening to the sound of my own breathing, the minutes ticking by on the grandfather clock in the study. Like droplets of water falling on my forehead.

Tick... tock.

Drip... drop.

Then a cool breeze tickles me between the legs as the rugged artist tantalizes my bare skin with his long paintbrush.

'Bastien, again... *please, mon amour.*'

'You're drunk, Sylvie... sloppy drunk, but you're beautiful.'

I wiggle my hips. 'Hand me my pills. And the brandy.'

I need it, crave it... I can't turn off the painful thirst for the alcohol circulating in my brain. My mouth is dry. I'm heaving up gulps of air. My eyelids are heavy as a profound weariness descends upon me. Weighing me down as if I'm bound by restraints, my feelings and emotions wrapped up in a realm of fantasy, knowing what comes next. Pure ecstasy.

'Where did you get these pills?' he asks. 'They're a powerful sedative.' He rattles the glass bottle of sleeping pills I sweet talked the studio doctor into giving me.

'I have my ways... give me the pills.'

'What if Hélène shows up and finds you here?'

'Who the hell is she?'

'My patroness...'

'You mean your posh whore.' I see him grin wide, his bare chest shiny with sweat.

'She's doesn't trust me.'

'Neither do I.' I smirk, then wiggle my hips again to get what I want. Him. And the pills.

'*Zut alors*, Sylvie, I can never resist you,' he says, handing me the pills and then the brandy. 'You're the most beautiful woman I've ever made love to.'

'Until the next one comes along.' I have no illusions about Bastien and his loyalty, or lack thereof, but the struggling artist is good for my ego... and my needs.

His fingers are cold, *colder* than I would have imagined when he touches me. I don't care. I'm all in a fever, wrapped up in darkness and secrecy and—

Desire.

Sending me to a place I both need *and* fear.

I hear the crisp snap of a matchstick hitting the iron bedframe and the scent of that fear mixes with the pungent odor of a familiar smell filling the outrageously red bedroom. A cool, damp musky smell that reminds me of rich earth.

Bastien inhales deeply and blows out the smoke before offering me the bud. I shake my head, preferring the lovely dream my pills promise. I down the rest of the pills with the brandy, then gasp when I feel his soft kisses teasing me, and then his curious mouth moving up and down my body, his lips dancing over my skin with a wicked playfulness both intimate and frightening.

My heart beats faster, my breaths frantic.

The room begins spinning around me. A nauseating dizziness takes hold of me. I shouldn't have taken so many pills. I'm powerless to resist their effect. I refuse to acknowledge I'm on a drunken, drug-induced binge, drowning my sorrows with a man I don't love but enjoy, except tonight he seems nervous. I assume that's because I dropped in unexpectedly, enticing him to soothe my lonely soul with his gorgeous body.

A pity, I remember little of what happens afterward except I'm never disappointed. All I recall is waking up with a raging headache and a lovely soreness between my legs and a woman shouting... then Bastien shouting back.

'She's a drunk and an addict,' the woman yells. 'Get her out of here.'

'Do you know who she is?'

'No, and I don't care. She's nothing to me. Get rid of her or we're through.'

'You don't mean that, *ma chérie.*'

'I'm not paying for this rattrap so you can bring your tart here. We have an agreement. I own you and you service only me. Toss her out now or you can sell your ass to another rich pigeon.'

Then a door banging... the grandfather clock striking three... someone picking me up and carrying me out into the chilly night.

And I pass out. Again.

9

JULIANA

ONCE UPON A TIME ON THE SILVER SCREEN

Burbank, California
Present Day

'My grandmother was Sylvie Martone, a famous French actress...?' I choke on the words. '*And* a Nazi collaborator?'

Rain pitter patters down on the large blue umbrella Ridge holds over me as we walk quickly by the soundstages so familiar to me, a path I've walked for years bringing me to a crossroads. I wave to actors I've worked with zooming by in golf carts, production people I've known since I first stepped onto the lot as a bouncy nineteen-year-old to give my first studio tour in French. I feel like everybody is watching me with curious eyes, asking themselves, *Did you know Juliana Chastain is related to a French actress who slept with the enemy during the war?*

The rain hasn't let up and neither have my insecurities. I keep telling myself it's a mistake. I can't be related to a traitor.

I am, according to Ridge. And he's about to show me the proof.

'I couldn't believe it either, Juliana,' he says, 'but pictures don't lie. I went through the historical footage in our company film library and that led me here where I found more info in the studio archives. Press shots of her sitting at Paris cafés with Nazi officers, newsreel footage of her publicizing her films in Berlin, even cozying up to a handsome SS captain in 1943.'

'I still can't believe it. Are you *sure* it's her, my grandmother?'

'Yes,' he says with a firmness not to be challenged. We enter the studio movie theater through glass doors and shake off the rain. 'I called in a favor and put the image you sent me through photo recognition software to identify her. Sylvie Martone was born in Paris in 1910, but there's no date of her death. She disappeared after the war. According to the French studio bio, her mother was an aristocrat, father unknown. Raised by pious nuns at the Convent of Saint Daria in Ville Canfort-Terre before she ran away at sixteen to Paris and spent her career under the tutelage of Emil-Hugo de Ville, a prominent director, also her manager.'

'None of this proves she was working with the Nazis.'

'If you're thinking she was forced to do publicity for Goebbels' film campaigns, that may be true... but there were rumors she had an affair with an SS officer.'

'*No!*' I cry out, wiping raindrops off my sleek trench coat. 'I won't believe my grandfather was a goose-stepping monster.'

Ridge gives me a friendly hug and doesn't let me go, comforting me. I admit I like it. He knows how much I'm hurting inside and is trying to get me through it. 'I thought you'd be happy to find out your grams was in show business until I started digging into her personal life and found the newspaper stories and press photos from the war. So I sorted through our film catalog of World War II newsreels in both English and French and came up with proof of her working with the Nazis.'

'Do you have the films?' I ask as he ushers me into the small studio theater where the producers, directors, and actors watch the daily rushes.

'Yes.'

'Okay, I'm ready... I think.' It's so quiet, yet I feel in my bones the place is reeking with ghosts of screen legends giving Sylvie Martone a thumbs down as Ridge dumps an old cardboard box of 35mm films on a table, then sorts through them.

I'm afraid to watch as he sets up the projector, my heart pounding.

I trust him. We started out in the film business together, worked our way up. Out of the corner of my eye, I see a young woman in jeans and college sweatshirt wave to me from the corner. I wave back. I've seen her around Ridge's office dropping off films from the studio. Harper is shy, spending her time huddled over old film, going over each frame for scratches and splits in the film.

As Ridge sorts the old films, I realize I've never seen him so over-the-top freaked out, rambling on about how Sylvie Martone was a major star in French cinema beginning with silent films.

'She had a successful career that started in 1926 and lasted throughout the war,' Ridge rushes his words, pulling out the round metal blue cans, finding what he's looking for, then threading the film through the projector.

'So she wasn't an innocent young girl seduced by the Nazi war machine,' I ponder, tapping my fingers on the plush seating. Sylvie Martone was a bona fide movie star just into her thirties when the Occupation began. She didn't save anyone but herself, her career.

I shake my head back and forth. No excuse for her behavior.

I sink down into my seat. I'm getting deeper and deeper into a situation that could have dire consequences... a sad, heart-wrenching feeling sitting on the edge of my brain that I should have let *sleeping film stars lie*, that I'm digging up a piece of history my mother tried so hard to spare me from and I have no right to do so.

I try not to think about it... not yet. First, I must see for myself this woman who betrayed France.

Ridge lowers the lights and shows me newsreels from the war years of 1940 to 1944 showing Sylvie smiling and waving into the camera at various locations in Paris. Cafés, movie theaters, *Le Grand Palais* – always with a Nazi presence close by. Then afterward, he hands me a large, untouched photo shot for a daily newspaper showing Sylvie smiling big and arm in arm with a handsome, sneering SS captain.

I don't know what to say when Ridge pulls up stories from the film magazine *Ciné-Miroir* on old microfilm about Sylvie before the war and later gossip tidbits in *Le Matin* and *Paris Soir* about her dining here and there with members of the Nazi party.

I translate the stories into English for Ridge and Harper until I can't read anymore. No doubt my grandmother enjoyed a brilliant career during the Occupation along with an active social life with the hierarchy of the Wehrmacht.

'From late 1941 to 1944, she starred in films produced by the German-owned Galerie Films during the Occupation,' Ridge says. 'Then her career fell apart when Paris was liberated and according to my source, she was accused of what the French government called *collaboration horizontale.*'

I squirm in the plush red seat. No need to translate. I grip the armrests, attempting to remain calm. Somehow she escaped to Switzerland, according to Ridge, and that's where the trail goes cold.

Or does it?

Something doesn't sit right with me, doesn't make sense. How did my mother end up at a French convent? Why did Sylvie leave her that photo dated 1949? So many questions and so far, all the answers point to a woman selfish and interested only in keeping herself in the spotlight.

Why did I ever start digging up the past, why couldn't I leave well enough alone? No wonder my mother never spoke about her family.

She was so ashamed. So am I.

Harper has been quiet up to now, waiting while I compose myself. She tells me Ridge asked if she could sit in so she could tell me about her restoration work. How hundreds of nitrate reels of silent films discovered decades ago in an outpost in Ontario were miraculously preserved under an old ice hockey rink. Silent films that made their way across the country from one movie theater to another and ended up there, all but forgotten until a construction crew unearthed them.

She tells me in a quiet voice reels of films starring my grandmother were in that cache of films, a woman I never knew existed until today.

'I went through the catalog we put together and found seven two-reelers listed starring Sylvie Martone from 1926 to 1928,' she says, sitting down next to me. Her dark blue eyes twinkle when she looks at Ridge. I smile. Have I been missing something? 'They're from a serial called *Ninette* shown in weekly installments. I can't wait for you to see them.'

An ache in my heart surfaces that I never expected. In spite of the evidence of Sylvie's betrayal of France, I *want* to see her.

Ridge loads up the projector with another reel. 'I know this has been a shock, Juliana, but you had to see it.'

'Shock? I can't breathe... my pulse is racing... I'm sweaty. I thought my grandmother was an actress or a Paris model. Not working with the Nazis. My heart is thumping out of control.'

'Sit back and relax and meet your grandmother *before* the war. When Sylvie Martone was beloved in all of France as Ninette.

* * *

Her lips move as I watch her on the silver screen, but her voice is as silent as light speeding through time and space. A young woman flirting with the camera in a film about a girl called Ninette in *Les Orphelins Perdus* (Lost Orphans). I lean closer, wishing I could hear her speak, but the actress with a twinkle in her eye keeps her secrets from me, secrets that rock my world, tear me apart.

I can't believe it. The girl with the mirth of a mischievous fairy is the younger version of the woman in the photo.

Sylvie Martone.

My grandmother.

Still, I watch. The luminous nitrate emitting from the old silent film hypnotizing me.

Heart pounding, my hand shakes as I massage my aching forehead to clear my vision. I've been staring at the screen too long, the *whirring* sound of the projector behind me and the arc of the light beaming off the ceiling in the darkened screening room giving me chills as it takes me back to a more innocent time. A time when wildflowers and ribbons graced this young girl's hair.

I'm breathless, a sense of self-awakening in me that both frightens and intrigues me. Like a curious hummingbird peeking through your window. Wanting attention. You can't look away.

From what I know about her, Sylvie made choices during the war I find unforgiveable. Deeds forged and executed like scenes in a film she starred in. I don't turn away. And that's what puzzles me, why I can't let it go, how it draws me to her to try to understand *why* she did what she did.

I catch my breath and hold my chest every time I think about it.

I blink several times. The silent film has scratches on the image along with numerous dirt particles. It doesn't dull the brilliance of the platinum-haired, sixteen-year-old girl filling the screen. According to Ridge, *Ninette* and her adventures was one of the most popular French serials of the silent film era. Each story featured a seamstress named Ninette, an angel with curly platinum hair framing her face sent to earth to do good deeds, chased and thwarted by the devil in different disguises trying to undo her good deeds and get rid of her.

The devil eventually caught up with her.

Wearing a Nazi swastika.

I tap my fingers on the deep-red, velvet armrest, wishing Sylvie had remained Ninette. A sweet child giving so much of her heart to the audience... the lost chord on a summer song that turned into a deep and heavy requiem as the years went by.

Not in this film. This was a time of innocence and a young girl's sweet laughter. I'm amazed at the depth of her performance, focusing on the intensity of her eyes to convey her emotions while the brilliant sunlight gilded her hair a striking platinum. She was 'in the moment' even when she stood still, her body language, whether it was a hand gesture or the sway of her shoulders, telling a story.

A story shot in Paris on a spring day.

When no one could guess the storm clouds that would rain down on the City of Light for four years when unspeakable horror befell the city when the Germans came to Paris in June 1940.

Before the actress playing Ninette went over to the dark side.

Before someone snapped a photo of her linked arm in arm with the handsome SS Officer.

I let a tear fall and it stings my heart like a slender, silver arrow. A small trinket you pin onto a coat lapel or a navy-blue French beret.

The diamond heart pin with the arrow must be a gift Sylvie gave to her daughter to remember her by along with the photo. I wonder where her name, Madeleine Chastain, came from. During the war, records were shoddy at best, and it would be easy for her to keep her child's father's name secret.

I take a minute to compose myself. What I've seen today changes everything. My body tingles, my ears ring, and I have a difficult time focusing on the rest of the film. What I've discovered about my roots unnerves me.

How can I go about my normal life knowing my grandmother was a Nazi?

* * *

Faster and faster we go, Ridge's motorcycle kicking up dirt on the backlot, me on the back with him pulling out all stops. Flying over dirt, brush... squealing around corners on the New York set... whizzing down Main Street in the Old West town with me hanging on to him for dear life.

Heart-pounding stunts that cleanse my mind of anything except surviving the next hare-brained turn.

Ridge insisted what I needed was a fast, crazy spin around the backlot to blow off steam. A way of pushing down the shock, fear, despair... and shame that hit me when I discovered my grandmother hung out with Nazis.

'Ready to jump over the swamp lake, Juliana?' he shouts back at me. In spite of the wind noise, I can hear him since we're wearing open-face helmets.

'Why not?' I play cavalier. 'You're the best in the business.'

His laughter flies back at me. I hold on tighter when he zooms *around* the lake, gravel flying up and splattering us in a spray.

I grab him tighter as he navigates another curve then picks up speed as we fly over a clickety, old wooden bridge, my breasts pressed against his strong back, my butt sliding left then right on the leather seat. I don't want to let go... or is it more than that?

Being so damn close to this man stirs up more than friendship in me. His skin burning hot, his arm muscles tense as he steers the bike around corners, up a hill. I'm uncomfortable with my physical reaction to him. I can't ignore his hard body pressed against mine. His warmth, his strength, they make me feel protected. I try not to think about how it good it feels to hug this man. Any girl would find him sexy as heck, but what he did for me today makes me even more determined to keep our relationship as trusted friends. Anything else is too dangerous.

A twinge of guilt hits me when I remember Harper's long, lingering looks at him. I don't want to mess up anything between them.

Then we race down a long straightaway at top speed, the onshore winds blowing the dust away, my heart pumping, before he slows down and slides the bike around the corner then slams to a halt, the motorcycle idling.

'You ready to talk about it, Juliana?'

I attempt a smile. 'I'm good.'

He turns off the engine and gets off his bike, removes his helmet. 'Are you?' His stare is direct, a shock of hair falling into his eyes that look at me different than before. Or am I imagining it?

I hand him the extra helmet he got from the property department.

'You got me. I'm far from being okay,' I admit and together we sit down on the porch steps of an old façade once used as the house where a popular TV family lived. Shuttered, the dirty yellow paint was cracked and peeling. A remnant from the past hiding its secrets.

Like Sylvie Martone.

'This is the worst day in my life since my mother took her last breath.' I sigh. A nagging and growing guilt comes over me, but I let go of my feelings. I need her strength. How she kept her secret all these years baffles me. I feel deep in my heart she'd understand why I have to share it with the only person who will understand.

Ridge grabs my hand, his dark hair falling in his eyes like an avenging superhero. 'I want to hear everything.'

I clear my throat. 'I need to figure out how I'm going to cope with what you showed me about my grandmother. The French newsreels with her smiling and waving to the camera and surrounded by SS officers. And the press photos showing her hanging out in Paris cafés with Nazis and riding around in a big Mercedes with tiny swastika flags blowing in the wind. It was heartbreaking to see my own flesh and blood cavorting with the enemy while Parisians were dying of hunger and beaten on the streets. Drinking and eating with them, and God knows what else.' I take a breath. 'Not to mention the rumor she had an affair with an SS officer, which means my grandfather—'

He cuts me off. 'Hold on, don't jump to conclusions. In spite of what we dug up, we need hard evidence, documented facts, not hearsay. I've been in the film business long enough to know photos don't tell the whole story. We need to research whatever archives and official records of the German High Command in France that survived and weren't burnt. I know a few suits in the legal department. We can get them started digging up records from the war so we can get to the bottom of this—'

I shake my head. 'No, this is something I have to do myself. I can't sit here and wait for bored government officials to plod through records that may or may not exist. You said yourself many records were destroyed. And what you said about photos makes me wonder if I'm looking at this in the wrong light.' I pull up the glamor shot of the beautiful blonde on my phone and give it another long, hard look. The photo signed by Sylvie Martone to her daughter Madeleine, my mother. 'I speculate *Maman* never opened that box... it remained sealed all these years holding the secret she couldn't face... so the question remains, why did she bring it with her only to keep it buried?'

'Sylvie Martone was a gorgeous woman,' Ridge says, looking at my phone. 'I see that same spark in her eye you have. And that adorable dimple, too.' He smiles at me, trying to make me feel better. 'Like her granddaughter, she doesn't give up. Give her a chance, Juliana. I have the feeling there's more to your grandmother than old newsreels.'

'Ridge McCall, you may be the most insane stunt driver, but you're the best friend ever.'

He kisses me lightly on the nose. I let go with a dreamy sigh, then catch myself. I can't even *think* about letting him kiss me. I've come to rely on his friendship and would die if I did something stupid to lose that.

'You're not alone in this. I'll do whatever I can to help you. Where are you going to start?'

'You said after the war the French government believed Sylvie Martone fled to Switzerland in 1944 or early 1945... but the date on the photo is 1949.'

'Go on.'

'My mother told me she came to the convent as a baby. I think Sylvie may have hidden out there... God knows for how long. She'd be over a hundred if she were alive. We have no idea when she died. It must have been when my mother was a child. *Maman* was adamant she grew up an orphan, but someone at the convent may still remember Sylvie. It's worth a shot.' I catch myself staring at him. He's a hunk of manliness worth staring at. I push those thoughts out of my head. 'At least I can pay homage to my mother and bring peace to her spirit.'

'What do you mean?'

'Sylvie Martone wrote on the back of the photo, *Someday you'll find out the truth*. I'm going to France, Ridge, to find that truth.'

* * *

I don't know when I made up my mind to go to France, when that crazy scheme settled in my brain. Maybe it was when I saw Sylvie Martone riding around in that Nazi staff car... or smiling at the camera squeezed between two Nazi officers. Something struck me as off. I know how actresses think, how they pose for the camera with their best side showing, their bosoms lifted, their lips moist from wetting them with their tongue. They *love* the camera. Sylvie's smile was forced, her brow wrinkled, her shoulders slumped. She wasn't a happy camper taking those pictures with the Nazi officers and that gives me hope.

I want to believe I'm not going on a fool's errand, but logic tells me I have to dig deeper into Sylvie's past, try to understand the woman before I pass judgment on her and pray there's more to her than old newsreels and flashy photos. I owe it to my mom. And to Sylvie.

Ma grand-mère.

I hustle together the 'go-bag' I keep packed for last-minute location shoots, grab my passport, and make online flight reservations. I'll fly into Charles de Gaulle Airport in Paris, then drive out to the small town where *Maman* spent her life. Ville Canfort-Terre. I found a small inn there and made a reservation. I checked to make sure the convent is up and running... the nuns are known for their lacemaking (is that where the lace veil came from?) and it's very profitable for them. I'm not telling anyone I'm coming. I'll play *tourist slash designer* looking for ideas for costumes for a show I'm doing. Partially true. That way, I can poke around without anyone knowing the real reason I'm there.

I work around the clock for the next ten days finishing up the prelim sketches for *Wings over Manhattan* and tell the producer I'll be back in time to meet with him and the actors before production starts.

There's no turning back.

My own personal D-Day looms before me. Amazing how over a week ago I didn't know I had a famous actress grandmother, now I'm off to learn everything I can about her.

Now I understand why my mother didn't want me to go into show business, why even though she loved visiting me on the set and seeing the actors wearing my costumes, she never seemed comfortable being around the movies. Like she found it disheartening. Sad, somehow. It reminded her of the life her own mother lived. The need to know more about this woman who had such an impact on both our lives pulls at me.

I wish my mother were going with me, but that never would have happened. When I'd ask her if she wanted to go back to France, she'd shake her head, her eyes fierce then teary. I chalked it up to her sad love affair and went out of my way to treat my mother to whatever I could. She never wanted anything but to see me. She'd sigh with pleasure whenever I brought her pink peonies like the ones that grew near her weeping willow and her favorite chocolate nonpareils. A treat the nuns gave her at the French convent where she grew up.

That's where I have to start. Sylvie disappeared after the war, but according to the photo, she was alive in 1949. Was she in hiding at the convent all that time with her little daughter? I feel in my gut I'll find the answers there. It's up to me to do what *Maman* couldn't. Find out the truth about Sylvie Martone.

I spend a long goodbye with Ridge on the way to the airport, my cell never out of my hand, a different emotion running through me as we talk, a new closeness between us that frightens the heck out of me. Yet also gives me courage.

Then I'm off to France. I thank *Maman* for her generous gift to me, which is paying for my trip. I believe in my heart she approves of spending my inheritance to clear *ma grand-mère's* name.

10

SYLVIE

THE ROAD BACK FROM MONTMARTRE

Montmartre

1935

Bastien dumps me on the steps of Sacré-Coeur to dry out, a fitting place since it was once a pagan site before the great basilica was built in the last century. I'm as godless as any druid, every bone in my body protesting when cold stones make hard contact with my flesh. My skin crawls from imaginary creatures digging into me, the putrid smell of vomit emitting from the jazzy-blue, velvet gown wrapped around my legs stings my nostrils. The taste left in my mouth makes me gag. Worse is the quiet before dawn taunting me with the idea of giving up and letting go...

I can't. Not yet.

'I need another drink,' I mutter, clinging to his warm, strong body so dangerously close to me I can smell his ripe odor. '*Please*, just one... then I'll be fine. I swear.'

I pull him closer, straining to hear the low whispering of his voice urging me to forgive him, that he has no choice, but I'll be safe here.

'Bastien, *please*...' my voice croaks as I scratch at my bare legs, try to make out his face as he leans over me but he's covered in shadows. I marvel at the strength in his arms having carried me halfway up the steep stairs before his breathing became labored, his chest heaving, his mission of abandonment completed. I have a vague recollection of him laying me down, kissing my dry lips, and then nuzzling his face in my hair smelling of perfume and brandy. 'I shall never forget you, *ma chérie*. I would give you my heart for always... if I were free.'

'*Merde.*'

I know a goodbye line when I hear it, even if I'm floating somewhere between heaven and hell in a drug-addicted high. I'm chilled and forgotten, my body heavy like sand on a beach crushed by a roaring wave pounding into me, making me dizzy, piercing my skull with the craving for more... *more*... till I'll do *anything* to get that high.

I hear Bastien breathing heavily. *Alors*, he's still here, waiting to see if I'll swear my undying love for him. Beg him to let me be his patron and in a make-believe world we live happily ever after in a garret with a view of the Seine and have six *enfants*.

The plot I have in mind is quite different.

I intend to drag myself to the closest café and drink a bottle of cognac and forget the reason I'm here. Forget my mother was a prostitute and then drink another bottle and forget I'm Sylvie Martone. The bone-chilling admission by Sister Vincent about my past only intensifies my need to be loved for *me*.

Even a horrible me reeking of booze.

'Go away, Bastien,' I moan. 'Leave me alone.'

'*Adieu, mon amour*,' he whispers, 'I wish it didn't have to end like this.'

A soft breeze carrying his male scent whizzes by my nose and even in my confused state, I can't help but inhale him, wish he'd hold me, knowing he won't. I tell myself I don't need him. I'm a big movie star. I'll find a new lover and then we'll...

Do what? Repeat the scene like another retake in my life? I'm too miserable to contemplate it, my head hurts too much and my belly is bloated. My hands are puffy. And my mouth is so dry... like it's stuffed with cotton. I climb a step, then two... it's too much for me. I lie down on the cold stone and cradle my head in my arms. I'll sleep it off like I always do, then I'll be fine. No one will notice me huddled on the steps. There are plenty of *les exclus*, homeless, in Paris. Besides, I don't need help. I can stop drinking any time I want to... of course I can.

I know that alcoholic's prayer by heart.

* * *

The cathedral bells ring in my ears, killing my eardrums.

Head pounding, I untangle my legs, numb from being twisted underneath me for hours, stagger to my feet on an early morning and wrap my long gown around my waist like a laundress doing her business. My feet are bare since Bastien tied my shoes around my waist with the long straps. I raise my left arm and my small beaded purse dangles by its chain from my wrist.

Francs, centimes. Identity card. Lipstick in gold case. Keys. The only thing Bastien stole was my pride.

I stagger back and forth, unsteady. *Bien*, I'm a drunk but I don't deserve this. Left out here with the cold west wind in my face to sober me up. The bells won't stop ringing, reminding me God is not impressed with my performance tonight or yesterday or a million yesterdays.

Bon. I don't need Him either.

I drag myself up a few steps, banging my bare toes on the stone, yelping from the sharp pain then, exhausted, I slump down. A sudden crying jag hits me hard and I can't stop—

'May I help you, *mademoiselle*?' I hear a man ask me with rich, melted tones, not sultry but arresting, making me shiver.

I wet my lips. My prayers are answered. I'll convince him to buy me a drink.

I squint at the persimmon-yellow sun trying to come out from behind the fog, wipe the tears away, and put on my public face. At least I try to. It's not easy when you've already spilled the contents of your stomach onto your lovely, blue velvet gown.

'If you'd be so kind, *monsieur*, to buy a lady a drink...' I burp, blink. Burp again. I feel sick, but I keep my game face on.

'Sorry, *mademoiselle*, I can't do that.'

I smirk. 'Who are you, *God*?'

He chuckles, folds his hands in his Roman cassock sleeves. 'No, I am His disciple. Father Armand.'

I shade my eyes with my hand, trying to get a better look at this man who pinged my ego with his curt rebuff. A swath of black billowing in the hilltop wind stands over me, white collar, large brim black hat.

A priest. He looks so young. I gaze upward. *Is this Your idea of a joke?*

'I don't need your help, Father. Go away.'

He smiles, a kindly smile that's neither wide nor nondescript but knowing. As if he's heard those words more times than there are stars in the sky. 'As you wish, *mademoiselle*, but you will not find me a bad companion on your journey.'

I laugh. 'I'm not going anywhere but—'

'There *is* another path, *mademoiselle*.'

'Not for me.'

He tips his hat. 'I see. Well then, since you've given up, I shall be on my way.' He turns to leave and his holy but arrogant attitude gets to me, making me uneasy. How *dare* he pretend to want to help me, and then walk away like my soul isn't worth a centime?

I scrape the skin on my arms with my nails, poking at my face, my whole body twitching. What did I expect? I'm acting like a scruffy streetwalker, talking back to a man of the cloth who offered to help me and I turn my back on him. No wonder he's walking away. Am I that much of a fool? Or is there another answer, one I don't want to face?

That my soul is lost forever, that I can never come back from this insanity I've created for myself. I *want* to get sober, but every time I try,

I slide back to my old ways. Lose myself in the bliss of an alcoholic stupor then face the deep, hidden pain of loneliness that resides within me like a constant sore that won't heal. An ache so deep inside me it comes upon me at the oddest times, reminding me of everything I've done, that everything I have is worth nothing without someone to share it with.

So I share it with the bottle.

A cold, heartless piece of glass that keeps my soul prisoner like a butterfly that will never be free. When I stop drinking, I shake, get so angry with myself, then fearful, anxious. So I have a drink and the bliss returns. Not for long. Once again, I end up tossed aside. I hate this feeling, more so now because this is the second time I've been turned down by a man tonight, even if he is a priest. It's time I assert myself and set him straight. I don't need him or whatever he's selling.

I pull myself up to my knees, sway back and forth until I'm close enough to grab onto the hem of his robe. 'You can't talk to me like that,' I cry out with an arrogance to match his. 'Do you know who I am?'

'I do, *mademoiselle.*' He leans down, cups my chin in his hands and looks into my eyes with a knowing spirit like he opened the confessional window. 'You are Ninette.'

'What...?' His words send shivers through me. 'How...?'

'I watched you climbing up the steps to the basilica after that man left you, your tormented soul in need of a prayer... and I swore I knew you. When the first ray of dawn broke upon your beautiful face, your platinum hair shining like an angel's, I held back, my breath wanting, my eyes not believing, Yes, it *was* you, a woman my dear mother adored... she believed in you, a star in the sky who taught her to have dreams when she went to see your pictures. Ninette gave her hope... and the courage to go forward even during the worst of times, and that hope can be as powerful as any prayer.

'She prayed I'd be chosen to serve God since I aspired to the seminary. But when I was a boy, we were too poor for me to even have a bed. I slept in a hammock. We lived in the suburbs of Paris, where my widowed mother worked in a button factory to support her three children and prayed every day for the two she had lost. Every Saturday when she got paid, she took my two sisters and me to the pictures. We'd watch you up on the big screen in the darkened theater. *Maman* never gave up believing I'd find a path to serving God because she believed Ninette showed her how to work hard and be strong for us. She found the courage to go on even when she became ill with the cough because it was what Ninette would have done.'

I stifle a sob, his gentle voice moving me in a manner that makes me listen. He's speaking from the heart, pulling up a memory so real to him that I, too, can see the picture he paints. No, he's not acting, spinning a pious yarn as do so many of his ilk. I know bad acting when I see it and the humble priest is as real as they come. Which does nothing to assuage the guilt slamming through my soul, the shame at him finding me soiled and damaged. I'm not surprised he recognized me. My face is everywhere. On kiosks advertising numerous products... posters bigger than life hung outside movie theaters.

I lower my head and bring my knees to my chest to hide from him.

He won't go away.

He bows his head, remembering. 'Her prayers were answered when a patron sponsored me at the seminary. I swore then I would do His work with every ounce of my strength. So when I found you here on these holy steps, I couldn't turn away, couldn't believe I was seeing the great Sylvie Martone so lost when she has given so much to France. I couldn't leave to chance you'd survive the night unharmed by the denizens who slither out of their holes to prey on the innocent, so I waited beside you, and no, you didn't know I was there. You tossed and turned, fretted and swore, called out God for abandoning you when you were a child. More than once you cried out, *Help me... please help me.* I believe God heard you and sent me here to guide you since most days I attend to the sick at this hour. Today I heard His voice telling me to go to Sacré-Coeur... now I know why, *mademoiselle*. He sent me to you.'

I smirk. 'Even if I believed your story, which I don't, why help me, a sinner?'

'We are all sinners, *mademoiselle*, but you're the reason I wear the cross today.' He holds my hand, doesn't let go. 'I'm so grateful to you for giving me those wonderful years going to the pictures with my mother before she died of tuberculosis. She was forty-five.'

'I wish I were more like Ninette,' I admit in a broken, harsh voice. I mourn for the loss of those early years when I was making the *Ninette* two-reelers. If only I'd grabbed onto the depth and sincerity of the character I played, the goodness of Ninette, and held it close to my heart, things would have turned out different.

'You are, *Mademoiselle* Martone,' Father Armand insists, helping me stand then guiding me up the stairs with a gentle hand and through the grand portals of the basilica. 'You wouldn't have come this far if you didn't have her strength.' We anoint our foreheads with water from the holy water font and make the sign of the cross. I lower my eyes and my need for alcohol is so powerful, I lick the water off my fingertips, wishing it were vodka. I catch the priest's questioning look. 'Do you believe in God, *mademoiselle*?'

'Yes.'

'Do you think He would put temptation in your path?'

'No. But the devil would.'

'You needn't fear him. He hasn't got the guts to come in here.'

His humor makes me smile. 'Now what, Father?'

'We pray.'

Prayer. I'm so mentally and physically tired, so emotionally drained, my will to resist his request is stripped from my mind. Deep-seeded comfort from prayer isn't something I coveted growing up, but it feels right. As if I *have* come home.

As we take a place in the brown, wooden pew, Father Armand has the hand of the Lord on his shoulder when he says the devil, whatever shape he takes – Emil, Bastien, or the others – can't come in here. For the first time since Sister Vincent took my hand that day my mother left me at the convent, I feel safe.

We kneel in the back of the grand basilica, my knees hurting.

When was the last time I prayed in a church? I shift my weight back and forth as the pew squeaks and the priest chants a prayer in Latin.

'*Actiones nostras, quaesumus Domine, aspirando praeveni et adiuvando prosequere...*'

I know enough Latin from the sisters to recognize the prayer; he's asking for the Lord's help before we begin our journey – a journey, if I'm honest, I'm not keen on.

How do you get an alcoholic to give up the one thing they want most in the world?

It's then it hits me, that with everything I have – I can buy anything, go anywhere – I chose alcohol and cocaine for my companions. What a sorry mess I am. There's no glamor to ending up in the sewer, stiff-legged and lips tinted blue like a bloated corpse.

I need help.

Or I damn well will.

I'm sober enough to know this is my last chance. Father Armand believes in me. His story touches me deeply and *damn* Emil and his control over me. I *am* Ninette and more determined than ever to quash any gossip about where I come from the best way I know how.

By getting clean and sober.

By being the film star loved by the people of France. I've never let my fans down. I choose only products I believe in to put my name on. My brand is everywhere – on face powder, stockings, and perfume. Magazine covers. I'm so well known on the streets of Paris, I often resort to wearing disguises to get a breath of fresh air in the Tuileries Gardens.

A cleansing breath escapes my lungs now.

I don't know how long we pray. Every time the doors open and a faithful follower comes in, a belligerent wind sweeps in with them and pounces on my poor body with its cold hand, making it clear to me how badly off I am. My chest hurts so much, I find it hard to breathe, like someone is trying smother me. I try to shake off the tremors that make me shake all over, the severe headache pounding in my temples. I can't. My teeth chatter.

Oh, God, please make it stop!

Sweats... perspiration dripping from my body... dreams... *voices*... anger, oh, so much anger because my body is craving alcohol... and drugs. That innocent sniff of white powder I took led to a habit that nearly killed me. It isn't my drug of choice, neither are the pills they gave me to lose weight. Alcohol is... it's a demon on my back I can't get rid of.

'Father Armand...' I tug on his sleeve. 'I need help.'

He stops praying and nods. 'It is time.'

He guides me to an alcove as the basilica fills and the Church goes about its business of saving souls. We enter a staircase hidden behind a plain wooden door, a secret passageway, he explains, left over from the building of the basilica by the workers when they were constructing the four main staircases. It leads to a storage room filled with vestments, votive candles, and crates filled with clothes donated to the poor of Paris by wealthy patrons.

'I fear leaving you to your own designs, *mademoiselle*, so I shall accompany you to your destination.' He lowers his eyes. 'First you must cover yourself.'

'Where are you taking me, Father?' I marvel at the pile of petticoats, long, woolen overcoats, shoes neatly arranged.

'I have a friend who can help you: a physician of the mind who aided me when I lost my mother and I... well, as I said, we are all sinners.'

I nod, my admiration for this young priest swelling in my heart. I *do* believe God sent him to me. He secures a long, velvet cloak cast with the sheen of the grey dawn from the donated items. Tattered at the bottom, most of the sequins on the shoulder are missing. A few sparkling stars wink at me, giving me hope I can shine again. I imagine this cloak belonged to a rich *bourgeoisie* who never dreamed it would save a film star from ruin.

I fasten the clasp on the cloak and put on my shoes, winding the straps around my calves. With a dramatic gesture, I dangle my beaded purse on my wrist. 'Is it far from here?'

'Outside the city... a place where you can heal filled with green woods and ponds with lily pads and happy frogs.' He smiles. 'I will need to secure transportation.'

I fluff my hair with my fingers, then wiggle my nose *à la* Ninette and hand him the keys to my red Bugatti roadster. 'Can you drive a motor-car, Father?'

11

SYLVIE

ONE DAY AT A TIME

Sainte Albertine, France
1935–1936

I thought it was hard to deal with my success in pictures. Dealing with overcoming my addiction... is a nightmare.

I check myself into the sanitarium outside Paris, a place where cowbells ring instead of cathedral bells, and the butterflies landing on my shoulder flutter their wings like I fluttered my eyelashes. Once an estate for a minor aristocrat who fell onto hard times, the Gothic buildings consist of a carriage house, stable, greenhouse, and main living quarters, and caters to anyone who wants anonymity as well as treatment.

I felt a sense of comfort when I arrived, aided by the presence of the fascinating Father Armand. I imagine it's the only time a patient arrived here in a red Bugatti roadster driven by a priest.

For years I ran from my addiction, years of pretending that I could be the fabulous Sylvie Martone every moment of my waking life. I worked hard at being a cinema star, but the fantasy of my perfect life in the magazines belonged to someone else, not me. I was unprepared to handle the pressure, the hounding by Emil to stay on top by sleeping with powerful men. The man I thought was family was more like a debauched uncle sneering at me. So I grabbed another bottle, a cigarette, a snort of white powder, then I'd find myself in a café signing autographs from British tourists who found me so French and glamorous.

The Sainte Albertine Sanitarium is anything but glamorous.

And detoxing is a hell of a mindbender.

The intense cravings, chronic nausea, trouble sleeping. My chest hurting so badly from the emotional outbursts I can't control.

Yelling... screaming. Panting hard, banging my head against the brass bed when I can't sleep, until I pass out. Then I can't get up, don't remember where I am, fighting the dizziness that rolls over me. All the crying fits that start and stop like someone yelling 'Cut!' make it clear to my subconscious I *am* a drunk. A fact that comes as no surprise to Emil when I wire him about my sudden departure from Paris. I'm seeking treatment and I don't know when I'll be back. Six months... maybe more. Although I kept my addiction from the press and Father Armand would never betray me, Emil knew about my fall from grace but chose to ignore it as long as I made pictures for him. The staff tells me he checks often to see how I'm doing. I don't want to see him. Not yet. How many times a day do I stare at myself in the mirror (how I wish this place were like the convent *without* mirrors), the drained, pale skin of a ghost staring back at me? Eyes red-rimmed, hair coarse like straw, lower lip trembling.

And I can't stop it.

The anger, the lashing out, the insane craving that takes weeks to simmer down. And when it does, then the downer, depression... and the craving for sugar hits you. Hits you *hard*. I want to devour everything I see, vanilla cakes and raspberry tarts with whipped country cream. The sweeter they are, the more I want it. I gain weight, but it's expected. Still, it's better than the alternative... a quick slide to Hell and this time there's no guarantee I'll ever come back.

It's not easy to kick an addiction... you don't get over it like a bad review. I'm trying a new therapy that's finding popularity across the pond about *taking one day at a time*. Knowing your triggers, knowing you have to give up your old friends and knowing you're never an *ex-addict*. You're an addict in recovery. Of course, I could say I was never an alcoholic, never addicted to cocaine and pills. That's like saying I never bleached my hair.

Today I sit by a tall, narrow window, pondering my state of mind as I tear at the seams of an unfashionable... no, *ugly,* chemise. Something a crone would wear in a film about a nineteenth-century workhouse, loose-fitting and washed so many times the threads hang together in an unholy alliance. For years, I was like every other alcoholic.

In denial.

I raced along making film after film, a few flops, mostly hits, emoting my heart out on the screen, trying to connect with my feelings. That fourth wall between you and the audience is a hard one to step through to find the right balance in your personal life. To find someone in your corner, to help you with the ups and downs, the good and the bad of show business. Yes, I was surrounded by sycophants eager to tell me what I wanted to hear. I had no one in the studio hierarchy looking out for me. They had their own agenda. I'm not making excuses or feeling sorry for myself. I wanted to be a cinema star more than anything, but I was young, *so* young. Sixteen, eighteen... I didn't know how to handle the success, so I turned to the bottle and the white powder to fill that void in me. Then those awful pills Emil got from the studio dispensary that amped me up, helped me starve myself.

I often wonder if I'd had a child, maybe I would have straightened up my life sooner, but I didn't.

I walk every day around the grounds, acres of wooded forest, searching for the secret to finding my way to being sober. It's not that simple. After months of therapy from caring physicians and nurses in starched white, I come to grips with the truth that I'm in charge of my own sobriety and only through hard work will I ever go home.

For now, I form an uneasy alliance with Emil when he shows up at the sanitarium today. His weekly check to see how I'm doing. I feel confident enough at this point in my treatment to speak with him. I should be flattered he's concerned, but I know him too well not to know he's up to something. He tugs at his extravagant black cravat, blows his nose numerous times (is he sniffing the white powder?), and manages to avoid answering questions from the psychiatrist about why he believes I'm here. Did the director see the signs of my drug use, they ask, was I sexually abused? Peeking through the door, I laugh at that last question. I'm supposed to be at a ceramics class, working with my hands to quiet my mind and its constant cravings. I'm also taking English classes to stimulate my brain and retrain my learning process, but watching him squirm is so much more therapeutic.

I can't let him go without telling him how I feel, that the old me is dead. I'm set to be discharged soon after six months of therapy and then spending more time learning how to live sober. I'm not going back to Paris until we have an understanding that things will be different between us.

I put pink wildflowers in my hair and slip my chemise off one shoulder in an attempt to look sensual. Then I waylay the director outside the front gate before he races off in his latest Citroën model, a yellow touring car.

I kneel down in the dirt where he can see me.

'Watch me, Emil,' I call out to him. 'This is the old Sylvie. Subservient, young, obedient.' Then I jump up and pull the wild-flowers from my hair, toss them on the ground and stomp on them with my bare foot. 'I buried her and she's going to stay buried.'

He smirks. 'You look terrible, Sylvie, like a tomcat dragged you home. Your hair needs bleaching and you've got bags under your eyes. Get some sleep. And lose a few pounds before we start your next picture.' He revs his engine.

'Is that all you have to say?' I demand, working on keeping my temper. It's not easy. I want to smash my fist into the hood of his car. 'Don't you want to know how I'm doing? Don't you care?'

'Of course I care or I wouldn't be here.' A smug look crosses his face he can't hide. A subtle smirk I know so well when he sweet talks a starlet to hike her skirt so he can check out her legs. 'Your fans are bombarding the studio with letters, asking where you are. They miss you, Sylvie. That's why I need you in tiptop shape.'

I don't have a fancy comeback. He hit me below the belt. My fans are the most important thing to me. 'What have you told them?'

'Nothing. The press doesn't know where you are.' Emil tells me how he made up a phony story that I went to London to take time off, but the rumor mills say I'm meeting with producers and entertaining an offer from a British film studio. The result is a tidal wave of protests when the publicity department of Delacroix Studios receives thousands of letters begging me to come back to France and not abandon them like so many European actors.

After he drives off, I think about what he said. How my fans are clamoring for more pictures from me. It's the news I needed to hear, the final step in my treatment.

I'm going home.

* * *

Paris
1937

My fans keep me sober.

After I return to Paris, I read the thousands of letters written to me in blue ink and florid handwriting on crisp white stationery, on brown butcher paper with chalk, letters begging me to come back to France.

Come and make us smile again, Sylvie, they write to me, telling me their woes, how they're struggling to survive in these hard times and miss my adventures on the silver screen. I tear up every time, my heart tugging at my soul to unite and help my body fight the terrible cravings, the desire to drink. It doesn't go away but I'm learning to control it. Cocaine also calls out to me, but I have more of a problem with the pills I became addicted to... some spiked-up concoction that takes away hunger.

I've found some respite in my daily walks around the *16e arrondisse-*

ment or the Tuileries Gardens where I've again started wearing a disguise. I've taken a liking to a particular one – a delightfully inquisitive aristocrat with a limp I call Baroness de Ravenne. Putty nose. Heavy brows. Fake beauty mark. Who knows? Maybe someday I can work her into a script.

For the moment, I'm more concerned in getting my career back on track. I sit in the main room downstairs in my spacious apartment on Avenue du Trocadéro, sunshine filling the rooms done in my signature tones of ivory, blue, and grey and lighting up the polished parquet floor and brocade walls with an exquisite Louis XIV floral design. I'm reading every newspaper I can find to see what pictures are making money and how my rivals are faring as the Depression lingers on.

What worries me is what I see *behind* the headlines. How Germany has evolved since the Nazi Party came into power with that horrid little man with a moustache who reminds me of the devil character in my *Ninette* films. I've never been to Berlin and don't want to go if he's in charge. How he's militarizing the country and citizens are being sent to what they call 'concentration camps' for being political foes. Free thinking is being suppressed and that affects the film business. Emil tells me actors and writers are fleeing Germany and he's hoping to sign them up for new pictures he has planned for me.

I don't give in to Emil's demands and assert my independence. I choose what scripts to read, but I'm smart enough to know we need each other. I'm impressed with the plays he brings me by a new screenwriter, Raoul Monteux. He comes to visit me at my apartment, bringing along his young daughter Halette. She's a big fan of mine and keeps staring at me as if I'm a goddess. I like the girl and we have long chats about what it's like to be a film star. Raoul tells me his daughter loves making scrapbooks and has one devoted to me. Watching the girl laugh and enjoy an ice treat on a hot day gives me bouts of sadness at not having my own child.

I'm twenty-seven... I have many years yet to fall in love, *n'est-ce pas*? I thought about that often at the sanitarium, how more meaningful my life would be if I had a special man to share it with.

For now, I have my film family, the newest members being Raoul and his daughter. I look forward to their visits (his wife Estelle is too ill to leave their apartment). We have long script meetings where we discuss his wonderful characters, exciting action, and clever dialogue. The idea of going before the camera again doesn't terrify me as much as I thought it would. Over the next eighteen months, I star in two films written by Raoul. Both hits.

Still, the fear of relapse looms in my mind. I get rid of anything in my dressing room that reminds me of drinking or using. I feel so alive, becoming someone else. I'm still wary of falling in love. My work is my cloak of invisibility so I don't get hurt by Emil's 'dates' who steal my heart, then toss it away. I become so good at inhabiting my character's skin, the reviewers praise me for my amazing transformations.

I receive the best reviews of my career since *Ninette* after I get sober.

And then as if the stars align in the sky just for me, the most magnificent thing happens when I get away from Paris on a film junket to Monte Carlo to publicize my latest picture about a female highway-man, *Madame Le Noir*.

I fall in love.

JULIANA

ASK AND YOU SHALL RECEIVE...

Ville Canfort-Terre, France
Present Day

I'm a terrible actress.

I fall flat on my face when I meet the Mother Superior in charge of the *Couvent de Sainte Daria*. Oh, if only I were more like *ma grand-mère*. My quick dismissal makes it obvious to me I'm no Sylvie Martone.

My short acting career begins after a quick look-see around the small medieval town located outside Paris when I talk my way into the convent by speaking French to a young postulant. She's so impressed with me coming here from California to find out about their lacemaking, she breaks the rules.

She allows me to enter their religious domain housed in an imposing limestone structure with four turrets.

Bon. Step one. Completed. As I step through the double portals, I'm in awe of the grandeur of the ancient chateau. From the material I read on the flight coming over, the village main street was bombed during the war, but the chateau came through unscathed. The town is known for its wool industry, beetroots, and flower market featuring the local prized favorite, the Canfort Lily. This is the first connection I've had with my roots. I'm overwhelmed to think this charming place with the overpowering chestnut tree standing watch at the gate is where my mother grew up. I bite my lip to keep from losing my composure and hold back the tears.

I can't cry. Not now, Maman. *I have a job to do.*

I arrive at the convent around noon, a busy time of day with nuns scattering to what I assume is the dining room for the afternoon meal, their rosaries entwined around their hands, whispering and glancing in my direction. My designer eye notes their plain white blouses, calf-length navy skirts and matching sweaters, black sensible shoes, their navy head coverings hanging down their back, some with bangs showing.

Quite a change from the wooly, black habits I imagine they wore when my mother lived here. I get a chill as I embrace the history of this place, noting the wall-size tapestry of knights and ladies adorning the Grand Hall and the intricately carved, high-backed wooden chairs and finely woven rugs on the stone floor. This is no movie set, but the real deal.

Before I can decide whether or not to sit down, I hear a whizzing sound behind me. A screech, then the overpowering scent of talcum tickles my nostrils. Curious, I turn around and see an elderly sister zoom by me in a motorized wheelchair. Dressed in a religious habit from another century with black tunic, long full sleeves, black apron cinched at the waist with a brown belt, her long black veil blows behind her as she makes a circle around me, humming and maneuvering her scooter-like wheelchair, all the while sneaking peeks at me. I spot the wires from a headset hanging from underneath her wimple. By the way she keeps eyeing me, I have the feeling she's more interested in me than the music.

I've intruded on her turf and she's letting me know it.

She looks me up and down with a curious eye as if she wants to say something, but doesn't.

I smile at her and have a flickering feeling that I've walked back in time. A connection that sparks my imagination to wonder how long she's been here at the convent. She must be at least eighty... could she have...? No, that would be asking too much of fate.

Before I can reach out to her, she zooms away but by the knowing smile on her lips, I don't think I've seen the last of her. Strange, I thought she was about to say something. Then I see why she made a hasty retreat and disappeared. I turn my attention to a nun I assume is the Mother Superior. I hear her admonishing the young postulant for admitting a strange woman into their midst. The girl's head is lowered, her hands folded across her chest.

Oh, no, what I have done?

I forget about the sister in the wheelchair and march over to the woman. I can't let the young girl take the blame for my crazy scheme.

I don't get the chance.

The Mother Superior sends the girl scattering away, then heads in my direction.

'If you wish to know more about our lacemaking, *mademoiselle*,' she says in perfect English and getting straight to her agenda with a forced smile, 'I suggest you check our convent website.' She holds up her cell to show me the lovely graphics on their site with photos of the sisters and their lacemaking craft. 'Everything you need to know is there.'

'*Oui, bien sûr*,' I say in French, hoping to win her over. 'But I'd so love to see the sisters at work and interview them about their lace-making process. I imagine they have some fascinating stories to tell.'

Stories, I pray, that will give me a lead that will substantiate my belief Sylvie came here after the war with her baby. 'We are a cloistered order, *mademoiselle*,' says the Mother Superior, arms folded high on her chest, 'and do not receive visitors.'

Step two. Shot down. I try a different approach.

'I'm interested in purchasing lace for costumes for a new film about to start production.'

Not true, but if she goes for it, I'll worry about what to do with it later.

Her eyes blink. 'You're from *Hollywood*?'

That got her attention, so I go with it. 'Yes, I work for a major film studio and I've heard your lace is of the finest quality with excellent workmanship and perfect for the period costumes I've designed.'

A brief silence. 'Do you know George Clooney?'

I shake my head. 'No, the film I'm working on takes place during the Occupation of Paris. I'm interested in the stars of the French cinema during that time.' I wait a beat before I toss out the name that's been on the edge of my tongue since I walked in here. 'Stars like Sylvie Martone.'

Her upper lip twitches. She tries to hide her surprise, but her voice quivers as she says, 'I regret to say, *mademoiselle*, I know nothing about this actress. I can't help you.'

'Are you *sure* you don't know her?' I persist, whipping out the glam shot of Sylvie from my purse. 'Here's a picture of her from before the war.' I flash the photo in front of her pale face, careful not to let her see the inscription on the back.

Her surprise turns to indignation. 'Where did you get that?'

'From a friend. I understand she was a big star during the war, then she disappeared. I'm fascinated to find out what happened to her.' I lower my voice to a whisper and repeat what Ridge told me when he dug into the bios of French film stars from the silent era. 'I also heard Sylvie Martone grew up here at the convent before she went to Paris to get into the movies.'

Her brows shoot up. 'You were misinformed.'

I shake my head. 'My source is *never* wrong.'

She smirks. '*Alors*, now the truth comes out. You work for a scandal sheet. You're here to dig up the past no one wants to remember.'

Why the attitude? I admit I don't understand the brush-off. The Mother Superior can't be more than fifty. She'd have no recollections of my grandmother other than as a historical reference.

'No one will ever forget the war, Reverend Mother, the heroes and the heroines of the Resistance—'

'Sylvie Martone was no heroine, *mademoiselle*. You'll find nothing about her here within these convent walls.' She pretends to check her phone, but I see her stewing. 'I must request you leave. I'm late for prayers.'

'*Wait.*'

She turns. 'Yes?'

'Please allow me to take the blame and not the young postulant for my barging in here. It wasn't her fault. I'd be grateful if you don't punish her for my insolence.'

'As you wish.' She seems surprised at my sincerity, but she still won't talk to me. She walks away with long strides as if she's afraid I'll run after her.

For a moment, my bravado leaves me. I'll get nothing out of her. Instead I'm filled with the uncertainty of what to do next.

Sylvie Martone is a forbidden topic around here. Why?

I'm reluctant to go home with my tail between my legs. I need advice. I check my phone. It's 4 a.m. in Los Angeles. I hesitate to wake Ridge with my bad news. Short of telling the nun Sylvie Martone was my grandmother, I can't do much. I've made a mess out of everything. She thinks I'm a snippy American reporter. If I tell her I'm the granddaughter of Sylvie Martone, she'll probably have me escorted out of France.

What to do next?

The problem is, I have no step three.

* * *

I try to shake off the disappointment that follows, the hollow feeling that stays with me as I head for the chateau's double doors, feeling like I've lost the only chance I had to do right by my mother. The whole time, though, I keep thinking about how *Maman* always talked about the pink peonies that grew near her weeping willow in the convent courtyard and her favorite chocolate nonpareils the nuns gave her on her birthday. A simple childhood memory, but aren't those the best ones? And to think I'm here where she felt the most vulnerable growing up without a family.

I shuffle along, pretending to be interested in the amazing carved ceiling at least twenty feet high. I stop in my tracks as a plan forms in my head.

Do I dare?

I look around me. The flurry of nuns I saw earlier has disappeared and the Mother Superior hightailed it out of the Grand Hall as fast as she could. I'm alone. No doubt everything here is done on the honor system, so who's to know if I leave or not? I can't come all this way and not see the garden where my mother played as a child and wrote letters to the man she loved as a woman. I've been on an emotional roller-coaster for so long... dealing with my mother's illness then trying to cope with her loss... then my discovery my roots are so unbelievable they could be a movie.

It doesn't take me long to find the inner courtyard after I sneak past the long dining room filled with chattering nuns. Glasses tinkling, silverware rattling, they don't hear me as I scoot past the open door and find my way outside to the convent grounds.

You can't miss the giant weeping willow tree. Its long, swaying branches blow in the afternoon breeze like the nuns' billowing sleeves as they passed through here on their way to chapel for hundreds of years. The distinct scent of fresh lilies wafts through the air along with the crisp, sweet smell of peonies dancing around me, tempting me to stand here and inhale. It's like *Maman* said it was. Pink peonies pepper the garden along with the lilies and a dash of bluebells. An enchanted garden that transposes me back in time. I sit down on a white stone bench. I swear I feel my mother's arms wrap around me with a protective shield, her spirit is so strong here.

'*Je suis là, Maman.*'

I let myself cry, the tears coming freely, as if we're reunited here. My mother, my grandmother, and me.

All three of us together under this willow tree.

A rustling in the willow makes me shiver, as if inviting me to stay. *Begging* me to stay, to not give up. Somehow I know with certainty the

Mother Superior is hiding something, some secret is driving her dismissal of me.

And I know just the nun who can help me unravel that secret.

* * *

'Why do you wish to know about Sylvie Martone, *mademoiselle*?'

I stand my ground before the elderly sister in her motorized wheelchair, her gaze sharp and questioning, looking me up and down. It didn't take me long to find her dozing – or pretending to – under the overhead trellis covered with sweet-smelling pink roses. Her eyes flew open when she heard my heels tapping on the ancient stone.

She didn't look surprised to see me.

'I'm writing a story about her,' I answer in French.

She shakes her head. 'You're too nice to be a reporter. Reporters are always hiding in corners, trying to talk to you, sneaking into your cell to look for clues under the mattress... *ah*, there were so many of them coming here after the war.' She giggles. 'They never found anything.'

I double blink. 'You were here then?'

'*Oui.* I came to the convent seventy years ago after my mother couldn't care for me any longer. I was thirteen and knew then I wanted to take the veil, so it seemed like the right thing to do.'

I suck in a breath, my heart thumping loudly. 'Then you knew—'

'Your mother, *mademoiselle*, Madeleine Chastain,' the nun says with a sun-kissed smile and mirth in her voice like an impish fairy.

I exhale. 'Then you know who I am.'

I admit, I never expected such a direct answer from the charming nun. She reminds me of a kind-hearted but feisty supporting character straight out of Central Casting who throws the audience for a loop with her wisecracking one-liners and snappy delivery.

'Oh, yes, I knew who you were the minute I saw you... I see her in your eyes... I see your grandmother, too. You have her grace *and* her dimple.'

This is too much for me. My knees wobble. 'You knew Sylvie Martone?'

She nods. 'I was a young girl then, but I shall never forget her. So kind and beautiful and risking everything to protect her baby.' She chuckles. 'Sylvie was right under their noses when the reporters showed up. Dressed as a Belgian nun, she'd answer their questions professing to know nothing, telling them how she spent the war helping refugees from her country make the journey through the German lines to France, including the little girl she brought with her.'

'My mother,' I say with a deep sigh.

'*Oui, mademoiselle.*'

An uncomfortable silence arises between us, as if we're each going back in time with our thoughts, sad and happy times. From what I learnt about my grandmother from Ridge, Sylvie was a beloved star of the cinema since she was a teenager, but during the war she used her influence with the Nazis to receive special 'favors' to get her films made after production started up again in Paris in the summer of 1941.

I feel myself wanting to rush forward with so many questions, but I don't know where to start. I look around the sequestered alcove, note the ripples of sunshine that filter through the ivy-covered trellis over-head, the serene pond with lilies floating in the calm water. I have a feeling this was a favorite place for Sylvie to come with her baby which is why the nun waited here for me. She must have seen me sneak out into the gardens and knew I'd end up here.

'My mother called me Juliana. Juliana Chastain.'

'I am called Sister Rose-Celine, *mademoiselle*,' she says, introducing herself.

I pause, *think*. Why does that name sound so familiar? Then it hits me.

'You're the nun who wrote to *Maman* after she went to California.'

She nods. '*Yes*, I prayed for her… and you. She wrote to me when you were growing up; she told me how proud she was when you gradu-ated from university.' She reflects a moment, then her eyes get moist. 'Then she stopped writing and it saddened my heart.'

'It wasn't her fault, Sister...' I don't know why, but I find myself spilling out my grief to a stranger about how my mother lost sight of everything in her life the past few years, including me. The light slowly leaving her eyes, how I felt her spirit never stopping trying to get through to comfort me. As I feel it now. I feel lighter somehow and for the first time, I know I made the right decision coming here.

'And now, *mademoiselle*,' Sister Rose-Celine says in that charming way nuns have when they're about to teach you something, 'you wish to fill in the gaps about your mother, things she never told you. God in His wisdom has sent you here to me.' She exhales. '*Alors*, where do I begin?'

* * *

Sister Rose-Celine keeps the conversation lively, the two of us sitting in the garden with her recounting stories about *Maman*. How the Mother Superior at the time, Sister Vincent, made certain Sylvie's baby was cared for after she died. How the nuns subscribe to a vow of silence about the goings-on within the convent walls. If they had any speculation among themselves regarding the Belgian nun who showed up here with the orphan baby after the liberation of Paris in 1944, they kept mum. Sylvie's secret was safe. Years later, the Mother Superior – Sister Vincent – told Sister Rose-Celine about a trust fund set up in the baby's name to pay for her education, most likely funded by Sylvie's exquisite jewelry that she sold on the black market during the war.

The sister also reveals during the 1960s, a rumor circulated about the Belgian nun, that she was the elusive French actress. Since only Sister Vincent and Sister Rose-Celine knew for certain she was Sylvie Martone, the truth was never known. The rumor resurfaces every few years and reporters and podcasters show up, trying to make a story out of it.

Then Sister Rose-Celine's eyes turn tender and her breathing slows when she talks about my mother.

'Tell me about *Maman* when she was a little girl,' I beg her, yearning to know what she was like before she became the reserved art history professor.

The sister claps her hands. 'Ah, she loved to have tea parties with her doll with the long, blonde braids, but your *maman* wasn't always quiet. I remember the time she was twelve and hid in the dungeon and pretended to be a ghost, moaning and groaning and rattling a chain. She scared the knickers off me.' The nun giggles. 'She was like a sister to me. I was so happy when Madeleine went to university and then returned here afterward to use her skills.'

'Do you have any photos of her growing up?' I ask.

'No selfies then, *mademoiselle*,' she says, making me smile. 'I do have a photo of the three of us – Sylvie, *ta maman*, and me – standing under the willow tree. Madeleine was six and I was thirteen. It's in my room, *mademoiselle*, though I can't say where. I promise you, I *will* find it, but first...' I can see her mind zooming back in time, remembering... questioning.

'Yes?' I beg to know what's on her mind.

'You have a right to know, *mademoiselle*, how *ta grand-mère* drove her motorcar off the road during a summer rainstorm in 1950 and hit a tree, killing her instantly.'

'Oh...' I feel the life drain from me, as if my body melts into a pool of sadness. 'I wish you'd told me, *Maman*,' I whisper. 'So I could comfort you.'

Sister Rose-Celine lays her hand on my arm and says in a whisper, 'It was very hush-hush, how the authorities determined the vehicle was convent property, but the driver was never identified. That an unknown woman stole the car and died in the motorcar accident.'

'Sylvie...' I say in a reverent whisper, my hand going to my throat.

'*Oui*, the Mother Superior confided in me that she knew Sylvie since she was a child and was privy to her innermost secrets, but she never broke that confidence. She used her influence afterward to make sure no one knew who was buried in the unmarked grave on the convent grounds... it was what Sylvie would have wanted: to protect her child from nosy reporters who might find out she was laid to rest here and unearth the truth she had a child. She wouldn't want her daughter to grow up with the stigma of her mother's alleged sins during the war. The Mother Superior made me promise to keep Sylvie's secret. I can't believe she did the terrible things they said she did. In my heart I prayed someday someone would find out what really happened during the war and Sylvie's true story would be told.'

I feel a tinge of sadness at knowing the exact year of her death. I was secretly hoping she'd lived a longer life, got to know her daughter, even if it was from afar.

'*Ta maman* and I had happy years afterward,' Sister Rose-Celine continues, 'filled with learning and prayer and nurturing the lily flowers for our special tea, then the road narrowed when she was a teenager and Madeleine was sent along a lonely path.' Her long, luxurious sigh releases a burden held so long.

'What happened, Sister?' I fear to ask.

'Madeleine found her original birth registration issued from the Neuilly-sur-Seine *mairie* or city hall in Paris, listing the actress Sylvie Martone as her birth mother. She had no idea her mother was famous and when she heard the colorful rumors about Sylvie being spotted here in the convent... *alors*, you can imagine the pain she suffered.'

'Oh, my God, no wonder she said nothing to me. How did she find the birth certificate?'

'She was working in the convent office after Sister Vincent passed away when she came across a sealed brown envelope with her name on it, along with a photo of Sylvie, a diamond pin, and lace veil. Stuffed away in a file cabinet and forgotten.'

'Where did they come from?' I urge her on, my heart pounding.

'When Sister Vincent became the Mother Superior after the war, I assume she found them hidden among Sylvie's personal items. She was waiting to give the envelope to Madeleine, but Sister Vincent left us when Madeleine was seventeen.'

'Didn't *Maman* ask about her parents when she was growing up?'

Sister Rose-Celine shakes her head. 'Madeleine accepted the fact she was a *war child* and her birth wasn't registered in *un livret de famille*.

Instead, Sylvie secured what the government called "anonymous birth", a way of dealing with children fathered by German soldiers. This allowed unwed mothers to give up their children at birth to orphanages. Those children never knew their parents' names.'

'Wouldn't Sylvie have been recognized when she registered her child as an unwed mother?'

'*Oui, mademoiselle*, unless someone else did it for her.'

My head is spinning as the mystery deepens when Sister Rose-Celine reveals Madeleine destroyed the original birth certificate and she could do nothing to stop her.

But she kept the photo of Sylvie, the diamond pin, and the lace veil.

Strange.

I can imagine how my mother felt, first believing she was the product of a rape or coercion by the enemy of an innocent French-woman. When Madeleine found out about Sylvie's nefarious dealings during the war, she went into a deep depression. She told anyone who asked she was an orphan and never knew her French parents. Madeleine became a lay sister and kept her mother's past as a noto-rious actress hidden.

I never knew any of this, never questioned my mother's roots in France. World War II was ancient history to me and for that I'm ashamed. I shouldn't have waited so long to embrace where I came from, but we don't always ask these questions when we don't know where we're going in life.

I do now.

I have my career and who knows... maybe someday I'll fall in love.

I can't let recent events make me question if I'm not *already* in love with Ridge and I've been too dumb to see it. Of course, he's not in love with me. He'd have told me, wouldn't he?

No time to ponder over my romantic notions that will probably go nowhere.

First, I need to come to grips with the past.

Old stories long forgotten that need to be found. A fragile thread entwining around my heart that tightens when I fear *what* I'll find. I've discovered what I needed to know about *Maman*, but what about Sylvie? The sister has no knowledge of the actress before she showed up disguised as a Belgian nun after Paris was liberated.

I can't contain my disappointment. Is this the end of the road?

Or did Sylvie leave behind any other traces of her existence?

'You mentioned files, Sister Rose-Celine. Did the Mother Superior, whom you said was close to Sylvie, leave behind any personal files, identity card, letters from her? Anything that would hint at what Sylvie did during the war. Photos, notes, scribbles... *anything*?'

Then she lays a bombshell on me.

'I believe God sent you here to retrieve Sylvie's belongings.'

I gasp. Loudly. 'What belongings?' This information sets my bell ringing.

'Be assured, *mademoiselle*, whatever boxes and suitcase Sylvie Martone stored in the convent chateau dungeon are safe,' she adds with a secret smile.

Boxes, suitcase?

Did I hear her correctly? My heart is fluttering like a schoolgirl's at prom, my brain going this way and that, not believing my hunch was right.

Sylvie left a trail for me to follow.

Then why didn't the current Mother Superior mention the boxes and suitcase? Or, if the mirth in the nun's eyes tells me anything, she doesn't know about them.

I try to concentrate on what she's saying while my pulse races out of control.

Sister Rose-Celine rambles on about how she couldn't bear to throw them out, hoping one day Madeleine would return for them. When I showed up asking questions about the French actress, she saw it as a sign from God the time had come to tell the truth...

'And you have access to the dungeon?' I beg to ask her, praying she isn't in the midst of an old memory with no truth to it.

She holds up a ring of keys. 'Where do you think I go to listen to my Chopin when the other sisters get too noisy?'

13

JULIANA

AN IMPETUOUS NUN TELLS ALL

Ville Canfort-Terre, France
Present Day

What is all this stuff? is the first thing that comes to my mind when Sister Rose-Celine shows me where Sylvie's things are stored in the dungeon among what she calls 'artifacts' piled up over the decades.

'It's forbidden but not unusual for some nuns to retain a feeling of individuality by *borrowing* a favorite hand-painted teacup or holy candle or a personal item.' She chuckles as if she's guilty herself. 'We called these acts *pious thefts* back when I was a young novice, though the practice fell out of favor years ago. Back then, such thefts were frowned upon and when discovered, placed here to keep the sinful deeds closed up.'

I have to hand it to my grandmother. What better place to hide the property of the beautiful film star than where it wouldn't be disturbed? It would also explain why the Mother Superior knew nothing about Sylvie's personal possessions stored here. I doubt the woman ever stepped into this creepy, old dungeon. Cobwebs and broken stones lay scattered everywhere among the objects tossed into wooden crates. Sister Rose-Celine told me electricity was installed down here during the Great War and later updated when the dungeon was used in the 1940s as a bomb shelter. Someone also installed a two-person lift big enough to accommodate her wheelchair. According to the sister, the lift was used to help Resistance fighters move weapons and ammo hidden here.

I wonder if Sylvie ever entertained joining the Resistance, or am I asking for too much?

'Were you ever tempted, Sister Rose-Celine, to look inside the boxes or the suitcase?' I ask, curious. I poke around the crates, but I don't see any suitcase. Is this just a lonely nun's fantasy to keep the past alive?

'*Oh, no,*' the sister says, blessing herself, 'that would be breaking my vows to respect the promise made by the Mother Superior to Sylvie.'

'Didn't my mother want to see them?' I have to know.

Sister Rose-Celine shakes her head. 'Sylvie instructed the Mother Superior if anything happened to her, she wasn't to tell her daughter about the boxes until Madeleine was eighteen. The new Mother Superior at the time found the notation in Sister Vincent's last will and mentioned it to her, but Madeleine was still reeling about discovering who her mother was months earlier and never bothered.' She lowers her eyes. 'I told her the good things I remembered about her mother, but that wasn't enough in her eyes to erase what Sylvie had done during the war.'

'Wasn't she curious? Why didn't she want to know more?'

'Like so many of her generation, Madeleine chose to accept what she was told about Sylvie. You must understand the shame felt by people after the war for what happened during the Occupation, a shame that's taken a lifetime for so many Frenchmen to accept. The grey line of resistance... and the even greyer line of collaboration with the enemy.'

I understand. Sister Rose-Celine is a sly old fox, leaving much unsaid, but I get the drift of what she means. How French women were often put in difficult circumstances, women whose homes were used to billet German soldiers and prostitutes forced to accept them as customers.

'You're saying there could be truth to the accusations Sylvie Martone went over willingly to the enemy.'

I don't want to accept it. I may have to.

'*Alors*, Juliana, I wish I knew. There have been cases of accusers who were petty collaborators trying to draw attention away from themselves.'

'I understand why *Maman* chose a reclusive life as a way of atonement for what she perceived as her mother's indiscretions, her sins. It was her way of coping in a time without the Internet and access to information.'

'*Oui*, you have much insight into *ta maman*. She did her best to serve the Church in her own way.'

I have to smile. 'She was also a romantic, Sister Rose-Celine, and dreamed of falling in love. No doubt that romantic part of her came alive when she met my father. When she realized she, too, had sinned, she took that as further proof she must bury the past... and she raised me without the burden of knowing about Sylvie's part in the war to protect me.'

'Unlike your mother, you're willing to accept your *grand-mère* for who she was?' she asks me, scooting across the stone floor, maneuvering her way around.

'Is this a trick question, Sister?'

'No, *mademoiselle*, just an honest one you must answer to yourself.'

The nun realizes she's given me a lot to think about because I don't have an answer. She continues looking for the box and the suitcase, knowing she's touched a nerve in me.

'They must be here somewhere. Could be,' she admits with a heavy sigh, 'the suitcase was emptied back in the late sixties when we had a leak and used to store books from the library, but I'm not sure.'

Perhaps if I show the nun the photo, it will jog her memory.

'Have you ever seen this photo of Sylvie?' I ask her. The sudden fluttering of her eyelids tells me she has. 'I found it in a box among my mother's things wrapped up in a lace veil.'

'Oh... *mon Dieu,* I never thought I'd see this picture again.' Sister Rose-Celine rubs her gnarled fingers over the glossy photo with a reverence that touches me. Her crinkly eyes look tearful as she says, 'She was so beautiful... and kind, *mademoiselle.*'

I smile. 'Call me Juliana, please.'

She nods, then continues in a wistful voice, enjoying the lovely sentiment of a day long ago. 'Madeleine asked me to keep the photo, pin, and veil for her. Perhaps she was afraid she'd destroy them, too, in anger and a part of her *wanted* to remember her mother. I wrapped up the photo in the lace veil along with Sylvie's diamond pin and slipped the slender box into her carrying case before she left the convent for America so she wouldn't know it was there till she was far away.'

Now I understand why *Maman* hid away the box, though I find it interesting how the sister said she didn't destroy the photo... as if she, too, harbored a deep-seeded wish Sylvie had a reason for doing what she did during the war.

'*Merci* for sharing that with me, Sister—'

A loud buzzing echoes in the old dungeon, raising the hairs on the back of my neck, but it doesn't rattle the elderly sister. She shakes her head in frustration, then reaches into the pocket of her tunic and pulls out the culprit. Her cellphone, ringing madly.

She shoo-shoos the notion of answering it, choosing instead to turn it off. 'I'm sorry, Juliana, I fear Reverend Mother will track me down here since I missed the noon meal.' She sighs. 'We haven't much time to find Sylvie's boxes before her lackeys find me. *Allons...* quickly... before they discover us.'

With the sister pointing here then there and clutching the photo in her hand, I move around crates, lamps, old clothes. 'I remember Sylvie marking a crate with red lipstick.'

'Are you sure?'

'*Ah, oui,* she told me it was a special lipstick because she'd first kissed the man she loved wearing it.'

My heart sings with a special joy at hearing that. So Sylvie *did* fall in love with my grandfather. He couldn't have been a Nazi SS officer, not if she had that much sentiment for him.

With renewed hope, I scramble over the newspapers scattered around my feet and shine the flashlight from my cellphone over crates on the far side of the dungeon wall. Embedded brass rings jut out from the stone wall along with rusty chains, making me shiver. A reminder of the cruelty of man which makes me only more determined to find out the truth about a woman I can't believe was involved with such depravity during the war. I make a wide arc with my light, looking at each crate until I hit a lucky streak and find one with *Les Orphelins Perdus* smeared on it with lipstick faded to a soft pink rose.

I grin. Of course... the *Ninette* film, *Lost Orphans*.

'Sister Rose-Celine, I see the crate!'

'*Très bien,*' cries out the nun with glee, clapping her hands.

Then, with more anticipation than I could have ever imagined, I open the crate and pull out a sealed box that must weigh at least twenty or thirty pounds. What's in it? I can't wait to find out. I'm not home free yet. Before I can tear it open, a bright light hits me in the face, blinding me.

I don't need to guess who when I hear a stern voice.

The Mother Superior.

'If you don't leave *immediately, mademoiselle,* I shall send for the gendarmes.'

I've never talked so fast in my life.

When I explain to the Mother Superior who I am, why I came to France, the pain I have in my heart finding out my grandmother was Sylvie Martone, a Nazi collaborator, and I can't believe it's true, I see utter confusion in her eyes. She lowers her flashlight and I see relief on her face. Her shoulders relax, and for the first time since I got here, she smiles at me.

'I think we both need a cup of tea, *mademoiselle*.'

She invites me to her office and, over hot lily flower tea with fresh lemon and a cherry tart, I tell her my story with Sister Rose-Celine chiming in with her own information about the lost boxes and suitcase. I see the Mother Superior's brows arch in amazement, but to her credit, she doesn't admonish the elderly nun for her silence all these years. If anything, she respects the sister's code of loyalty to Sylvie and my mother.

'And you believe Sylvie Martone, your grandmother,' Reverend Mother asks again for clarity, 'was *not* a Nazi collaborator?'

'Yes. I know it sounds crazy, that I don't have proof, but my gut tells me there's more to Sylvie's story. And, I admit, in my heart I want to give her a chance to tell her side. I believe she left the box and suitcase filled with information about her life during the war for my mother to find, but *Maman* never looked for them. She remained in denial my whole life about Sylvie's past. I came here on a hunch when I found her photo and this note Sylvie wrote on the back.'

The Mother Superior reads the inscription on the back of the photo and her hand goes to her lips, parted in awe. Smiling with a warmth I never expected from the woman, she hands the photo back to me. 'I've heard the rumors for years Sylvie Martone hid here after the war. There was even speculation she'd borne a child, but the baby perished in a bombing. It was only hearsay. As you are aware, we make our sustenance from our lacemaking to keep the convent running smoothly. I've always felt it was my duty to protect the sisters from any more scandal.' She pauses to sip her tea and I have the feeling my entire mission rests on what's going through her mind. And her heart. 'You're not the first one to show up wanting to know about *Mademoiselle* Martone. However...'

'Yes, Reverend Mother, I know.' I grab Sister Rose-Celine's hand and she grips mine tight.

'All the others who came wished to sell their newspapers and make a mockery out of our Order for hiding a Nazi film star. I could not let that happen.'

Heart thudding, I say what's on my mind. 'I want to prove Sylvie's innocence.'

'And if you're wrong?'

'Then I will go away and Sylvie Martone's connection to the convent will stay hidden. I promise you.'

The Mother Superior ponders the situation, weighing up all the factors, but having Sister Rose-Celine on my side helps my case. Glowing like a Christmas angel, the elderly nun hasn't touched her cherry tart or her tea. She's been hesitant to speak and looks like she's going to burst until she has her say.

'*Please*, Reverend Mother,' Sister Rose-Celine pleads in a steady, determined voice. I can't believe the sister is eighty-three; she's as spry as a perky robin and as lucid as a bright, shiny star. She remains calm as she recites what Sister Vincent told her about Sylvie, that the war years were difficult ones for her and how she found peace here afterward. The degradation the film star went through after the liberation was devastating to her. The nuns didn't judge her. *It wasn't their place*, she says, the Mother Superior then reminded them, for only God knew the truth. Sister Rose-Celine harbored the notion the woman knew more than she was telling and it pained the nun to keep silent. 'God will be so pleased if we can right this wrong to a woman I knew to be good and pure of heart.'

The Mother Superior nods. 'So be it. You have my permission to stay, *mademoiselle*. And may God help you. The truth is in His hands now.'

'*Merci beaucoup*, Reverend Mother.'

I squeeze Sister Rose-Celine's hand and she squeezes back. Yes, together we'll find out the truth about Sylvie Martone.

The truth... and whatever it is, I'll have to accept it.

* * *

Having received the Mother Superior's blessing, I feel certain I'll find the answer to the mystery of Sylvie Martone quickly. That isn't the case. What I find in the sealed box is a red leather diary filled with Sylvie's precise but feminine handwriting in large, elegant capital letters. The diary looks brand new, its shiny, smooth cover kept sealed and away from the scurrilous hand of daylight for nearly seventy years. I open it and the pages are still fresh-looking... as if Sylvie wrote them yesterday.

I can't wait to read it.

We also find reels of film and a photo album. I feel it's important to discover the personal side of Sylvie before we tackle the films. We're like two kids opening up presents on Christmas Eve, huddled together in the study which was *Maman's* room when she lived here.

I breathe in the past, still so evident here in spite of the renovations. The elegant wooden cornices from another era give the room a feeling of solidity, comfort. Two long, arched windows add a spiritual essence along with built-in bookshelves with elegant mahogany scrolls that remind me of a lordly manor. I feel *Maman's* presence here. I imagine her spending her days working on her medieval manuscript translations, attending prayers in the chapel, and dreaming of what life would be like for her and her child.

Did she ever think about her own mother? I suppose I'll never know. For now, I embrace her spirit in this lovely room decorated with a brown leather divan with old-fashioned, handmade lace doilies made by the sisters and a throw rug the color of a muted sunshine interwoven with a blue woolen design. I love the antique desk with a million drawers, jade-glass study lamps, and an electric burner plate to put the kettle on, as the sisters like to say. The young postulant who helped me earlier keeps it humming with hot water and the nuns' own brand of tea. A soothing, sweet chamomile infused with lemon and lily flower.

Over the next few days Sister Rose-Celine and I are never far apart. I swear the nun has more energy than I do and speaks enough English to fill in the gaps for me in French; translating odd phrases or current expressions on my phone only goes so far. I'm delighted the Mother Superior insists I stay at the chateau instead of the village inn where I'd booked a room. Never have I been happier for this chance to reconnect with my mother's past. The convent modernized several years ago to keep up with the times and the once sparsely decorated rooms with the barest essentials now resemble a modern dormitory with Internet and Wi-Fi. My mother's room is our workroom, but Sister Rose-Celine assures me I'll find the guest room set aside for visiting clergy most comfortable. Again, I feel like I'm on a film set with the brick fireplace and marble mantelpiece, eighteenth-century writing desk and chair, and snow-white canopied double bed.

I call Ridge and fill him in on everything that's happened. To say he's amazed is an understatement. I pray I'll soon have good news to tell him.

And now for the most anticipated moment in my life. We go through Sylvie's diary with blue lines and black ink detailing every aspect of her life from the time she was brought to the convent when she was three years old, growing up with Sister Vincent as her mentor, and then later discovered for films at sixteen by the French film director, Emil-Hugo de Ville. Her diary paints him as a controlling man in a white Panama hat and not the paternal image she sought him to be, selling her like a piece of property to the studio, how he manipulated her to get her to stardom and then keep her there. She speaks lovingly of her *Ninette* films (Sister Rose-Celine has never seen them and I promise her Ridge will somehow make that happen so she can watch them on her phone), then more films. Pills, alcohol, men. Emil is there guiding her career and encouraging Sylvie to engage in them all. A quick Google search turns up a film biography of the director that makes my head spin, adding to what I already knew about Sylvie from the research Ridge and I did before I left LA. For thirty years Emil guided young starlets through the ups and downs of the film business. Sylvie was his greatest success.

Unfortunately, Emil also disappeared after the war.

Which doesn't give me any leads to follow regarding Sylvie's activities during the war. Besides his work directing and producing Sylvie's films, Emil wasn't involved in any scandals except for spending too much money on women and cognac at the Hôtel Ritz and making money on the black market. From what I can tell, the director falls into the 'grey' area of resistance against the Nazis. He kind of did... he kind of didn't.

He was considered a genius in his time and the Nazis were so involved with making a positive mark in French film production, they left him alone as long as he produced hits, and he did. Besides the *Ninette* serial films, he produced two of Sylvie's biggest hits, a circa 1931 Weimar era film and a historical drama about the Sun King.

After three days of going over every page of Sylvie's diary chronicling her rise to stardom and asking Sister Rose-Celine for help with unfamiliar phrases (when she's not dozing, the poor dear), I come to the end of 1937. Sylvie has documented her life up to then with a conscious effort at honesty, not holding back. She spends time chronicling her slide into drug addiction and alcohol and later recovery, and how difficult it was for her to stay sober. I come away with the idea she was very proud of attaining her sobriety and keeping clean during the difficult years that followed.

Which again makes me question how such a woman could collaborate with the enemy.

Such a woman would be lazy, ruthless, hedonistic... everything Sylvie wasn't. It didn't make sense.

I sit back in the comfortable chair in what was once my mother's room, listening to Sister Rose-Celine's gentle snoring since the hour is late. I feel guilty reading another woman's diary, even if she is my grandmother. My brain is wired with so much information, my reading skills maxed out trying to interpret the actress's precise, perfectly shaped handwriting cascading across the pages. She does a lovely job of making me feel her intense highs, how the work is all that matters. How she creates her characters and the extra spice that gives a character flavor with the right makeup and wardrobe (*Merci, Grand-mère,* for understanding how important the job of the costume designer is), and the sincere love she has for her fans. Which makes me wonder how she could let them down by working with the Nazis. Then her world spins into a different direction when she talks about the darkness she lived under during that time. My heart suffers with her when she speaks about the years of torment she endured under Emil's control, her road to addiction and back, her sorrowful track record of falling for the wrong men.

And her intense desire to have a child.

Then a big surprise lights up before my eyes as I turn the page to 1938.

My heart flutters, my eyes tear up.

The years leading up to the war reveal a torrid love affair Sylvie had that keeps me turning the pages...

14

SYLVIE

FALLING IN LOVE... C'EST SI BON

Monte Carlo
1938

When I walk through the swinging doors into the casino and see the suave rogue in the white dinner jacket and black bow tie steal a wad of British pound sterling notes from a young woman's purse, I switch gears.

Instead of grabbing a vacant chair and watching a ball spinning around the roulette wheel and losing several thousand francs, I decide to play the avenging angel.

I continue to ponder my options, grinning as I study this handsome specimen of masculinity. Thief or not, I allow my needy, hungry senses to take as much time as they want to drool over him. I'm not going anywhere till I have my fun. It's part of the game of being a film star, *n'est-ce pas?* When Emil insisted I go on a junket to promote the film, I agreed. I love the attention, the glamor. The studio wardrobe department outfitted me with spectacular clothes. Wearing a black wig and a slinky, white silk jersey dress with a low, hanging back that hugs my curves, I could be anybody. A Castilian countess. A rich American heiress on holiday.

Or even a spy.

I admit this trip is a good test of my sobriety. I spent all afternoon at a press party avoiding the champagne *and* a Swedish producer trying to con me into going to his hotel room. I need some fun. And the casino is a short walk from my hotel.

I never expected to stop a crime.

I stand near the four floor-length mirrors in the corner of the gaming room, observing the gentleman thief with more than a casual interest. This gorgeous man is the most handsome villain I've played against, upping the stakes on what I believed would be a quiet but boring evening after I dumped the bodyguard Emil set on my tail.

We had the usual argument earlier about me having a night off.

After a long day meeting with the European press jamming the Hôtel de Paris to interview me, an American reporter told me in broken French I should come to Hollywood. I replied back in decent English, *Never say never.* I don't see myself going to the States, but Emil is in talks with the biggest film studio in London about dubbing my films in English and hiring me to do the voiceover. Why not? I studied English during my stay at Sainte Albertine.

I sigh. Ah, that seems so long ago. The detoxing. Shivers. Sweats... and the intense mental deprivation of a normal life when I was under the influence. Sobriety is a road with many pitfalls. Unfortunately, in my business, I'm never too far from a drink.

I exhale a breath, let the moment pass.

And keep my eyes riveted on the handsome thief.

Enter from stage right Sylvie Martone. Angel and temptress.

I sashay across the salon with fire in my blood and sex appeal in my walk. I move with the sleekness of a tigress, catching the eye of more than one gentleman daring to look away from the roulette table to take a peek. I'm more interested in the sexy rogue with the broad shoulders who makes my breath catch.

I find it surprising the cad had the gall to make his move on the young English girl.

Uh-oh.

They've progressed to a heated exchange with the young woman stomping her foot. She's upset about something, but she hasn't looked in her purse yet.

Odd. She's not backing down from his stern rebuke, rather pressing her hands on the gaming table to stake her claim. The rogue smiles. I know what he's thinking. There's nothing more intriguing to a con man than a willing mark who doesn't *know* she's willing. Him and his soldierly moves. A command decision to steal from his mark in one, easy manipulative sleight of hand. Even if he does have strong shoulders a dinner jacket can't hide, he needs to be taken down a peg.

I wet my lips with my tongue, prepare for battle. This kitten needs rescuing more than I first believed. Wasn't I that way when Emil found me at sixteen?

I make my approach. If I thought his appeal put my hormones on notice before, they spike the closer I get. After years of exposure to good-looking actors, you'd think I'm immune to such a man. Apparently not.

'*Pardon, mademoiselle,*' I say to the young girl, then continue in English, 'If I were you, I'd dump this phony Romeo before he steals more than your money.'

The young girl widens her eyes in surprise then stares at me like she wants to say something but doesn't. She looks me up and down, assessing my gown, my jeweled pin, while the sexy rogue shoots around so quickly, I have to step back. *A graceful slide out of the dragon's lair,* monsieur? my eyes ask him. Ah, yes, I see a temper sparking in his eyes, snapping at me with disapproval for exposing his game.

His jaw tightens and I get a better look at that handsome face. Everything around me comes into sharp focus when he moves on me, the distinct musk in the air giving off the scent of a primal male used to getting the female he wants, the golden glow emitting from the dim casino lighting illuminating his tanned face against his white dinner jacket.

He leads me by the elbow away from the young girl looking both miffed and confused. The warmth rushing through me from the human contact with this stranger surprises me.

I don't pull away.

'I beg your pardon, *mademoiselle*? What did you call me?' He raises both brows. A complete feign of innocence lights up those gorgeous, dark smoldering eyes. He's got his moves down, I'll give him that.

'You heard me, *monsieur*. *Beat it*. She's not your type.'

The thief slides his hand down my arm, his gaze *and* his words direct.

'And you *are* my type?' His eyes twinkle, amused. I slink away, breaking the heated contact between us, though part of me doesn't want to. The man with the arrogance of a highwayman is asking me if I'm coquette or lady.

'That's for you to find out, *monsieur*.' I take a beat, the urge to have him take up the challenge so strong, I lower my eyes and whisper in a low, husky voice, 'If you dare.'

'How do you know I won't steal from *you*?' He flicks his finger over the diamond pin on my gown, his eyes so bright and piercing as he peeks at my cleavage they give me a chill.

I don't back down.

Instead I raise my chest, pushing my breasts out in a deliberate tease. 'What I've got to offer, no man can take.'

'That's a gamble I'm willing to pursue.'

'A lady's got to look out for her reputation.'

A confident smirk plays upon his lips. 'I can help you with that.'

'Can you?' I ask, moving closer as if any physicality between us is because *I* call the shots, not him. 'Are we making a bet?'

'If I kiss you, you'll lose.'

He's backed me into a corner. 'You don't give a girl much choice.'

'Afraid you'll like it?'

'I'm afraid of no man, *monsieur*,' I shoot back. *Except falling in love and having my heart broken.* I must have given myself away, the loneliness in my heart seeping into my eyes.

'I'd never break your heart.'

The look I catch him giving me is mesmerizing. Heated. Hungry. Confident. As if he's acknowledging a fervent interest in upping the stakes. I exhale a deep sigh. I feel caught up in a game I have no intention of playing. Yet I can't help myself.

'I trust no man, *monsieur*, especially a con artist.' I roll my shoulder, tilt my head to catch the sparkle from the chandelier in my eyes.

To seduce him farther away from his mark, I saunter over to the table near the entrance of the Salle Schmidt. I look over my shoulder, inviting the gorgeous man to follow me. There's nothing a devilishly handsome rogue likes better than to enhance his image by seducing a woman who won't fall for his game. He gives me a stony gaze, his blue eyes deepening in color, alerting me I've hit a nerve.

He's at my side in two long strides. 'Well played, *mademoiselle*. Have we met before?'

'We have now, *monsieur*.' Forcing my emotions to remain behind the carefully crafted mask I forged for this evening, I don't hesitate to say, 'If you're looking for someone who can match you in your con game, pick on me, not the innocent girl.'

His square jaw tightens when I don't back down, don't crawl at his feet.

Interesting.

He ventures to smile into my eyes, searching for more than a playful answer from me. 'And what *is* your game, *mademoiselle*?'

'Relieving a gentleman of his winnings. Especially the ill-gotten ones.' I nudge my hip against his jacket pocket where he stuffed the bills. He stiffens. So he's not in control of *everything*. *Bon*. A point for me. 'Now if you'll be so kind as to return the roll of British pounds sterling you lifted from the girl's purse, I won't call the snooty inspector and tell him you're a Big Bad Wolf disguised as a gentleman.'

He lets out a low whistle. 'And if I don't?'

'Then you'll have to answer to me.' A direct challenge. A warning that in spite of my interest in him as a man, he's still a thief.

He refutes my words with a rock-hard resistance that sends a shudder through me. 'I answer to no one, *mademoiselle*.'

'You're British, *n'est-ce pas?*'

'Is it that obvious?' The rogue's retort, not to mention the flash of danger in his eyes, invite me to continue the game. Sure of himself, isn't he?

'Your arrogance is,' I snap back, enjoying myself.

'And you're so deliciously French.'

I strike a pose. 'That *is* obvious.'

'And you're also very beautiful. Who are you?' He slides his arm around my waist, a daring move. In Monte Carlo they say nothing good or honest ever happens here, so I'm not surprised at his arrogance.

'That's not important, *monsieur*.' I sidestep him with a swish of my long, slinky gown. 'After you return the money, I suggest we take this conversation elsewhere, like the Hôtel de Paris, where you won't be tempted to lure any more young girls into your trap.'

'So you can lure me into yours?' Again, that low and gravelly voice tempts me to go beyond playing a game with him, a treat for my poor battered heart, but I promised Emil I wouldn't cause a scandal while I'm here. Having a one-night affair with a rogue gambler, no matter how much he stirs my loins, is off limits. Believe it or not, there are times I agree with him regarding my reputation and the consequences of an impulsive affair.

Yes, I have changed since I got out of the sanitarium.

Yes, I'm wiser now.

Yes, I'm lonelier than ever.

Which is why I don't run. I'm hungry for a man's touch so long denied me. I can't get it through my brain to walk away. There's something about this man that makes me want to know him – even though I know him to be unscrupulous. Why is he driven to stealing from beautiful women? Has he lost fifty, a hundred, a thousand francs tonight? Why is he gambling so heavily he has to resort to stealing from an innocent girl?

Is it my job as an avenging angel to also save *him*?

What a deliciously wicked idea.

A rising emotion makes me sigh and want and burn. A feeling

I've suppressed so long I'm desperate to rediscover it. He's no rudimentary gentleman shy of fancy talk when conning a feminine bit of fluff – which he knows I'm not – so he's changing his playbook. I can see it in his eyes, dark with secrets he's not ready to reveal to me. Not yet.

'Do you think I'm a spy?' I ask, hiding the lower half of my face with my gloved hand and peering over my fingers, sending him a piercing look. Would it hurt to play along a little longer?

'Everyone here has something to hide, *mademoiselle*. Whether it's a heart broken by a road not taken, or a passion burning for the unattainable, we've all lost something... or someone. So we come to the gaming tables at Monte Carlo and watch the little ball make its descent into the pockets on the wheel... red or black... it doesn't matter... hoping we'll be lucky this time.' An arrogant smile, then, 'Including you.'

I sense a note of curiosity, then hope I'll take the bait in his deep baritone voice.

'And why would you say that?' Deep in the pit of my stomach, my game of subterfuge turns into something more revealing. Never before have I cared about the results of my roleplaying. Whoever this handsome man is, he's found a way to unsettle me and I don't like it.

His eyes narrow. 'I think you know the answer.'

He waits for me to speak, then smirks when I catch him looking at my cleavage as if he's already tasting the salt on my skin with his warm lips.

Bad enough I'm flirting with him, now he's challenging me to reveal who I am... or is he bluffing? After all, he's a player. I can feel the dizzying pounding of my heart when I let myself fall for a man and I *am* falling for him.

I don't have a chance to find out. The young girl marches over to us, holding up her empty purse. 'The lady is right, Jock, you took my spending allowance,' she says, annoyed. 'How could you?'

I can't hide my surprise. 'You *know* this thief?'

'He's no thief.' Her gaze wanders past me to the tall gentleman taking out a platinum cigarette case *and* giving me a victorious, sexy glance. 'He's my brother.'

'You see, *mademoiselle*, I'm not such a bad sort after all.' His eyes are full of mirth, enjoying his deception as he lights a cigarette. Again, he can't take his eyes off me, sweeping his glance up and down my body in approval. 'You might say I'm a good sport, seeing how you almost got me arrested with your accusations.'

His sister's eyes widen with shock, then amusement. 'Jock, she *didn't*.'

'I did, *mademoiselle*, since I was concerned when I saw your *brother* remove the money from your purse.' I don't know whether or not to be angry or amused at his ruse. What's more disconcerting is the physical arousal this man evokes in me. 'I should have him arrested for his duplicitous game.'

'I like her, Jock.' Her amusement turns into a huge smile that shows her pretty, white teeth. 'She's got more guts than the silly women you usually hang around with.' She plants her hands on her hips. 'Now if you'll return the money Nana gave me for my birthday, I'll leave you two alone.' She winks at me. 'Good luck, *mademoiselle*, and I don't mean at the tables.'

Her brother narrows his gaze, focusing on the young woman, then returns the money to her. 'No gambling, Winnie. Understood?'

'Promise.' She crosses her fingers. 'Keep him occupied, *mademoiselle. Please.*' Then she trots off without another word, looking over her shoulder and glancing at us with a big smile.

Jock shakes his head. 'She lost ten thousand francs yesterday at *trente et quarante.*'

'Let her go. She's having fun.'

'At my poor grandmother's expense.' He narrows his eyes. 'How do I know *you're* not a thief?'

'You don't. This could be a trap.'

'A very beautiful trap, *mademoiselle*,' he says, smiling at whatever sensual thought occupies his mind. 'Can I buy you a drink at the bar?'

'Spies don't drink with their target.' The words come quick.

Dangerous territory for me when it comes to the bottle and I don't want to spoil our interlude. I like the game too much to ruin it.

'Too bad. I would have enjoyed being seduced by a Mata Hari who happens to be a famous French film star.' I see merriment in his eyes. He made me and he's enjoying every minute of it. It doesn't, however, stop his eyes smoldering with midnight-blue flames.

It's my turn to tip my hat to him. 'When did you know who I was?'

'When you mentioned the Hôtel de Paris, I remembered seeing you in the lobby earlier wearing that same gown and surrounded by press photographers. I overheard the hotel staff talking about the beautiful blonde actress from Paris.' As he looks at me remembering that moment, his eyes wrap me up in velvet, sending a pleasurable ache slithering through me. 'I couldn't take my eyes off you when your diamond pin sparkled as flashbulbs went off and you rubbed the horse's front leg for good luck on the Louis XIV statue.'

'It's already brought me good luck.' I wink at him, a brazen move. I don't tell him the diamond pin is a fake from the studio wardrobe department. A prop I coveted from *Madame le Noir* to go with my gown. 'I never expected anyone to recognize me in a black wig.'

'You underestimate your fans.'

'You're a fan?'

'I am now.'

I'm struck by the sincerity in his voice. It warms me in a way I haven't felt for a long time.

'I want to thank you for looking out for my sister Winnie.' His handsome features are etched with brotherly concern. 'She's very impetuous. I was impressed by how you protected her from what you perceived as a threat. I've never met a gorgeous woman who would do that. You're nothing like the other actresses I've gone out with, most with enormous egos.'

I laugh. 'Not where I come from.' I don't elaborate. 'I'll never forget the poor seamstress role that made me a star. I like to think of myself as Ninette, an angel saving the world from bad villains.'

'*Mon bel ange.*' Jock smiles at me and the word *angel* takes on a whole new meaning for me. A fluttering in my heart I won't easily forget. 'Winnie's lucky to have a famous actress watching out for her.'

'She's lucky to have such a handsome brother.'

Gorgeously handsome, but I won't tell him that.

'Call me Jock.'

'Sylvie... but then you already know that.'

Ah, mon Dieu, how I don't want this conversation to end. It won't be easy to let him into my heart, if he's even *interested* in me beyond flirting. Rather like placing a bet on the roulette wheel with your eyes closed. The hunger to win, the need to connect outweigh the fear of losing it all.

Suddenly I don't care when I hear him say—

'There's a lot more I'd like to know about you, Sylvie.'

15

SYLVIE

WHO IS MY PRINCE CHARMING REALLY?

Monte Carlo
1938

Does the night ever end in Monte Carlo?

The casino closes at midnight, but the stepping stars of lights from the hotels and the nearby sporting club, the yachts anchored in the harbor... the laughter drifting on the cool evening breeze... all make the evening magic. After our unique introduction, Jock and I hold hands as we wander down the steps to the almost deserted terrace of the casino chairs near the balustrade. As far as our wildly sensual banter goes, we trade it for a more relaxed camaraderie between us that goes deeper than quips and innuendos. The simmering emotions we let go so freely when we didn't know where the play would lead us find a new course. We're no longer hiding behind masks of anonymity and I find him a fascinating enigma I can't wait to unravel.

'I owe Winnie a debt I can never repay.' Jock squeezes my hand.

'You do?' I say, squeezing his hand back. The scent of roses dances by on a wistful breeze adding to the romantic moment.

'If she weren't an adorable little troublemaker, we never would have met.'

'Oh? I don't believe you. You had me in your sights at the Hôtel de Paris.'

'I did... but I'm a gambling man and I was waiting for the right moment to—'

'Kidnap me?' I tease him. 'I hear there's a local superstition that it's lucky to abduct a French actress and hold her close and inhale her perfume when you make your bet.'

'Like this?' He picks me up and drapes me over his broad shoulder, paying no mind to my meek protests and carrying me away from the bright lights of the casino. My worst acting job ever. I moan with a deep pleasure, yielding to his will when he puts me down near the sumptuous garden. I imagine the sleeping blossoms opening and peeking at our antics when he holds me close to his chest and slides his hands up and down my body, his gaze locked on me.

'Yes,' I whisper, 'most definitely like this.'

'Sylvie... you try a man's soul. I've never met a woman like you.'

'Is that good or bad?' I ask in an unsteady voice, surprised at my own question.

'Very good... but you're a famous film star and I'm—'

'You're a man and I'm a woman... that's all that counts.'

'If only it were that simple.'

He cups my chin as I look up into his eyes, trusting him, baring my soul to him, a man I hardly know. Every part of me aches to feel him kiss me, explore my hidden places. He smiles at me in a way that tells me he's finding it painful to tamp down his passion for me. That he's on edge, holding back. I sense he's keeping something from me.

A flippant breeze flirts with the lingering night as the minutes tick by. Neither of us moves, the heat of our bodies touching so pleasurable we embrace the sheer joy of it.

'I want to keep holding you, Sylvie, but I'm only human and I won't last much longer,' he whispers, nuzzling my hair with his face. 'I'll escort you back to your hotel before I do something we'll both regret.'

I nod. I can't speak, my throat tight. I thought he was going to kiss me. He didn't. Would I have resisted? Or leant into him, matching his hunger with my own?

I'll never know.

* * *

In the days that follow, we keep in contact by telephone, but we don't speak about what happened that night. As if we've called a truce to our physical need for each other. I'm not sure why. Again, I have the feeling Jock is keeping something from me. It can't be another woman. Winnie would have spilled the beans if there was. I put that thought out of my head and jump up and down like a schoolgirl reading a billet-doux when Jock shows up at my hotel with orchids and chocolate. I can't get enough of his deliciously warm charm and his vast knowledge. He's brilliantly educated and filled with utter confidence, a Renaissance man, while I'm a lowly player on this earth on what the Bard called a stage.

Yet that doesn't stop me from challenging myself.

I've had an education in life and, thanks to reading script after script, I'm familiar with the classics, but I realize deep down I'm still that little girl from the convent.

Jock doesn't care where I come from. He's impressed with my film career, how I started out at sixteen and fought my way to the top.

Over the next few days, as I drool over this millionaire rogue, I'm fortunate Emil is tied up with meetings with British film executives and, after letting the bodyguard go for failing to keep track of my whereabouts, he's willing to loosen the leash as long as I show up for press events. (I don't miss any of them.) He doesn't want any scandal attached to my visit to Monte Carlo, something that could upset the Brits during his negotiations for the English film deal. He's well aware how touchy they are about scandals.

All the more reason for Jock and me to keep our relationship away from the press (my black wig becomes *de rigeur* on our jaunts around Monaco).

My favorite moment, the one I'll always remember, comes at a time when I least expected I'd suffer such a romantic reaction to a man. An undeniable attraction to having him in my life for as long as I live, an attraction that threatens to unseat my current state of stability. I've worked so hard making my films, fulfilling my publicity obligations, writing to my fans. Every time we're together, the sun feels warmer on my face, the moonlight makes everything brighter. My need for him surges like a great sea, ebbing only when I lie in his arms and know I'm safe... then surges again until I see him.

Tonight, Jock whisks me away in a 'borrowed' Mercedes, into the deepening night. Somehow he arranges for us to visit a villa high on a cliff surrounded by orange groves and overlooking the sea – just us, no servants or attendants. A cold buffet laid out for us. Wine. Champagne. Sparkling lemon water. (I'm not induced to imbibe alcohol when I'm with him.) Beautiful roses and daffodils. He says he wants me to see something I'll never see anywhere else. I thought he may try to take advantage of us being alone together, and if he does, well, I'm more than tempted.

The seduction he has in mind is the lovely illumination of—

Fireflies.

Hundreds, *thousands* of them nestling near the tall, marble fountain in the sumptuous floral garden and glowing like live fairy dust. We stand holding each other as we look out over the lighted city of Monaco, so bright, and filled with no tomorrows. Surrounding us is the beauty and brilliance of nature's little torchbearers.

'I can't tell you how much this week has meant to me, Sylvie,' Jock whispers in my ear, 'as if the rest of the world and its mayhem don't exist.'

'I wish we could stay here in Monte Carlo...' I leave the rest unsaid, raising my hand to run my fingertips over the stubble on his face. My man is in rebel mode this week, pushing aside society's rules. No tie. No hat. I unbutton his white shirt and get a peek at that broad chest and start drooling again.

He's never kissed me. Why?

'And live here with me in this villa?' He heaves out a heavy sigh. 'I'd like that. No schedule, no telegrams, no rules...'

'Oh, there'd be rules,' I tease him, tugging on his collar. 'You'd have to kiss me at least once an hour. Morning, noon, *and* night.'

'You know I *want* to kiss you,' he says, reading my mind. 'Kiss you madly, take every inch of you into my arms and smell you, taste you... make you moan with pleasure.'

'Then why don't you?' I ask now.

'Because I don't want to hurt you.'

'Hurt me? How?'

'We're complete opposites. You're wild, unpredictable. I'm a moody Brit. Always by the book. You believe in love at first sight. I find love to be complicated... and messy.'

I feel let down, but not crushed. Jock's honesty makes me want him more.

'*Alors, mon chéri,* I have a plan. We agree to enjoy each other's company without any expectation of seeing each other again. No questions about our private lives. But no holding back either... no putting what we have in a box. Instead, we'll be like the fireflies... lighting up each other's lives with a dazzling brilliance and when it's over... we'll have the memory of a glorious time that will never dim.'

He studies my face. 'Is that what you want?'

'I want you...'

'Even if it can't last?'

'Yes, I want you and if you think I'm going to shy away and play hard-to-get like the proper ladies you're used to, you've got the wrong girl. I make no excuses for who I am,' I admit, though my hands are trembling. 'And I'm no angel.'

'Oh, but you are, Sylvie,' he murmurs as he brushes my lips with his mouth. 'The angel who dared to confront me to right a wrong.' His voice goes deeper. 'At first, I thought we could have a few laughs, enjoy each other's company in this paradise. It didn't turn out that way.'

I arch a brow. 'What do you mean?'

'I'm falling in love with you, Sylvie. You've turned me into a mad, crazy, impetuous fool and I can't stop myself.'

'Then don't, *mon amour*... kiss me.'

I lean into him as we enjoy a searing, burning kiss in the moonlight that doesn't end even after our lips part. The kiss turns into a passionate rhythm as our bodies move against each other, exploring, probing... then resisting the temptation. He holds back, though barely, insisting he'll wait to take me in a bed of silk and satin when I ask him to... but not until I'm sure it's what I want. I can think of nothing else when I'm with this gorgeous man who tells me he loves me, how for the first time in my life I've bared my soul to a man and he doesn't try to change me or take advantage of me. My heart has been broken before. Not this time. I want to believe I've found true love with Jock and nothing can change that, our bodies bathed in the glow of tiny fireflies, their nocturnal lights slowly fading as dawn cast her spell over them.

And us.

I'll never forget I'm wearing my favorite red shade of lipstick from my *Toujours, Sylvie* collection when we shared our first kiss on this night of nights.

I shall keep it always.

* * *

I never find out how Jock arranged for us to visit the villa.

Business connections, I imagine. As agreed, we made a pact not to discuss our private lives. I don't talk about show business and he doesn't mention where he made his money. I guess manufacturing. His cool calculations at the roulette table suggests a mind used to making quick decisions and his esteemed knowledge of the gambling principality suggests he visits here often... business, politics? It's well known that certain British lawmakers and royals aren't shy about stopping here on their way from Cannes to Paris.

I don't care where he comes from. I want to be with him, though

I'm not about to make the mistake of falling into bed with him. I don't need sex. I need a man's love. I know he's rich. So am I. I don't see that as a problem, which gives me hope this time I can fall in love.

Even if I'm scheduled to return to Paris. I've done my job for the studio, promoted the picture, even Emil is pleased with my efforts. The head of production wants me back in France.

But how to tell Jock?

Has it been three weeks already since I came to Monte Carlo?

'I hear the Duke and Duchess of Windsor might be stopping by here at the Hôtel de Paris next week,' I begin after tea is served in my suite by a uniformed waiter. Jock is sitting on the divan reading a British newspaper. 'It's a shame I won't be—'

'*Bonjour, Mademoiselle* Sylvie...' Winnie bounces into the hotel room with a burst of energy. 'I can't wait to tell you what happened today.'

I admit I'm relieved to put off telling Jock and hug the girl warmly. 'Come and join us for tea, Winnie.' I notice a brunette following behind her, a shy girl looking at everything in the opulent suite with curious eyes. 'And your friend, too, *mademoiselle*...'

The girl mutters her name but I don't catch it as Jock grabs me round the waist and Winnie, too. 'I'm a lucky man with three beautiful women for tea.'

'I'm the lucky one, Jock,' I say with a twinge of guilt for not telling him I'm going back to Paris. 'You two girls have a seat while I pour the tea and tell me about your day.'

'*Sit?*' Winnie laughs. 'Not after spending the morning trekking up the hill on a donkey to visit a ruined old castle.' Her eyes sparkle with mischief as she accepts a steaming demitasse of tea with milk. 'Then the loveliest thing happened. We went to the Palace of the Prince of Monaco and his official secretary asked us to sign the guest book.' She hugs her teacup to her chest, swooning. 'Maybe we'll get a royal invitation to a party. Wouldn't that be grand?'

'What's *grand*,' says Jock, 'is you're keeping your promise not to gamble in the casinos.' He nods toward her friend sipping tea, alerting me the quiet girl is a classmate from boarding school and a local resident. 'Citizens of Monaco aren't allowed to gamble.'

'I'm proud of you, too, Winnie,' I acknowledge, but resist the urge to tell him I saw a glint in her eye that tells me she's up to something. Because I'm up to something, too. I just don't have the courage to tell him.

I'm leaving in two days on the *Calais-Mediterranée Express*.

The Blue Train.

* * *

'Has my brother kissed you yet?'

I shake my head at Winnie, amused. A simple, direct question only a teenage girl in love with love would ask.

It's late and the two of us are in the middle of a wild, jazzy move when she tosses the question at me. Winnie asked me to show her the dances we do in Paris so she can impress her friends back in London, turning on the radio and the two of us raising a ruckus in my suite.

'*Ah, ma chère* Winnie, your debonair brother is a wonderful kisser,' I tell her in a playful manner, and she lets go with a long, wistful sigh. I'd never tell her his kisses are not brushes on my lips, but hot kisses on my jaw, my dimple, the side of my neck... *everywhere*.

'I knew it!' She reaches toward me and squeezes my hand tight. 'Jock is quite a catch, you know.' She bites her lip, baiting me, waiting to see what I'll say.

I ignore her probing. 'I bet you have a beau, Winnie, *n'est-ce pas?*'

She shakes her head. 'No, Mummy doesn't approve of me dating and since she's not well I'd never go against her wishes since I haven't been presented at court yet—'

'*Pardon?*' I raise a quizzical brow and she tries to change the subject like she's said too much.

'Is this how you do the dance step?' she asks, batting her eyes as she pirouettes then shimmies her hips.

'*Très bon!*' I give her a thumbs up, chalking her comment up to

her earlier remark about hoping for a royal invitation to the Palace of
the Prince of Monaco. 'You must come visit me in Paris... you *and*
Jock.'

'And *you* must come to London.'

I cross my fingers. 'I may have a voice-dubbing deal at a British film
studio soon.'

'Brilliant. We'll have a swell time. I'm certain Jock will invite you to
our country house during the hunting season. Do you ride?'

'Did you see me in *Madame Le Noir*? It's about a female highway-
man.' I let out a big sigh. I'm already picturing me riding alongside
Jock on a high-stepping bay mare like a proper English lady. 'I spent
more time in the saddle than in a corset.'

* * *

My pipe dream of spending time in London with Jock takes a wrong
turn the next day when Jock and I stroll arm in arm along the Boulevard Albert 1er. I'm scheduled to leave for Paris tomorrow but if Jock
asks me to stay, I plan to tell Emil about us and beg him to understand
since I don't start a new film for two weeks.

I'm filled with a familiar desire to please this man who's captured
my heart, wearing a slim, silk floral dress with a billowing overskirt,
wide brim hat, white gloves, and holding a small, ivory lace parasol
over my head. I dance over the stone walkway like a fairy princess
walking on a cloud, not knowing what's waiting for me around the
corner. Jock looks devastatingly handsome in a white summer suit with
a blue tie. He's hatless and the sun embraces his handsome, tanned
features with a glow, his dark eyes holding mine until—

'I didn't know you were still in Monte Carlo, Your Grace,' says a
dowager British woman approaching us, her sagging bosom matching
her chin.

I spin around. Who's she talking to? I don't see anyone behind us.
Oh, she was addressing *Jock*...

'We thought we'd missed you,' she finishes, laying a hand on his sleeve and confirming my suspicions, making my heart palpitate like firecrackers popping.

She's well dressed, with a pointy nose. Her friend is about the same age with the same sagging bosom, but she's more interested in looking me over.

We nearly ran into them... or did they go out of their way to run into *us*?

'We had the pleasure of chatting with your dear sister when we checked into our hotel.' She clears her throat. 'Lady Revell said you'd returned to Kyretree Castle.'

I double blink. *Lady Revell...* Winnie?

Who are these women? Why did Winnie tell them Jock had returned to England?

They look horrified at me hanging onto him in a most intimate manner. My dress reveals my curves, ruffles emphasizing my décolletage, and my lipstick is red... too red for their pale tastes.

'You must invite us for tea, Your Grace,' asserts the first woman. 'When you're not occupied with *other* matters.'

I'd like to wrap my parasol around her neck. No doubt those 'other matters' refer to me, talking about me as if I'm not even here.

In her mind, I'm not.

'Lady Hensworth, Lady Devon,' Jock begins, his voice pleasant but firm. 'May I present Sylvie Martone, famed star of French cinema.'

His mouth tightens as he digresses into a mundane nonsense one says to women of that ilk, all the while knowing they're cataloging me in their minds and not in a nice way.

A Frenchwoman, my word. And an actress. What next?

That isn't what sets every nerve in my body on fire.

They addressed him as *Your Grace.*

A term I came across in a British script Emil wanted me to read to prepare me for dubbing my films into English. A *royal* term for—

It has to be a mistake, a game he's playing with me. My eyes plead with him to tell me so. He smiles at me, shining love at me that doesn't go unnoticed by the two women.

I have no idea how we get back to the hotel, but everything changes between us as we enter the lobby and head for the lift.

'You didn't tell me you were a duke.'

'You didn't ask.'

'As if I go around asking every man I meet if he's a duke.' Now I know what Winnie was hiding from me: her family's royal blood. 'You told Winnie... I mean, Lady Revell, not to tell me, didn't you?'

'Yes, Lady Winifred Revell. I call her Winnie. I didn't want to scare you away, *mon bel ange*.'

'That's why you were so careful not to let anyone see us together. And I thought you were trying to help me avoid the press.'

His voice lowers, rich and heavy with the emotion of a man who's used to getting what he wants. 'I planned to tell you who I was on my terms, when the time was right.'

'And when would that have been? After I was back in Paris?'

Jock senses my frustration mixed with a pinch of drama regarding the direction of this conversation. He tilts my face up to his, giving me that wicked look of his that makes me sigh like a handmaiden summoned to his bedchamber.

He ignores my question. 'It's not a sin to be a duke.'

'It should be.' I force a smile and refuse to squirm in front of him. 'The way you go around seducing women with your inimitable charm, you act more like a king.'

'Then you shall be my queen,' he dares to cajole me, setting his big hands on my shoulders and pressing my flesh with his fingers. The effect of his touch on me is instant. Mesmerizing. I can't resist him. I close my eyes, letting my anger diffuse, waiting for him to kiss me and make me swoon...

Instead he presses a soft, gentle kiss to my forehead. 'Now will you stop acting like a child before I—'

'A child?' I sputter, my eyes shooting open and my adrenaline spiking. '*You're* the one who said you were falling in love with me without mentioning you're a royal pain in the ass duke. A minor detail you omitted. No doubt to test me. See if I'm a gold digger out to snag you *and* your title.'

He runs his hand through his dark hair in frustration. 'I admit I should have told you sooner, Sylvie, but you're so damned independent, I didn't know how you'd act. Well, I was right. You're acting the way I thought you would. You can't accept the fact I fell in love with *you*, the angel with a heart, not the shimmering blonde film star.'

'You did?' I ask, hopeful.

'Yes, I did. And *nothing* you say will change my mind. Ever. I love you, dammit. And whether or not you want to admit it, you love me, too.'

I should turn my back on him, not let him see the heat flaming my cheeks, not only in anger but desire. I don't.

Instead I walk away from the lift and head for a shadowy corner, then tell him what he wants to hear with one powerful word, not caring if I appear a fool, for that's what I am. A crazy, loving fool who can't let this wonderful man, duke or whatever he is, walk away without knowing how I feel.

'Yes... oh, *yes*.' I can't believe that husky, powerful word came out of my throat, that tense awareness that I mean it with all my heart. I *do* love him, but I don't want my heart broken. I don't want to end up at the bottom again.

This time I won't make it back.

'You make me happy, Sylvie, what does it matter if I'm a duke? I inherited a blasted string of names. It doesn't make me who I am.'

'*Mon Dieu*, how many titles do you have?'

'My given name is John Lawrence Revell but I answer to the Earl of Aspenbrooke, Fifth Duke of Greychurch, and the Baron of Candemore.'

'Oh, my, that's all?' I utter with more than a twinge of sarcasm and the raising of a blonde penciled brow. 'What's the royal world coming to?'

'*This*, my darling.' He pulls me into his arms, stroking the bare skin on my back with his fingers, leaving trails of fire that singe the soft ruffles fluttering on my shoulders. I don't pull away though I should, begging for one more moment in his arms.

'I've never met a woman like you, Sylvie. We have something beautiful between us. Let's not ruin it.'

I shake my head. 'I wish I could say, "yes, we can make it work", but I know how this story ends. I've played too many poor shop girls who fall in love with the handsome lord of the manor only to have their hearts broken by the end of the fourth reel.' My nerves are stretched taut, my emotions ablaze with regret when I say, 'I can't see you again.'

'I don't believe you.'

'I'll always remember Monte Carlo... and the fireflies. *Adieu.*'

I turn on my heel and walk briskly out of the hotel and back toward the casino. He calls after me, but he doesn't follow me. Did I expect him to? I won't go running back. I have my pride. I feel played.

I'm an actress, he's a duke.

End of story.

16

SYLVIE

ONE FOR THE ROAD... MAYBE

Monte Carlo
1938

'Brandy... make it a *double.*'

I order a drink at the casino bar, then stare at it for I don't know how long. I've been sober for a while and this is the first time a glimmer of temptation triggers me to take a drink. I ignore the curious look from the elderly gent sitting next to me nursing an empty pocket-book with a bottle of vodka, pressing in as close as he can to see if I'm who he thinks I am. I keep my head down. I don't need him butting in. If I want a drink, I'll have one. Funny, I never had the craving when I was with Jock *before* I found out he's a duke, never went down that road.

The road that leads to heartbreak. And it's crushing my willpower.

I put the brandy to my lips, then somehow put it down... I know it's waiting there for me. The craving is so strong I want to gulp it down like a common drunk, be done with it and then hate myself. Then start all over again. Instead, I sniff the pungent smell of alcohol like it's an elixir promising a soothing, wonderful, healing relief. A pretty story I tell myself to put a lovely spin on it so I can wash away the guilt.

Something holds me back.

Call it instinct or the tools I learnt at the sanitarium to deal with my addiction, or plain luck when a too-suave gent with the heavy smell of garlic and cigar smoke on his breath sits down next to me on the other side and starts chatting me up.

Whatever the reason, I push away the brandy.

I want that drink. Instead, I grab a vacant chair at the roulette wheel and plunk down my derriere on the red velvet cushion. I toss down five thousand francs, all the time berating myself. How could I let myself fall head over heels in love with a man who can never love me back?

Me. The illegitimate child of a prostitute falling in love with a playboy duke.

It only happens in moving pictures.

Except this is no picture.

This is real life. Mine. And there is no happy ending.

I gather up the chips the croupier gives me in exchange for the cash and the wheel turns. That horrible clicking sound fills my ears and all I hear is, *Do it... do it... get a drink... you know you want to.*

And I do. I don't want to feel pain anymore, I want to fall down, *down* into that abyss of nothingness and float away in a dream.

Just one sip and I'll be okay...

The heat inside me grows with every moment I sit at the gaming table, watching the spinning ball, my head twirling, my entire being craving a drink so bad it feels like someone stabbed my gut with a knife. I clench and unclench my fists. Anything can trigger a relapse. Anxiety. Devastating disappointment. Sorrow. I fought it before, but this is different. My heart isn't just broken, it's stamped with a big red X, reminding me what I am. I'll never be good enough for Jock and I'd die rather than the gossips find out about me and hurt him. I can see the headline in the London scandal sheets. '*Playboy Duke breaks the heart of French actress in Monte Carlo*'. Then the reporters will go digging like they always do, and the studio will feed them my official bio, find out I'm three years older than Jock and they'll use the 'older woman' angle. That's bad enough – what if a royal watcher finds out the truth? I'm flattered Jock wants to be with me though he's flaunting tradition, dating a commoner and an illegitimate one at that.

I need a brandy, champagne cocktail, vodka. *Anything* to wash away the pain.

I grab a handful of chips and squeeze them tight. Maybe if I stay at the table... maybe I can beat the craving... *maybe.*

I toss down one chip after another... white, pink, not caring if I win or lose. A numbness spreading over me I haven't felt since that night in Montmartre.

I make a wager with myself, the same wager every alcoholic makes when they're ready to relapse. *If I win the spin of the wheel, I walk away; if I lose, I drink the brandy.*

What are the odds of me winning?

Right... I want that drink.

I linger a minute, then two, planning my move, thinking; the anticipation is almost as good as the high. I put all my chips on one number.

Rien ne va plus... no more bets.

The ivory ball spins round and round. I can't stop watching it. I see my life spinning out of control. My hand shakes... my bottom lip trembles... and suddenly I see the face of Father Armand and his caring eyes bluer than a summer sky, his warm hand taking my cold fingers in his and helping me up the steps of Sacré-Coeur... then the stink of my sins making me gag when I enter the holy place... and afterward how it took months to wash away the smell of what I was.

A disgusting drunk. And an addict.

Is that you want again? The vomit stuck in your throat? The shakes... the smell of urine coming off your silk dress because you're too drunk to go to the loo?

No, I don't.

Then think of Jock. The man loves you. Even if you let him go, you don't have to let go of your pride. Never forget, you're a star and if you take that drink, you're letting down that sixteen-year-old who had the guts to take the ridicule and insults to get where you are.

Are you such a coward, you can't take this now?

A long shudder goes through me, like I'm waking up from a bad dream. Instead of that horrible clicking, I hear the sound of rushing water in my ears... a cleansing.

I can't relapse. I can't. I've worked too hard, too long to find my sobriety.

I get up from the table and don't look back. I hear the croupier announce the winning number. I'm not listening. Not this time. It doesn't matter to me where the ivory ball lands.

I've already won.

* * *

'I'm not letting you go like this, Sylvie. I must see you again.'

I should be surprised when Jock waylays me at the hotel. I'm not. I look at him with longing, but I can't linger. The express train leaves tonight from Menton station less than ten kilometers from the hotel. My reservation is for tomorrow, but I can't wait. Can't keep my passion for this man under control if I stay. I'll take any seat available. First class, second... third, whatever.

'I'm leaving Monte Carlo, Jock. Or should I say, Your Grace. I'm taking the Blue Train back to Paris.'

'Then I'll come with you.'

'You can't, my manager Emil won't understand.'

'*You* don't understand, Sylvie.' Jock rakes his hand through his dark hair, frustrated. His suave charm has been forsaken and replaced by a raw hunger in his voice that torments me so when he says, 'I'm in love with you.'

'You don't know what you're saying, Jock. If you were John Lawrence Revell, British millionaire, we might have a chance. But where I come from, dipping your toe into the royal pond can stir up a whole can of worms that can't be put back. I don't fit into your world. Believe me, it's better this way, no one gets hurt.'

'I can't change who I am, Sylvie, neither can you. That doesn't mean we can't be together.'

'Don't you see, Jock, this is all a dream. I'm under contract. I have film commitments.'

'And I have lands to run, family business to oversee, financial dealings to fulfill, political obligations. It doesn't stop me from loving you. We're in this together, to support each other, love each other. With the shape the world is in right now, God knows how long before Hitler plants his boot into the rest of the Europe.'

My eyes widen. 'You don't believe that.'

'I do.' He holds my gaze as he slowly and with great care runs his fingertips over my cheek, then settles in the dimple on my left cheek. 'You'd be surprised what you hear at the baccarat table. I've been privy to certain conversations with British dignities and the consensus is *not* good. The Foreign Office is convinced over the next several months, Hitler won't stop with enslaving the German people with his politics. He won't be happy until he has all of Europe under the Nazi flag.'

'He'd never try that in France.'

His deathly silence worries me.

The Germans in Paris?

Impossible.

'I'm coming to Paris next month, Sylvie. Please, I want to see you. Besides, Winnie says you're good for me, how she hasn't seen me smiling so much since I met you.'

I nod. 'She's a charming young girl, full of promise.'

'Don't I know it, and she admires you, Sylvie. I'll bring her with me. She can be our chaperone. After all, *mon bel ange,* I never would have met you if it weren't for Winnie.'

Then before I can pull away, he kisses me and crushes me against his chest, the faux diamond pin on my red gabardine suit digging into my chest. My lucky charm because it led me to him. Everything I told him is true. I'd be giving the gossips the keys to a scandal that could ruin us both, but the way he looks at me, holds me, I can't let him go. Jock has made up his mind and so have I. We have to be discreet, carry on like secret lovers meeting in out-of-the-way hotels or rented villas. I'll never let go of our secret... or the faux diamond pin... or Jock. Every excuse I have melts under his kiss. I should stop him, but I can't.

How can I turn down a duke?

I hold on to him tight and his promise our love will survive.

Even as the tensions in Europe escalate and the world prepares for war.

17

JULIANA

A PICTURE IS WORTH A THOUSAND HEARTBREAKS

Ville Canfort-Terre, France
Present Day

I can't resist peeking at the last page of Sylvie's diary from 1939 and it's a doozy.

A cliffhanger. Like one of her *Ninette* serials.

I sip my warm tea; I'm getting used to its sweet taste. After reading this, I need something with a kick as I try to focus on the handwritten pages. I never imagined my grandmother was so passionate.

And an alcoholic. The pain she suffered tears me apart, reliving what I went through with my mother all over again albeit in a different way. Alcoholism is a disease. And watching Sylvie nearly relapse brings back so many memories as I watched my mother's dementia steal *her* life away. I try to hold back my anguish, but the tears running down my cheeks end up in my tea, salt mixing with its sweet taste. Like Sylvie's fantastic life. It makes me sad, yet I'm so proud of her. It's a lot to take in and even more so when I'm struggling to find out what made her turn against France. From what I read in her own words, it doesn't sound like her.

Then why did she do it?

I sit back in the sixteenth-century walnut chair and finish my tea, thinking.

I cry over the heartache Sylvie went through with Jock, laugh at their meeting in the casino, sigh over their romance, and then totally freak out when Sylvie breaks up with him.

Such different times they were, how people had such disdain for children born out of love without marriage. How my own horizon changed when I found out I was the child of an unwed mother, though I never faulted *Maman* for her choice. It's different in the twenty-first century (then why am I so hung up on my roots?). It's not something I'd discuss with Sister Rose-Celine. I wonder if she'd understand. She's such a darling, sitting with me for hours and listening to me lamenting over French idioms I haven't used for years and struggling with interpreting Sylvie's looped and flowery handwriting. I'm disappointed the sister isn't here now. She left to take a well-deserved nap (I hate seeing her falling asleep in her wheelchair in what has to be an uncomfortable position). I often forget she's in her eighties, she's so dedicated to our cause to find out everything about Sylvie.

I can't wait to tell her what happens when Sylvie meets this dashing duke.

* * *

'I thought you said Sylvie and the duke broke up, and now they're hanging out in Paris together?'

I try to explain to Sister Rose-Celine their on-again, off-again, on-again relationship as we switch between English *and* French.

'It was a crazy time with the world on the brink of war,' I tell her, 'but upper class Parisians didn't want to believe their city was in danger from invasion by the German Army. Champagne flowed and pretty women in haute couture ruled the day.'

It's like a romantic soap opera. According to the diary, they continue to see each other through the late summer of 1939 and throw caution – and propriety – to the wind and fall in love. What I find odd is Sylvie never mentions the duke by his given name. Only as 'Jock', a nickname, as if keeping her word not to reveal anything about their love affair.

Which presents an interesting dilemma.

Without a name or where he lived, it's nearly impossible to find him.

I could do a search on the Internet on every duke from the era and try to figure out who he was, but I'm running out of time. I'm hoping Sylvie names him somewhere, in a second diary perhaps... and gives us clues where to find it. I can't believe she didn't continue the story. In the meantime, I send a text to Ridge filling him in and while I'm waiting to hear from him, Sister Rose-Celine and I devour the rest of the diary.

'And it wasn't just Paris, Sister,' I tell her, grabbing a handful of chocolate nonpareils. 'All over Europe, the society crowd wasn't paying attention to what was happening in Germany and the rise of the Nazi Party.' With Sister Rose-Celine's charming pleading, the nun heading up the kitchen is only too happy to give me a never-ending bowl of chocolate candy. 'Sylvie talks about their exciting adventures from summer 1938 to early autumn 1939. Yachting off the coast of Ireland, dining in London at the Savoy, touring the flamenco bars of Madrid, and then...' I pause for emphasis. 'Hiding out at the Hôtel Ritz in Paris to escape the watchful eye of the press.'

'*Ooh la la*,' Sister Rose-Celine says with a chuckle. 'This is getting juicy.'

'*Sister!*' I admonish her.

'I'm not so old-fashioned I don't watch movies on my phone, *mademoiselle*,' she says wryly. 'Tell me what happens next.'

She makes me smile with her adorable sense of humor.

'If you won't be offended, Sister, but I have to warn you, it's not always roses and lollipops for Sylvie and her duke.'

She loves my American expressions.

'I won't be.'

'*Bien*. Then I'll tell you Sylvie writes about the wonderful, romantic nights they spend with each other both at the hotel and her apartment in the Trocadéro, then meeting secretly in her old place in the Faubourg Saint-Antoine.' I explain how Sylvie is fond of her old neighborhood and keeps the place as her hideaway even after she's famous.

The sister wrinkles her nose, sniffing. 'I wonder if the duke was your grandfather.'

I shake my head. 'My mother wasn't born until 1944.' I sigh heavily. 'I don't think we'll ever know...'

I won't even whisper the creepy thought in my brain, that he could have been a Nazi SS officer.

I can't go there.

I continue. 'Sylvie writes they both know nothing can come of their affair, how her duke commands the role of wealthy landowner, dutiful son to a mother he adores, protector of his society-wild, little sister, and how he took his place in Parliament as Hereditary Peer after his late father's death.'

A major clue to his identity. I bet Ridge can help me, but I'm not ready yet. I want to do this on my own.

'What else does she say?'

'She's at the height of her career,' I read, munching on chocolate while Sister Rose-Celine grabs a handful, too. '*I'm no fool*, Sylvie writes. *If I want to stay on top, I have to build security for myself. I have no one.* Except her duke, she adds, though she fears he may be lost to her if there's pressure to end their affair. *We write secret letters to each other and meet in Marly-le-Roi, eighteen kilometers outside Paris in an old hunting lodge turned* hostellerie. Sylvie fears their affair is doomed as storm clouds gather over Europe. It's 1939... and her lover is tapped for a position in the Foreign Office with the rumblings of war echoing loud and clear.'

I stop eating, chocolate halfway to my mouth. 'I can't believe it, Sister. Her duke returns to England, weeks go by before she hears from him. And then...'

'What does she say, *mademoiselle*? *Please*.'

'She says the news is devastating. Something about the duke doing his duty to God and country... and his family, and it's over between them. She doesn't explain more than that.' I look up at the nun, feeling lost. 'That's the last page in the diary, Sister. It's dated 5 September 1939 and I have no idea what happened to Sylvie and her whirlwind romance with her duke.'

How could you do this to me, Sylvie Martone?

I'm more confused than ever.

What happened next?

* * *

If a picture is indeed worth a thousand words, then the only hope I have of continuing Sylvie's story is to decipher what I can from the photos and old films neatly compiled in the box where I discovered the diary.

I hunch over the box, the muscles of my neck and shoulders tightening as I reach inside and pull out the heavy photo album. It's filled with press clippings, publicity photos, and folded-up movie posters from Sylvie's films.

I also find what appear to be well-preserved 35mm nitrate prints of her films, *Le Masque de Velours de Versailles* and *Angeline*, along with boxed small reels of home movies. According to the labels on the boxes, the rare color film was shot in Paris and on location on a movie set in Versailles during 1942 and 1943.

I'm dying to see the home movies, hoping they'll shed light on what happened to Sylvie. When I ask the Mother Superior if the nuns have an old film projector, I'm delighted when her eyes light up.

'We may, *mademoiselle*. When I first came here as a young postulant, the Mother Superior at the time was keen on preserving the history of the village during the war. From what I understand, when the movie theater in the village was bombed in 1943, the projector survived, and the theater owner showed films here on Saturday nights in the Grand Hall to keep everyone's spirits up.'

'Do you know where the projector is?' Bold on my part, but I see enthusiasm light up the Mother Superior's grey eyes.

'No, but I believe what you and Sister Rose-Celine are doing is important work.' She grins. 'I shall set a committee of sisters in motion to find it.'

'*Merci beaucoup*, Reverend Mother.'

Which leaves us the massive photo album.

After two hours of reading press releases and looking at publicity stills of Sylvie in various films, Sister Rose-Celine and I both gasp. I swear our hearts stop at the same moment.

'*Mon Dieu, mademoiselle.*' Sister Rose-Celine puts her hand to her mouth and makes a gurgling sound.

I can't believe it either.

Stuck in the back of the album is the original photo from the Paris newspaper Ridge showed me on old microfilm. The picture isn't so grainy, the photo crisp and new-looking, Sylvie smiling and holding on to the arm of a dashing Nazi SS officer and standing with him in front of a black Mercedes touring car on the streets of Paris.

Why did she put such an incriminating photo in the box for her daughter to see?

Or that matter, for anyone to see?

I don't understand it.

I'm at an impasse. The diaries chronicling Sylvie's life as a film actress end in 1939 with nothing more. Publicity photos, *yes*, old home moves, *yes*... there's got to be more. I'm determined to find out the truth about Sylvie. I can't believe this is a dead end. Maybe the best solution is to take the films back home with me and work with Ridge while the two of us go about identifying Sylvie's royal lover.

I turn the photo over and my pulse races when I see something written in French to my mother:

I saved him the day this photo was taken, mon enfant... saved the man I love... your father... and fooled the entire SS. I've never given a better performance.

Saved who? It sounds like she means my grandfather. She can't mean the SS officer in the photo with her. It doesn't make sense.

I sigh. Another part of the puzzle that's missing so many pieces.

I show the writing on the back of the photo to the nun and she makes the sign of the cross.

'I don't know what to do, Sister. I have more questions now than when I arrived here.'

'Look again in the box, *mademoiselle*,' Sister Rose-Celine implores me. 'God has His ways of coming to our aid when we need Him.'

I wipe my forehead with the back of my hand, wet with the sweat of my frustration, then dig in. Old newspapers from 1950 rumpled up into a ball. Another folded-up poster stuck under the newspapers. Then guilt washes over me for giving up so quickly when I find something shaped like a large spiral notebook neatly wrapped in tissue stuck in the bottom of the box. My heart pounds. Sister Rose-Celine was right. I close my eyes and cross my fingers.

I pray it's another diary.

18

SYLVIE

WHEN ONE DOOR CLOSES... ANOTHER ONE OPENS

Paris
1939

The day starts out with a 6 a.m. call for hair and makeup. I'm finishing up a modern drama about a woman who leaves her husband for a racecar driver. Lots of racing action, romance, great clothes. I've been so busy shooting the interior shots here on a soundstage in Paris, I haven't seen Jock for two weeks. Resting between takes, I sway back and forth with a smile on my face when I remember the riotous last evening we had together. Dining on *Langouste en Bellevue* and *petits eclairs* filled with chocolate cream at our favorite restaurant near the royal park in Marly-le-Roi at the *hostellerie*. We enjoyed slow, leisurely bites of the rich meal, taking turns feeding each other with forks said to have graced the table of Marie Antoinette. Juices dripping on chins, busy tongues tasting, licking. A lovely anticipation heating bare skin yearning to be touched. A more sensual meal I've never had... nor a more passionate night with my royal lover in the charming *hostellerie* outside Paris with its original seventeenth-century décor. A place where we can escape...

Jock carried me up to our room along the narrow winding staircase where we collapsed on the canopied four poster, laughing. Our need for each other flooded the room with life, love, and hope. My world spun when I arched up to meet him and he leant down and whispered, '*Je t'aime, Sylvie Martone.*' When I woke up in semi-darkness to see *la madame* moon bidding goodnight to her cast of sparkling stars, I remember thinking, *I could live with this man forever.*

We bid *au revoir* in the morning with promises of ending this idyllic summer in each other's arms.

Then I heard nothing. As if Jock had vanished.

I can't deny, I'm worried.

Meanwhile, Winnie writes to me often, telling me about her beaux and I sense she's trying to keep me cheerful. She came to Paris for a few days to visit me on the set and I introduced her as Lady Revell, a charming fellow traveler and fan I met in Monte Carlo. We were careful not to give any indication she's more than a casual acquaintance.

She's also my go-between when I can't make direct contact with Jock.

Winnie whispered to me that Jock was tied up night and day with politics. He couldn't turn his back on his duty when he received a personal plea from the PM's office to give his take on the current state of affairs in Europe. A small, embarrassed smile crept onto her face. A sign of truth about what they were doing in Monte Carlo. Seems he and Winnie did a lot of traveling on her birthday grand tour. A 'look-see' on Jock's part to do casual spying in the major European capitals. Also, Jock received news about Winnie's friend from boarding school that was quite disturbing. She won't tell me what it is, only that it affects my relationship with Jock.

I was so naïve, I didn't see anything but him, making me wonder if I wasn't merely a diversion for him. I toss that aside. No, he wouldn't have taken the enormous risks to be with me if that were true.

Before she left for London, Winnie slipped me a note.

Jock will call you on Friday and explain everything.

* * *

Today is Friday, September 1st. Late afternoon. I'm alone in my dressing room when my phone rings.

'*Allô?*' I gush into the fancy black receiver, my throat tight with nerves.

'Sylvie—'

'Oh, Jock, I've missed you so... when can I see you?'

I hear him breathe heavily into the phone. 'I only have a few minutes, *mon bel ange*... I'm calling from Scotland.'

'Scotland?' I mutter, unable to keep the surprise out of my voice. I was hoping we could rendezvous in our usual place by the royal park. That dream is dashed.

'Yes, I can't tell you where. I'm meeting with several important political figures from the PM's cabinet.' A pause. 'Sylvie—'

'Is the lake monster as big as they say?' I interrupt him with a tease in my voice.

'I'm tangled up here in meetings. I have no time for rendezvous at fancy hotels to indulge your whims. I have to cancel our engagement in Paris.'

His cold words course through me, as if he's rehearsed what he's saying. I notice a distance in his voice, as if he's reading the words. When he didn't laugh at my joke, I knew I was in trouble. Jock and I have an intense, sexual relationship. We also love to play silly games, tease each other with not-so-subtle innuendos... write letters in code. I wish we didn't have to be so secretive. No doubt the pundits would argue an English duke linked with a French actress with a questionable past is political suicide if he wishes to advance his career in Parliament. Yet I can't tell you how happy I am when we're together. But in my heart, I know it's over between us. I can't move, can't think.

I'm no fool. I imagine the stuffy political sods advising him made it clear that if he continues our affair it leaves him open for accusations in the scandal sheets, how he's neglecting his national duties during a momentous time of upheaval in Europe to gallivant around Paris with a flighty actress.

What if Jock is trying to protect me? My career has had its ups and downs, but never a major scandal with a royal. It could go either way. Either I gain sympathy from my fans for being 'dumped', or they turn against me for hiding the affair and tarnishing my image.

What burns me is when Jock tells me his superiors discovered our affair from an unlikely source.

Winnie's friend from boarding school.

Her name is Princess Claudina and she claims her title from a minor Italian principality before she took up residence in Monte Carlo a year ago. She's alleging Jock promised to marry her so she could stay in England. Ridiculous. She just turned nineteen. She's a mere child. Jock is twenty-six, seven years older than this girl, and she *is* a girl. Not a woman. Round face. Dark eyes that followed me everywhere when we had tea that afternoon in Monte Carlo. I thought then she still had her teddy bear sitting on her pink chenille duvet.

I know differently now. She was planning to unmask me all along.

When Jock wouldn't agree to the engagement, she went to an old connection of her father's and spilled the whole story about how she met me and saw Jock and I together several times in Monte Carlo. It didn't help when the two English snoops validated her story.

'I'll tell the concierge at the *hostellerie* we have other plans, Jock,' I acquiesce, keeping my voice even, plaintive. I love him too much to make it any more difficult for him.

'*Godammit, Sylvie*, you don't think I *wanted* to say those horrible things?'

'Jock... I don't understand...'

'I wish I could take back everything I said, that I'll be there to hold you in my arms. I can't. I made that ridiculous speech about having no time to see you to give you reason to break it off with me. The truth is I love you. I'd defy the whole damn system and marry you tomorrow if I didn't believe we're in for a long, terrible war with Germany.'

'I'd never ask you to turn your back on your country, Jock, my darling. Like I'd fight for France.'

'How did I ever deserve a woman like you?' His voice is warm, wanting.

'Because you're the most wonderful man and I will never love another.' Desire for this man threads through me.

'I can't stop seeing you, Sylvie. I love you too much.' I hear him inhale sharply. 'I'll figure something out.'

'Surely this Hitler business will be over soon. Till then, never forget me, my darling,' I whisper, a tear spilling down my cheek. My voice catches when I finish, 'And I'll love you always.'

* * *

There. It's done. Jock and I must go back to the way things were before we met. He alluded to a suspicion Princess Claudina is a German spy... which makes it even more important he doesn't compromise his position with the Foreign Office. Our love affair makes him vulnerable to scandalous talk that could expose his clandestine comings and goings. What if the British press follows him to Paris to see me? And I can't go to London – that would make matters worse.

Which kills Emil's deal with the British film studio to dub my films. The project is put on hold.

I didn't think I'd get hit in the gut like this on the same day Hitler invades Poland. I head back over to the soundstage to shoot the next scene. The intense heat from the hot lights sits on my face, melting my makeup as I attempt to say my lines, everyone on set waiting... waiting... while I try to process what Jock told me minutes before Emil ordered me back on set.

I get so rattled I flub my lines. Over and over... I can't concentrate, I can't find my mark. Emil halts shooting for the day.

I call for a studio car to take me back to my posh apartment in the Trocadéro, order the driver to stop at a my old haunt behind a chocolate shop, a centuries-old wine and spirits cave where I toss down enough francs for several bottles of their best brandy, then go home. I put my feet up on my black suede ottoman, grab the brandy, and lament over how I can't escape this damn Nazi Party screwing up my life.

I gulp down the alcohol straight from the bottle.

I never meant to go off on a drunken binge in the middle of shooting a picture. But my world is shattered. My brain has been knocked out of my head, my heart is bleeding, and I can think of only one thing. What goes through an alcoholic's mind when they're triggered.

Just one... I can stop... just one.

Then one turns into... well, this time I can't fight it. I relapse. My impulse explodes when the early September weather in Paris gets so stinking hot. I grab another bottle and guzzle it down.

Jock can never find out I slipped. There's nothing more heartbreaking for an alcoholic than to let down the one person who means the most to you.

My body shivers with an uncanny premonition when I catch part of a special radio news broadcast about Hitler's army devastating the Polish countryside with bombs, destroying the railroad lines, then tanks and soldiers ransacking the soul of the country with their guns and swastikas. I can't imagine such a thing happening in France... and never Paris. No, the French people who brought down a monarchy won't stand for that little man and his funny-looking moustache muddying up our beautiful Champs-Élysées with his dirty, hobnail boots.

Besides, Poland is more than fifteen hundred kilometers from Paris... God will save us from this monster. He can't keep closing His eyes to this horror, can He?

I ignore the headache already pounding my brain and remember what I told Jock in Monte Carlo. The shop girl always loses the lord of the manor at the end of the fourth reel. I told him it wouldn't work between us, but like every girl who comes to see my pictures, I wanted to believe it would. He did, too, but with the craziness in the world and his place in politics, our love story has come to an end.

I've fought long and hard to have control over my life, to battle against the bad guy on screen and off. But this time, I'm up against a madman in Berlin who's determined to rule the world.

I can't let a scandal involving me ruin Jock's work with the Foreign Office. The world of espionage is a delicate balance between truth and fantasy, something I know about, seeing how I played a spy in *Retour à Venise*. His public persona must remain above suspicion. I can't take him away from the important business of stopping Hitler because he's worrying about me getting hurt by scandalous talk.

So we've ended the affair. It's better this way.

That doesn't change anything. I love him. I always will.

* * *

'I refuse to do this script, Emil.'

I throw the pinned-together notebook across the room. This part *isn't* me. I've made a few bombs in my time, but my pictures are stories about strong women in unconventional roles overcoming hardship and fighting for their man, their home, their children. This is a silly comedy with bad dialogue and too much slapstick. My fans don't want slapstick and Emil knows that. He's trying to take advantage of me at a weak moment with a lousy script acquired from a questionable source. An investor who wants to make money, not art.

Emil is no slouch. He ducks the script I throw at him *and* my outburst. 'You have no choice, Sylvie, you're under contract to do another picture.'

'Then find me a new script the fans will love. Not another divorcee melodrama with a swooning lover draped all over me and a cigarette holder hanging out of the side of my mouth. The world has changed with Herr Hitler writing his own scripts. We're at war, Emil.'

I calm down, think this out. I have every intention of fulfilling my contract for another picture, but it's got to be a good story.

I stand up and look out the wide window of the bedroom of my Trocadéro apartment. It's rained steadily all day, big drops that splatter against the glass. Down below, a sheen of mist glistens on the wet pavement. The hot days of August then September have vanished, but some things never change. The Eiffel Tower stands strong even in the thrashing rain. What *has* changed is, Britain is at war with Germany.

And God help me, so is France.

There's nothing like a war to put things in perspective. I've been sober for thirty days and I intend to stay that way. I'm so ashamed of how I acted, relapsing because I had to let Jock go. His work is vital to the British government. I'd never stand in the way of that. I'm lucky the studio didn't fire me, but they need the picture finished and distributed to the movie theaters as soon as possible. No one knows what's going to happen with everyone scrambling to meet the government's demands to fight the Nazis, increasing the French Army to massive proportions, and scaring everyone in Paris with training on what to do during an air raid and turning Métro stations into bomb shelters. What's next... rationing? Then what goes? Going to the pictures?

Is the Nazi threat going to jeopardize that, too?

We finish the picture on time after I go on a regimen of strong coffee, strawberries, and fish to detoxify my body. I refuse to take those pills the studio doctor pushes on me. Three days of an alcohol binge and I'm done. They say relapse is normal. The strange thing is, I'm stronger. Even if my heart still aches. Winnie gives me updates on Jock which amount to 'he's safe'. It's enough.

For now.

I owe it to my fans to stay sober. They never let me down. They helped me through this before and they'll do it again. Which makes me more determined to give them the best film I can to take their minds off the fear we live with every day since the invasion of Poland as the Nazis gobble up Europe. A fantasy to capture their imagination. Wrap them up in a tragic, rolling romance and let them fall in love all over again with Sylvia Martone.

It's when I run into my old friend Pierre Limone I get an idea. We talk about the good old days and his amazing makeup techniques, and how much fun we had making the *Ninette* pictures and the interesting characters we played in *Retour à Venise*. How the enduring fantasy of good versus evil always works.

Wouldn't it be fun to update it?

Make the male lead a Prussian war hero, a physician who lost his power to heal during the Great War... a beautiful aristocratic heroine whose life he must save or he'll lose her. A gangland villain who wants the heroine for himself and to destroy the soldier-hero.

And I know the screenwriter for the job.

Raoul Monteux.

* * *

'Did you see this piece of *merde* Emil brought to me, Raoul? A box office bomb.'

I give my cooling espresso a sip as I wait for him to scroll through the script, his expert screenwriter's eye catching the lack of a good story.

I begged him to meet me this morning at Café de la Paix. The sun is shining today even if the war news isn't good. We're in what they're calling *'drôle de guerre'* (Phony War). What amazes me is how Parisians carry on as if nothing is happening. Scurrying about the boulevards like rabbits sniffing for a new carrot in the shops, the patisseries, the cafés. Happy bunnies while Hitler is digging up the entire cabbage patch of Europe.

I can't think about that now. I wait patiently for Raoul's opinion. The tall, lanky man cocks his black beret to the back of his skull and stretches out his long frame under the tiny table and shakes his head. Raoul is in his mid-thirties though he appears much younger. He trained as a playwright but he got into pictures when one of his plays caught my eye. I feel a flush of pride at having discovered him. I love his witty banter, strong emotional connection between the characters, plot twists. I brought the play to Emil's attention and he hired him on the spot.

I study him now, thinking he looks different. More serious. Like he's worked up about something, but he won't talk about it.

His dark brown hair is cut unevenly, like he did the job himself. His dark eyes hooded by heavy lids from lack of sleep. His angular face bears a long scar running along the side of his nose, from a fight I heard he got into in the Marais district when he saved his wife's father from hooligans beating up the old man because the family is Jewish. His wife died a few months ago and Raoul took it hard. Nearby, his fourteen-year-old daughter Halette is nose-deep in a book of poems, pretending not to listen to our conversation but she keeps peeking at me, curious.

I smile at her, and nod. Embarrassed, she hunches her shoulders and tries to hide behind her book.

'You're right, Sylvie,' Raoul says, slapping the notebook down on the round table. 'The story has no heart, only jokes.'

'You've *got* to write a script for me, Raoul.'

'I just finished a spec script about the Sun King and Versailles... intrigue, action, romance—'

'I have no doubt it's fabulous, but I've got an idea for a story that's perfect for these times... and my fans. Wait till you hear it.'

'*Pardon, mademoiselle*, may I listen, too?' Halette asks, moving her chair closer.

I hesitate. 'It's a scary story, Halette.' I look to her father for his approval.

'Go ahead, Sylvie. I don't keep anything from Halette. She's going to have a hard enough time as it is growing up in this world with Hitler and his gang.'

I nod, understanding. He rarely lets Halette out of his sight since Estelle succumbed to a rare blood disorder.

I look at Raoul and Halette, and then begin. 'I see the story as a mystery thriller about the gang underworld... and a Prussian war hero who was once a physician and saves a beautiful girl, a postulant, from death after she's attacked by slave traffickers... very bad people.' I look over at Halette. She's not the least bit shocked.

'Like the Nazis?' she asks.

'Yes, that's a wonderful idea, Halette. What do you think, Raoul? Why not set the story in Berlin in the early 1930s during the decadent Weimar era and make the fictitious gang bear a strong resemblance to the brownshirts I read about in Germany?'

'*Très bon*, Sylvie. I like it.'

My hands fly through the air, moving this way and that, my wild gestures expressing my excitement. 'In the script, the soldier-physician and the postulant bring down a murderous gang while trying to find her kidnapped sister sold into slavery... and fall in love, the hero doing his best to save her as he works to find a cure for her illness, knowing if he doesn't, their love is doomed.'

'Are we doomed, Papa?' Halette begs to know.

She looks to her father for guidance. I have the feeling this subject has come up often between father and daughter. I know Raoul considers himself and his family French first, Jewish second. Like most Jewish intellectuals, they came to Paris to find the freedom and tolerance stripped from them in other parts of Europe. But the fierce crossing of his brows tells me he's worried. He also has a sister with a lazy husband and five children who run a doll and candle shop on Rue des Rosiers in the crammed Marais district. An area filled with tenement buildings housing Eastern immigrants trying to make their daily bread.

A pang of guilt hits me. I know Raoul needs money, but he won't take charity from me. He confided to me he made poor investments with the funds he received from his last script to help pay for Estelle's devastating and costly illness and he's nearly bankrupt. And he has Halette to care for. She's smart and more than once I let her stay in my dressing room when her father takes meetings at the studio, reading or cutting out pictures of film stars out of *Ciné-Miroir* and pasting them in a scrapbook. She confided to me I'm her favorite.

I've no doubt Raoul is worried about his daughter's future... and is wary of the climate in Europe with Hitler on the move. He confides in me he needs the money to take Halette to America.

'What can I do to convince you to write the script, Raoul?'

'You know I can't refuse you, Sylvie. I owe my career to you and I'll never forget how you visited Estelle in the hospital and made sure she had flowers till the end. I admit, I was ashamed when you paid for her final expenses... I'll pay you back, I promise.'

'You can pay me back by writing a wonderful script. I'm only as good on the screen as the words you write.'

Raoul grabs me and kisses both my cheeks. 'When does production start?'

* * *

The next few weeks move quickly with Raoul coming up with a complete script quicker than I thought possible. Next, I'm thrilled when a celebrated actor is cast opposite me.

Angeline is on a grueling production schedule in 1940 to get into theaters as the dark clouds of war get closer to Paris. I insist Raoul come to the set, changing lines at my request and driving Emil crazy. During the entire production, everyone is on edge as Hitler continues his insane plan for conquest, invading the Netherlands and Belgium, and England introduces rationing and evacuations of children to rural areas.

I think of Jock... wonder where he is, what he's doing, if he thinks of me. I accept our relationship has to remain on hold during this war, that afterward we face an uphill battle. I'm willing to wait. For now, all that matters is defeating Hitler. Making pictures may not be a frontline battle, but it's what I can do to give the French people courage and hope.

And the will to fight for freedom should the enemy get too close.

I pray that never happens.

19

JULIANA

A GIRL NAMED ANGELINE

Ville Canfort-Terre, France
Present Day

I open my eyes and all my frustrations and hopes and fears come out in one big *whoosh.*

It's not another diary I find, but the complete script for Sylvie's film, *Angeline.* I don't see how this will help me, but I can't resist reading the production notes to Sister Rose-Celine, copious notes detailing the characters and key plot points. It's not only a poignant love story, but a social commentary on the world at the time.

'Berlin, 1931.

'Count Peter von Stryker, war hero and physician.

'Wild, reckless, he's lived with the loss of his ability to heal since the end of the Great War. When a young woman dressed as a postulant and with a saintly aura enters his realm, his world is brighter, not so black.

'Peter can't deny he's drawn to this innocent in ways he never imagined. She isn't like the other dancers he meets in Berlin. Angeline is a French runaway from a convent here to find her kidnapped sister. She makes him want to strip away the pious sanctity of her religious cloth to reveal to him

the sensual woman underneath, a woman seething with a ravenous need to let go of the guilt that forces her to choose a life of abstinence.

'*He's determined to have her. Will she sell her soul to him to find fulfilment as a woman? Or will she hide behind her religious veil and never experience the passion, the depth of a great love?*'

'I remember this film, *mademoiselle*,' Sister Rose-Celine says, sighing heavily, 'and the handsome Prussian officer every girl fell in love with.'

'You're not alone. I'm falling for this guy already and I haven't read the whole script.' *Because he reminds you of Ridge?* 'I've got to find out more about the heroine.'

I keep reading, stumbling a few times over phrases, but the sister joyfully comes to my rescue with the proper translations.

'*Angeline can never fall in love. Like Peter, she lives with a deep loneliness even her strong belief in God cannot cure.*

'*She'll do anything to find her sister – even if it means aligning with the mysterious count who promises to help her. She should run and never look back. She can't. She ignores the prickling of her skin as she stares up at the mysterious, looming structure silhouetted against the gloomy sky overhead. Obscured from the lack of sunlight, she can't read the faded name plate on the dilapidated building as if the street has no name. Angeline will never forget that first night when she enters the domain of Count Peter von Stryker and he awakens in her a heated desire she can't ignore.*'

I keep flipping the pages and come upon the villain… and oh, is it juicy.

'*A different pain grips Peter when he encounters Lord Helmut von der Mein, a fellow ex-Army officer. A Blood Lord who taints the honor of the secret society when he flaunts his aristocratic heritage but acts like the devils he's cavorts with. Drinking and carousing with party members of the national socialists.*

'*They are the new evil emerging, professional soldiers loyal to no one but their commanders. Peter witnesses the rise of men believing Germany can rule herself without the influence of the Kaiser. They must be stopped.*'

'The Nazi Party… what a daring idea, Sister.'

'Sylvie must have based the heroine Angeline on her own life in the convent.'

'This is my favorite part: *It's a strange path the elusive soldier and the young postulant must follow as they become entwined in each other's lives.*

'Peter resides in a world of midnight black, while Angeline lives for the promise of the white veil when she becomes a holy sister – a novice.

'But it's the color red – blood-red —that enflames their passion for each other.'

According to the Internet, it was one of her biggest hits, grossing more than her previous two films. Why did she put it into the box with the diaries and the photos and films?

Is Sylvie trying to say something about her activities during the war?

She marked certain scenes in the script, comparing them in her notes to the mood in Europe with the National Socialist German Workers' Party in Germany.

Notes I believe she made *after* the war.

Why didn't I encourage Raoul to leave Paris before it was too late? she writes in the margins.

Why didn't I protect Halette from her great loss?

Why didn't I use my talents sooner to save others?

I'm unfamiliar with the screenwriter, Raoul Monteux, and a quick Internet search turns up little information – as if he disappeared off the face of the earth after the Berlin film. I have no idea who 'Halette' is. What loss is Sylvie referring to? Hopefully, she left additional clues, clues that will show the world Sylvie wasn't a willing Nazi collaborator.

I check in with Ridge via Skype. He's excited about what I've found, including the script for *Angeline*.

'And you also found a print of the film?' he wants to know. I've caught him working late in the studio. His dark, silky hair is mussed like he hasn't slept for two days with a stubble beard that draws my attention to his manly appeal. He's up to his eyebrows in metal vintage octagonal film canisters.

'Are you eating tacos from Olvera Street without me?' I question, miffed. For years we've been doing Taco Tuesdays at this hole in the wall with the best Mexican food. My mouth is watering for a bit of home. Or is it Ridge I'm missing? 'Just you wait till I get back to LA. You *owe* me—'

He cuts me off with a ripple of laughter and then a wink right into the camera with that sexy smile that makes me hungry. And not for tacos. I wish he'd stop flirting with me and making my cheeks hot and my toes curl. I feel embarrassed, considering I'm having sexy thoughts about him. He's gone super casual in a black tank top ripped across his chest so tight I swear I can see his muscles straining underneath.

I find this side of Ridge intriguing and it worries me when he comes back at me with, 'I'll wait for you as long as it takes, Juliana.'

What is *that* supposed to mean? That he's waiting to see me so we can talk about my adventure? Or he's into me in a romantic way? I'd never get over it if I was wrong. So I go back to my safe place where I don't react, and let his sexy retort fly right over my head. I don't know what came over me. I *never* flirt with him like this. I can blame it on my romantic longing heating up after reading about Sylvie and Jock's amazing love affair. Like I said, why ruin a beautiful relationship? He's the best guy ever and so supportive in this crazy time in my life. I don't want to lose that.

'Yes. And Sylvie's Versailles film, too,' I tell him, keeping a straight face. 'I can't wait to see them.'

We chat about the photos and home movies I found, then the hot weather in LA while Ridge munches on his taco but never takes his eyes off me. I'm reminded of Sylvie and Jock and their sexy lobster meal with more than a twinge of embarrassment tinting my cheeks. Thank God, he has no idea what's going through my head.

Then with a shaky smile, I click off with a promise to call him with any news.

Before I make a complete idiot of myself.

* * *

Late into the night, I sit in what I refer to as 'Maman's study', surrounded by artifacts and paintings from centuries gone by, reading the *Angeline* script, fascinated by the story.

Then I find a torn diary page in French stuck between pages that sets my heart racing:

I find great joy writing down my life for my dear Madeleine so she won't forget me. But I'm such a slow writer... Sister Vincent says, am I not a great actress? (Her words, not mine.) Why don't I record my thoughts instead?

What a wonderful idea!

Sister Vincent secured a recorder for me and blank tapes from Paris with funds I gave her, telling the proprietor the nuns' choir wants to record their songs in the library. We have no choir, but he didn't know that.

And so I shall begin recording what happened to me during the war... how I fought the Nazis...

I can't believe my luck; my hands are shaking. I'm overcome with excitement.

My God, to hear my grandmother's voice telling her story, it's too fabulous. Heart pounding in my ears, I sift through the films in the box, hoping in my excitement I mistook a film for a reel-to-reel tape... *nothing.*

I clutch the script tight to my chest, willing it to whisper its secrets to me.

I hear nothing but the night wind outside the window doing a final dance before the dawn settles it down.

Tears well up in my eyes. I'm disheartened.

Where are the recordings?

20

SYLVIE

THE QUIET BEFORE THE NAZI STORM

Paris
Spring 1940

I park my red Bugatti roadster outside the carriage gate in the Faubourg Saint-Antoine and even before I get out of the motorcar, I'm mobbed by fans.

'*Salut*, Sylvie!'

'We love you, Sylvie!'

I gush with excitement at seeing so many people from the old neighborhood cheering for me, tossing daisies and violets into the air, showering me with flowers and affection.

'*Bonjour, mes amis*, I'm so happy to see everyone.'

I close my eyes and imagine myself as that sixteen-year-old again on the first day I came here with Emil, so scared and frightened, but excited to be in pictures. I had fire in my belly then that's since ebbed and flowed, but has never gone out, even in my darkest days. I conjure up in my mind Jock at my side, so strong and handsome, his dark eyes intense, holding onto my arm and sharing this moment with me. I think of him as I give out publicity photos. A new photo, so glamorous, my fans love it. I'm wearing the white slinky gown and the heart-shaped diamond pin I wore in Monte Carlo when I met Jock. I'm wearing the pin today on my houndstooth suit... no one knows it's a fake. It's as real to me as my love for Jock.

When this war is over, mon chéri... we shall meet again.

I pray that's true. Winnie writes to me he's involved in what she calls the 'spy squad'. I think it's more a romantic musing on her part than reality. Most likely, he's sitting behind a desk at the Foreign Office signing paperwork and trying to deal with England's 'Phony War' while fielding intelligence about Hitler's plan to invade Scandinavia.

I remember the last time we met here in the Faubourg... so long ago. Before France was at war with Germany. I've heard whispered reports the government believes Hitler himself will be in Paris by summer.

But not today.

Today is my triumphal return since Jock and I came here after Monte Carlo to the place I'll always treasure. I'll never give it up. I bought the seventeenth-century first floor apartment where I started out when I first came to Paris at sixteen. Overlooking a quiet street, the place is my solace, my home for all things heartfelt in these times. Emil thinks I should give up my fantasy of being a 'star of the people' like a modern Joan of Arc, that I must understand filmmaking is a business.

I'm doomed by sentiment to spend my life striving for that.

I paid cash for the two-bedroom residence with the high ceilings and iron-paned wide windows. Why not? I've earned it. *Angeline* secures my spot as a premiere star of French cinema, according to *Ciné-Miroir*. The tragic love story of Peter and Angeline sends swooning audiences into tears. Everywhere I go, I'm mobbed by fans.

No more than here in the Faubourg.

I ask the laundress's daughter to help me distribute the flowers and sweets I've brought for everyone. No one goes home empty-handed. I adore my fans in the working-class neighborhood. I have warm memories of wandering in and out of the passageways and courtyards, talking to the inhabitants – woodcarvers, furniture makers, and textile weavers – getting ideas for my *Ninette* stories. How many times have I acted them out for Emil and the writers on my films?

Especially Raoul.

I'm worried about him and Halette as I hand out pink and yellow coconut bonbons to giggling little girls with ribbons wound in their hair. I called him at his sister's shop in the Marais district and invited them for coffee and raspberry tarts yesterday at *Aux Deux Magots*, but he couldn't make it. His voice caught on the words. I didn't question him, like he was afraid someone was listening on the phone.

I'll stop by the shop tomorrow.

For now, I owe it to my fans to sign autographs.

I take a wide panoramic look at their bright, eager faces and I can't help but feel lighthearted. Here I can put away the fears and insecurities that still hit me every time I face a camera, that I'm not good enough. My illegitimate background has soiled my soul with a red stain I can never erase. My whole career is built on a lie. Here it's not true. They love me as Ninette or Angeline or whatever part I play that moves them to cry or laugh or love. This is my haven away from the camera where the world of make-believe becomes real because *they* believe in me.

Where I can break bread with Lili, a laundress, over hot coffee.

Trade gossip with feisty Madame Frenier who dances with *La Goulue* from the Moulin Rouge at the yearly post Lenten fair.

I bend over and tickle the pink cheeks of *petit* Jacquot, while his mother, Emmeline, and her mother, both widows, carry on the family's textile trade.

These women give me so much. It's true what they say, an actress's most important tool is her keenness to observe, to find the soul of her character, and what souls these *femmes de Paris* have shown me.

I pray they never change.

* * *

'I need your help, Sylvie, to secure passage to America for Halette.'

I clutch onto the Dutch doll I've been admiring and shoot a blank stare at Raoul, not certain I heard him correctly. We exchanged small talk when I arrived at his sister's shop on Rue des Rosiers in the Jewish quarter, then I waited while Raoul sent Halette to bring me a coffee. I always enjoy browsing the charming array of dolls dressed in everything from eccentric Victorian costumes to flappers along with the scented candles that take me back to another time.

I never expected my dear friend to ask me for a favor that will break his heart.

'Why would you want to send your only child so far away?'

'I'm desperate, Sylvie.'

'Desperate? Why, Raoul?'

'I've been worried about her safety ever since Hitler invaded Poland, dreading the day when the unthinkable might happen.' He wrings his hands and the long scar on his cheek reddens. 'What will happen if the Germans take Paris?' he continues. 'So many Jewish writers, actors, and directors left Vienna when Hitler annexed Austria to the Reich... will I be forced to do the same? Or God help us, will it be worse?'

'Hitler's a madman, but he's not a fool. One hundred and fifty thousand Jews live in Paris and our industry is filled with talented, dedicated Jewish *artistes* who contribute greatly to the success of French cinema, including you and your outstanding writing talent. I don't know what I'd do without Yvette who does my hair and makeup, or Marcel who does such a fabulous job lighting me for the camera. Two French-Jewish citizens I depend on. That France depends on. You can't destroy an entire people because der Fuehrer has an itch up his backside.'

'I hope you're right, Sylvie, but after losing Estelle, I can't lose Halette.' His eyes grow fierce, making me wish I could be certain what I said was true.

I'm not.

I fumble with the long, golden braids on the Dutch doll, thinking. His fears aren't unfounded. I can't ignore the gossip going around the studio, from the grips to the makeup girls to the suits in the executive offices. Everyone's on edge. Anyone Jewish or married to a Jew has a right to be frightened. I've heard speculation the Nazis could prohibit Jewish 'participation' in filmmaking as they seek to 'Aryanize' the arts like they've done in Germany.

'Can you check on passage for Halette on a ship leaving for New York, Sylvie? I fear playing my hand in the open... you never know who's on the Nazi payroll. Fifth Columnists are here doing their dirty work.'

'Why don't you go with her?' I have to ask, not understanding. 'Halette is very responsible, more so than most girls her age, but it's dangerous for her to travel alone.'

'It's *more* dangerous for her to stay here in Paris.' He leads me over to a corner in the shop where the smell of lavender and rose from the candles is overpowering. 'I can't leave Paris.'

'Why not?'

'My younger sister Hela needs help to run the shop and to buy milk and vegetables and chicken to feed the children.' For a tall, proud man, I see what's running through his mind is difficult for him to accept. 'My lazy brother-in-law gambles away the store's profits.'

I put down the doll and grab onto his shirtsleeve, staring up into his eyes. He's desperate to keep his child safe. I love this brilliant man as a brother and I'm grateful he doesn't push me away when I grab onto him tight. I want to embrace this dear soul into my heart and help him every way I can. I tell him what we both want to hear to assuage his guilt, quiet his mind from worry, and soothe the pain in his heart aching from losing his beloved wife.

'France is strong, Raoul, *we* are strong... the Germans will never make it past the Maginot Line. And Paris? Unthinkable.'

* * *

I'm wrong... the Nazis invade France through Belgium.

And I regret every word I said, that I could be so foolish not to believe it could happen.

I groan in anguish, clutching my heart when the Germans march into Paris on 14 June 1940 because I know then nothing will ever be the same.

It's the beginning of an extraordinary shift in my film career I never see coming.

21

JULIANA

BE CAREFUL WHAT YOU WISH FOR

Ville Canfort-Terre, France
Present Day

I can't find Sylvie's reel-to-reel recordings *anywhere*.

I'm at a crossroads. I don't have much time left to clear her. I have to go back to LA to meet with the producer on the new show or I won't have a job.

I've doubled checked where we found the box in the dungeon. *Nada*. I've talked to the Mother Superior who's willing to do her best to help me. She has her staff check the numerous storage closets for anything looking like it's at least half a century old, but the young postulants and the nuns find nothing. When the convent chateau was modernized in the nineties, anything deemed of no value was tossed.

Which means the recordings could have been destroyed.

I'm heartbroken. The photo we found showing Sylvie arm in arm with the SS officer as well as the newsreels Ridge showed me all point to her voluntary collaboration with the Nazis. I have no idea what's on the home movies... I'll find out when we set up the projector. Yes, the Mother Superior's posse found the old movie theater projector and are checking it out for me.

I decide to give the dungeon another look, then it hits me. Sister Rose-Celine mentioned there was also a suitcase. Maybe it *wasn't* a suitcase, but a carrying case for a 1950s tape recorder?

Then where are the tapes?

Didn't Sylvie mention the choir 'recording songs in the library'?

A clue, perhaps?

I go on a mad search through the library with Sister Rose-Celine's help – opening up cupboards, going through bookcases, looking for a storage compartment when, hidden behind a wall, we find a cache of nineteenth-century books, a grey, dusty carrying case – the tape recorder – *and* a large, brown satchel with two thick straps and big buckles.

I hold my breath. I open it up and—

Oh, my, it's filled with reel-to-reel tapes marked: *'Sylvie Martone – The War Years, 1940–1944.'*

Then in smaller letters: *'Narrated by the actress in summer 1950.'*

My chest tightens with excitement, a million different scenarios playing out in my mind as I anticipate what I'll find.

Redemption for Sylvie? Or the final proof of her guilt?

Praying the old recorder works, I load the first tape, turn it on, and listen.

I can't tell you the thrill that goes through me when Sylvie's voice comes through loud and clear in exquisite French. I have to rewind the tape several times to catch a phrase, but with Sister Rose-Celine's help, I'm transported back to the chaos that ensued when the Germans invaded France and headed toward Paris... how at Emil's coaxing, Sylvie fled the city to the Côte d'Azur in the South of France with the idea of making films for the Vichy. She hints this was a painful time in her life, seeing how French men and women were falling all over themselves, trying to believe 'everything was normal' when it wasn't.

Finally, she had enough.

Sylvie returned to Paris and speaks about how she felt when she first saw the Germans marching along the Champs-Élysées...

* * *

Life during the German Occupation when I returned from the Free Zone in the South was nothing like what I expected.

The glorious yellow sun warmed the pavements with a soothing heat while the Napoleonic blue skies overhead assured us life would go on. No matter if the boulevards trembled with the sound of black hobnail boots, we were aware of the quiet hush over the city. We adjusted, we had to. Curfews. Rationing, no gasoline. Parisians rode bicycles everywhere.

I stood in long queues for bread, cringing at seeing swastika flags flying over the luxury hotels. When I went out, I pretended I was auditioning for a part in a film, going about my business in disguise. Laundress, teacher, old woman. Looking for food became the primary mission for each day. We feared catching the eye of a Nazi and giving him reason to demand our papers.

You may ask, 'But you're Sylvie Martone, star of French cinema, why did you stand in line for bread?' Because, ma petite, *I was afraid. When I arrived in Paris with Emil complaining all the way along the crowded road about the Vichy and their obstinance to allow him complete freedom to make the pictures he wanted, my Trocadéro apartment was filled with Nazi doryphores ('beetles' we called them because of those unfashionable helmets) looking for alcohol. The German Army wasn't particular about which 'abandoned' apartments they pillaged and spared no one. Including me. The joke was on them since I'd been sober for a while. They didn't believe me and searched my apartment like impertinent rats looking for cheese. How I hated those miserable creatures and their primal instinct to enslave, making me fear France will never be free again. That was the moment I grabbed what I could and stormed out of my apartment after they left. I wasn't the only tenant 'inconvenienced' by the search. Some tenants left, others stayed, resigned to the Nazis' unannounced visits under the New Order. (I hid my jewels in the trunk of my car.) I needed to get my affairs in order so I could draw out funds. Were my assets seized? No one at my financial institution could tell me what was in my accounts – they were too scared they'd be reported since I was listed as 'missing' when the local* Kommandant checked the whereabouts of major depositors. So I went back to the Faubourg Saint-Antoine. There I found peace away from the maddening crowd of German soldiers laughing and cavorting like naughty schoolboys on a holiday.

To be safe, I told no one but Emil about my return to my old place in the Faubourg Saint-Antoine and took to wearing disguises to keep a low profile. My old neighbors were lovely and I adored them, but they gossiped. I didn't trust the German High Command who had a habit of seeking out famous personages to do their bidding. The Nazis had their spies in Paris long before they marched into the city, checking out buildings, residences, brothels. No doubt they checked out anyone popular in the arts and the cinema.

I couldn't hide forever, I needed to work, but I wouldn't make it easy for them to find me.

As I went about trying to survive, I found I liked the old lady disguise the best. She gave me the freedom I needed to move about Paris undetected, poke my nose in places where I could sting the Nazi beast with small indiscretions to irritate them (when I saw German soldiers looking at a map of Paris, I gave them wrong directions), but she was in the early stages of character development then. I didn't know how important she'd become to me later on... I'm getting ahead of myself. Alors, mon enfant, life took on a new normal in late 1940. By 1941, we were back to making pictures... surprised, non? Me, too. I was thrilled when Emil insisted it was time my presence in Paris became known to the head of Galerie Films, a new German-funded film studio. I believed I could make a difference for my fans, for the people of France. I didn't know then what I was getting into, which is why I'm recording these tapes for you. So you know the truth.

I shall go and check on you now, my angel, watch your sweet face as you sleep, the way your nose crinkles when you smile when I tickle your tummy. You're still mon petit enfant even if you're almost six years old now. Then tomorrow we shall play with the Dutch doll I gave you... do you remember the doll with the long, blonde braids? She was a gift from my dearest friend, Raoul... that story will be for another tape. A terrible time when my heart broke and everything changed and things started that I couldn't stop. I had to embrace the core of a terrible evil to keep you safe... and others, too. I shall tell *you soon... bear with me because those times are most difficult for me to talk about, but if I'm to free my soul, I must.*

Till next time... bonne nuit à toi... *and always remember,* ta maman *loves you.*

I turn off the tape recorder, exhausted, though a spirit of hope comes over me as I listen to Sylvie's innermost thoughts, revealing the life of the French actress that fills me with new understanding... and new fears.

What unspeakable event turned Sylvie Martone into a Nazi collaborator?

22

SYLVIE

THE MAN IN THE BOWLER HAT

Paris
1941

Emil insists I meet him at Café de la Paix. He may have film work for me. He sent word early this morning by bicycle messenger since I don't have a phone in the Faubourg apartment that works. We made it through the harsh winter of 1940, but going to the pictures has never been more popular with Parisians.

I've been in hiding for months, keeping a low profile after selling an emerald bracelet on the black market. Then I discover someone tipped off the German High Command I was in Paris. Emil, of course. He made no secret of his whereabouts – or mine – when he discovered a new organization called the *Filmprüfstelle* (they answer to the military command and are in direct contact with Berlin) is in the process of permitting French film production to begin soon. A new film company called Galerie Films is founded and entirely funded by German money.

'What do I care where the money's coming from?' he insists when I call him out on it. 'We're making motion pictures, not invading North Africa.'

We watch Parisians and Germans alike strolling along the boulevard near Café de la Paix. Parisians... heads down, shoulders hunched, reluctant to catch anyone's eye. German soldiers... scrutinizing the scene around them, everyone with a posture that says everything from arrogance to bewilderment. We keep our voices low since two German soldiers are enjoying a beer next to us. The cafés are hotbeds for Nazi spies eavesdropping for anti-German sentiment talk.

I order another coffee and ignore the stares of the two soldiers who haven't taken their eyes off my legs. I shift my position so my bare legs are tucked under the table, then say to them with a big smile, 'No more free looks, *mes amis*. Next time you'll have to pay to see these legs.'

Yes, I said those words before when I was a sixteen-year-old kid knocking around the movie theater with big dreams. I was young, smelling of rotten tomatoes, tears flooding my eyes, but I meant every word. I mean every word now. I could not have imagined I'd be sitting here years later muttering those same words.

The two soldiers nod their heads, grinning from ear to ear while they toast me with their warm beers.

I thank my lucky stars they have no idea what I said.

* * *

My money's running out... my shoes need fixing... and I fear going back to my apartment in the Trocadéro to pick up my clothes and grab some shoes lest I find it filled with Nazis again. Still, I'm not as bad off as some in the film industry. Thousands of people have no jobs, no income, and if they're Jewish, they fear what will happen next.

Everyone in the motion picture business has suffered one way or another since the Germans are hell bent on confiscating films contrary to the beliefs of the Third Reich (Emil assures me they haven't gotten their hands on the original negative for *Angeline* and gives me an extra print for safekeeping). Some directors flee to the Unoccupied Zone in the South with the negatives of their unreleased films, some films are lost in the chaos, and other classic films are hidden in basements and attics.

Meanwhile, the Germans waste no time reopening movie theaters to show Nazi newsreels. God help any poor soul who boos when the German Army goose-steps across the screen – they remedy that behavior by leaving the lights on.

A mental torture, if nothing else.

Then what every filmmaker fears, happens. The Germans form a committee to head up government control (as in Nazi control) over the motion picture industry. What next? Can it get any worse? Then, this so-called committee receives permission to resume production in Paris.

Emil can't wait to share the news with me at our daily meet at the Café de la Paix. He doesn't come to the Faubourg – the less my neighbors know the better, though it's no secret since my presence in Paris is well established with the Propaganda *Abteiling*. According to Emil, the Nazis have decided they will 'flatter' French culture, let it flourish, and that includes shining praise on film stars like me. An idea that pleases Emil... he didn't find success in dealing with the Vichy in the South and he's only too happy to pick up where he left off in the French capital with his biggest star. I find this talk of admiring French culture ludicrous and insulting to me as an actress since they changed the name of the Sarah Bernhardt Theater to *Théâtre de la Cité*.

What next?

* * *

Today I got upstaged by a cow.

Mooing and wagging her tail, flashbulbs from the press popping when she knocks me over and I land on my butt. For the past hour I've been waving to crowds at a Nazi propaganda exhibition in the *Grand Palais*, though it's more like a county fair. Fifi got away from her handler as I'm addressing the press about my *Ninette* films. I'm promising new motion pictures from me soon when she knocks me over with her jaunty gait and swinging tail. The press love it, since the whole day has been nothing but boring talk about the new social and economic order between Germany and France. Why I was commanded to speak today, I don't know. Once the Nazis get an idea into their twisted brains, there's no stopping them.

Emil follows the PR stunt at the *Grand Palais* (the headline reads '*Sylvie Martone mooing around*') with more appearances so he can raise my profile in the eyes of the Propaganda *Abteilung*.

And so *he* can make money. Gambling debts, drinking, and he's heavily into the black market. Then again, who isn't? What's uppermost on his mind is getting me front and center in the *eyes* of the public.

So where does he put me?

On the radio.

'... and I want to thank all my fans who came to see me at the *Grand Palais*...'

Me or Fifi the cow?

'And let you know how happy I am we're going to make new pictures for each and every one of you...'

When the Nazi high horse gets off his butt...

'So until I see you again on the silver screen, let us give thanks to our German friends who are helping French culture flourish and blossom...'

What? Who wrote this? Not me.

'With movie theaters opening up again.'

I want to gag. I *do* gag. I garble the last sentence so nobody can understand what I said. It makes me sick.

Who changed my words? I had an uplifting speech written about celebrating our French culture in film... not this trash. Someone rewrote my script, putting words into my mouth that show the Germans in a positive light.

'*Pardon, mes amis*, something got caught in my throat,' I continue without missing a beat. I'm wary to look anywhere but down at my script. When I arrived at the last minute, I noted the radio studio filled with visitors. The heel on my black pump cracked and I had to make a stop at my Trocadéro apartment to pick up another pair of shoes (I was delighted to see the German soldiers hadn't been back, thank God). I didn't have time to look over what I thought was my approved script shoved into my hand.

Someone censored my words. *Who?*

There's dead silence except for my heavy breathing.

I continue with an adlib that would never make it past the Nazi censors, 'I'd like to end this evening with a quote from one of my *Ninette* films about surviving in these difficult times. As my humble angel character said to the two orphans she rescued from the devil's clutches, "We must believe in the unseen power in us to overcome evil if we stick together." *Merci et bonne nuit.*'

I imagine Emil is smoking his cigar overtime and I wouldn't be surprised if two Nazi guards appear and escort me out of the building. Emil can't wait to dig into me when I leave the control booth.

'You're going to ruin us, Sylvie, with your obstinance. You're an actress, not a politician.' His face is so red I wonder if he's swallowed his cigar.

'If more of us actors took a stand when the Boche invaded, I wouldn't have to be.' Reckless words since the word 'Boche' is *verboten* to be spoken anywhere, but I'm angry. 'I'm no better than the words I speak. Fans listen to me. I can't let them down.'

'Why did you go off script with that not-so-subtle quote?' he demands, looking over his shoulder at the man in the black leather trench coat scribbling on his crossword. He looks up, smiles at me. Dark eyes with heavy, overhanging lids that shield his thoughts, but not his piercing look. He gives me the creeps. I have no doubt he's Gestapo. I breathe a sigh of relief when he retreats into the shadows.

'Do you want my fans to come to our pictures? Or spit at us on the street?' I stare at the dark corner with uncertainty. Is he still watching me? 'Being honest with them is the only way to win the hearts of the people.'

'I'm afraid this isn't over, Sylvie,' Emil warns. 'You may have gotten your way for now, but our new German friends are *not* happy with you.'

'They're not my friends,' I toss back at him and head toward the studio door leading to the corridor guarded by Nazi soldiers. Then I have to go through more guards to get to the street and pray my red Bugatti has enough gasoline to make it back to the garage where I've been storing it. Since it's an older model I wasn't 'requested' to bring it to the Hippodrome so the Nazis could decide whether or not to purchase it. I enjoyed the privilege of using my motorcar today because I'm on 'official German government business'. I have the feeling that privilege is now revoked.

'May I have a word, *mademoiselle*?'

I spin around, my heart in my throat. My hand is on the door lever, but I can't move. The rat has come out of his corner, a big rat who enjoys crossword puzzles.

The Gestapo man.

'Of course.' I give him my star charm, the big dimple smile I'm famous for. I refuse to cower before him, though the rumors I've heard about the reputation of the persistent and treacherous secret police – the most hardened political dissident can be broken and beg for mercy – are not to be ignored.

What does he want with me?

He stuffs the newspaper into his pocket and removes a small note-book. 'I enjoyed your radio address, *Mademoiselle* Martone, however...'

His stern, dark eyes deepen as he flips through his notebook, making me believe Emil is right and this time I went too far.

I go on the offensive with, 'Would you like an autograph, *Monsieur*...'

He grins. 'Avicus Geller, *mademoiselle*, of the Gestapo.'

'Oh, how *fascinating*, *Monsieur* Geller. I've heard so much about your organization.' My voice comes out high and hollow sounding, like a young girl gushing over a new party dress.

Can it. That singsong reply isn't going to make it with this mug. Do you see how he wets his lips over and over?

I shiver.

'That's excellent, *mademoiselle*.' A slow grin comes over his full lips, then he shoves the black notebook at me... and a pen. 'Your auto-graph... please.'

'My pleasure.' I take the pen though I swear he holds onto it longer than necessary, and sign my name on a blank page. Not my best signa-ture. Wiggly with large capital letters. Nerves, I imagine. It's not my overly zealous handwriting that worries me, but what's written on the opposite page that sends a rolling chill across my shoulder blades.

Herr Geller has made notes on me. Yes, *notes*.

I can't believe what I'm reading:

Sylvie Martone... beautiful blonde cinema star... charming... people like her, could use that talent for our work in Paris... however, she's obstinate... doesn't follow orders, which could be a problem... with the right incentives, I've no doubt we can tame her rebellious spirit.

He doesn't blink when I give him back his pen. Instead he closes the notebook with a loud snap and then tips his bowler, knowing full well I read the notes. '*Merci, Mademoiselle* Martone, I pray we meet again.'

His words chill me. I race out of the studio, eager to change my clothes and take a long, hot bath to wash off the lingering smell of his threat, but the stink won't go away.

Life in occupied Paris just got a lot more dangerous.

23

SYLVIE

PUTTING ON THE RITZ WITH THE SS

Paris
1941

'You're lucky the Gestapo man is a big fan of yours.'

Emil hustles me into the jet-black Mercedes coupe before anyone sees us. *Bon.* I avoided catching the glance of anyone, especially German soldiers eager to meet a French girl. Too many times I've seen a startled young woman approached by two soldiers and cornered into having a beer with them lest she invite trouble. For the most part, girls travel in pairs and several keep their hair pinned up tight, a subconscious act to keep their virtue wrapped up as well.

'I wouldn't call him a fan, Emil.... more like a tiger waiting to pounce.'

Emil doesn't laugh at my attempt at humor. I don't blame him. We're both on edge. Our usual morning chat changed from the Café de la Paix to this passageway with a car and driver waiting for us after we each received a cryptic message from the Propaganda *Abteiling* to meet here. As predicted, after deviating from the radio script, I lost the right to drive my red Bugatti and Emil is no longer allowed to race around the city in his yellow Citroën. The Germans consider it too 'flashy'.

We're lucky we enjoyed the privilege as long as we did since the Nazis often requisition private automobiles.

Now we're relegated to following orders (yes, I'm taking Herr Geller's threat seriously).

I'm still shaking from my encounter with him. Since then I find myself looking over my shoulder every time I leave the safety of the Faubourg, which isn't often. No film roles have come my way, but I refuse to give in to the Nazis' demands I speak publicly about the positive effects of the Occupation. All I see is how the Nazis are stifling the French people. Curfews, food shortages, no motorcars allowed.

Riding around on the open streets in a German car makes me feel like a traitor.

Emil doesn't see it that way.

'Be grateful you're on Herr Geller's good side, Sylvie. From what I've heard, it's not a pleasant afternoon if he requests your presence at 84 Avenue Foch.'

'Then that's not where we're going?' I dare to exhale in a big breath. It's well known the German Intelligence Service appropriated several buildings in the fashionable *arrondissement*.

He snickers. 'No. It's a surprise.'

'I don't like surprises, Emil. What are you up to?'

'I hope you realize it's in your best interest to work *with* the new regime.'

I don't answer him. I'm uncomfortable with all this secrecy. I've been careful to keep a low profile. I won't listen to German-controlled *Radio Paris* and its propaganda, but I admit to listening to the message of hope from *Radio Londres* in the quiet of the night. I wonder if things would have been different with Jock and me if there hadn't been a war, if we could have overcome the obstacles in our path. I like to believe so, but when the clear dawn arrives with its stark reality, I know I'll never see him again. How can I with Paris occupied? I have no idea where he is, though I pray he's safe in London doing his job with the Foreign Office.

Still, I've never stopped loving him.

Emil won't give up with his chatter about how the tide has turned and we're a step closer to getting permission to make a new film. For once, I'm grateful for his obnoxious persistence in getting things done. I'm not flattered to believe it's because he likes me. I'm his main meal ticket since several of his stars stayed in the Unoccupied Zone and others fled to England and Portugal. For the benefit of our nosy driver who keeps looking at me in the rear-view mirror, I'm careful to answer with enthusiasm when Emil points out the *Deutsches Soldaten Kino* (movie theaters for German soldiers only) and emphasizes how popular my pre-war films are with the soldiers.

I'm not so enthusiastic when the Mercedes pulls up to the Hôtel Ritz and he mentions one SS officer in particular who insists on dining with me.

Captain Karl Lunzer.

The name means nothing to me, but I have an idea he was among the officers I snubbed at the radio studio. Emil insists if I don't want to end up in one of the German brothels in Paris, I'd better get cozy with him. They need him to influence the right general to greenlight a film.

I tell him I'd rather sleep on the pavements with the vermin.

* * *

'Herr Geller told me you're more beautiful in person than on the screen, *mademoiselle*. I didn't believe him till I saw you at the radio station.'

So I was right. Another rat who wants his piece of the cheese.

Captain Lunzer bows low, clicks his heels, and kisses my hand. I stiffen. 'He insisted I make your acquaintance.'

An excuse? Or does everybody in Paris kowtow to the Gestapo?

'Herr Geller has a way with words, *n'est-ce pas?*'

The captain takes my arm and we walk down the long gallery toward the restaurant when I notice Emil isn't behind me. I turn around and see him disappearing through the revolving doors. The coward. He baited the trap and now it's sprung.

'Everything all right, *mademoiselle*?' the SS officer asks, his gloved hand moving to surround my waist. If I'd been wearing a corset in one of my period films I couldn't have felt more confined. I can't breathe.

'Yes, Captain, everything is just the way you planned.'

He smiles and I accept the fact I have a part to play in this Nazi melodrama while we dine on exquisite caviar and truffles, then poached salmon, though I beg off the champagne. I'm not going to relapse because a damned Nazi captain wants to get into my pants. I know what's expected of me, but I'll only go so far.

We linger over coffee and an overly sweet strawberry-orange tart with the flakiest crust I've ever tasted, talking about... well, about the captain. His exploits, his passion for polo. Then he pulls out a map for German officers and soldiers marked *Pariser Plan* in bold Germanic script and, in not so subtle words, requests me to show him the *real* Paris. (I wonder if that includes my Trocadéro apartment.) I admit the tall, broad-shouldered officer has the blond good looks of an SS poster boy and the swagger to go with it. I don't reject his attentions, but I don't encourage him either. I play it down the middle. I hope that will be enough to keep the Gestapo man from making more notes about me in his book. I admit Karl is handsome with a cleft in his chin, a patrician nose and the physical prowess of a university athlete.

'Like our Fuehrer, I'm Austrian by birth,' he's quick to tell me and I'm surprised he doesn't click his heels under the table. *Or did he?* 'I'm honored to do my duty for my country.' He moves his chair closer to mine. I squirm. 'As I expect you will do for yours.'

'I'm here, *n'est-ce pas*?' I don't hide the sneer in my voice, but he chooses to ignore it. I sense he enjoys playing our little game and would be disappointed if I acquiesce too easily.

'I'm a big fan of your work in cinema, *mademoiselle*. I'm looking forward to seeing you make new and better films now that the Party is in charge of production.'

'My fate is in your hands, Captain.' I flutter my eyelashes at him, keeping the mood light. I have nothing to gain by pitting him against me. Yet I'm taken aback by his next comment when I mention I can't wait to work with my old crew again.

'Some crew members won't be returning.'

'Oh?'

'I'm sure you'll agree the film industry runs more efficiency without Jews, *mademoiselle*.'

'*Pardon*, Captain?'

'Fortunately, they've either fled the city or will soon be taken care of.'

I choke on a strawberry. God knows what he means by that. I strive very hard to be pleasant but stern when I say, 'I don't agree. What's happened to Jewish *artistes* is a persecution of a valued and talented group of individuals who make my films the wonderful experience they are.'

'My dear Sylvie... may I call you Sylvie?'

'*Oui.* *Do I have a choice?*

'It's not a persecution of Jews,' Karl continues (he insists I call him Karl), 'but a matter of security under the New Order to keep France safe.'

Perhaps I raise my voice a bit too high when I counter with, 'I still believe the *Party* made a mistake by allowing only non-Jews to own and distribute films. What's next? Barring Jewish writer, actors, and directors from the studio lot?' I realize I've gone too far when a Nazi general sitting nearby signals to a German solider to approach my table. Then I hear a loud cough and I see Herr Geller come out of the shadows and wave him off, then nod at me.

The deadly look in his eyes chills me. A warning.

Do it again and you will regret it.

I push away my cream tarte. It doesn't taste so sweet now.

* * *

In spite of the frightening incident at the Hôtel Ritz, I continue to spar with Karl over everything from the German invasion of the USSR to

Why are Jews no longer permitted to have radios? He laughs at my question, insisting for the same reason they're barred from universities and the medical profession.

They're not Aryans.

It's a crazy theory I don't buy and I don't care how many dinners at the Ritz Karl wants to buy me, or how he can make certain I receive more food than my *carte de rationnement* allows, I can't be quiet, sit back, and not stand up for my Jewish friends. Skilled tradesmen and women I work with, including Raoul.

Karl stops sending the black Mercedes coupe for me. The brush-off, I assume. *Très bon.* I'm tired of playing his game. (I always meet the driver at the same place in the secluded passageway. What would my neighbors say?)

I prepare to sell another bracelet. Diamond cuff set in platinum, a gift to myself with the success of *Angeline.* Funny thing. I keep the faux diamond pin I wore when I met Jock in a special box. It's more precious to me than any jewelry I own.

Oh, how I miss you, ma chéri.

I admit, I *almost* relented with Karl to agree on something, like how nice it would be if der Fuehrer visited Paris again (he came once) so I can ask him to look into why the Germans seized my bank accounts for 'audits'.

I couldn't even bring myself to do that.

I hate the Nazis. Hate what they're doing to Paris, to France. Damn it, I hate what they did to my Trocadéro apartment, trashing it that day. That's the strange thing... they haven't been back since, but I'm still afraid to stay there alone. I prefer the Faubourg where I'm among friends.

At the same time, Emil has also been strangely absent in his pursuit of me to star in a new film. How long since our last café meeting? Two weeks... no, three. Strange, I miss his constant nagging and wonder what happened to the big deal he was working on for me to make pictures for Galerie Films.

I decide to find out.

24

SYLVIE

A STAR IS BORN... THE SEQUEL

Paris
1941

'*Mais non,* Madame Martone, I have nothing for you today.'

'It's *Mademoiselle* Martone, *Fräulein,*' I say with a snicker, not caring if she's French or German. The overly rouged brunette enjoys ribbing me when I ask her if there are any messages for me. I stomped into the main reception of Galerie Films on Rue de Rivoli wearing an elegant white suit with a black braid trim and that diamond cuff platinum bracelet sparkling on my left arm. I dangle it in front of her, enjoying it while I can.

I'm off to pawn it after this.

'Perhaps tomorrow, *mademoiselle*... but I wouldn't count on it.' She goes back to her typewriter, squirming in her seat and pecking at it like a hen about to lay an egg. She can't wait to get rid of me.

'Emil-Hugo de Ville... the *director*, left me a message to meet him here,' I lie.

I tap my fingers on the counter, but the brunette won't look up from her typing until another factor enters the picture.

I hear a soft baby voice behind me say, 'Oh... are you meeting Emil here today, too, *Mademoiselle*...?'

I spin around. 'Sylvie Martone.'

She double blinks. '*Pardon*...?'

'The *actress*,' I emphasize. 'I made the *Ninette* films when I was about your age.'

'Oh, of course.' She giggles. 'Then again, your films were before my time.' In spite of her dipsy mannerisms, she has a certain appeal. Curly red ringlets fall loosely around her shoulders, a full bosom, round hips. Green eyes.

'*Really?*' I raise a brow. That hit me in the gut. Unfortunately, she's right. She can't be more than eighteen. A light goes on in my brain as I slide my extravagant bracelet up and down my forearm to keep my nerves from exploding. 'I imagine Emil promised you a part in his next picture, *Mademoiselle*...'

'Bibi Charmont. *Enchanté.*'

'*Enchanté*,' I repeat, surprised when in a gesture of camaraderie, she extends her hand and smiles big. 'You're a pretty girl, Bibi,' I say, meaning it, 'but you've got to project your voice if you want to impress Emil to give you a speaking role.'

She gives me a smile that says there's more to her being here than a walk-on. '*Pardon, Mademoiselle* Martone, Emil is *starring* me in his next picture.'

'*He's what*...?' My mouth is hanging open.

'Emil says he can make me a film star if I leave everything behind and become his protégé.'

'Oh, did he now?'

Where have I heard those words before? How can I ever forget them? He said the exact same thing to me when I was sixteen, hungry to act, and so vulnerable.

For once I'm caught without a snappy comeback. Now I know why Emil hasn't contacted me though I sent messages to him at the Hôtel Ritz. He's found a new protégé.

'Ah, Sylvie, I see you've met Bibi.' Emil arrives with a sweep of his white Panama hat in a grand gesture and drags me away out of hearing. Bibi doesn't notice. She's too busy chatting up the brunette and showing off her new red manicure. 'What are you doing here?'

I refuse to play nice and meet his dark eyes with a piercing stare he won't forget. 'What did she mean she's *starring* in your new picture?'

He's not the least embarrassed I found out. 'Face it, Sylvie, you didn't play ball with the Nazis. I had to find someone else. Bibi is young, ambitious, a new face. Granted, she doesn't have your talent and Captain Lunzer made it his prerogative to demand I produce the charming Sylvie Martone, but she's more than willing to cozy up to him when he returns from an assignment in Berlin.'

'Just like that, I'm old news?'

'These Nazis control everything, Sylvie, even us. On the outside, the film business tells the world we're run by the French. The reality is Herr Goebbels pulls the strings from Berlin.'

'So I'm on *his* blacklist, too?'

I was warned this would happen by my 'friend' Herr Geller. I didn't believe it.

'That's the funny thing about these Germans. They're so worried about what the rest of Europe and America thinks about this Occupation as well as here in France, they will go to great lengths to keep up a good front with their propaganda. Including showing life in Paris in a flattering manner and keeping French film stars like you out in the public eye.'

'What are trying to say, Emil? Spill it.'

'If you change your mind about cooperating and I mean *cooperating in every way,* you know where to find me.'

'You mean collaborating,' I shoot back, feeling the sting of what he's suggesting hurting my pride.

'How you interpret it is up to you.' He puts his hat back on. 'Now if you'll excuse me...'

Without another word, he rejoins Bibi and the brunette personally escorts them to the executive film offices. Emil doesn't glance back at me, though I have the strangest feeling he's hoping I rethink my position.

His tossing me aside for a younger actress hurt. Far more than I thought it would.

Like an old rag doll with her stuffing kicked out of her, I spend the rest of the afternoon walking the boulevards. Up and down the grand avenues filled with German soldiers and their damned tourist maps, drinking beer, singing while someone plays the accordion. Nazi officers speeding through the streets in their open touring cars like kings in shiny, black carriages. I've never felt so alone, so useless. How can I fight them? I should try to get to London like other actors have done, make anti-Nazi films, but I'd feel like a traitor to France if I abandon my country *and* my faithful film crew in their time of need. God knows if I'll get to work with them again.

One thing I know for sure.

I see the writing on the wall. I'm thirty-one. I'm a star.

But for how much longer with the Nazis in charge?

* * *

I wish I had an angel like Ninette to give me the strength to get through this.

I do. The girl smiles like an angel and reads books and is everything a young Parisienne should be with big, beautiful doll eyes.

Halette. Raoul's daughter.

I've seen how she takes care of her father since her mother died and is so willing to help with her young cousins. And she's such a champion for my pictures – she boosts me up when I'm down, reminding me I worked hard to get where I am, that it didn't come easy.

I find myself walking in an eastwardly direction toward the doll and candle shop, toward the Rue des Rosiers in the Marais district, looking for a friendly face. I turn down a somewhat narrow street with high stone buildings and see an old man sitting on a stool, carving in wood. An old woman pushing a cart filled with rags. A young woman with a baby on her hip, tickling the child under the chin and laughing. Quiet, normal life in this section of Paris where Jews have lived since the thirteenth century. No German soldiers anywhere. I say a prayer of thanks. I need to step out of the idyllic fairyland the Nazis have created on the boulevards with their 'smiling, happy French people' propaganda they want to show the world.

I stop by the doll and candle shop, looking for Raoul. He's not here, but Halette is watching the shop so her Aunt Hela can find milk for the little ones.

'You look so sad, *mademoiselle*.'

'Do I?'

I find her making a classic display of tall, scented lavender candles surrounded by costumed dolls. The Dutch doll I saw the other day is among them so I pick it up and start unbraiding her hair. A nervous gesture and Halette notices.

'What's wrong?' she asks.

'Do you think I'm old, Halette?' I don't look up from my menial task, enjoying the repetitious action of re-braiding the doll's hair as a form of therapy for my tortured soul.

'*You, mademoiselle? Mais non*, you're as beautiful now as when you played Ninette.'

I look up at her, surprised. 'You weren't even born when I made those films.'

'No, mademoiselle, but they show the old films at the Gaumont when they have nothing new. I like them the best.' She sighs. 'I wish you'd make new films filled with romance and pretty costumes, like the dolls wear.' She holds up a doll dressed like Marie Antoinette and claps the doll's hands together. '*Oui, oui, mademoiselle!*' she mimics the doll's voice and cocks her head at an angle. 'We don't like those awful German films... *off with their heads!*'

I can't help but laugh at her jubilance. 'Oh, how I'd love to go back to work and entertain people and tell the stories they love. I don't know anything else but acting, and in my heart, I know it's what I do best.'

'That's what Papa says, too, *mademoiselle*.'

'Call me Sylvie, please.'

She smiles at the intimacy of calling me by first name, a grown-up thing for this young girl with so much charm of her own. '*Merci...* Sylvie. Papa says you're a wonderful actress, the best he's ever worked with.'

'And your papa is a wonderful writer.'

She puts down the doll and exhales. 'No one will hire him since the Germans came to Paris.'

'He's not the only one, Halette. I can't get an acting job unless I...' I let my thought hang in the air like the scent of lavender wafting toward me. I finish braiding the doll's hair, my moment of grace ended. I have to make a decision. 'If you had to tell a lie to do something good, Halette, would you do it?'

Unfair of me to ask her, but sometimes the best wisdom comes from someone so young who see things clearer than I can.

'Well,' she begins, 'it's like when the German soldiers come into the shop poking around, I don't tell them they're horrible people for making everyone so unhappy, but I don't say I like them either. I just smile. Papa says they can't arrest you for that.'

In spite of myself, I grin. Her logic strikes me as true.

I can agree to make pictures for Galerie run by the French even if German investors are behind it. In doing so, I'm not saying I *like* the Germans, but in their eyes I'm not working against them either, which will please Emil. And Herr Geller. That man terrifies me.

'I hope you get an acting job soon, Sylvie. It's so difficult to get through the days. I can't see my friends, Aunt Hela is always rushing about trying to get food, and Papa spends long hours away from home... If I could go to the pictures and see a beautiful story with you as the heroine then I could forget the Nazis for a little while.'

I see the longing in her eyes for a way to escape the yoke of the German occupiers and I realize she's not alone, there are thousands of schoolgirls, secretaries, mothers, grandmothers... all who need a way to find the strength to get through this.

I'm not so vain I believe I can save Paris, but I can make life better.

I hold onto the doll tighter, like I wish I could hold onto Halette to save her from what I fear is coming. These are dangerous times for anyone of the Jewish faith. The French police did a roundup of foreign Jews, mostly Polish, with rumors of more arrests coming.

I can't stand by and not do something. Some women fight behind the lines blowing up railway lines, others distribute pamphlets decrying the Occupation.

I'm a cinema star. I must use that to fight the Nazis.

I come to grips with the idea of playing a new, dangerous game to achieve the most important thing I've ever done in my life. To keep my Jewish friends safe. I can do that by keeping my ears open and spying on Captain Lunzer and his military cronies for information. To do so, I'll pretend to fall in line with Emil's request to tow the mark with the SS officer, not that I'd ever sleep with him. I'll have to rely on his hunger for me to keep him at bay.

Of course, I tell Halette nothing of what's brewing in my mind.

We chat for a while longer as the afternoon beats through the windows, heating up the shop with bursts of sunshine. The glass is so shiny, it's like a shield against everything evil outside these walls and I pray it is, that nothing happens to my dear friend Raoul and his family.

'If the Nazis *do* come and make a show of authority, you won't be safe here, Halette.'

'But I will, Sylvie.' She grins. 'Come, I will show you a secret no one knows.'

Halette closes up the shop and locks the front door. Then she unlatches the gold-leaf mirror cabinet holding the precious antique dolls and pulls a lever, and *voilà*, the cabinet opens revealing a small hiding place behind it big enough for one, two people.

'Papa says this hidden alcove was used to store arms and gold during the Revolution,' she says, getting inside and closing it, then opening it from the inside. 'The owner hid a beautiful aristocrat here who frequented the shop and was kind to his children.'

'I pray you never need it, Halette.'

We clasp hands, embrace, then before I bid her au revoir, she insists I take the Dutch doll. 'Papa would want you to have it,' she says and wraps it up in soft peach tissue paper.

I will treasure it always.

* * *

'I'll do a picture for Galerie Films, Emil, on one condition.'

'Ah, so my beautiful Sylvie has come to her senses at last.' He narrows his eyes. 'You want a bigger salary?'

I hold back a smile at his comment though the moment is difficult for me. It took me all morning to get up the guts to return to our table at Café de la Paix. I found Emil here alone... reading the newspaper and watching the pretty girls stroll by.

'I want Raoul to write the script.'

Emil balks. 'He's Jewish. The answer is no.'

Has it come to that?

In one word, yes. Jewish bank accounts have been seized and their safe deposit boxes ripped open. No wonder Emil is running scared.

Even more heartbreaking is when Raoul confides in me he's worried he can't get Halette to America since the Nazis have forbidden Jews to move from their current homes, as if they're taking an official count. A count of Jews, but for what? More disheartening, the word 'Jew' must be stamped in red on their identity cards. To get past the Occupation authorities, Raoul needs new identity cards for Halette and himself and Hela's family – false ones – and that costs money.

The money he gets for writing the script will pay for those identity cards.

'He can write the script under a pseudonym,' I offer up, talking so fast he can't say no again. 'You can pay him in cash. Who will know?'

Emil smirks. 'We have to choose our battles these days, *ma petite*,' he says. 'You can't ride two trains at once.'

I huff and puff. This is ridiculous. 'What's going to get you a box office hit, Emil?' I counter. 'A good script by Raoul? Or a lousy script by a hack?'

'You know the answer to that.'

'Listen to me, Emil. The public love costume dramas. I remember a script Raoul told me he'd written about the Sun King and Versailles before we did the *Angeline* film. A big, action-filled melodrama with romance and intrigue. Just what the fans want.'

He taps his fingers together, purses his lips. 'You have a point, Sylvie, who would know? The Propaganda *Abteilung* wants results and doesn't care how we get them.' He turns to me and takes my hands in his. They're shaking. He's not doing as well as I thought. 'Bibi isn't working out, Sylvie. She's a terrible actress.' He gives me a kiss on each cheek. 'Get me that script by Raoul and we have a deal.'

I force myself not to turn away, though his touch makes my skin crawl. I wrestle with telling him off and keeping my pride, but my need to help Raoul wins out.

It isn't the first time Emil has used me and it won't be the last.

25

SYLVIE

LIGHTS, CAMERA... ACTION!

Paris
1941

It's unimaginable a film can get into production in six weeks, but it
happens.

Production on *Le Masque de Velours de Versailles* (Velvet Mask of
Versailles) begins in late 1941. It's like the Occupation doesn't exist
when we're shooting on the soundstages at Delacroix Studios. The
entire team is humming with good feelings and big smiles, none as big
as mine. It feels so good to be in front of a camera again. I revel in the
early 6 a.m. call, the fittings and blocking. Everything moves at a rapid
pace.

Raoul, under the name 'Henri du Pons', did a fast script rewrite,
and the casting director assembled a wonderful group of actors within
days (the line for actors reached around the block for the casting call).
The costume designer called in a favor from another studio and pulled
rows of costumes from a seventeenth-century drama made years ago.
Table readings, screen tests for makeup and costumes, then rehearsal.
Sets appear almost by magic – we pulled them out of storage in a
studio property warehouse overlooked by the Nazis. (They were too

busy looting artwork from famous collectors.) Thankfully, my set designer, Bertrand D'Artois, knew where to find the flats, backdrops, and set dressing we needed.

It's a grand welcome home party the first day on the set. The whole gang is here, including my old crew, at least those who didn't flee to the Unoccupied Zone in the South and are trying to their best to make Marseilles the French Hollywood. What they don't realize is in the *real* Hollywood, the Nazis never win. Here they do. I'll take Paris any day. I greet Marcel, who's a genius at lighting me and making me look years younger. Annette, who does my makeup and hair (oh, God, do I need my roots done). Orval, who always knows how to conceal a few extra pounds in my costumes. Bertrand, who has such an artistic gift for sets I convinced him to come back.

And of course, Raoul.

Where they've been, no one asks. All that matters is we're eager to get back to work when film production begins again in the City of Light with an exciting and bold new historical drama.

For everyone's safety, no one knows Raoul wrote the script.

Because he's Jewish.

So are Marcel and Annette, and I question their decision to stay in Paris. They insist they won't leave the city where they've lived their whole lives, where their friends are, their family. Besides, where else could they work for such a big star as Sylvie Martone?

I smile at their kind words when we hug, the warmth of those words flooding me with hope we can do this... Deep down, I have my doubts. The events of the past few weeks have changed me... new fears haunt me... a Gestapo man following me... a handsome SS officer pursuing me. Some nights I don't sleep at all, questioning if I'm doing the right thing for me... for France.

I'm happy to be working again with my crew, but I'll never forget the series of events that brought me here today.

I assure you, what I had to do to make this film happen does not make me proud.

* * *

There's much to be said in the world of filmmaking about the power of coincidence in the story, like when the heroine misses seeing the hero off at the train station by minutes, or a telephone call that goes unanswered that could change a lonely widow's life, or a road not taken.

When coincidence happens in real life, it can save lives.

Jewish lives.

As the door of my dressing room opens on a rainy, late winter morning, I don't look up but continue flipping through the costume sketches approved for the exterior scenes. I'm expecting Bertrand to burst through the door any minute with his layout of the gardens and gazebos we plan on using when we gather up the entire crew and the actors and go on location to the Palace of Versailles for two weeks. We're awaiting the final permission from a Nazi general who's not too happy an entire film crew is about to invade his privacy as he's taken over rooms in the palace as his personal retreat.

I notice Bertrand keeps a close watch on me whenever we have a certain 'visitor' to the set, a curious Nazi official who wants his picture taken with me. I admit I like his protective presence.

I look up quickly when I hear a loud sneeze. It's not Bertrand I see, but a rain-drenched Halette bursting through the door, wet white scarf tied around her dark hair, rumpled tweed coat, soggy galoshes.

'Halette, how charming to see you. I wasn't expecting you until tomorrow.'

Emil requested two new pages of dialogue and since no one knows Raoul wrote the script, the screenwriter called me at my Trocadéro apartment and said he was sending Halette with the pages.

'Papa gave me what you asked for, *mademoiselle*,' Halette says, surprising me by keeping to formalities. I fear something is wrong with the child as she lays the envelope down on my makeup table. She's shivering and her eyes and nose are red, like she's been crying. 'I'll be going now.'

'You'll do no such thing, Halette. I appreciate you bringing me the new pages, but you're not going back out in that rain. Stay.'

'I can't, *mademoiselle*... I'm worried about Papa.'

'What's wrong?' I ask, concerned.

She lowers her voice to a whisper. 'He's worried the Nazis are going to close Aunt Hela's shop and take her and the children away because my uncle is in big trouble.'

'What kind of trouble?'

'Papa said he cheated Germans involved in the black market, promising them goods hard to come by, then pocketed the money and disappeared.'

So that's why the elusive uncle hasn't been around.

'Then Papa says he lost thousands of francs at the horseraces and he owes bad people a lot of money.'

'Oh, dear God...' I'm taken aback, knowing what agony Raoul is feeling. Their identity cards are marked in red, identifying them as Jewish and making it impossible for them to leave the city. 'We *have* to get them out of Paris... but how?'

'Perhaps I can help, Sylvie.'

I look up. Bertrand.

How long has he been standing there?

* * *

It's that friendship and trust Bertrand and I have for each other that now comes into play.

After I send Halette to the wardrobe department to get dry clothes, Bertrand and I find a quiet spot among the rows and rows of hanging costumes where we won't be overheard.

'You can get Raoul's family new identity cards?' I keep my voice low, the smell of mothballs and dried human sweat emanating from the costumes makes it hard for me to breathe. I wonder how long it took for Bertrand to decide to spring this on me. The funny thing is, I'm not surprised. I always thought he'd make a great cloak and dagger character in my films with his inquisitive nature and powerful strength.

'Yes, but I'm not certain how long it will take.' He checks over his shoulder to make sure no one is listening. 'I promise you, it won't be easy, but I *will* get them false identity cards.'

'Why are you risking your life to help me... and Raoul?'

'Because you both love France as much as my friends and I do.' He doesn't speak for a moment, and his blue eyes go wide with excitement, then confirmation. 'I wasn't sure if I could trust you with my secret, but when I overhead you and Halette, I decided not to wait. I'm taking a chance by asking you to join us, but the Resistance needs patriots like you, Sylvie.'

He tells me about a secret location where members of the Resistance meet, how they use the underground passages to move agents and refugees between locations without being seen.

'I'm an actress, not a soldier.'

'We're all soldiers now. We need to know what the Nazis are thinking, planning.'

'And you think because of my public image, I'm above suspicion?'

'Yes. I know you're on the Gestapo's watch list, but you're too much of a beloved public figure for them to do more than throw idle threats your way. Once this picture is finished and distributed, you'll be a bigger star than ever.'

'And a bigger asset to the Resistance.'

'*Bien sûr.*' He holds my hands in his. 'Will you help us, Sylvie? The work is dangerous, and there's no guarantee you'll always entertain the gracious admiration of the Nazis. If they find out you're helping us—'

'They won't, if no one in your organization knows who I am.'

'What are you thinking?'

I smile. An idea has been forming in my mind as we speak... a character so familiar to me since I was a teen sneaking into *Monsieur* Durand's theater, then later useful when I wanted to move about the city unnoticed, a way of helping free my country from these Nazi madmen unique to me.

'I will meet your friends, Bertrand, but only you will know my true identity. You will introduce me as a widowed baroness with a worthless title but a sharp mind, a woman who can get into places no one else can.

'A woman named Fantine.'

* * *

With my plan in place, I'm all smiles when Herr Geller pays me a visit on the set. He's pleased with my willingness to make a new film for my adoring fans – French and German alike.

'How could you ever doubt me, Herr Geller?' I coo his name sweetly to please him, noting the two Nazi soldiers at his side. He's not as easily manipulated as Captain Lunzer.

'I was testing your loyalty to the Party, *mademoiselle*.' He looks around, making notes. 'And that of your crew.'

'I assure you, everyone here is an *artiste* interested only in making pictures for the French people. We're not political creatures by nature.'

'Perhaps... perhaps not.' He sniffs around the lighting equipment, takes a seat in Emil's director chair, and then peers through the camera lens. What's his game? I'm grateful Emil isn't here, but instead giving a young actress a tour of the studio during a break in filming. 'We shall see, but that's not why I'm here today.'

'Oh?'

'The director of the Propaganda *Abteilung* is in need of an actress to make a short film about shopping hints for Paris department stores for our female German auxiliary workers. You will do the part in French and we will add German subtitles.'

'Why me?' I'm afraid to ask.

'The order came directly from Herr Goebbels. He's seen your films and chose you personally for the honor.'

Talk about a royal command.

'We're under a tight production schedule, Herr Geller—'

'*Auf Wiedersehen, mademoiselle*.'

He tips his bowler and with a nod he's off, his two German lapdogs clicking their heels and then following him.

I breathe a sigh of relief after the Gestapo man is gone. Obviously, I have no say in the matter. I'm the new spokesperson for what Parisians call 'Grey Mice', female German workers.

Me-ow.

* * *

Blindfolded, I shuffle though the double portals, pushing aside the overgrown plants poking in my face, the scent of sweet jasmine filling my nostrils. Then cool dampness as we walk down a steep ramp. Like we're underground. Keeping my head down, my lace veil over my face, I limp along with Bertrand as my guide, the pathway twisting and turning. He chuckles, amused at my disguise. It's a non-glamorous role I covet, donning a scraggly wig I cover with the lace veil Sister Vincent made for me, extreme makeup with my putty nose, heavy brows, and fake beauty mark, and a harness to give me a limp. I'm wearing an elegant, thread-worn purple brocade dress and black coat, black stockings, and brown laced-up boots.

'Are you certain you want to do this?' he asks me in a deep whisper, then removes the blindfold. The leader of the Resistance unit requires new recruits secure a scarf over their eyes before being led through the secret passageway to their meeting place.

I grin. I know where I am, any actress worth her mascara would. The Art Deco design on the walls mixed with Asian artifacts piled up in the corner tell me we're under the stage of a charming Oriental-themed, deserted movie theater in the 7e *arrondissement.*

'Yes. I need a way to share whatever intelligence I gather from my SS officer as well as staying clued in to the resistance movement,' I answer in my normal voice, then louder with a dramatic accent I call out, '*Zut alors, messieurs,* do you always blindfold your guests?'

A ruffled-looking man with a beret and a pipe stands off to the side, speaking with two other men. Workmen wearing caps. Smoking. A young woman wearing round glasses sits in a tattered bamboo chair knitting.

They all look up, curious.

'Meet the Baroness de Ravenne.' Bertrand introduces me as a feisty aristocrat widowed twice, penniless, but with a sharp mind for sabotage.

The partisans Bertrand introduces me to have no reason not to accept me, but it's up to me to prove myself.

I give the character a background, telling them I'm from a small town in the Unoccupied Zone (making it harder to trace my story), both my husbands died, and the last one was a minor noble giving me the title Baroness de Ravenne.

'I believe she will be a valuable asset to our movement,' Bertrand adds. 'She has entrée into numerous literary salons here in Paris as well as impressive connections in the black market.'

True. As Sylvie Martone. But no one must know my identity.

'You can call me Fantine,' I add quickly. 'I believe you need my help in securing information about a certain shipment of arms from Hamburg the Nazis are keen to receive.'

'*Mais oui, madame*, you know the railway route?' asks the man with the beret and pipe.

'Yes. Using intelligence I gathered, Bertrand has made a map for you with the coordinates, terrain, and Nazi outposts located nearby.'

Bertrand hands him the map he drew with his artistic flair and the leader passes it around.

He's not convinced. 'How do I know you're not a German spy?'

Bertrand steps forward. 'I trust Fantine with my life, Yves. You can, too.'

Yves nods. 'No one in our unit has been successful in securing details about this shipment. How did you come by this information?'

'A Nazi *Kommandant* with a big ego,' I answer honestly. Bertrand told me how difficult it is for them to get accurate intelligence at the highest levels of the Wehrmacht. 'And two bottles of aged cognac my late husband won from a Munich banker back in 1935 in a game of poker.'

The truth is, Captain Lunzer invited me to dinner at the Hôtel Ritz to impress a rotund general eager to brag about his exploits. A tickle under his chin and a knee bump under the table and he was talking so fast, I ran to the powder room to write down the information with my lipstick. Amazing how years of learning lines from a script takes on new meaning in these troubled times. Though it pains my heart, I have more to gain by showing the world I'm collaborating with the Nazis.

Even more importantly, it gives me the freedom I need to make the films that give the French people hope.

Hope to once again see a free France.

'If your information proves correct, Fantine, and the mission to blow up the railway line is successful,' says Yves, the leader, 'next time you won't need a blindfold.'

26

JULIANA

CONFESSIONS OF A RELUCTANT MATA HARI

Ville Canfort-Terre, France
Present Day

As I turn off the tape recorder, the double-clicking sound punctuates Sylvie's words about how she became involved with the Nazis and it's the happiest moment I've had since I found her old photo. How she never wanted to 'collaborate' with the enemy... that whatever she did was to save her Jewish friends – and for France.

I want to jump, sing, and hug Sister Rose-Celine. More than that, the nun can't hold back her emotions and pushes herself up off her scooter and dances.

Yes, *dances*. I join the sister in celebrating and we dance around in that funny circle you do when you're kids, singing, '*Sylvie was not a Nazi... Sylvie was not a Nazi...*'

I can't wait to tell Ridge. I go to text him right away, then hold off on sending it when I realize he's still asleep. He's already put up with my texting at odd hours. I want him to hear Sylvie's voice when he's *not* in the middle of a deep sleep. I miss him, even more as I listen to Sylvie's heartbreak and loneliness...

We dance till we're both exhausted, exhilarated by the tape from

1941 about how Sylvie got back into making movies. I admit, after hearing her voice catch several times and nearly crack, I'm worried sick about what happens to Raoul and Halette, Hela and the children...

Sister Rose-Celine and I head off to the convent kitchen to celebrate our victory with hot cocoa and chocolate nonpareils. Imagine our surprise when Mother Superior arrives with a flurry of several '*Pardon, mademoiselle...*' and says she has a surprise for us.

'What is it, Reverend Mother?' I ask, curious.

'We located the old movie projector in the chapel storage room.' She looks puzzled. 'Who put it there, I have no idea. I asked the gardener if he knew anyone who could operate it and he knew someone...' She waves her arms about, too excited to finish the story. '*Alors*, we got it up and running and the first reel shows *Mademoiselle* Martone at a café...' She pauses, blesses herself.

'Yes, Mother?' I ask, waiting.

'Drinking with Nazi officers.'

* * *

Oh, dear.

Again my mouth is moving as fast as it can to explain to the Mother Superior what I think, what I *hope*, is going on in those films as we gather around to watch the world as it was back then in 1942 and 1943 unfold in extraordinary brilliant color.

Red and black and white Nazi flags hanging from the Hôtel Meurice. Parisians decked out in fancy pink and peach hats in the Tuileries Gardens. Green, green trees and glistening white boulevards. And those dreaded awful olive uniforms of the German soldiers everywhere. *Beetles*, Sylvie called them, and she was right. It's with a strange fascination the film rolls before our eyes.

I'm not convinced Sylvie isn't a willing participant.

I study Sylvie's home movies with her showing off the SS officer I presume to be the Captain Karl Lunzer she mentions on the tape. Handsome in an alarming Aryan way that doesn't translate well in our times as appealing, more like terrifying. Escorting him around Paris, laughing, smoking, drinking champagne. *No*, I shake my head. I never see her drink the champagne. Toast with the officers, yes, but never drink it. A ray of hope. She kept to her sobriety... that's true. Does that mean the rest of her story is also true?

Flickering images of Sylvie Martone going to the Moulin Rouge, posing with the SS officer in front of the Eiffel Tower (a chilling image since it's reminiscent of Hitler doing the same thing), sitting with the captain at *Aux Deux Magots* frequented by known collaborators.

I've seen her pictures, her *Ninette* films, heard her voice, but this is Sylvie Martone unmasked. It's no path to redemption I see unfolding, but further proof of her collaboration with the enemy. Sylvie is dressed in the height of haute couture in a red fall suit with what they called a peplum back then – a short, flared skirt attached at the waist, black gloves and black Fedora cocked at a fetching angle. She looks so pretty, her face shiny though her cheeks are fuller than in her glam photos – her dimple nearly disappears – her figure a bit thicker... no, *wait*, I check the date on the small square box holding the reel of film. It was shot in late 1943. Was Sylvie pregnant with my mother here? Is that why she went to all this trouble to write the diary, make the recordings, because she can't admit the SS officer she's cavorting with is my grandfather as I first suspected?

The idea sickens me, but I keep it to myself.

Another thought rings a bell in my head. What if the famous actress was trying to fool *Maman* into believing she wasn't guilty of cozying up to the Nazis during the war?

What proof do I have Sylvie wasn't pulling off an elaborate hoax?

* * *

I sit by myself in the kitchen, nursing a cup of lily flower tea as I wrestle with my emotions. After a quiet discussion among ourselves after the film, no one questioned why I wanted to be alone. I have to make a decision. Either I'm going ahead with believing this was *not* a hoax by

Sylvie to sugarcoat her gallivanting about with the Nazis... or she was a bona fide spy.

Just saying that to myself gives me a sense of power I'm not sure I have the right to, but I owe it to her, to *Maman*, Sister Rose-Celine, Reverend Mother, and every dear nun or nun-in-training who sat through these upsetting home movies tonight, to pick a path and stick with it.

It's when I remember a certain little boy I saw in the film I make my decision.

Besides the Paris romps of Sylvie, we also watched movies of Versailles when the film crew went there on location. We saw Sylvie hamming it up for the camera with extras, including several children dressed up in Louis XIV wigs and costumes. My favorite was a boy about four or five in a lopsided, white powdered wig and satin breeches who makes me forget why I'm watching the film. He was smiling and waving until a brooding Nazi general stepped into the frame and mouthed a *'Sieg Heil'* and then gave the Nazi salute which sent Sylvie back into the frame. She picked up the little boy and handed him over to the general who had no choice but to hold him. I chuckled as the boy took off his powdered wig and plopped it onto the general's bare head.

Then the boy waved again into the camera.

Everyone was laughing so hard, I told the projectionist to turn it off. We'd seen enough.

The funny scene with the little boy and the Nazi general showed a lighter side of Sylvie's involvement during the war that no one ever saw. She had nothing to gain by pulling a joke on the general and everything to lose. I believe she was making a statement about what she thought of the Third Reich.

It doesn't change anything.

To the outside world, my grandmother collaborated with the Nazis.

And I don't have enough evidence or information to disprove that.

I can't sleep. I text Ridge to tell him we're making progress on clearing Sylvie's name, but my enthusiasm from earlier has dissipated and when he calls me to talk, I don't say much. He doesn't mention it, but I know he's detected something in my voice he can't figure out. Neither can I.

After I click off, I listen to another tape. Alone.

I need to feel at one with my grandmother, catch the nuances in her speech – anything I don't understand I can ask Sister Rose-Celine later. For now, I turn on the recorder and listen to a tape marked late fall 1941.

* * *

I'm on a train going back to Paris, Madeleine, returning from the convent in Ville Canfort-Terre to obtain food from Sister Vincent for Raoul's children when I hear about the Japanese attack on Pearl Harbor. It's been several months since the Germans attacked Russia and with both America and the Russian Bear in the war, there's hope they will defeat the Nazis.

Nothing stops the intense hunger invading the daily lives of Parisians. I discover my new 'job' as pretend collaborator has its advantages. I'm less hungry, often dining at restaurants and, with a careful placing of a note on the waiter's tray, securing extra food wrapped in a red and white checkered cloth to take home. Karl ignores my game, trying to charm me with his exploits in Berlin or unraveling the black market here in Paris. What pains me is whatever extra food I secure from restaurants is not enough to nourish the five children of Raoul's sister. I'm worried about them. Like so many children in Paris, they face the real possibility of contacting rickets from lack of good nutrition. So I make several trips by train to the convent and fill my suitcase with meat, milk, canned vegetables, eggs, dried fruits, and preserves. I always go in disguise, veil covering my face, no makeup, hair pulled back.

I should have known Sister Vincent would see through me.

On one of these trips, giving me a wink, the nun remarks how God works in strange ways, how He once sent her a girl with a deep dimple on her left cheek for her to save, a girl pinched by an angel when she was born. I will always remember that moment when the nun recognized me as the wayward girl who ran away to become a movie star.

It's on such a trip I hear the news America has also declared war on Germany.

With America in the war, will there once again be a free France?

I keep listening, grateful for the quieting of my pulse, though my head pounds with information overload as Sylvie runs through what she considers important moments in her life to explain her choices to her daughter. Her hope for a quick sweeping of Nazis from France is dashed as America builds up her army and navy and concentrates on the war in the Pacific.

Life in Paris continues on as before under the Nazis with more hunger, more fear, more desperation.

Sylvie gives a quick run-through of the next few months, talking about making personal appearances at movie theaters, and getting Raoul's Versailles script approved, casting completed, and additional crew lined up.

I hate making personal appearances, but I find it's a way of using my platform to make clever innuendos about the lack of German fashion savvy. When I see the rich wives of German officers shopping on the Rue de Rivoli. I call it 'puff pastry' fashion, my way of spitting in Goebbels' eye.

I hope I make you smile, mon enfant, *but I don't always get away with my stunts. I was called to another meeting with Herr Geller, the Gestapo man telling me I'd best be a good girl if I want my film project made and anyone I care about not questioned at the secret police headquarters at 84 Avenue Foch. I shivered. It is a place I will speak about later... What's important is the cold fear that went through me when he waved a page in his notebook in my face listing the names of crew members I've worked with, their movements detailed in his large handwriting.*

A sobering moment... a threat I can't ignore. It's a painful lesson for your maman. *Just when I thought I was ahead of the game by pretending to go along with these Nazis, I realized with a painful stab to my heart even a movie star loved by the people of France isn't immune to the whims and dictates of the Nazi war machine. Alors, I've heard rumors about death warrants issued by the Gestapo against another actress who broadcast anti-German sentiments on French radio right up to the Occupation. I continue to acquiesce. I don't want to be tortured like anyone who gets in their way.*

So, enough of that.

I must not let up in my story, for I have so much more to tell you...

Then the tape goes silent. I check the recorder... there's plenty of tape left. I wonder, have I come to the end of the recording?

My tea is cold and the first light of dawn peeps through the window shade, making me yawn. I wait another minute, then two, and heave out a big sigh, ready to catch some shuteye when the tape begins again.

I beg your patience, Madeleine, I thought I was recording but I wasn't. I got so emotional when I started speaking about the events of spring 1942, I couldn't stop the tears...

Satisfied I shall get *no* sleep tonight, I put on the kettle for more hot water and prepare to greet the dawn head on. Then I sit down and listen to Sylvie speak in a quiet voice filled with emotion that tugs at my heart.

I shall speak about a time so filled with horror I shiver still when I think about the dark days beginning in late May. A time when every Jew over the age of six was told to wear a yellow Star of David on the left side of their coat... including Raoul's sister's children.

All except four-year-old Gavriel.

Random conversations I picked up disturbed me. Whether I was dining with Karl at the Hôtel Ritz, or riding with him and members of his staff in that Mercedes open touring car, I became convinced I must get them out of Paris. Not easy. Bertrand ran into a problem getting them new identity cards when the shop was raided by German soldiers and they barely had time to destroy what forged cards they had. They moved locations, leaving me waiting for news.

Raoul remained in hiding after finishing the script rewrites (he joined the Resistance). Halette was helping take care of the children, so she was forced to wear a yellow star, too. I saw myself in the young girl, now sixteen. Unlike me, she lived in fear of that loud knock on the door, the Gestapo wagon pulling up and dragging her away. I wanted to hold her tight in my arms, brush her soft hair as her mother would, knowing what a hollow place it is in a girl's heart without her maman.

I lose it then, all the grief I've shoved aside as I work so hard on clearing Sylvie's name comes gushing out of me in buckets. I let go with a torrent of tears I didn't know I had left in me. I feel such pain in my soul... for Halette... my own mother... and Sylvie. All of us reaching across time like a daisy chain... connected to each other through the loss of the dearest woman in our lives. *Our mother.*

When I calm down and dry my tears, I take note of everything I've heard and I *swear* this doesn't sound like a woman caught up in her game working for the Nazis.

The tape continues.

Should you become too sad, sweet Madeleine, I shall digress and tell you a story I know will cheer you up.

About how I made a fool out of a Nazi general.

I can hardly wait.

After months of going through red tape and script rewrites by the reclusive M du Pons, the nom de plume of my amazing writer, Raoul, filming begins on location on Le Masque de Velours de Versailles in the nearby town in June 1942.

But alas, production is anything but smooth. Emotions run wild. The weather won't cooperate, raining down on the outdoor locations in the gardens, making the grounds muddy in places, ruining costumes, not to mention a snoopy Nazi general and his 'lady friends' getting in the way. We have no choice but to treat them as guests since the general was staying at the palace and gave us permission to film here if he could remain and watch the filming.

Making matters worse, for the first time I feel the sting of the consequences of my game with the New Order when several crew members hired for the film give me the cold shoulder because I've been seen dating an SS officer. I wouldn't call it dating, but Karl insists he's madly in love with me. So far, I've been able to keep him at bay, making his slow seduction of me a game he enjoys playing. I was reluctant to take advantage of his vulnerable state to gather valuable intelligence. My mind regroups and I realize I can save lives when he starts rambling about how he must return to headquarters, that someone leaked information to the French police about a roundup of Jews coming soon...

I pass on the information to Bertrand, knowing he was 'cozy' with a blonde grey mouse, a female German auxiliary worker. 'Find out if she knows anything,' I beg Bertrand. I have no doubt my lovable friend will charm the woman into giving him the information he needs...

Now for a story, ma petite, *that will make you smile, about how we get Hela and the children out of Paris...*

'Mademoiselle Juliana, you've not gone to bed?'

Sister Rose-Celine zips into the kitchen on her motorized scooter, eager to hear what I've found out. I fill her in, telling her Sylvie had intel on the *Vel' d'Hiv* Roundup, and together we listen to the story detailing how Sylvie got Raoul's family out of Paris.

'I was a little girl... five years old, *mademoiselle*, but I learned about this terrible event in school,' says the sister as I grab onto her hand. 'In July 1942, the Nazis orchestrated the infamous roundup of more than thirteen thousand Jews, including innocent children torn from their mothers' arms who never returned to their homes, but were sent to concentration camps in Germany.'

'How horrible and inhumane, Sister.' I have no other words, and we both bow our heads for a moment in remembrance before I turn the tape recorder back on.

Sylvie's next words are about Halette. I'm both afraid and curious to hear what happened to her.

One thing I regret is I didn't keep a more watchful eye on Halette. When I shared with her what I knew about the coming roundup of Jews, the young girl ran away to warn her father. I had no idea he was hiding in a farmhouse used by the partisans on the outskirts of the city. How she got there I'll never know. I have to admire her spunk and loyalty to her father. As for me, I was trying so hard to get the children out of Paris, I felt like I let the girl down. For days I was beside myself with worry while we shot the interiors in the palace because of the rain. Then Raoul got word to me, sending phony 'revised script pages' via a charming old farmhand only too happy to deliver them for a pack of Gauloises.

Raoul and his daughter were safe... but what was to become of his family?

Thanks to Bertrand who secured new cartes d'identités *for them and the elaborate network of* résistants *who helped refugees escape across the border to Spain, we executed the plan without a hitch.*

And here, ma chère Madeleine, *is where ta maman had her shining moment. With Bertrand's help and one of his* résistants, *we hid Hela and the children in a truck transporting seventeenth-century costumes and painted backdrops needed for filming in Versailles. Oh, the fun we had with the five children and their mother, dressing them up in satin costumes and white powdered wigs so they could work as 'extras' on the set along with local townspeople.*

And Gavriel looked the cutest of all.

I turn off the tape, bawling my eyes out. Oh... my... God. The children I saw on the home movie in Versailles dressed up in white powdered wigs, silk hoopskirts, and breeches were Raoul's nieces and nephew hiding in plain sight before Bertrand got them out of France.

And there was Sylvie, rubbing the general's nose in *merde* by posing him with the children. He had no idea the little boy he held in his arms, the daring, wonderful child who plopped a white powdered wig on the Nazi's head was Jewish and, with his sisters and mother, would soon be on their way to Spain and out of his clutches. Forever.

Bravo, Sylvie!

Another tear falls onto my cheek. I wonder if Sylvie used the home movie film as a way for Raoul to see the children in case anything happened to her.

I turn the tape back on, not daring to imagine what to expect next, and the first words I hear send me off to a place I never dreamed... and give me new hope for my *grand-mère's* happiness.

I never dreamed, my dearest Madeleine, in late summer 1942, I'd find a man waiting for me, hiding in the shadows outside my Trocadéro apartment. In my garden where he wouldn't be seen by passers-by. A tall, handsome, wonderful man with a British accent, wounded, exhausted, and ready to collapse.

And my world is forever changed.

I turn off the recorder.

I dare not breathe... can it be...?

27

SYLVIE

I'LL BE SEEING YOU... MY BEAUTIFUL ANGEL

Paris

1942–1943

I awake late this morning after a routine appearance at a theater last night signing autographs for German soldiers when I hear the incessant fluttering of birds outside my window, their nesting disturbed. Wary, I tiptoe out onto the veranda, praying the Gestapo hasn't resorted to hiding in my garden and peeping through my window, when big, strong hands grab me and a man kisses me.

It's like a scene out of a wartime script.

A tall, handsome RAF pilot with stubble beard shows up at my Trocadéro apartment and pulls me into his arms and kisses me. Hot, trembling... I recognize those tempting lips and hear the words I long to hear, '*Mon bel ange*, I've missed you so.'

Dearest of all moments in my life, it's real, *he's* real.

Jock.

'*Ah, mon chéri*, is it really you? Here... *in Paris?*' Running my hands up and down the torn blanket the color of a sour pumpkin, stained with dirt and blood, wrapped around his shoulders, I thrill to his touch as his muscular arms grip me tighter. Under the blanket, he's wearing a brown bomber jacket, the sheepskin lining peeking out and hugging his neck, hair tousled, and... is that dried blood I see on his forehead?

'Yes, my beautiful Sylvie, it's me.' He tells me his plane was shot down in an open field outside the city and he's the only survivor. 'Now let me kiss you.'

We absorb all the air in the shadowy alcove. I'm beside myself, touching his face, holding him, kissing him, I can't let him go. How did he get here? Tired, hungry, wounded with a bum shoulder, he's huddled in doorways for days, he says, no sleep, in pain. He wouldn't stop till he found his way to my apartment. He climbed over the stone wall late last night and waited, praying I still lived in the two-story building flanked by tall bushes, the garden in the back with its numerous potted lemon trees and Victorian penchant for odd, covered doorways making it the perfect hiding place.

We mumble questions, answers between kisses.

How long have you been in the RAF?

Long enough to get shot down.

I thought you were working for the Foreign Office.

The War Department had other ideas... or rather I did. I won't let Hitler win... he's got to be stopped and our boys in the air are the best... besides, I was hoping once we beat these Jerries and take back Paris, I'd see you again.

Seeing him is maddening, making my pulse race out of control when he presses his chest against my breasts covered by a light silk pink kimono.

I'm excited *and* frightened by Jock's sudden arrival – did anyone see him in a neighborhood crawling with Nazis? My fear doesn't curtail my physical reaction to the basest need of my sexual desire. But I'm scared.

Scared he'll be captured, and then God knows what horrors await him at the hands of the Nazis in a POW camp. If he were lucky, he'd be transferred to an *Oflag*, camp for officers. That was iffy at best.

'You can't stay here, Jock,' I moan, his kisses trailing down the curve of my throat as we stay out of sight in the shadowy alcove of my veranda.

'I understand, Sylvie... if I could just get some sleep...' His voice trails off and he stops kissing me, his body fueled by passion but the pain reminding him he's a wounded man in both body and soul. I pray he doesn't collapse in my arms.

Where to hide him?

My apartment in the Faubourg Saint-Antoine. I can trust my neighbors there not to say anything if 'Fantine' is hiding a downed flier, an 'evader'. I pray Emil doesn't drop in unexpectedly, drunk and with his usual abusive manner. I don't trust his motives these days. As long as Jock stays inside the apartment there until I can make contact with Bertrand and get him a forged identity card, he'll be safe. The Gestapo will never find him.

'Oh, my darling, I want you to stay here.' He flinches when I pull away from him. 'But I'm entertaining an SS captain and his Nazi friends later...'

His dark eyes that once smoldered with desire for me stare back at me, bewildered. I need to steady myself, knowing what his reaction will be. He's livid, his whole body stiffens, his eyes blaze hot and his breath hotter as he breathes the words into my face in a choked voice, 'Why is an SS officer coming here? Are you—?'

'Good God, Jock... no... *never*, my darling, but I can do more for France by putting up a pretense of helping the Germans. Entertaining Karl and his friends keeps my profile as a prominent actress in a good light in the eyes of the Gestapo.'

'By cheapening yourself... cavorting with these madmen...' he bellows, an unsettling darkness coloring his rich voice with fear *and* anger. 'Not only is it dangerous, it's—'

'Collaborating with them?' I say with a spark of truth. 'Don't you think every time I have to smile at a Nazi officer and ride around with him in that big, ugly motorcar in the streets of Paris, I don't die a little? Who else is going to fight for the French people if I run away? Yes, I hate it, despise the bastards who've taken the soul out of Paris and wrapped it up in drab olive green and goose-stepping and expect it to sparkle. It never will. I tried to defy them, but it got me nowhere. This... this *cavorting* as you call it allows me the freedom to do what's necessary to fight back in the only way I know how. With my art. It's how I got my dear Jewish friend Raoul's family out of Paris and over the border into Spain before the Nazis rounded them up and sent them to a concentration camp.' I take a breath and stand up straighter, pulling my kimono tight around me. 'I'm proud of what I've done, Jock. And now, my darling, I can use that same network to help you escape.'

* * *

'How about another song, Sylvie?'

Karl nuzzles his face in my hair as I sit at the piano pretending to play while a bespectacled lieutenant with new bars on his shoulder dances his fingers over the keys in a melody I can't name. A favorite of the Reich, I presume. Dressed in a red silk gown cut low to show off my bare back, I'm putting up a good front since I had no choice when Karl insisted his buddies needed a place to 'unwind'. Get drunk is more like it. I chuckle at his attempt at humor, laughing and flirting with the lieutenant. The elegant, white upright piano came with the apartment and though I can't play, I've faked it enough times on screen to make it look like I am.

Everyone is too drunk to notice.

'The lieutenant here is the real star of the evening.' I give him a saucy smile. 'Why don't you play something, Lieutenant, we can sing along to?' He nods and ripples the keys from one end of the keyboard to the other, giving me a break.

I smile as Karl takes my hand and kisses it, the hunger in his eyes telling me he wants more than that. The party's been going for over an hour and a half after Karl and two SS officers showed up with two French girls in tow and three bottles of Dom Perignon. Two bottles of the expensive champagne are already gone. The Germans barely touched the local cheese and what fresh fruit I could talk the chef at the Ritz into giving me (it's amazing how dropping Karl's name makes things happen). The two French girls devoured the strawberries and pears. Food isn't on my mind.

All I can think about is Jock.

Waiting in the cellar.

Listening at the keyhole, desperate to hear what's going on in my apartment with my Nazi guests and ready to storm the Bastille if he has to.

After I dressed the wound on his forehead, he made use of my tub then I insisted he shave (he'd stand out with that week-old beard). I found milk for him and added a good dose of brandy, then I demanded he let me ditch his clothes. My trip to the Hŏtel Ritz also produced a jar of hot chicken soup (I told the chef I was coming down with a cold and couldn't afford to pass it on to an SS officer). I had a leftover baguette in the pantry to give him with some cheese I didn't put out for the party. Then I made a quick stop to a pawn shop I know well and bought clothes for him (I plan to retrieve my diamond bracelet as soon as I receive my salary on the Versailles picture from Galerie Films). Nothing flashy. Old jacket, rumpled shirt, cravat, beret. The owner grunted, took my francs, no questions asked. With his sunken eyes and scraggy hair black as a witch's kettle, he looks like something out of horror casting call, but he can be trusted.

Next, I hid Jock in the cellar.

Blankets, pillow. More brandy.

Before I was halfway up the staircase, I could hear him snoring.

* * *

Getting a downed RAF flier out of my Trocadéro apartment with a shrewd SS officer watching my every move turns out to be a testament to my ability as an actress.

I relax my attention on Karl, trying to draw his eye elsewhere by talking to the two French girls. They profess to be fans of mine, gushing and hiding their mouths when they tell me how honored they are to meet me. Then they go back to flirting with the handsome German officers (do they even know they're SS?). I'm not comfortable with this. I find their eagerness to participate in a dangerous game that defies their everyday existence of food rationing and curfews upsetting. I imagine they haven't had fresh fruit on their plates since the Occupation began. I judge them to be in their early twenties, dressed in poplin and tweed.

The two French girls drink more than they sing and I wonder if they're aware they're collaborating with the enemy. So many young women see dating a German soldier as a way of getting more ration stamps or they just want to have a good time. Cabaret girls are highly sought after, but these two remind me of shopkeepers' daughters. There's an innocence about them that tells me they don't know what they're doing, that their desire to 'have fun' could cost them.

Then a more heart-wrenching thought crosses my mind.

Do they see this partying with the Nazis as acceptable because the film star Sylvie Martone is also doing it? In *her* apartment, no less.

If so, that's a byproduct of my game I never saw coming. It disturbs me. I'm influencing young women to go out with German soldiers and yet they have no idea of the serious consequences for them or their families if the 'date' goes sideways. It pains me, but tonight I can't play the good fairy and watch over them.

I have to get Jock out of my apartment, then make arrangements for him to travel by railway from Paris to the pickup point where he'll travel over rough terrain to cross the border into Spain, then back to Britain via Gibraltar or Portugal. Bertrand tells me the routes are becoming more dangerous since they suspect a traitor in their midst. As much as I want to keep my love close to me, I have to let him go. My 'arrangement' with the Gestapo to publicly promote French culture in films won't change.

Which means I can't give up seeing Karl.

What terrifies me is, I couldn't live with myself if Karl gets too friendly with his hands all over me and Jock witnesses it.

He'll try to kill him.

I'll lose Jock forever because of my game and I can't live with that.

A daring plan hatches in my brain.

I open a window, knowing Karl is watching me slowly sway my

hips. The drawing room is spacious with a high ceiling and parquet wood floor, but it feels stifling. I hear him draw in his breath. I imagine he's conjuring up a long night of sexual activities with me naked beneath him, my body flushed with desire, my voice low and husky, begging him to come to me.

I have a different scenario in mind. Knowing Jock is in the cellar waiting for me is an agonizing, slow death until I put my plan into action to help him escape.

I won't forget this evening for the rest of my life.

A throwback to my days as Ninette outwitting the devil with my daring stunts.

I pour more champagne for the German officers (I pray they pass out before they can come on to the girls), then cozy up to Karl, making him believe I've had too much to drink. I let him think I've had a sudden and most curious rush of desire to get to know him better. Knowing how he likes to be in control when he's around pretty women and show off his authority, I take a chance he drove here tonight. I fumble with the buttons on his uniform to draw his attention and, using the sleight of hand I perfected in *Madame Le Noir*, I pick his pocket.

And retrieve the key to his Mercedes touring car parked outside.

Holding the key tight in my fist, I make my play.

Laughing and singing along with the lieutenant banging on the piano keys, garbling words that make no sense, I pretend to take a sip of champagne then toss the glass against the white marble fireplace. Rolling my eyes and swaying my shoulders in a provocative manner, I do a grand slide across the parquet floor, throwing my head back in a wild, sexy laugh and—

Sacré bleu, my eyes say, *oh, my!*

Down I go, sliding across the shiny, polished floor like a slippery mermaid riding in on the crest of a wave. A perfect stunt. Like the old days when I was the queen of pratfalls.

Ouch. Except I'm not sixteen anymore and that *hurts.*

Karl, ever the dashing SS officer, sweeps me up off the floor in a grand manner and is about to kiss me when I beg off, telling him I need to go upstairs and rest my poor ass. Laughing, I steer him toward the girl with the ribbon in her hair. She's only too happy to play footsie with him while I go lie down... except I don't. The minute I see Karl pulling the satin ribbon from the girl's hair and nuzzling his face in her soft tresses, I jam down the cellar stairs.

'*Jock!*' I call out in a loud whisper. 'We have to go... *now!*'

He comes out of the shadows dressed in the clothes I bought him. 'Are the Jerries upstairs?'

'Yes. And, I might add, they're blessedly drunk.' I want to wrap my arms around him, tell him how sexy he looks with the navy blue cravat around his neck. I don't. Instead I cock his black beret at an angle. 'There. Now you *look* French.' I grab his hand. 'We have to go.'

'Not before I take a poke at those Nazi bastards.'

I stop, startled at his insane request. I can't keep out the pain in my voice when I say, 'I *know* these bastards, Jock. They're drunk but armed, which makes them *more* dangerous. Besides, there are two innocent girls up there who have no idea what these Nazis are capable of. I don't want to see them hurt... or you.' For a moment I feel a surge of panic I haven't felt since Monte Carlo. 'I found you again, *mon chéri*, I don't want to lose you. Besides...' I dangle the Mercedes key in front of his nose. 'We're traveling in style, courtesy of the Third Reich.'

* * *

Strange things happen in Paris after curfew.

But nothing stranger than the sight of the Mercedes-Benz touring car speeding down the boulevard along the Seine with me at the wheel and a downed RAF flier hiding inside.

What is a time of calm and civility on the streets becomes the roar of the eight-cylinder engine under my novice guidance. I'm used to driving an Italian roadster with an engine that purrs at my touch, not this giant metal grey monster.

I keep punching the gas pedal, then jamming it to the mat, sending the long motorcar skidding like a slithering serpent along the grand boulevard. I find it difficult to see where I'm going since the Germans require the headlights of all motorcars be equipped with a blue material that allows only the narrowest of light to shine through. I know the way back and forth by heart, though I'm grateful for the occasional streetlight that's still working. I pick up speed, not unusual since German arrogance dictates nothing else whenever possible. I'm lucky it *is* dark, but if anyone looks closer, all they'll see is a Nazi SS officer wearing a cap, black leather gloves, overcoat with the high collar pulled up, commanding the steering wheel and out for a jarring night spin.

I smile. And wisps of platinum-blonde hair escape from her cap.

I hit a pothole and I hear a loud groan from the floor of the rear passenger seat.

My dearest love wasn't happy when I 'requested' he ride in the back under a blanket. I go as fast as I can under darkness from the *16e arrondissement* to the *11e* in what is a fifteen-minute drive during the day. The six-wheeled G4 staff car will get up to over sixty kilometers an hour. I don't dare go too fast and have an accident.

I drop him off a block away, give him the key, and remind him it's the apartment with the blue door. Number 23. I don't give him time to protest, though by the firm squeeze to my waist and brush of my cheek with his lips, I have no doubt he's surprised at how I outmaneuvered him to get my way. I refuse to let tears fill my eyes at leaving him again so soon. My heart is heavy with longing when he takes a piercing look back at me before racing around the corner and down the dark passage.

I'll count the minutes till I see him again.

With my lips stinging for the kiss we promise each other with our eyes, I jam back to my Trocadéro apartment, park the touring car out front, and race into my fancy residence through the back entrance near the kitchen. I take a moment to catch my breath, then put phase two of my plan into action. A way to knock the compass of my SS officer into a direction he never saw coming. I've often heard the snide remarks of other SS men at the cafés when the chatter gets around to their favorite 'pastime': a French girl wearing nothing but heels, a German officer's overcoat and cap, and scanty underwear.

Now it's Karl's turn to gain bragging rights.

At my expense.

I'll do anything to save Jock from the Gestapo.

With the Nazi cap pushed back on my head, I throw off the long overcoat, drop the key into the pocket so he never knows it was missing and has me arrested for stealing Nazi property, and then strip down to my chemise, garter belt, and silk stockings.

Then I slip the coat back on, pull down the cap to cover my eyes, and wet my lips. It's as if I hear Emil's voice yell '*Action!*' as I grab a bottle of vodka I picked up for tonight's entertainment (I haven't touched a drop since the Nazis marched into Paris) and prance into the drawing room, swinging the vodka back and forth.

'Anybody miss me?' I call out.

Then I rip open the long overcoat and strike a glamor pose in my sheer chemise, garter belt, and silk stockings.

A loud cheer erupts from the lieutenant playing a soulful melody, while the other officer is passed out on the divan. The quiet blonde girl is nowhere to be seen, and Karl is tying the white ribbon around the brunette's bare thigh, her dress hiked up to her waist. His trousers are half buttoned – and an empty champagne bottle lies nearby.

'*Liebling!* You look *magnificent. Heil Hitler!*' Karl slurs his words as he makes the Nazi salute and – hard to imagine his short blond haircut looks askew but it does – makes a grab for me. 'Come join us.'

With the agility of an overfed, fat lion, he attempts to get to his feet, at the same time displacing the also drunk brunette from the divan and tossing her onto the parquet floor with a loud *thump*. She's so shocked, she runs to the WC.

I find the moment comical but resist the urge to laugh and go straight for my target – the very drunk SS officer, panting and desperate to get his hands on me.

'Karl, *chéri*, what you need is another drink.'

'What I need is *you, Liebling.*'

I open the vodka and he guzzles it down straight from the bottle while he stares at my cleavage. His eyes bug out as I drop the strap, revealing the curve of my breast. He's salivating, his eyes glued to my perky nipple pushing through the silk, but that's as far as I'm willing to go.

'Why don't you finish the bottle, *Liebling,* then we'll...' I coax him with a promise I never intend to keep. Eyes glassy, tongue hanging out, Karl obliges me with the determination of a field general, but even the staunchest member of the SS can't handle the amount of liquor he's imbibed tonight.

Ogling my bare back as I stand up and shimmy my hips back and forth until he's dizzy watching me, the happy and contented lion exhales a long, heavy sigh—

And passes out.

So ends the strangest night of my life.

* * *

Only the upper class of Parisian society have the funds to travel and pretend there isn't a war on. In the weeks that follow after I secure Jock in my apartment in the Faubourg Saint-Antoine, we do the same. We have no choice but to escape the city. It's too dangerous for Bertrand to orchestrate the journey to the Spanish border.

Although I find no joy in recent events, a part of me is secretly happy we have time together to pick up where we left off before the war. Also, it's a time of respite for me after the grueling filming on my Versailles film.

I talk Karl into allowing me the use of my red Bugatti, complaining about my bad back after my fall and telling him I need a rest in the country. He's so smitten with me after what happened that night, he signs the requisition order without question. He regrets he can't accompany me, but there's some nasty business at a concentration camp he must attend to and he won't be back in Paris for an indeterminate time. He admits he doesn't remember every detail of that night. I have the feeling he's convinced *more* happened between us than did. Since I have the feeling he became intimate with the brunette while I was gone and won't remember *who* he made love to, I let him believe it.

Of course, I don't tell Jock that.

We drive to Marly-le-Roi outside Paris to the same small *hostellerie* where we stayed before the war. I find our return here amusing since close by in St Germain-en-Laye is the head of the Nazi Wehrmacht. Throughout our stay here in late summer 1943, he never finds out an RAF pilot is right next door. I have fond memories of that time we spent here after meeting in Monte Carlo back in 1938. A fun, sensuous time when we carried on our love affair, yet knowing we could never marry because of our backgrounds.

Him a royal. Me the illegitimate child of a prostitute.

A sunny interlude brings us out on the restaurant terrace, a plate of local grown fruit, cheese rich and smooth from a nearby farm... you'd never know there's a war on until the talk turns to what might have been. Jock creases his forehead. 'I often wonder what would have happened between us if Hitler hadn't invaded Poland.'

'I'm not sure it would have changed anything, *mon chéri*. We're from different worlds.' I grab a handful of grapes. My eyes never leave his.

He picks off a plump grape and swallows it, mulling over what he wants to say. 'I had my bags packed and a flight to Paris booked when news of the invasion came.'

'You never told me, Jock,' I say in a hushed whisper. My throat is tight.

'I kept telling myself the war would be over in a few months and we'd be together again.' He leans toward me and cups my chin. 'I love you, Sylvie, more than ever. I can't think about being with anyone else.' His expression of love changes to frustration. 'My plans went to hell when my political cronies kept pressuring me to acquire a wife and family to complete my image as a peer in Parliament. So many times I wanted to toss it all away and come back to you. Then Mother took a turn for the worse and Winnie ended up marrying a Churchill cousin.'

My heart cries for his *maman* and overflows with happiness for Winnie.

His next words are sobering.

'I couldn't jeopardize my family's position by seeing you again.'

'All that's in the past, Jock. All that matters is we're together now.'

'When the war is over, I don't care *where* you come from and hang what my stodgy political friends think. I'm going to marry you.'

'You really mean it, don't you?' I manage, struggling to contain the unexpected joy in my heart.

'Yes. Winnie will insist on being your maid of honor,' Jock tells me as we abandon the terrace for a walk through the wooded grounds across from the *hostellerie* named after the Sun King. 'She adores you, Sylvie.'

'As much as you do, Jock?' I ask, squeezing his hand.

'No one could love you like I do, *mon bel ange.* I regret I didn't see sooner how wrong I was to keep to tradition, Sylvie. Forget all that pompous nonsense. These past few days have taught me I want to be with you, build a life together.' He holds me tight, shielding me from the war everywhere around us, saying what he has to say to me before the day comes and he must leave Paris. 'Promise you'll marry me, Sylvie?'

'This is my answer, *mon chéri.*'

And here in the wooded forest where royals once romped and played games, kissed and flirted, I kiss *my* royal, not giving a damn if the whole German Army marches through here. It's my turn. We're betrothed like so many of the historical heroines I've played.

Marriage. The thing I've dreamed about since Monte Carlo.

Is it possible?

Then a child... I sigh with pleasure, remembering everything passionate, thrilling, and wonderful about our nights together here. A dream fulfilled between satin sheets.

Mais oui, a baby is *very* possible.

* * *

Keeping Jock safe at my Faubourg apartment when we return to Paris opens up a new stage for me over the coming weeks. I become more involved in the Resistance. Delivering coded messages to my unit regarding German troop movements, names of political prisoners being transported out of Paris (Bertrand and his men saved a renowned French chemist from execution because I told them the route they were taking, thanks to an evening at a cabaret with Karl and a talkative colonel), even the hiding place of several pieces of art looted from a Jewish banker. I will always be thankful to Bertrand for trusting me that night to introduce me to his friends. They have no idea it's Sylvie Martone who is privy to café talks with SS officers. I dine at the Hôtel Ritz, and I often eavesdrop on Nazis who've taken up residence in my Trocadéro neighborhood.

The members of the Resistance don't know where my information comes from, but my intelligence is good, my loyalty to France profound, and I can tell a whale of a story to keep them laughing.

On the other hand, as Fantine, I can infiltrate places the actress Sylvie Martone can't go. Shops where German military wives frequent. Cafés, hair salons, open markets. I pass on valuable information to the Resistance about the Gestapo's nefarious comings and goings.

That's the part I *can* control.

What I *can't* control is Jock. He won't stay put, wanders around Paris in his 'French disguise', making me fear someone will get suspicious and turn him in. There's always an informer on every block, someone you can't trust, and that worries me.

He insists on becoming more involved in his own escape plans, so I put on my Fantine disguise (which he finds amusing and keeps calling me *madame)* and introduce him to Raoul. He's been helping Bertrand with hiding refugees and securing intelligence, with Halette acting as his courier. As the post-production on *Le Masque de Velours de Versailles* wraps up, I miss them more than ever, but we decide it's best if Raoul and his daughter don't return to Paris.

I send them whatever information I can glean from Karl. I'm saddened by the news I deliver that Raoul's brother-in-law was arrested by French police. He was out past curfew (eight o'clock for Jews) and rounded up. When the French police found out he was on the Gestapo's wanted list, he was sent to a concentration camp. The man was a miscreant, but I regret not saving him. It never gets easier seeing anyone snatched up in the web of the Gestapo. Crew members, neighbors... disappearing without a trace. Jock tries to console me, saying it's not my fault. Still, I swear I'll help as many people as I can. I haven't gotten over the roundup last year, mostly Jewish women and children. I'll always wonder if there was something I could have done, what happened to them, where they were sent.

When a reorganized escape line opens up, Jock wants to get back into the cockpit but he stays back to help secure passage to the Spanish border for his fellow downed fliers. RAF, Canadian, American. Then he receives word from London via a cryptic radio broadcast on *London Calling Europe*: 'The duke and his friend the baroness are summering in France instead of returning to Cornwall', code for meaning he and his French agent, Fantine, are doing great work and Jock is to remain in Paris.

Even the best laid plans of spies can go awry...

When my film *Le Masque de Velours de Versailles* opens in Paris in fall 1943, I receive word from Bertrand that Jock is in danger if he returns to my apartment in the Faubourg Saint-Antoine after his latest mission.

I have to warn him right under the nose of the SS.

28

JULIANA

THOSE OLD, FAMILIAR PARISIAN PLACES

Ville Canfort-Terre, France
Present Day

I believe Sylvie's fantastic story about how she joined the Resistance and created Fantine, about spies and counterspies, but will anyone else?

I need to find someone who can corroborate her story.

I confer with Sister Rose-Celine.

The sister disappeared for a while this afternoon as I was listening to Sylvie's story about how she and Jock put one over on the SS officer Karl. When she returned, the nun was smiling and beaming, her round cheeks pink and flushed. She mumbled she found something she'd lost. When I asked her what it was, she clammed up tighter than her wimple.

'Is there anyone in the village, a daughter or granddaughter of someone who knew Sylvie during the war?' I ask her. Someone who heard different stories than those circulated about *ma grand-mère* collaborating with the enemy.

She nods. '*Oui*, Sylvie did receive one visitor,' Sister Rose-Celine tells me. 'Sister Vincent was nervous the whole time the young woman was here, the daughter of an old friend Sylvie knew from her days as an actress, she told me, and that I was to say nothing to anyone. She brought her daughter, who was about three years old, with her.' She put her hand to her mouth. '*Mon Dieu*, could it have been—?'

'Yes, it must have been Halette. She survived the war and had a child.' I hug the sister and she smiles, holding her rosary close to her chest. She knows what's on my mind and she's praying for me. What the sister doesn't know is...

I have a secret weapon.

Ridge.

He has extensive connections in France at different film studios. It doesn't take him long to trace the daughter of Raoul Monteux through official records and accreditations of film projects written by French film screenwriters. He's certain she's still in Paris, but won't tell me where until he can verify the information. I'm hoping Halette's daughter may have diaries, letters, anything that will help prove Sylvie's innocence. '

I'm off to Paris tomorrow to find her.

* * *

'So, my taco-loving friend,' I begin, calling Ridge on my cell when I arrive in Paris, 'did you track down Halette?'

It's early in Los Angeles, but Ridge is expecting my call. I imagine he's at the gym, which brings up a sexy image of him working out. I need to keep reminding myself we're best buds, though my heart is questioning why I won't admit I want more.

I push my longings aside and grab the *croque-monsieur* I ordered at a sidewalk café. I had a chilling moment when I sat down, wondering if German soldiers sat at this table with Sylvie, ogling her and drinking beer. Whimsy on my part, but her story has affected me so I see her everywhere. Movie theaters, especially.

'You sound cheery this morning,' he teases.

'I am. I'm talking to you.'

Slow down, girl. Ridge will get the wrong idea.

I become sober for a moment, reflecting on what I've learnt, seen, and heard during this strange journey with Sylvie. 'Oh, if you only knew what the French people suffered under the Nazis. It makes me so grateful for everything I have...'

'I *have* heard the stories. The camps, the starvation, the beatings.' He takes a moment. 'Your journey to unravel Sylvie's past has changed us both, Juliana.'

'The journey's not over...' I mumble something that won't incriminate me because I'm seeing a new side of Ridge that warms my soul and I like it.

We both leave so much unsaid. They'll be time for us to reflect on what happened during the war. It means so much more to us now than before. I'm ashamed I was so ignorant of what went on during the Occupation of Paris. How the Jewish people suffered and the Resistance saved so many downed fliers. I hope I can find some way when I return home to pay tribute to Sylvie and everyone involved.

I listen to what Ridge has uncovered about Halette's exact whereabouts.

'You won't believe this, Juliana. After the war, Halette settled in at the apartment in the Faubourg Saint-Antoine where Sylvie once lived.'

'No... that's incredible. What happened to Raoul?'

'No one knows. He disappeared in 1943.'

A heavy sigh escapes me. 'That's around the time of the last recording I listened to from Sylvie.'

I have a feeling when I hear more tapes, it won't be good news. I don't say it. Not till I know for sure.

'Halette's daughter still lives there,' Ridge continues. 'Sylvie made certain Halette received the deed in her name.'

* * *

'I'm sorry, *mademoiselle*, my mother never talked about the war or Sylvie Martone.'

Halette's daughter, Denise, is in her seventies, a delicate-boned Frenchwoman with a silver pageboy bob.

'Do you believe Sylvie collaborated with the Nazis?' I ask her in French, grateful I find Halette's daughter at home in the Faubourg. It's exactly as Sylvie described it with the blue door, the ivy, even the swinging iron gate. I get chills just being here. When I showed her the glam photo *Maman* left me showing Sylvie in the white evening gown, she invited me in.

'Why are you asking these questions, *mademoiselle*?' Hands clenched, her mood is defensive. 'Are you writing a book?'

I sit for a moment, my mind stilled by her question, wondering if I'm doing the right thing by coming here, if this elegant woman will understand my urgent need to right what I believe is a wrong. If she'll insist I don't dig up the past and send me on my way.

I have to take that chance.

'No... I – I want to clear my *grand-mère's* name.'

'Strange you should say that.' She relaxes, her fingers unclenching. 'I often wondered when I was growing up what the real story was.' Denise shuffles through books and magazines on her bookshelf and way in the back she pulls out a worn, deep blue scrapbook. 'I was a teenager when I found my mother's film star scrapbook filled with pictures of Sylvie Martone. I kept it along with other teenage souvenirs.' She opens the book filled with the stories and photos from *Ciné-Miroir* Sylvie talks about on the recordings. 'The captions written on the pages never made any sense to me.'

My heart stops. They do to me.

I explain to Denise the captions written underneath the photos and stories from the magazines mirror the events Sylvie spoke about in her recordings.

Notations about her movements as Fantine, though Halette didn't know about her disguise. She knew only that Sylvie was helping the Resistance.

'Dates, meeting places...' I tell her, pointing them out. 'For example, *Aux Deux Magots 13 September 1943. Aux Trois Quartiers 21 November 1943.*

Then initials beside the dates. Code I imagine for the fliers they helped to orchestrate their departure from Paris along the escape line. Sylvie must have trusted Halette to enlist her help when she needed it, to keep this record for her where the Gestapo would never look, and then made her promise never to speak about it.' I give her a grateful smile. 'Your mother kept her word.'

Denise insists I take the scrapbook with me and kisses me on both cheeks. I see her eyes grow misty as I thank her and we promise to keep in touch.

I head back to the convent, thrilled I'm on the right track. I feel confident Sylvie's story is true. A scrapbook filled with cryptic notations is helpful, but it isn't enough to clear her.

What now?

29

SYLVIE

NINE MONTHS... AND COUNTING

Paris
1943

I've never felt so scared as I do that day in the Faubourg when I leave the yellow daffodils for Fantine, scared not only for Jock but for my baby.

Because of my desperation to save him, I almost lose the child.

I act carefree and happy like a glamorous film star should, strong and confident, not backing down when Karl tries to control me, but I'm merely acting the part. If the truth be known, that flighty woman in the red peplum dress and black Fedora I show to Karl, my Faubourg neighbors... *everyone* – is scared out of her wits. Everything is too crazy, too frantic, the danger coming at me when I'm most vulnerable, everything hitting me at once. I must keep up the ruse that Fantine is a real person I hired. It's not easy being two people at the same time. Especially when we're both pregnant. I keep putting off starting another film, telling Emil the stress of Herr Geller watching my every move and Karl making more demands on me is making me rundown, nauseous. For the first time in my life, I have no script to follow. I've always had a script in my head, a way of coping when I feet anxious, threatened.

Not today.

After I drop off the daffodils, *Le Grand Rex* overflows with Nazi brass when we arrive in Karl's Mercedes staff car, people booing at us. They're quickly dispersed by rifle-pointing German soldiers, but the effect lingers in my heart. What I find so disheartening is these same people will clamor to see the film next week, but their open disapproval of me here is a stab to my heart that hits me hard.

I stumble through the evening, the endless chatter in the lobby, Emil hobnobbing with the top brass, my co-stars posing for pictures, the photographers flitting around like worker bees for the Party, snapping shot after shot of me posing with so many officers in uniform, they all blur.

I beg off with a smile, retreating to a corner when a prickly jab hits me in the lower belly. Subtle at first, then intensifies. I shrug it off. Nerves.

A bell rings, calling us inside the theater like we're attending a grand opera.

A sarcastic smile crosses my lips as Karl escorts me to my seat.

The tension escalates when I find myself seated next to a sleazy general with grabby hands, pushing up my skirt when the credits roll. Running his hand up and down my thigh in the darkened theater. Snapping my garters against my skin. Whispering how lucky Karl is and why don't the three of us have dinner at the Hôtel Ritz after the film and then who knows...?

Disgust fills me. Two Exit lights are out, so the theater is darker than usual. Karl is not privy to my dilemma. Even if he was, I doubt he'd do more than scowl. Cross the general, he warned me earlier, and I'll find myself having a long conversation on Avenue Foch. My body makes an impassioned plea to get this creep off me, but I risk offending the military man. He's a decorated hero from the Siege of Warsaw, Karl whispers in my ear. Thinking about the horror this Nazi inflicted on those innocent people sends me into a state of panic. My body reeks of female hormones in overdrive, spiking from mixing with my spicy perfume. I'm flushed, my skin catching fire every time the Nazi rubs his thumb against my inner thigh.

I feel sick.

Horribly sick.

The jab in my belly hits me so hard I double over.

I want to retch all over his hated, grey-green uniform, but I'm no fool. Karl will insist I see a doctor, then they'll be questions I refuse to answer. Karl will be shocked then... *pleased*? Whatever *didn't* happen between us that night at my Trocadéro apartment won't matter.

He'll think it did.

And I'll be more of a prisoner to the Nazi ideal of womanhood than I am now because everyone will believe I'm carrying an Aryan child.

I work myself up into such a state, I don't see it coming, don't want to admit pregnancy brings a whole new set of rules to my game of espionage. I can't let go of my fear for Jock. I nearly gave myself away earlier when I found the note slipped under my plate at the café.

Yellow. Danger.

I was trapped.

I risked Karl's anger if I feigned a headache. Insisted he take me home so I could sneak out and wait for Jock to show up at my place in the Faubourg. His ego reigns supreme in his decisions. He'd never escape the reprimand from his superiors, not to mention jibes from fellow officers, if he couldn't produce the glamorous star of the film. So I made the daring decision to leave the flowers. The yellow daffodils are meant to warn Jock to stay in hiding and not make his way to the train station tonight to meet up with a *résistant* to escort him to the pickup point.

A Gestapo stooge will be waiting for him instead.

The Germans found out about the mission from a partisan they turned, a man as French as his beret who knows the streets and cafés of Paris so well, he was never suspected by his fellow *résistants*. Bertrand unearthed the informant who sold his soul to the Nazis for promise of a grand sum of money he planned to use for his own escape.

He won't have need of francs now. He met an untimely end for his betrayal.

All I can think about is, *is Jock safe*? Did he get the message?

When will I know? We said our goodbyes earlier. What am I saying? We've been saying goodbye since he first showed up at my apartment. We knew this day would come, but I keep to the faith he'll be safe... now I don't know. I didn't tell him about the baby... why give him more to worry about?

Then the pain jabs me again. I groan. Dizziness hits me. Hard.

I'm fidgeting with the peplum on my skirt, my knees tightly closed, trying to concentrate on the dueling scene in the picture when I take down the pirate captain who kidnapped my little sister when I keel over.

For real.

The last thing I remember is landing face down in the general's lap.

* * *

'A brilliant stunt, Sylvie,' Emil says, wiping my brow with a towel. 'Everyone's talking about it.'

'*Ooh*, what happened?' I moan, trying to sit up. I'm lying down on the divan in the powder room, alone with Emil. He told the press I'm suffering from exhaustion and shooed Karl and the general out of the room, insisting I need air.

A chilly breeze blows through the tiny window high about my head.

I need more than air. I need a doctor.

The dizziness abates, but there's an unsettledness within me, a trembling that tells me I've pushed my body to the limit.

'Don't try to fool me, Sylvie. I saw the distress on your face when you arrived and glanced over the unfriendly crowd. You pulled off this charade to gain sympathy so the press will write about how hard Sylvie Martone is working to make wonderful pictures for the French people. How much she loves them.'

I can't stop breathing heavy. 'I *did* faint, Emil, but not because I need good publicity.'

'Then why...?'

'I'm pregnant.'

* * *

Telling Emil about my condition could have been either a complete lapse of judgment or the best move I made tonight.

Fortunately, it's the latter because he takes me to a 'friend' in a quiet neighborhood not far my apartment in the Trocadéro who looks me over in the back room of his clinic. The physician works at the American Hospital in Paris and is an old friend of Emil's, having financed several of his pet film projects in better days. Seems the wily director has a redeeming quality in that cold heart of his. He brings the doctor much needed medical supplies he purchases on the black market.

I can't ask him why and blow my cover, though I suspect the doctor has been helping patch up wounded 'evaders'. All that filters through my mind is what the friendly physician with a penchant for wearing a monocle tells me.

'Nothing to worry about, *mademoiselle*.' He smiles and I believe him. 'You've been working too hard and under extreme duress. From what I can tell, your pregnancy is progressing normally. I would suggest you make regular visits here to the clinic so we can prepare to deliver your baby in a discreet manner.'

I want to cry. I've been worried about what to do, praying I could find a midwife somewhere outside the city where I can hide out when the time comes. All I can do is nod.

'My advice is to stay off your feet as much as possible and eat a good diet rich in iron.' He sighs heavily. 'Not easy to do in Paris these days, I'm afraid.'

'I'll find a way.' I can't tell him I dine on the best cuisine in the city, that to my fans I'm a Nazi sympathizer.

Then, as if he reads my mind, he takes my hand in his. 'I know who you are, *Mademoiselle* Martone,' he says in a voice low and comforting. 'I also know what you did for the family of a former patient of mine. Her husband is a screenwriter you've worked with. I attended to his wife until the end.'

No names.

No judgment.

Of course. Raoul. I wonder how the doctor found out. I don't believe Emil told him. The director suspects I'm involved with the Resistance, but he'd rather look the other way to protect himself should he ever end up in a Gestapo kitchen.

If he knows nothing, he can tell them nothing.

I smile as I pat my stomach and say a little prayer of thanks for my baby, then whisper, '*Bonne nuit, mon enfant.*' I bid *adieu* to the doctor, promising to make regular visits to the three-story house surrounded by well-tended rose bushes. In disguise, of course. We're not far from Avenue Foch.

Emil drives me back to my Trocadéro apartment in a black Mercedes coupe he commandeered from the general with the excuse of taking me home so he and his staff could enjoy the rest of the picture.

'Tell me, Sylvie,' Emil says, never taking his eyes off the road, 'who is the father?'

* * *

My so-called 'fainting stunt' works.

Parisians attend showings of *Le Masque de Velours de Versailles* in record numbers throughout the city *and* the suburbs. Prints are smuggled across the border and into the Unoccupied Zone. Emil is thrilled, excited, and doesn't ask me again who the father of my baby is. I gave him an evasive answer that night, citing his credo of preferring not to know anything about my nocturnal activities.

Which gives me breathing room.

I admit I find the rest rejuvenating, my body changing in ways I never imagine, including a tummy bulge I proudly look at in the mirror each morning. The looking glass is the only witness to my daily ritual. I keep my visit to the physician to myself. No one but Emil knows about my pregnancy.

I'm worried about Jock. Bertrand tells me when the French police found the body of the informant and reported the incident to the Gestapo, their plan was foiled. This allowed the formation of a new plan where the downed flier or 'evader' is moved from house to house using numerous hidden tunnels under the closed cinema until the evening of their departure.

For Jock, it's tonight.

I have to see him, though I have brief contact with members of the Resistance at meetings. Always in hushed whispers, me as Fantine, as new plans are discussed, then changed and changed again. Tonight, I listen intently, looking at Jock when the lights dim, knowing though I can't see his face clearly, he's watching me, too. Then I close my eyes and lovely images of the two of us at Monte Carlo, Marly-le-Roi, and my place in the Faubourg flash before me like a montage of film clips. When the night is so still and the sky a deep purple holding up the stars, a scene so vivid and intense, I feel his body moving against mine...

'It's time, Fantine.'

I open my eyes. It's Bertrand.

I nod.

I wrap my long flowing veil around my head and shoulders and without another word, another look, we prepare to head for Gare d'Austerlitz for the evening train to Toulouse.

'The lieutenant is going with you two,' Bertrand announces before we leave. A sheepish young man, who looks like he should be attending university, gives us a salute. Canadian, we're told.

I'm to accompany Jock and the downed airman to the meetup point where they'll be met by a local guide. He'll take them over the high Pyrenees and sometimes hostile terrain to the Spanish border and from there to Gibraltar.

Then to London.

This isn't the first time I've made the train trip with Allied airmen. But this is the man I love. I know the Foreign Office is anxious to have him back in England. He hints there's talk of him returning as an SOE – Special Operations Executive – agent and parachuting back into France. I can't think about that now. I want to go with him tonight in spite of the danger.

We trek to the train station in the dark, hiding in alcoves, crossing the Boulevard Saint-Germain then making a sharp left on Rue Dante and continuing along the Seine to the station in case anyone is following us.

I forgo the limp.

We need to move fast and if the Canadian thinks anything is amiss, he doesn't mention it.

Once aboard the train we take seats in close proximity and since it's late, not many passengers are interested in chatter. It seems longer than the nearly seven hours before we reach Toulouse. A difficult length of time for my two compatriots to keep quiet.

Especially Jock.

He mumbles a few words in French that mean nothing to anyone but me. My eyes *shush* him. It's too dangerous. The Canadian smiles. I suspect he's catching on to our game, though I imagine he's wondering how such a dashing RAF pilot could be flirting with a dispassionate French woman with the sex appeal of a snapping turtle.

A German officer saunters by, giving everyone surly looks if for nothing else than to make himself look important. When he asks the Canadian a question, Jock answers for him. Curt. Not too friendly, indicating the boy is mute.

I grin. I'm always surprised why the German soldiers on board the trains never wonder why so many 'Frenchmen' are hard of hearing when asked a question in French or mute. Then the German turns his attention to me. He runs his fingers along my lace veil trailing on the floor of the railway car. It slipped off my shoulders.

'This would make a beautiful gift for a pretty *mamselle* I know in Paris,' he says in broken French. 'How much, *madame?*'

Which means he wants to confiscate it in the name of the Reich.

Jock jumps to my defense. 'You should have more respect for a woman her age, *monsieur*,' he tells the Nazi in French. 'A woman disabled with a limp.'

If the situation weren't so frightening, I'd let go with a chuckle.

But I'm worried.

I love this darling man for coming to my defense, but few if any of the men I escort speak the language well enough to be a local. I imagine a missed idiom or two flies right over the Nazi's head. Still, we can't take that chance, so I always advise them not to speak.

Jock just broke that rule.

I pray we don't pay for it.

The Nazi officer is the only German in the railcar and is none too happy when the rest of the passengers rile up against him.

'*Have you no heart,* monsieur? *Harassing an old lady.*'

'Bien. *She could be your mother...*'

'*It's cruel to take the scarf from her when you Nazis have already taken so much.*'

A daring truth, but the Boche wants no trouble and, with hunched shoulders, moves quickly down the aisle and onto the next railcar.

This is the first time I see a German officer back down.

Outnumbered, I suppose. His Nazi pride wounded.

It's a small victory in a war that still must be won.

When the train stops, we get off at the station and we move quickly to the meetup point – a safe house I've been to before – and here I must say *adieu*. I grab the basket of food and water left for me before I catch the next train back to Paris. A chance then to close my eyes and rest and dream of him. Till I board that train, I must keep my identity secret, but nothing could have prepared me for this moment. We can't go off alone together to say our goodbyes. What if we're seen? Jock and I stand at a distance from each other, leaning inward, our body language speaking volumes. We can't kiss goodbye, hold hands, *anything* lovers do when they're being torn from each other for what they believe will be the duration of the war.

'*Merci, madame*, for your help,' Jock says, exhaling loudly. I see the love in his eyes for me.

I want to say *something* that will let him know how I feel. Give him a memory that will always be in his heart no matter what happens. Something so strong, he won't have to think, just feel and he'll remember this moment.

I pat my stomach and his eyes widen, amazed.

I smile. It couldn't have been any clearer that I'm pregnant.

30

SYLVIE

A PERILOUS JOURNEY INTO ENEMY TERRITORY

Berlin

1944

The Nazis lied when they said Berlin was as beautiful as Paris.

It's not.

Bien, Berlin has the Hotel Adlon across from the Brandenburg Gate where the posh society people and foreign diplomats hang out. And a palace or two still standing that haven't been bombed by the RAF.

It also has the Reichstag, the Parliament building that burnt down after Hitler came to power. I wonder if it will suffer a similar fate when the Allies and the Soviets reach Berlin.

Meanwhile, I'm stuck here in this city with more Nazis than I ever want to see for the rest of my life. Marching, goose-stepping, crowding everywhere.

I hate it.

But I have no choice.

My world is turned upside down when I'm invited – no, *ordered* – by Emil, with Herr Geller breathing down his neck, to Berlin on a touring excursion to promote my Versailles film with German subtitles. I've resisted going on one of these junkets – Goebbels' idea to show off

French *artistes* – but Herr Geller requested me personally. I can't afford to invite scrutiny from the Gestapo and jeopardize my work with the Resistance.

Besides, my soul is in limbo with Jock gone.

Doing his part with the RAF.

Here in Berlin, I'm doing mine. *If* my grand idea works...

I grit my teeth, holding a bouquet of red roses thrust upon me by the president of the German Cinema *Abteilung*, pushing down my volatile emotions as I smile for the camera and wave to the crowd swarming our entourage of French *artistes*.

Three actresses.

And a male crooner.

All playing our part for the Reich. Just planting those hated words in my head makes me die inside. But I'm here and I have to make the most of it, trying out German phrases from the pamphlet the studio publicity department provided to connect to the 'locals', if not for anything else but to keep up my cover.

And, I admit, checking the lens on the hidden movie camera in my traveling bag, to do a little spying. Daring or stupid? Both, I suppose, but I'm an actress. I've been making films since I was sixteen. I live, *breathe*, filmmaking. I can't let the opportunity pass by to film what I see here in a city that proudly states it's been 'cleansed of Jews'. What strikes me as odd is the nonchalance of the populace. Young people queuing up to see my film seem oblivious to what's happened. They become more upset when during a showing, the film is stopped for a temporary cut in the power. Yet they show little understanding when I ask in a casual manner in German while I'm signing autographs if they miss their Jewish friends. Blank stares, an occasional show of concern. One girl looked genuinely horrified I would ask such a question and warned me in high school French the Gestapo could be listening.

I imagine the newsreels show me all smiles as I visit Berlin movie theaters and wave to adoring fans, but I have little tolerance for this phony world the Nazi High Command has created. How they can keep the people so blindly in line frightens me. Yet aren't they doing the same in Paris? We have the Resistance, I remind myself, and word reached us in Paris last year about an Underground movement here in Germany led by students till it was quashed.

There must be more *résistants* in Berlin... who knows what they're planning?

I pull my autumn haze mink coat tighter around me to keep out the chill that makes my heart shrivel with sadness. Yes, mink. And a stylish mink hat to go with it, courtesy of the studio wardrobe department. To keep their star warm and cozy in the cold Berlin weather? I doubt it. More likely to keep up appearances in front of a foreign audience.

The voluminous coat with its high collar has the added benefit of concealing my pregnancy, but it can't protect me in case of another RAF attack.

The irony is, I could be killed in my sleep, bombed by a pilot I saved.

Which is why I have to film as much of the city as I can. Whatever I capture on film could be helpful to the Allies.

Buildings... burnt and bombed by the RAF at night.

Buildings still standing... ready to be bombed.

I'm pleased with how Bertrand and I accented my carryall tote bag with large, glass buttons. One of the buttons is a round hole, exposing the camera lens of my 16mm home movie camera hidden inside the bag. Whenever I want to record, I pull on the hanging chain with the long, decorative cord and point the camera. I'm never sure if I've got the focus right and the windup power supply causes me moments of panic when I forget if I wound it or not (I blame that on 'pregnancy fog').

Then our journey is cut short due to weather. It's not *that* cold. I imagine our early departure has something to do with what Bertrand told me before I left Paris.

The rumor is the Americans will soon begin the daylight bombing of Berlin.

I can't say I'm sorry to leave, though we escaped the embarrassment of an unpleasant lunch with Goebbels. It's been canceled. Unfortunately, I've used up less than half the film. I've had a few missteps. I bemuse the fact I may be a good actress, but I'm not the best camera-man. I thought I was filming Nazi officials huddled together in a brief argument in the theater lobby and I wanted to chronicle their presence in Berlin, thinking it might be useful to the Resistance, when I realized I didn't wind it up.

I got nothing.

We board the private railcar to take us back to Paris, each of us lost in our thoughts about what we'd seen in Berlin. The indifference of the German youth to anything not in their world, and how the older people blotted out what they didn't want to see... the salutation to der Fuehrer ringing in our ears everywhere we went. Even if we wanted to discuss what we saw, we won't. Not here, but privately, when we're behind closed doors. I should be filming what I see out the window as the train speeds by the countryside, but I'm exhausted. I've got shooting pains in my swollen feet from so much walking and my lower back has had better days. I'm not complaining. I'm grateful to be returning to Paris which seems like an oasis after what I've seen in Berlin.

The Nazi officer in charge (treating us like we're a nuisance he'd like to be rid of) keeps the temperature warm in the railcar. I keep my mink coat on in an effort to hide my starting-to-show baby tummy. Closing my eyes, I settle back in the royal blue velvet seat and dream of Jock and me, a loving moment I allow myself, letting my mind wander, a place not even the Gestapo can peek into—

When the locomotive whistle blasts loudly in my ears and the train screeches to a halt.

Shaking us awake.

Sending us to the windows to see what's happened.

'Where are we?' I ask the Nazi officer in charge.

'A most distressing incident has forced the train to stop near the French–German border, *mademoiselle*,' he answers me in French.

'Mechanical problem?' I prod him.

The Nazi officer, a nervous, young lieutenant who keeps checking his watch, blurts out without apology, 'We've been inconvenienced because of a boxcar of dirty Jews.'

I clench my fists to my side, all the anger building inside of me coming to a head.

'They're human beings, Lieutenant,' I tell him point blank, poking my head out the window. I see where the train ahead of us broke down, leaving a rustic-brown, closed boxcar with four tiny windows on the side sitting idle on the tracks.

'Are they, *mademoiselle*?' he says, smug.

I hesitate to make myself a target. A sudden bout of dizziness reminds me I have my baby to think about, but his superior attitude angers me. 'How can you be so sure who's in that boxcar?' I ask. 'I don't see anyone.'

'You have my word as a German officer of the Reich, I've seen many such boxcars and they are *all* filled with Jewish, Romany, and political prisoners.'

A roundup from outlying towns, no doubt, like we had in Paris in 1942.

'Where are they going?' I have to ask. I can't let this go. I have an idea.

'If you must be so curious, *mademoiselle*, they're on their way to a concentration camp where they will work for der Fuehrer.'

He means death camp, the coward.

'What about giving them food, water...?'

His brows shoot up in surprise. 'Jews are not entitled to such privileges.'

I can't believe what he's saying in that cold, nasal tone, what horrors await those poor people.

I take a bold step I can't take back. 'I want to see for myself.'

He's as surprised as I am by my brashness, but he doesn't stop me when I grab my tote bag with my hidden camera and get off the train. Why I don't go back to my seat and my lovely dream, I don't know. I feel compelled to do something, though I'm shaking all over, sweating in spite of my fur coat. The other members of my troupe watch me with disbelief, the lieutenant warning me to hurry. A seven-seat staff car is being dispatched for us from a nearby Nazi command post and will be here in precisely ten minutes, he says, tapping his watch.

'German efficiency at work,' I mutter under my breath.

I remind him I'm an important film star and his personal responsibility. That doesn't sit well with him, but I've made my play.

An unforgiving, cold wind is at my back when I make my way down the three railcar steps, but my determination to record this first-hand account of what the Nazi officer admitted were inhumane conditions takes me out of myself. I become the conduit for what I believe is an important visual document.

I freeze when I hear the screaming, the crying coming from inside the boxcar... crushing my soul with the incessant wailing that will haunt my dreams for the rest of my life. And the smell. A decisive blow to my senses I never would have imagined. Human fear mixed with lost hope and unwashed flesh. A stink so profound it's gone straight up my nostrils, bringing on a headache so blinding I can't think.

Go back, go back!

I can't, I won't.

I've led men to freedom, risked my life. I can do this.

Ignoring the muddy terrain around the railcar, I inch closer, my black suede pumps sinking into the goo. As I make my way, I hold my tote bag steady and, with a careful tug on the chain, I secretly film what I see.

Hands reaching through the four small, broken windows on one side of the boxcar. Tossing scraps of paper onto the ground.

So many hands, so many stories, each one heartbreaking.

I can tell it for them. My camera doesn't record sound, but I believe anyone who sees this film will 'hear' their anguished voices pleading for mercy.

Minutes tick by... I'm well aware the lieutenant is watching me.

I imagine his obsession with efficiency overrules his curiosity. *A frivolous French actress without a brain*, I can hear him recount later to his beer-drinking buddies.

I move closer, trying to get a better shot—

'*Halt, Fräulein!*'

I do nothing. No doubt I've been spotted by a German guard from the transport train. Any quick movement could be my last.

I turn around... slowly... and come face to face with a disgusting German sergeant. Pudgy, gross manners. He yells at me to go away while brandishing his Luger at me.

I grin slightly... hoping what I do next works. I give him what I call my 'Hollywood wave', putting him off balance while my secret camera keeps filming.

'*Bonjour, bonjour!*'

The man has no idea who I am, but he's not fool enough to shoot a snoopy Frenchwoman in a mink coat. Not when he sees a big, silver Mercedes touring car race to the scene and screech to a halt nearby. No doubt this is the vehicle the lieutenant mentioned.

He lowers his weapon, clicks his heels, and gives me the '*Heil Hitler!*' salute. Then he walks away. I nearly faint with relief.

And have a surprising moment that warms me in spite of the cold.

My baby kicks.

I'm imagining it, but it's a good feeling that stays with me. In my haste to get to the waiting motorcar, I underestimate the usefulness of high heels in mud. I take a few steps when I notice scraps of paper sticking to my shoes. *The notes from the prisoners.* A sense of duty overtakes me and I gather up as many as I can and stick them in my suit jacket pocket. I reach down for more when I stumble, almost dropping my tote holding the hidden camera.

Oh, no... no!

Before I can contemplate the foolishness of my action, I hear the tramping of boots running up behind me and in a shocking moment, the dutiful lieutenant grabs me from behind and picks me up in his arms. I can't express the panic that races through me.

Thank God I didn't drop the bag and lose my camera.

The lieutenant grunts, not expecting to find a *zaftig Fräulein* in his arms. He wobbles, steadies himself, and I do my best not to grin. With

the heavy mink coat and the kilograms I've put on during my pregnancy, he's huffing and puffing by the time we get to the touring car.

Der Fuehrer's army isn't in the shape it should be.

I thank the Nazi officer for his trouble, wanting nothing but to get
going, get this film to Paris and tell the world, but he insists on holding
my large cloth bag as he hustles me into the Mercedes. I manage a
smile, but I don't take a breath all the way to Paris as we speed off with
my military escort holding the bag with the camera and precious roll of
film. I doubt if anyone ever experienced a stranger series of events. The
adoring crowds in Berlin and the fanfare for me – an actress. Then how
strange afterward to find myself standing in the mud near the train of
anguished prisoners, desperately filming what I see so no one will ever
forget.

All I can think about is how dangerous it was to record on film the
prisoners begging for mercy. It could have turned out differently if I
had been discovered. I'd be tortured then shot. I'm not sorry. It's never
been clearer to me what atrocious actions that defy the core of human
decency the Nazi party will stoop to in their march across Europe.

I can't stop the shudders going through me, well aware I could be
caged in that boxcar... or Bertrand, Raoul, or Halette.

I make a promise to myself.

I'll do *anything* to keep them safe.

31

SYLVIE

ADIEU, DEAR FRIEND... TILL WE MEET AGAIN

Paris
1944

'The Gestapo have Raoul.'

Chilling words I prayed I'd never hear. *How did they find him?* I ask Bertrand. I blame myself for not being here to keep this from happening.

Someone betrayed him, he tells me.

Who?

A misty rain falls outside the old, deserted cinema in the *7e arrondissement*, our meeting place. I rushed over here as soon as I received his cryptic message to meet him here at the appointed time.

The film begins at 14:00 hours.

'From what I gather, Halette was on a mission for her father and didn't return to the farmhouse for two days. Raoul was worried sick about her and ventured back to Paris.'

My stomach plummets. Again, my fault. I should have been here, helped him find her. 'What happened?'

'Raoul checked the safe house, but she wasn't there. Word on the street is Halette had important intelligence to leave at the drop-off point near the Louvre when she witnessed her contact being dragged off by the French police.'

'Did the man betray Raoul?'

Bertrand shakes his head. 'No... he never made it to the police station. They shot him when he tried to escape.'

'Oh, my God.' My heart thuds in my ears. I didn't know the *résistant*, but there's no mistaking a good man was lost, his bravery saving *mon bon ami*. This heartless action of the police strengthens my resolve to continue the fight. 'And Halette?'

'She ran off before they spotted her and hid in the doll and candle shop. The Germans ransacked the building during the roundup last year, took what they wanted, then left. The place is deserted and she knew she'd be safe there.'

I nod. Halette showed me the alcove hidden behind the glass cabinet showcasing the antique dolls.

'Where is she now?'

'She's here, Sylvie. Frightened but safe.'

He takes me to her and my heart cries for the young girl who's suffered such a nightmare. The child stirs in an uneasy sleep. Her soft, brown hair in long plaits wrapped around her head like the Dutch doll she gave me, dried tears on her cheek. I hold her hand, whisper to her not to worry, though in my heart I fear the worst.

'She turned her ankle escaping from the French police,' Bertrand explains, 'and hid in the shop for two days without food or water, resting her ankle till she could make her way back to the farmhouse.'

'Raoul guessed where she'd go.'

'Yes. He found her hiding in the shop, she told me, got her food and water, but he was so worried about her, he wasn't careful about his comings and goings.' He draws in a heavy breath, works his jaw.

'An informant.' My voice is flat, but inside I'm seething. Every apartment has a concierge whose duty it is to know every merchant, report everything, an insufferable human being ready to betray their neighbor for money.

'The French police showed up within minutes and arrested him.'

From what Bertrand could find out from a frightened neighbor, Raoul gave himself up without a fight before they could enter the shop and tear it apart.

My heart swells. He gave himself up to save his daughter.

'Where did they take him?' I ask.

'At first, we believed he was interned in the Gestapo torture chamber near the Eiffel Tower.'

I panic. I've heard about the place. Soundproof, prisoners tied to wooden posts for execution.

'... but he was moved to 84 Avenue Foch.'

The headquarters of the SS counterintelligence.

I have a chance to save him.

I breathe a ray of hope, praying my relationship with Karl can help me... In the past, I've paid outlandish bribes to clerks there for special privileges, including more ration books or gasoline for my motorcar.

I make my decision. 'I'll go.'

'I should come with you, Sylvie.'

I shake my head. 'No, Bertrand, you're too valuable should something go wrong.'

He cocks a brow. 'Nothing is more valuable than the secret you carry, *ma belle* Sylvie.'

I should have known I couldn't keep my condition from this big, powerful man who watches out for me. 'Who else knows besides you and Emil?'

'No one, *ma chère*. I'll be waiting nearby if you... well, if you need me. These are strange times we live in. You never know if there's a tomorrow. I don't want you to feel that you're ever alone. *Allons*, let's go save our friend.'

* * *

'You've made a terrible mistake, Lieutenant. Raoul Monteux isn't a political dissident and God knows, he's not a threat to the Reich. He's a writer,' I plead to the SD officer in charge. The SD is a fearsome offshoot of the notorious SS known for its torture methods. 'He's a dear friend of mine *and* Captain Karl Lunzer of the SS.'

The obstinate lieutenant scans the notebook in front of him with a pencil, moving it up and down the rows of names.

'I see here in the film registry, his name was struck from the credits of several films because he's Jewish.' He looks up, balancing his tiny pince-nez on his short nose. 'This *Juif* is a friend of yours?'

'Yes... yes, he is.'

'I see...'

'I've known him since I made my *Ninette* films,' I argue, telling a white lie to gain sympathy from the stodgy SS officer newly arrived from Berlin. The prison cells are located here. Knowing its reputation as a torture kitchen, I'm wondering if I *should* have come alone. I convinced Bertrand to wait for me at a nearby café and if I'm not back in thirty minutes, to make his play.

The first lieutenant isn't impressed.

He's never heard of *Ninette*.

'It will be difficult to arrange for you to see this Jewish person before he's transferred, *Mademoiselle...?*' He looks at me quizzically, searching for a name.

'Sylvie Martone... the cinema star.'

'Ah, yes, I saw your Versailles film last week at the *Soldatenkino* on the Champs-Élysées.' He removes his tiny glasses, looks me up and down. 'You look different in person.'

'The camera adds ten pounds,' I joke, knowing I'm twenty-five pounds heavier and not expecting this pencil pusher to get it. I'm panicking, wondering if Raoul is to be tortured.

From what I was told earlier, he was brought here for questioning and encouraged by the Gestapo to 'give up' other Jews in hiding. Names, locations.

'Raoul has written wonderful speeches for me,' I toss back at the SD officer with a sway of my hips, my low, husky voice. 'Would you deny the French people the talent of this accomplished writer? What would your superiors say if they knew you were interfering with orders from Herr Goebbels to encourage the arts between our cultures?' I make my big move. 'I just got back from Berlin where I spoke to the Minister of Propaganda—'

'You spoke to Herr Goebbels?' His glasses slide off his nose.

'Yes.' I smile. 'A most charming man.'

'I see.' He picks up the phone. 'Bring *Monsieur* Monteux, *schnell*,' he orders when—

'Ah, Mademoiselle Martone, I pray when you spoke with Herr Goebbels, he was in good health.'

The hairs stand up on the back of my neck. I freeze when I hear that gruff voice behind me.

I spin around. 'Herr Geller.' I choke. I can't move. He knows I didn't meet Goebbels in Berlin. What's his play?

'I couldn't believe it when I heard the great Sylvie Martone was seen entering the building,' he says, surprised. 'And now she's pleading for a Jew's life.'

How long has he been listening?

'Raoul is no threat, Herr Geller,' I repeat.

'He's a Jew and we must protect our people.'

'He's a writer, not an activist.'

He narrows his eyes. 'You would swear to this?'

I think carefully before I answer, pray my baby doesn't kick me when I say, 'Yes.'

'Most interesting.'

I feel a great wave of dizziness. The Gestapo man didn't call me out for telling the SD officer a lie. Now the man I both revile and fear is using that lie to trap me. I'm afraid if I don't keep talking, I'll faint.

'I'd be willing to do anything for the people who made me a star. No matter what their faith. I'm certain der Fuehrer would understand how important it is to protect those loyal to us.'

'You're a good actress, *Mademoiselle* Martone,' Herr Geller says, 'and I admire your performance, but you needn't worry about acquiring future assignments because you worked with this Jew. Your trip to Berlin proved you're a valuable asset to the Reich.'

I raise a brow. 'What do you want from me, Herr Geller? I'm not a fool.'

'Neither am I, *mademoiselle*, but I fear you've been spending too much time in your make-believe world of films and are misguided in your plea.' He leans closer to me, staring at me like he can read into my soul. Do I see more lines etched on his stodgy face? More anger in those burning eyes? 'I have it on the best authority from the French police *Monsieur* Monteux has been identified as a member of the group behind several railway incidents causing delays to our transport trains.' He snaps his fingers. 'So you see, your plea for this Jew is for nil. He's an enemy of the Reich and will be dealt with as such.'

I refuse to back down and allow him this abuse of power.

'I will swear—'

'The Gestapo man is right, *Mademoiselle* Martone. I'm not the man you think I am.'

Raoul.

He's standing in the doorway, flanked by two German guards, his hands tied behind his back. Hatless, his clothes torn, his face bruised a deep purple, the scar along his cheek open and oozing with fresh blood. He shakes his head, his fierce eyes begging me to play along.

'*Monsieur* Monteux... Raoul.' I act surprised, praying the Gestapo buys it.

'I *could* interrogate you as well, *mademoiselle*,' Herr Geller snarls at me. 'You may have heard information about Resistance activities from *Monsieur* Monteux since you're so chummy with him.'

A direct threat.

My game of passionate film star trying to help a writer I admire has turned a new page. My muscles are tense, bracing for an attack I'll never be able to endure.

He'll find out you're pregnant.

Torture you till you give up the father's name.

And you'll lose both your baby and any chance of seeing Jock again.

I try to focus but can't. The love I have for my unborn child rips through me with such intensity, I touch my stomach and a small vibration from deep within my womb makes me shiver.

'I – I, uh...' I stumble, reading Raoul's body expression as being one of a man facing sheer terror. Not for himself. But for his child. And for the first time in my life, I also know that terror. For *both* our children. What a fool I've been. I've been so cavalier trying to save my friend, I neglected to realize I could get caught up in the Gestapo's cruel web of duplicitous deceit. Two traitors for the price of one, not that Herr Geller has reason to suspect me. I have no doubt he doesn't count sheep at nights, but how to trap innocent lambs for fun.

No, I can't let this vile man win.

I know when to let the other actor have their moment in the spotlight and react. *Acting is reacting.* I remain quiet but solemn as the German guards drag Raoul away. I see in his eyes a clear message as he mouths the words, *Save Halette.* We both know Herr Geller has no grounds to hold me here. I can walk out, free. Besides, the Gestapo man has more to gain by keeping tabs on me, praying I slip up.

Before I'm escorted out by a Nazi guard, I give Raoul a slight nod. I understand. He'll do anything to save his daughter.

Including giving up his freedom... *and* his life.

* * *

Bertrand is waiting for me outside the courtyard of the elaborate SD headquarters, pacing up and down, smoking a cigarette. When he sees the fear on my face, he says nothing. He follows me without a word.

'It was a trap, Bertrand,' I tell him in a hushed whisper when we're far enough away from the dreaded place. 'Herr Geller knew I'd show up to help Raoul.'

'*Merde*, if I ever get my hands on that Gestapo bastard—'

'Raoul saved me but condemned himself.'

Bertrand grabs me by the shoulders and squeezes me so tight, I feel like I'm going to cry. I've never seen such anguish in his eyes.

'*I beg you*, Sylvie, not to take chances. You have the child to consider.'

I nod. We agree not to meet till things quiet down.

I walk back to my Trocadéro apartment, Bertrand tailing me at a safe distance to make sure I'm not followed. Once I get home, I pull off the two-piece suit I'm wearing. The smell of despair clings to my clothes. A metallic, sharp smell. Alcohol and bleach. I can't wait to wash it off. I slip on a lavender-smelling kimono and wait. Two hours later I let Halette in through the back entrance.

When I hear a rustle of the bushes, I know Bertrand is gone.

* * *

'Take the yellow Star of David off your sweater, Halette, and then we'll burn it.'

'*Oui, mademoiselle.*'

The girl is quiet, *too* quiet. I don't press her. She dutifully rips off the cloth star, then I see a moment of regret. A sniffle and intake of a deep breath that tears me apart. It may be a tool of the Nazis, but the star is also a link to her father, her faith.

And now she's lost both.

I sit with her for a long time, my arms wrapped around her as best I can in my condition, her head on my shoulder. I like to think she finds comfort in the warmth of my body, a mother's warmth when she needs it most. And my baby. A comfort to me.

Halette said little when I explained why I insisted Bertrand bring her to my Trocadéro apartment, she had no resistance left after I told her in a soft voice what happened at 84 Avenue Foch. I didn't tell her they beat her father or what would happen to him, only that he'd be interned at a camp. I pray I'm right, that he has a chance to survive.

Then I remember the boxcar of prisoners I saw on my way back from Berlin.

And I cry.

Softly at first as I unwrap the sleeping girl's arms from my waist and lay a paisley blue soft blanket over her. I leave her sleeping in the den and go upstairs to my bedroom and sob so hard I can't breathe. I can't control the hatred rushing through me for the injustice I've seen played out today. I will never forgive myself for not convincing Raoul to go to America.

Instead, what did I do? I pleaded with him to stay in Paris and write for me. A hit I needed. Who cares about a damn movie? Because of me, he stayed. I shudder at how my dearest Raoul played down our friendship to keep the Gestapo off my back.

I can do nothing more to save him.

But I *can* save Halette.

I'll hide the girl here in my Trocadéro apartment and if anyone asks, she's my new maid. I start tearing through my wardrobe, looking for suitable clothes, shoes for her. We're the same size... *or we were*, I smile, before my body changed. I pull together conservative outfits, comfortable flats I haven't worn in years, sweater, socks, coat—

A knock on my front door slams the breath out of my chest. I bend over to protect my baby, listening, going through every horrible scenario imaginable.

Who... what?

Another knock. *Loud.*

I make my way downstairs... The knocks becomes louder. My brain hurts from flipping through so many scenes.

It's Emil. He has a habit of showing up drunk.

Raoul escaped... no, impossible.

Herr Geller never believed a word I said and sent his goons to pick me up.

The last human being I expect to see when I open that door is Karl.

His SS cap askew on the back of his head. His blond, Aryan looks distorted with a hellish look of blatant lust.

Uniform collar unbuttoned.

Snarling at me and very drunk.

What happens next moves so fast, I can't put it together in any logical order. All I know is, I have two children to protect and one despicable SS officer trying to take them both away from me.

Karl pushes his way inside with his black hobnail boot kicking the door in, then he grabs me around the waist.

'I heard what happened at Avenue Foch, *Liebling*... how you defended that Jew prisoner.' He tries to kiss me; I turn my head and his sloppy lips lick the back of my neck. The disgust I feel overwhelms me, choking me.

'You're drunk, Karl. Go home.'

'Who is he, Sylvie... your lover?'

'Don't be ridiculous.' I push him away, pull my kimono closer around me, but he grabs onto the thin silk, pulling it off my bare shoulder. I turn my back on him to shield my stomach. It's then I hear a slight creaking of footsteps on the winding staircase.

Halette. *How much did she hear?*

'Do you think you can insult an officer of the Reich and get away with it?' he yells. 'Not after what you and I had together.'

He's referring to the night he *thinks* we slept together. So that's what this is about.

He's jealous.

'I was trying to help a friend.' I suck in my breath, knowing I must choose my words carefully. 'Herr Geller made it clear to me what my position is.'

'No more games, Sylvie. You'll do as you're told.' He nuzzles my neck. 'Kiss me.'

My face gets hot. I feel numb.

'Please, Karl, you're upset. It won't happen again.'

I hate myself for placating him, this ugly feeling of submission I have every time he touches me. A horrible realization washes over me. That's what I've been doing since I agreed to this insanity of working *against* the Nazis by working *with* them. A puzzling fear grips me. I'm in too deep. I can't back out now. Everything I've worked for will be lost if I don't find a way to placate him. 'Let me get you a vodka.'

Could I fill him with booze so he passes out? It worked once. Will it work again?

If not, then what?

He doesn't want a vodka. He wants me.

'I'm ordering you, *Fräulein*, to remove your robe or I shall tear it off you.'

I no longer feel in control, like I'm being hunted. The use of the German word shows his mindset, his intent to treat me as his personal property. He stands with his arms folded. Eyes narrowed into slits. I see their accusing blue stripping me. I freeze.

'Karl—'

'Do it.'

When I don't move, he slaps me hard and I fall to the floor, my life suddenly becoming a living hell. I try to move, but can't. I see Halette out of the corner of my eye. I shake my head, motion for her to run. Karl's back is to her, so he doesn't see her trembling, visibly shaken. I attempt to move farther away, give her a chance to escape out the front door, but every effort I make to get away from him is painful.

'I'm asking you, Karl, to remember you're an officer of the Reich, a soldier.'

'You will do as I say, you French whore—'

He grabs the hem of my kimono and holds it tight in his fist as he drags me toward him.

'Karl, please...'

'Do as I command... *now!*'

He pulls me to my feet as if I'm made of straw and with a seediness low and base and inhumane, he rips my kimono open, exposing my belly so round and filled with a new life. The shock reaching across his facial muscles is a slow wave of surprise, then an intense hatred that sends my pulse racing so fast, making me acutely conscious of his every action, knowing I'll have to defend myself with my fists, my nails. Bite him, if I have to. He yells at me in German, ugly words I don't understand. A pitiful excuse to take me down to his level.

Then he strikes the fireplace with his polo whip, chipping the marble.

'On your knees, *Fräulein*.'

'You don't want to do this, Karl. I'm no threat to you.'

'No? You're carrying the Jew's bastard.' He cracks the whip again, then tosses it away before drawing his pistol. He points it at my belly. I curl up in fear, my eyes searching for something, *anything* to use as a weapon. 'You leave me no choice—'

A swift movement in the shadows behind him alerts my senses... the sound of footsteps slow and steady. I catch a brief glimpse of Halette, holding a heavy Louis XIII vase in both hands, a deadly determination in her eyes. In a slow, concentrated sweep through the air, she raises the vase up high, her intention clear. I gasp, my heart in my throat. I can't stop her, a frightening punch my brain absorbs in slow motion. It's all over in a few seconds.

The SS officer never sees it coming.

Crash!

I scream when she smashes the heavy porcelain object on the back of Karl's head. Pieces fly everywhere... in his hair, on his shoulders, the floor. He staggers, disbelieving, before hitting the parquet floor with a dull, horrifying thud.

Knocking him out.

'*Is he dead?*' Halette cries out, her fist going to her mouth. She's shaking badly.

I search for a pulse on the side of his neck with my fingers. Weak, but steady.

'No, he's alive,' I tell her, relieved, 'but we'll end up in a concentration camp if he's found here.'

I hear her heavy breathing behind me. The words she heard about the baby seared her soul, the pain ripping through her.

'Is it true about the baby, *mademoiselle*?' her voice croaks. 'Is my father...?'

I smile, a soft and tearful moment as I try to assuage a difficult situation, find the right words. Halette is in a delicate state of mind having nearly ended the life of a feared Nazi, but pushing heavier on her mind is whether or not I betrayed her.

'No, Halette, your father is the most honorable man I've ever known and faithful to your mother.' I rub my belly to calm the child growing inside me. 'All I can tell you is the father of my child is someone I've loved for a long time, someone I never thought I'd see again until he was shot down...'

She smiles wide. 'You have my word I will keep your secret.'

Strange, how female bonds are born from shared sacrifice.

Tonight, here in my apartment we share both the guilt for what we've done, albeit in self-defense, as well as the pain of what happened earlier at Avenue Foch, and the joy of my impending motherhood.

A bond forged in war. I pray it endures when we find peace again.

I call Bertrand and tell him I have a package that needs delivering. His sharp intake of breath tells me he's been fearful for my safety. When he arrives and sees Karl lying on the floor and my ripped kimono, he's livid with anger. I assure him the SS officer had an 'accident' before anything happened. I make no mention of Halette's courageous act. Better for her safety if no one knows but me.

Dousing Karl with more alcohol, Bertrand loads him onto his shoulders while I make sure no one is about outside. Somehow, he has commandeered a German uniform and a military motorcycle with a sidecar. No one will question a tipsy SS officer being driven about the streets with his aide.

'What will you do with him, Bertrand?'

Whatever happens to him because of me, I will have to live with that.

'He's so drunk, he won't remember anything when he wakes up in a brothel in the Pigalle.' Bertrand smiles wide. 'Without his uniform *and* his identity papers. He'll have a hard time explaining *that* to his superiors.'

32

JULIANA

FILMS, PHOTOS, AND NAZIS, OH MY

Ville Canfort-Terre, France
Present Day

What if I can't clear the name of my fabulous grandmother Sylvie Martone? Show the world she was working in disguise as 'Fantine' for the Resistance? The evidence is all circumstantial. I need official proof of her involvement with the SOE, Special Operations Executive, the group organized to conduct espionage operations during the war Jock mentions, how impressed the *hush hush* organization was with their work helping what Sylvie calls 'evaders' along the escape line to the Spanish border and then on to Gibraltar. *Someone* in the Foreign Office must have known about Fantine, but Sylvie makes no mention of anything official that left a paper trail.

All I've got are the recordings, the scrapbook, and the diary.

What worries me is I've also got films showing Sylvie cavorting with the Nazis in cafés and photos of her riding with the SS in a motorcar with miniature Nazi flags flying.

A picture is worth a thousand words they say... a moving picture has to be even more incriminating.

People will believe what they see with their own eyes.

They won't believe an actress telling her story on old reel-to-reel tapes. Where's the proof what she's saying is the truth?

I feel a soft, weathered hand on my shoulder. Comforting me.

'It's getting late, Juliana. I must be off to evening prayers.'

Sister Rose-Celine. Trying to console me. We've spent all day making notes, cataloging what we've got and trying to figure out our next move.

'I'm going to stay here for a while,' I tell her, the twilight breeze keeping me company. I find peace here under the willow tree. It's become my anchor to both *Maman* and Sylvie. 'I want to call Ridge.'

She giggles like a schoolgirl, then she's off on her motorized scooter. She's convinced Ridge is my boyfriend and I don't have the heart to tell her we're just friends.

Or are we?

Something unsettling is happening to my everyday world since I got here. I didn't realize till I was thousands of miles away how well Ridge and I work together. How much I look forward to talking to him. Miss him.

I sigh. Leave it to a romance-loving nun to make me see it. I don't know what I'd do without her. Sister Rose-Celine has changed my view of life in ways I never imagined. That getting older doesn't mean you have to lose your curiosity, your zest for something new, and you don't have to be afraid to reopen the past.

I won't say it's made losing *Maman* any easier.

Just different. I think the best explanation I can give is, spending time with this extraordinary nun has made see that I gave up my personal life when my mother was ill. I became trapped in *Maman's* world. Yet, I felt that doing anything else was selfish on my part. That if I wanted time for myself or to see a friend – Ridge never stopped asking what he could do to help, but I was too proud to accept his offer – that I was being disloyal to her. Not true. She was a loving, caring woman; she'd want me to have someone. And somehow, I know she'd be proud of me for wanting to clear Sylvie's name and doing what she couldn't in her time. And I respect that.

Meanwhile my life back in LA continues down this strange new road when Ridge sends me a text, asking if I need him to start a Sylvie Martone fan club yet. There he goes, making me smile when I'm in a quandary. Still, I have to be careful. He's helping a friend, I tell myself. I'm reading too much into this.

So then why do I call him?

Because you like him. Always have, but you're too busy having a career.

'Hey... Super Stunt Guy,' I gush into the phone, thinking how lucky I am to have a friend who listens to my crazy ideas. 'You still driving that motorcycle like a wild man?'

'You know another way? Hey, it's lonely tearing up the backlot without you on the back of my bike.'

'So that's what I am to you,' I tease him. 'A partner in crime.'

'Yep.' I have the feeling he wants to say more but won't. Why did Ridge bring that up now? Because I opened the door the last time we went on a talky taco binge via Skype? I wonder if there's something else he wants to say, something bothering him he needs to get off his mind. I sense he's holding back like he always does when the conversation gets too personal. I accept it, always have. For a world class stuntman who lives for danger, the man can sure clam up when it comes to saying what he feels. So I'm not surprised when he gets back to my grandmother.

'Anything new on Sylvie?'

I bite my lip. 'I've got some amazing first-person accounts from Sylvie on her tape recordings, but no way to prove what she says is true.' I tell him the latest.

He lets out a low whistle. 'Sylvie was a brave woman, Juliana. An amazing human being to risk her life like that.' He pauses a beat. 'I know a lot of people who'd like to see that film if it exists, including me. I've come across heart-wrenching footage of the Holocaust here at the studio, but nothing like what you described. It would be an extraordinary contribution to the remembrance of what Jews suffered during the war.'

I feel the heat of his passion in his voice, his words giving me the push I need not to give up. It's so important I find enough evidence to complete my mission.

'You're right, Ridge, and it could be the proof I need to help prove her innocence, show what she was trying to do, but I don't see the film anywhere. Just the reel-to-reel tapes she made. I have two more left.' I'll be sad when I've listened to the last tape. I'm going to miss my interesting conversations with my grandmother. *Afternoons with Sylvie*, I call it. She talks on the tape and I talk back to her. Sometimes when I turn the tape back on, she answers the question I have on my mind. Strange, but I don't try to understand it.

'Didn't you tell me your grandmother left the box and the tapes in the chateau dungeon?'

'Yes.'

'And she was killed in a car accident?'

'Yes.'

'I have the feeling she used the dungeon as a storage place until she could make her case. Gathering up her notes, the diary. Then putting the recordings in order. That she never intended to leave her materials there indefinitely. You may not have found everything.'

'There's so much stuff down there... it could take weeks to go through it and I've got to be back in LA for my meeting with the producers in less than a week.'

I give out a lonely sigh. I can see him in my mind. Smiling, his strong jaw covered with sexy stubble, his dark eyes swimming with ideas about how to help me, but knowing how much it means to me to stand on my own.

'Hey, call me if you need anything. I'm here for you.'

* * *

The possibility of me finding the film rattles my brain with impossible odds, but I embrace the job with a vengeance and go on a treasure hunt anyway.

It's like winning the lotto. You can't win if you don't buy a ticket.

It's late, but fueled by Ridge's belief in me, I poke around the convent dungeon to see what I can find. It's hot down here, no air, my palms are sweaty. Waving my flashlight around, I almost expect to see a ghost. I push aside boxes, get tangled up in old curtains, knock over a rocking horse, and then nearly slip on an old metal roller skate. Before I can grab it, the skate goes flying across the floor and slams into—

A large round, blue model case with the initials *S.M.*

Sylvie Martone.

I'm beside herself with excitement, not believing my luck. I tear into the hat box and pull out a stylish, black velvet suit with black jet beaded trim, black gloves, black pumps still crusted with dried mud, silk stockings – *and* movie theater lobby cards in German for *Die Dame aus Versailles.* Sylvie must have been so horribly affected from her trip to Berlin she wanted to preserve everything as it was so she'd never forget. I imagine she returned the mink coat and hat to the studio wardrobe department.

I also find an old home movie camera from the 1940s in a pristine, brown leather case. I inspect it closer and find a roll of film inside the case never developed. I can't control the chills running through me. This must be the film Sylvie shot when she saw the prisoners on their way to a concentration camp.

Ridge is beyond excited when I call him.

'Everything fits, Juliana... the clothes, the muddy shoes. You've struck gold.'

Holding the precious film close to my chest, I want to cry.

'I could kiss you, Ridge, for giving me encouragement when I needed it,' I tell him, not realizing what I said till I said it.

I hear him suck in a deep breath, then a long pause before he says, 'Can you send me the film? I want Harper to see it, too. She's great with restoring old nitrate negatives.'

'Oh, yeah... Harper.'

I almost forgot about her. Nice kid, but the idea of the two of them working together in the darkroom does nothing for my ego. I beat myself up for acting like a ditzy groupie, but I don't know how to walk it back. Seems I don't have to. Ridge keeps talking about the film.

'Send me the film the fastest way possible. We have a guy here who handles our film imports from Europe. He can expedite getting the package through customs.'

'Oh, that's amazing, Ridge, thank you.'

We both agree if the film is what Sylvie said it was, along with her personal tape recording of the event, it could help exonerate her.

He'll get on it right away and send me anything important ASAP. I doubt if he'll get a moment of sleep till the film arrives.

Neither will I. And it's not the film keeping me up.

I keep thinking about him... and Harper in that darkroom.

Jealous, are you? My, my...

Early the next morning, I can't believe my luck when I find an overseas shipping office less than a half hour from Ville Canfort-Terre. With Sister Rose-Celine's help, we box up the film and I hop into my rental car and drop it off (*merci* for GPS) while the sister takes her nap. I cross my fingers. It could take two to four days to get there but with Ridge's help, the package will speed through customs.

I settle in and listen to another tape, my heart in turmoil at realizing I want a lot more than a 'best friends' sticker from Ridge. What took me so long to see it? I know how Sylvie felt without her love. I gain courage when I hear her recount how she saved Jock and countless other 'evaders' by leading them to the Spanish border, always as Fantine so they never knew her real identity.

Except one person.

Sister Vincent.

I wonder, did she ever write down her memories of Sylvie after the war? And why didn't she come forward with her knowledge of 'Fantine' to clear her?

So many unanswered questions.

I listen to the last tape.

33

SYLVIE

THE FINAL CHAPTER IN MY LIFE AS A SPY

Paris
Spring 1944

Ask any actress what her favorite role is and she'll tell you it's the one that makes the audience cry.

Ask me... and it's the one that makes *me* cry.

Fantine.

My audience consists of downed fliers who never know they're part of my greatest performance. One or two evaders tailing along with me from the Gare d'Austerlitz in Paris on a crowded train till we arrive at Toulouse and I lead them to the pickup point. There we meet up with their guide to the Spanish border.

When we're alone without the sniffing Nazis within earshot, I speak in English as I limp along with my lace veil wrapped around my head, making them laugh, telling them about my escapades with two departed husbands, my life as a baroness in a drafty old castle, how I broke the bank at Monte Carlo...

I make up the script as I go along.

When we arrive at the safe house, we chat over bread and cheese with the guide.

'Where are you from?' I ask a young man with tousled hair.

'Manchester,' he says, his mouth filled with cheese.

'What about you?' I ask the other pilot.

'Blackpool.' He sighs deeply. 'I miss my girl Annie.'

'Annie...' I repeat. 'I'm sure she's lovely.'

'Take a look.' He whips an oval-shaped photo of a pretty girl out of his pocket. I see where she wrote on the back, *'Love you forever, your sweetheart, Annie.'*

'You can't keep the photo, Lieutenant. You have to destroy it.'

'You ain't taking my Annie from me.'

'I *must*, Lieutenant, for your safety.'

'Why, miss?' asks his friend.

'The photo could be his undoing.'

'How?' asks the lieutenant, disbelieving.

'If you're captured,' I tell him, 'and the Nazis find the photo, they'll use it against you. Make your mind spin with doubt and pain and the fear of losing your girl to the guy back home. Enticing you to give them information about planes, dates, missions, so you can get home faster.'

A form of psychological warfare.

Something the Gestapo is good at, I remind myself. How Herr Geller entices me to act my part with a sly glance over my shoulder to see if he's watching, or the fear on my face when he pops out of the shadows. An overwhelming fear. I'm never sure if this is the day he arrests me and slips on those shiny, silver handcuffs.

I caught sight of them when he pulled them out of his pocket along with his newspaper to work a crossword puzzle. He dangled them in my face then slid them down my neck, over my breasts. A strange, creepy feeling shot through me. A sexual gesture I'll never forget. A provocative dance he enjoyed playing with me because I upset his orderly mind. He can't put me into the little boxes on his crossword puzzles and predict what I'll do.

That intrigues him.

And keeps me alive.

The somber moment passes, then panic causes a major upheaval in my swollen belly when the guide talks about the girl who broke *his* heart. I'm glad no one else notices when he points out an advertisement in a Paris newspaper for my Versailles film.

A provocative illustration of me.

Lips parted, blonde hair blowing.

'For years, I was in love with Sylvie Martone,' he says with a sneer. '*Ah*, so beautiful she is. I went to see her films every Saturday. Now she sleeps with the Boche.'

Then he spits on my picture and tears it up.

The day turns darker.

I wonder if I'll ever be able to tell the people of France the truth.

* * *

Emil yells, '*Action!*'

Sweating under the hot lights on the indoor set, I react to an actor reading lines off to the side. *Smiling, a sneer... listening intently.* Pickup shots for a scene he filmed yesterday with my stand-in Halette pretending to be me in the long shots.

I notice my acting has a depth to it in the close-ups I've never experienced before when Emil shows me the daily rushes later. A crying in my eyes that speaks of pain, loneliness. Yet there's also a light of hope.

'You should get pregnant more often, Sylvie,' he snickers, complimenting me on my scenes when we're alone.

'Be careful what you wish for,' I tease him, resting in my dressing room with my feet up. His eyes bug out. 'Just kidding.' I smile, then in a serious tone, 'Have you thought about what will happen to us, Emil, when Paris is liberated?'

He chokes on his cigar smoke. 'Where'd you hear that?'

'Backstairs gossip.'

'I'm in no hurry.'

'You wouldn't be. You've never had it so good.'

'Neither have you, Sylvie. I thought we were done when sound came in, then the Depression, but we kept at it, you and me. In spite of the shortages in getting film, raw materials to build sets, and losing talent, the Occupation hasn't stopped us.'

Talent like Raoul?

I'm still reeling over his arrest, his eyes pooling so deep and dark with an uncanny fear. As if he'd accepted his fate, but he couldn't let go of a debilitating fear if his little girl – nearly a woman – were caught, she'd face unspeakable horror at the hands of the SS.

Since then, I've heard rumors Raoul was sent to Natzweiler-Struthof, a concentration camp in Alsace hundreds of miles east of Paris.

I pray he survives.

A blade cuts through me every time I think about him, making me wonder if I'm existing in a false security believing I'm helping defeat the Nazi war machine by making pictures.

Emil says the head of Galerie Films is so pleased with the record crowds in Berlin promoting *Die Dame aus Versailles*, he'll have no problem getting another film greenlighted. I wonder how long I can conceal my pregnancy by wearing boxy coats and voluminous capes. I feel guilty taking advantage of Emil's insistence his 'star' takes up residence at the Hôtel Ritz, lavishing me with great meals while the rest of Paris lives in a state of acute hunger. (Halette remains at my apartment.) I took Emil up on his offer to keep my baby nourished or... no, I can't think that way. I'll do *anything* to secure the safety of my unborn child.

Dealing with lower back pain and fatigue, spotting, and worrying about Jock, I'm filming a nineteenth-century costume drama titled *La Dame avec les Yeux Verts (Lady with the Green Eyes)*. The script isn't my favorite. What writer can compare to Raoul? We're shooting the film in Paris where Emil directs me on a closed set. Only my wardrobe designer and cinematographer know it's not me in the exterior scenes shot around Paris, but Halette wearing wigs and extravagant cavalier hats with trailing, wavy feathers.

The film is shot in less than two months while everyone in Paris holds their breath, waiting for what's coming.

The Allied invasion of France.

Fortunately for me, I no longer have to deal with the unwanted attention of Captain Lunzer. At first, I believed Karl was shipped off to the Eastern Front because of me. Then I picked up conversations at the Hôtel Ritz from unhappy officers preparing to depart Paris, how the Wehrmacht ordered their top soldiers to leave the city. It seems der Fuehrer needs more bodies to put on a good show and die for the Reich as the battle escalates. I've heard hushed talk at the cafés the Germans are suffering the worst casualties of the war.

I shudder. As a girl raised in a convent, I should be forgiving, but I no longer feel compelled to acknowledge my uneasy alliance with that man. Karl would have raped me, killed my baby. I wrap my arms around my belly to protect my unborn child, my body trembling just *thinking* about that SS madman.

Unfortunately, the Gestapo isn't going anywhere.

They're staying in Paris. Ramping up arrests, torture.

Which means Herr Geller will be a part of my life for a while to come.

* * *

I say nothing about my fears and what happened that night in my apartment when Jock returns to Paris, so filled with joy I am at feeling his arms around me. Kissing me with such intensity I can't breathe. We don't dare meet in the open, so we're underground. I have to stand up on my toes to wrap my arms around his neck, my navy cloak swinging around me like a swirl of saffron fog, our voices echoing in the cool, damp passageway under the city. He slides his hands up and down my body, his fingers digging into my flesh, rolling up my lightweight housedress to stare at me. I've never been happier to show off my big belly than to this man. He's in awe at the sight of me, the vein at the side of his neck pulsating from the near miss of a Nazi bullet earlier when he was spotted after curfew.

I grip him so tight he flinches. I'd die if anything happened to him because of me.

We're engulfed in a comforting semi-darkness as we speak. I can't let him go. Jock couldn't be happier about the child. He speaks the words with a mixture of joy and amazement, adding that he loves me more than anything. Our baby is lodged between us as we embrace, the unborn urging her parents to stay as close together as possible. *Mais oui*, since all my weight is spread out around my middle, I'm convinced I'm having a girl.

I keep my thoughts to myself, listening to every word from Jock, how he wanted to return sooner, but he saw heavy hand-to-hand combat with Nazi patrols after he picked up three airmen. He's keeping them hidden in safe houses around the city till it's safe to travel.

I find it so hard to listen to him talking about leaving again, my hands covering his as he holds me with a firmness both comforting and protective. I instinctively suck in my protruding stomach. Jock never stops asking if I'm feeling well, if the baby is okay, *what can he do to help*? I tell him having him here means everything to me. And the baby. *Mon amour* stands close to me until I relax, his loving hand resting on my belly, his lips brushing my hair, making me feel warm inside and happy. I feel complete. Loved. Pretty.

Am I selfish to want to keep him with me? Of course I am. What woman in love isn't?

These moments may have to last me for the rest of my life.

He cups my chin, kisses me, not with heat but with the promise he'll protect me. A notion so far removed from my psyche, it takes me a moment to accept it. I've always been on my own, had to fight for everything. Now in my greatest moment of need, when I'm determined to be stronger than ever, I let go, not feel guilty if I close my eyes and be as one with my unborn child. Because Jock will be there, watching over both of us.

For now. This moment.

I'm not fool enough to believe it will last, not with Paris again on the brink of armed conflict. Air raid warnings are becoming more common-place. The Resistance is going on the offensive, skirmishing with the Germans out in the open. Strange, we've had nearly four years of occu-pation when Parisians got on and off the Nazi merry-go-round while others – like the Jewish roundup – were pushed off with reckless aban-don. I'll never come to grips with it. When Jock confirms what I heard about a major Allied invasion coming soon, I pray the ride is nearly over.

And the Nazi machine will fall apart like a house of cards.

Which presents me with a new set of problems. When the Allies come... what will I tell them? I had no choice but to make it appear as if I cooperated with the Nazis?

Will they believe me?

A raw fear grips me. A weak excuse, if best. Yes, I started out openly defiant against the Nazis. It didn't work.

So I embraced what *did*.

I used my status as a film star to gather intelligence to help the Resistance. Then created Fantine. A fanciful adventure at best. I notice the air in the passageway is suddenly stifling and the smell of black deeds from centuries past rises up around me, the spirits pointing their bony fingers at me, accusing.

We don't believe you, mademoiselle.

A nervous humming escapes from my lips.

I can't prove a damn thing. I don't care for myself. But what about my child?

I keep humming like I used to do when I was a little girl, playing among the roses and violets in the convent garden, picking up the fallen petals. Feeling as lonely as each petal cast aside, I'd try to put them back together to make a new flower.

It always fell apart.

I pray that won't be me when the Allies come.

Jock must have known by my nervousness and all this talk about invasion what's on my mind. He gives me a number to memorize... *a service number*, he says. He sent a coded message to London via a trusted wireless British operator dropped into France. (I'm saddened to learn the operator was later picked up by the Gestapo and sent to a concentration camp.) The British officials responded with the number, acknowledging my work as Fantine with the Resistance is known to a 'Mr Peeps' in the Foreign Office and what I've accomplished is registered with the SOE F (French) Section in London with a notation of my true identity.

Sylvie Martone.

French actress.

No other record exists.

Then he kisses the tip of my nose and tells me he'll love me always... and he's off on a dangerous mission soon.

But first, he insists on marrying me.

* * *

I never expected I'd say my wedding vows with an armed Nazi guard as a witness.

Before I get ahead of myself, it's not a real wedding and it's not a real Nazi guard.

Bertrand again dons his German soldier disguise to give our ceremony the guise of being sanctioned by the Party when we enter Sacré-Coeur late at night. He drove me here in the sidecar of his military motorcycle with Jock meeting us outside the basilica.

Father Armand is waiting for us, the kindly priest more than pleased when I asked him to marry us. He's never spoken of that time in my life when I abandoned God, but welcomed me over the years when I come here to pray. A simple word to the father-on-duty in the confessional earlier and he received my message I need him. Tonight. To marry us.

He asks no questions.

But he records our names in his journal for proof of the religious ceremony after the war. Other than that, we don't go through the legal formalities – how can we? Jock would have to establish his residency for at least two weeks to obtain a marriage license. I find a bit of mirth in that, imagining how he'd explain to a French official he 'dropped in' by parachute and he had no permanent address because the Gestapo is on his tail. I whimsically conjure up an image of me wearing a wedding gown made from his white silk parachute. Instead I choose a loose blue frock with a white collar that hides my rounded figure and cover my head with my trailing lace veil.

We say our vows to each other in clear voices and Father Armand gives us his blessing.

No marriage certificate.

No ring.

But it's a union blessed by God.

And that's all that matters to me.

* * *

Our wedding night lasts a mere six hours.

I hide my new husband in my apartment in the Faubourg Saint-Antoine swathed in a night of blessed darkness. First he insists on carrying 'us' over the threshold. The baby and me. I beg to imagine what my nocturnal neighbors will think if they're out past curfew and see a pregnant woman, her face hidden by a long lace veil, being lovingly brought inside, then the door kicked shut with the man's boot.

Should questions be asked, Fantine will tell them the daughter of a dear friend needed a place to hide with her Resistance-fighter husband until the heat died down, that a Nazi detail was following them after a mission. No one will question her.

Not me. I'm too busy enjoying marital bliss.

Kisses abound for the *first* hour... perhaps longer.

Hours *two* and *three* see us rolling around the four-poster, our bodies tense and distraught for so long easing up and trying to find a position where we can get as close to each other as possible without injuring the baby. Comical, funny, staccato moves. Wild facial expressions like we're making a silent film.

Fourth hour we lie in each other's arms, exhausted. Smiling, contented, the wild fever in us satiated. For now. We speak in hushed undertones about the baby. Our love for each other. And us.

'I pray our child will be born into a France free from these horrible Nazis,' I whisper, laying a hand over my belly. Jock puts his hand over mine.

'The invasion is coming, Sylvie, and I shall fight to keep you and the baby safe.'

I trace his jawline with my fingers. 'We'll raise our baby to never forget the long road to peace, *mon amour*.'

'And she'll speak both English and French,' Jock insists, kissing my stomach.

'And we'll spoil the little royal rotten... a pony, dolls, ribbons for her hair...'

'And she'll be pretty, like her mother.'

'Did I tell you I love you?' I whisper, hungry for him again.

'Not for at least five minutes.' He wraps his arms around me. 'Let me *show* you.'

We kiss again, a warmth igniting between us that hovers over us like an invisible aura I shall remember always as I reach up to stroke his thick, dark hair. We're safe and happy here, but we're aware of the hurdle we face regarding us getting married.

'If we can defeat the Nazis,' I tell Jock, 'and I'm sure we will, we can overcome the prejudice of stuffy, old British bureaucrats.'

'My enchanting Sylvie,' he says with a chuckle, 'they have no idea what they're in for.'

My aching back rules the *fifth* hour with Jock kneading, probing with his fingers to relieve the building pressure in my lower back, pressing hard enough to relieve the pain and evoke in me a pleasant wave of release. I cry out, a surprised moan erupting from deep with me. Then I sleep for a precious few minutes.

It isn't until the *sixth* hour we rise up to accept our responsibility we have a job to do in this war. Jock received a wireless message earlier telling him he has SOE agents being dropped tomorrow night at a field outside Angers, nearly three hundred kilometers from Paris. I dive under the fluffy quilt on my bed, teasing my love to join for one more heated embrace. As I sigh in his arms, I wish I could turn back the clock and relive tonight. I can't. It's only after he leaves and I accept the fact it will be a while till we see each other again, that I embrace a new truth.

I'm a wife in the eyes of God.

No one has ever loved me enough to risk everything, to make me feel so wanted, so happy. I love Jock with everything I am and it thrills me that he's embraced that love. Given me his undying devotion and a name I am proud to own if only in my heart.

Madame John Lawrence Revell.

The Duchess of Greychurch.

* * *

My baby kicks me hard when I see the kindly physician with the monocle arrested by the French police for hiding Jews.

I panic, my steps a slow and steady pace near the apartment on Rue des Belles Fueilles, the contractions getting more painful, my dear Halette urging me to run the other way, hide. I can't. My shoulder muscles tighten. Everyone knows the *Milice*, a French paramilitary organization, is controlled by the Gestapo. The shock is settling in, the fear twisting, turning in my gut. I can't shut out the yelling in my head, the accusations hurled at the poor man by the commander, calling him out so everyone can hear his 'crime' of concealing a Jewish family in the empty apartment in the building.

God sent me a warning... I can't leave him like this.

I wrap my cloak around me, *think, think*. I must help him.

'There's nothing we can do, Mademoiselle Sylvie,' Halette cries out, pulling on my arm. Her skin is as pale as a porcelain doll, her eyes exploding with the harsh reality of our situation. She insisted on coming with me and I'm grateful for her loyalty these past weeks. Massaging my lower back, bringing me tea, insisting I put my feet up. Watching over me after Jock left on a dangerous mission in advance of the Allied invasion. The glow of our union hasn't worn off, nor the urge to wrap my arms around his neck and bury my face in his chest. At nights the feeling is so intense I forget my changing body. Then a wild kicking in my belly alerts me I won't be alone. That doesn't make the memory of our parting easy, remembering how he left me with a passionate kiss and a promise to return before the baby is born.

Since then, I've been keeping Halette busy acting as my courier to get intelligence, giving her instructions on how to proceed if anything happens to me. I still have my room at the Hôtel Ritz, but we spend more time at my Trocadéro apartment, coming and going at odd hours, fearful of running into our Nazi neighbors, but things run smoother here than in the poorer *arrondissements*. Meanwhile, Emil is busy in post-production, which suits my purpose. Bertrand spends more time disguised as a German soldier than not, his tall powerful image sending fear into both German and French alike.

And my baby is overdue.

Which is what brings us here this morning.

The surreal scene of this stalwart man being forced into the black Citroën holds me fast.

I clench my fists to my side. 'I can't stand by and do nothing.'

'We *must*, Sylvie... think about the baby.'

'Yes... my baby.'

I rub my stomach under the voluminous navy cloak hiding my impending motherhood. Along with the white nurse's cap and sensible white shoes I commandeered from the studio wardrobe department, I donned a black wig and wire-rim glasses to hide my identity. No one pays attention to me when I make my pregnancy visits to the doctor's residence a short walk from my Trocadéro apartment. To anyone spying, I'm a nurse from the nearby American Hospital of Paris come to deliver an important message to the doctor. Since the hospital is farther north of his residence, I go to the extreme of circling round the street should anyone notice I'm approaching from the wrong direction.

Now I'm grateful for my caution.

Hopefully I've aroused no suspicion, though I imagine had I

arrived earlier, I could have been caught in their mousetrap, a Gestapo operation where they don't take their target into custody right away, but wait around for other suspects to show up and snag them in their net.

'*Merci, mon enfant*, for saving us,' I whisper to my unborn child for keeping me home until I couldn't wait any longer. Contractions coming then abating since early this morning when Halette and I were discussing her future over tea and biscuits. I told her I've made certain the deed to my Faubourg apartment is also in her name. Not an easy feat. Using her false identity card and calling in a favor from the studio solicitor, I achieved my goal.

Then the contractions started coming closer together. *Too* close. Regular intervals, which I could deal with by slowing my breathing. When my legs cramped, I got scared. Then the nausea. I couldn't use the telephone to call the doctor's residence for help. The line is down again.

What if I *had* called? Could he have warned me? Not as easily as pulling the curtains closed, a signal often used to indicate 'stay away'. My heart is breaking seeing this brave physician being treated like an animal.

I've been coming here since that night when I fainted in front of the Nazi general. A lucky break for me rather than trying to get to the clinic on top of Rue des Martyrs when my time came. The doctor and I both agreed it would be safer for me to have the baby here at the private clinic in his home, but he assured me he'd hide me in the hospital if necessary. Bertrand later confirmed my suspicions the French physician is friendly to the Underground and has attended to several wounded evaders. He keeps them safe from the Germans by forging their identities on their medical charts as Frenchmen, or listing them as deceased and then moving them very much alive along the escape lines to freedom.

His wonderful work will cease and I beg to wonder how many Allied soldiers will never see home again because we've lost him to the Gestapo.

The last time I see the esteemed doctor, he's being shoved into the motorcar without his monocle.

I turn and walk down the block, motioning for Halette to run off in the opposite direction down a narrow passageway so we're not seen together—

When a black Mercedes rolls up behind me as silent as a devil-ghost.

What's going on?

I cross the street.

The motorcar cuts me off.

I zigzag, my head down, clasping my cloak tight around me. The motorcar must have been waiting around the corner, engine running, for someone to snare in its claws. Thank God Halette escaped from his clutches.

The black metal monster moves forward and nearly clips me. Heart racing, I jump back. The car stops, the driver side door opens and why am I not surprised when Herr Geller gets out, his eagerness to confront me affecting me in a frightening manner.

I can't move, my senses spiking with a strange smell up my nostrils. It's the scent of decay that clings to him like a shroud. Yes, it's in my mind, but the horror that races through me every time we meet singes my skin on fire. Every nerve in my body taut, heart pounding in my chest so hard, I can't breathe.

Another contraction... then another, the pressure building in my back.

Oh, God, I can't stand the pain.

'Need a lift to the hospital, *mademoiselle*?' he asks in that syrupy sticky voice that crawls all over me like a thousand ants.

'*Non, merci.*'

Say nothing.

'You live in this neighborhood?'

Don't lie. He'll follow you and you'll blow your cover.

'No. I like to walk after my shift... now if you'll excuse me.'

'I find Paris in early summer too humid for my tastes. I'd rather ride... wouldn't you?'

He's toying with you. He knows you were on your way to the physician's home. Why? his brain is asking. Who is she?

I've got to get out of here before he asks me for my *papiere*. In my haste, I left my phony identity card at the apartment. You don't think about damn papers when you're in labor for hours.

'Unless you're in need of medical assistance, *monsieur*, I won't waste any more of your time.'

I turn sharply away from him. Wrong move.

A loud growl, but he's quicker than a hungry fox, surprising me when he grabs me by the shoulder and spins me around.

'I've not dismissed you... yet.'

I glance up, catch his penetrating gaze. His eyes are searching as if he's trying to see something, but he's not sure what. I didn't put on face makeup, just a black wig and glasses. Now I chide myself for my haste. Who would see me? I never expected to come face to face with the man I despise.

'Are you new at the hospital? You look familiar. And your voice...' He thinks a moment. 'Have we met, *mademoiselle*?'

'I'm certain we haven't, *monsieur*. I – I've only been in Paris a short while.'

'Yet you know the boulevards well enough to wander around on your own.' It wasn't a question, but a piece of the puzzle forming in his brain. 'I *swear* we've met before.'

Herr Geller is cleverer than most Gestapo. I think those crossword puzzles he's obsessed with fuel his brain to come up with schemes of torment that go beyond the physical, a mental torture to rob his target of the one thing we cling to under the worst physical torture: our souls.

Like now. Waiting outside in his motorcar for an unwary mouse to get close enough to spring his trap and then *bam*! Another victim he can jibe with his sharp tongue.

I wince then force back a groan when a big contraction hits, using all my strength not to faint. My body doesn't know I'm in fear for my life. I double over. I can't help it.

His brows shoot up in surprise. 'Are you ill?'

'No.' I shake my head vigorously. 'It's something I ate... you don't know what you're getting these days.' I force a smile, but my ridiculous attempt at humor comes out flat. I wipe my face, sweating profusely as I sway back and forth, realizing my wig is loose, hair – is it blonde hair? – sticking to my forehead.

Then before I can turn and run...

My water breaks.

I freeze, bracing for whatever comes next, closing my hands into fists, shielding my belly. The Gestapo curses at me in German, his nostrils flaring. I've ruined his game and he intends to make me pay. He rips open my cloak, looks me up and down, but he doesn't touch me. Then as if he's working a puzzle and the answer pinged his brain, an almost tender look plays over his face.

'*Herr Doktor* was your physician.'

I nod. I can't speak till the pain passes.

Then he laughs. A big guffaw that shakes his rotund body so hard, the black leather of his trench coat stretches at the seams. 'You nearly had me fooled, *Mademoiselle* Martone. A clever disguise on your part to escape publicity,' he says, ripping off my wig and nurse's cap. 'A glamorous film star can't afford to have a child out of wedlock. It will tarnish your image, *n'est-ce pas?*'

So he *did* recognize me.

'I admit *nothing*, Herr Geller.'

'No? You came to SD headquarters that day to plead for the Jew to throw me off track, *mademoiselle*, making me question if he was your lover.'

Where's he going with this?

'I've had my suspicions for weeks you were hiding something... of course, SS Captain Lunzer is the father of your child. When I picked him for you, I wondered how long it would take for him to seduce you. Karl never was discreet. Before he was called to the Eastern Front, he bragged about his passion for you and how beautiful you are in the moonlight without...' He smiles. 'I shall leave the rest to your imagination.'

I must be having a moment of sheer insanity. *That lying SS bastard.*

But a force bigger than me, the need for survival overtakes me and I keep silent. Let him think what he wants. My baby will be born on the pavements if I don't get help.

I make a stand. '*Now* am I dismissed?'

He smiles. 'Get into the car, *mademoiselle*. I shall drive you to the hospital myself.'

34

JULIANA

AND THE CRADLE WILL FALL

Ville Canfort-Terre, France
Present Day

I can't stop shaking, my heart in my throat listening to the tape.

Sylvie and that horrible Gestapo man unmasking her and then driving her to the hospital.

Sylvie talking about how she saved downed pilots.

Sylvie and Jock getting married in Sacré-Coeur.

The French actress speaks in a clear, lovely voice, telling Madeleine she wants her to know everything as it happened, her work for the SOE, how she nearly lost Jock, what happened the night she was born. The emotion, the feelings, the wonder of it all when, in the midst of utter chaos and heartbreak, betrayal and then victory, she gave birth to a baby girl.

I know deep in my heart, Sylvie wanted Madeleine to know her mother was no mythical creature with wings like in her *Ninette* films, but a woman. Strong yet vulnerable, determined and faithful under the most horrible circumstances. She made mistakes, some small, others that made her heart break, but she did it for her child... and for France.

I'm still shaking when I turn the recorder back on and listen to what happens next.

* * *

I delivered my beautiful baby girl at the American Hospital in Paris four hours later. Never in my life have I been more filled with joy than when I pressed my skin against hers and she began to feed. Soft, pink with all her fingers and toes. A gift from a benevolent God not even the Nazis could take from me.

I cherish that time with you, ma petite.

Then Allied Forces landed at Normandy and the end to the Occupation of Paris began.

Not everyone believed the invasion was real. Hitler slept late that morning, surmising the news of troops landing at Normandy was a decoy and the invasion would come at Calais.

And what I thought was a generous move by Herr Geller to help me was another ploy to use me.

The summer days turned hotter... July then August. Jock made daring visits to me in the Trocadéro... I hesitate to speak of our passion, ma petite, *but I want you to know you were born of that passion and it never cooled.*

Not even in those dangerous times.

I'm still stunned by the missions we pulled off, the men we saved, but the Resistance made mistakes. The fighters needed weapons and the Germans lived up to their reputation of efficiency experts, keeping destructive arms other than guns and grenades out of our hands. So when Halette brought me a message from Bertrand saying they'd located a cache of weapons in an underground cave used by the Germans, I volunteered to get the word to Jock.

On our last meeting he told me he was staying at a safe house on the Left Bank belonging to a philosophy professor at the Sorbonne.

I gave you a kiss on the forehead, Madelaine, praying I'd hold you in my arms again soon, then I set off into the moonlit night in my nurse disguise. No one would challenge me on a mission of mercy.

Big mistake.

Herr Geller was watching my apartment.

He followed me across the city like a mythical creature with heavy, flapping wings and when I got to the Pont Saint-Michel, Jock saw me and I rushed into his arms, not knowing I'd led the Gestapo man here. Then out of the shadows like a medieval gargoyle, his eyes flashing with a satisfied amusement, Herr Geller ordered me to step away.

I didn't move.

The Gestapo man was an evil man I never wanted to look too closely at. That night, I did.

I locked my gaze on him, studying his face, from his straight black eyebrows to his nose off center, to that cruel mouth. His stodgy body so alive with anticipation, I could smell the sweat sticking to his leather trench coat.

With his revolver aimed at Jock, he ordered him to surrender.

Jock folded his arms across his chest. 'Go to hell,' he said in English, 'you Nazi bastard.'

His defiance infuriated the Gestapo man.

'You British think you rule the world. That's over. Long live the Reich!' yelled Herr Geller.

He stared at Jock with eyes gone black with fury, his delayed reaction frightening me more than if he'd shot his weapon.

When I least expected it, he moved as quickly as a rat with his tail cut off and grabbed me by the collar of my cloak, nearly choking me, 'Come any closer and France will be mourning the death of its most famous cinema star.'

'Don't listen to him, Jock! He wouldn't dare.'

The Gestapo man held me tight. 'Wouldn't I?'

Jock started to rush forward, then stopped. The rage on his face was replaced by fear, his words of contempt shouted at the Gestapo man coming hot and fast. Trying to talk him down, offering to give himself up, but let me go first.

No, I pleaded. He'd kill Jock. Shoot him before I could catch a breath. Then I remembered the handcuffs Herr Geller kept in his pocket. The left one. I slipped my hand inside and grabbed the cuffs, then slung the heavy metal upward and hit him in the eye.

'You French bitch!' he cursed and cursed. He let go of me and dropped the

revolver. Jock grabbed the gun, but Herr Geller rushed him before he could get off a shot. They fought and the gun went off.

My heart stopped.

I looked up to see Jock toss the dead Gestapo man over the bridge. A loud splash.

Then silence.

We never spoke of what happened, never questioned our actions. A man who tortured, maimed, and killed innocent partisans had met his fate.

We went home.

We didn't make love, we held other tight with you, ma petite, *lying on the bed between us until it was time for Jock to go. His mission couldn't wait. He had orders to keep the Nazis from getting supplies as the Allies pushed through France toward Paris, blowing up as many rail lines as possible to help weaken the German defenses.*

With sweet kisses and a loving look at his baby daughter, Jock disappeared into the darkness.

We were a family that night...

For the last time.

I turn off the recording.

Shaking so hard, I suffer such severe chills it scares me. Then a fever in me rises up from the horror of what Sylvie want through that night. Knowing they had no choice. I've been on the set and felt my heart skip during wild dramatic scenes like this one. Then I go home. Forget about it.

Sylvie *lived* it.

How did she cope with her feelings, her emotions afterward? Did the horror of everything she'd seen slowly lose its fever, like hot tea turning cold? When she made this recording in 1950, she sounded calm, resolved, as if she'd accepted these events as the price of war, knowing in her heart she was about to pay the ultimate price.

Losing Jock.

No last name. No title. I still have no idea who my grandfather was.

Waiting to hear Sylvie tell me *how, when*, is killing me. My nerves fraying, my distress so acute, I don't thread the empty spool on the recorder right and ribbons of tape unwind before I can stop it. What else can I think? No other answer makes sense as I wind up the tape in painful slow motion. If my grandfather *had* survived, I wouldn't be here listening to their story.

I wouldn't be here at all.

There's little comfort in knowing that, but I'm so proud of them both, that my grandfather was a brave RAF pilot (I still can't grasp he was a duke) and a member of the Resistance, and because of his sacrifice, he also gave me life. *Maman* would never have met my father.

More than ever, I'm grateful for the life I have. And for the man who helped me uncover the truth about Sylvie Martone.

Before I turn the recording back on, I call Ridge.

My voice shakes as I ramble on about God knows what, hardly letting him get a word in, making no sense as I try to explain how Sylvie and Jock took down the Gestapo, that I can't bear to listen to anymore, and I wish he were here because I can't face Sylvie losing the man she loves.

Like I could never face losing *him*. His awful jokes... his wild streak... his friendship.

Then, before I break down completely, I click off.

Knowing that after my crazy, insane rambling and wearing my heart on my sleeve, our relationship will never be the same.

35

SYLVIE

FAREWELL, MY LOVE... I SHALL NEVER FORGET YOU

Paris
Summer 1944

With Herr Geller dead, I assume my life will no longer be a living hell.

I'm wrong.

The veracity of the German High Command to show the people of Paris they're still in control reaches a point of insanity in the weeks that follow.

Especially the Gestapo.

The stodgy man in the bowler hat who loved to taunt me was merely one of the ubiquitous men (including French) in black or brown leather trench coats. They push their power to the limit with a fierce intensity, continuing to round up Jews, arrest anyone on the word of an informant, and execute hostages.

When Jock returns to Paris, we decide it's best if we don't meet as often at my apartment. Yes, we've gotten away with our clandestine meetings under the cloak of darkness, but those threads are becoming worn and thin as the Nazis become more desperate. I don't go anywhere near Avenue Foch or my place in the Faubourg. Paris is like a pot of chicken stew boiling over with too many bones and not enough meat. The Abwehr or German counterintelligence has slim pickings to interrogate with everyone hiding under their bed. Waiting.

For the Allies to come. And the Germans to go.

Anyone can be picked up at any time.

Especially when Herr Geller's body is fished from the Seine.

I receive the news from an unlikely source. Emil. He's upset because the Gestapo man looked the other way on his black market deals in exchange for information. He twisted more than one arm to allow Emil freedom to get good distribution deals for his films. He's nervous about our latest film getting into the theaters. I think he's *more* nervous about American films invading France when this is over. He's been sitting on top of a candy mountain since we returned to Paris. Like so many sweet things made of spun sugar, they don't last. I find it humorous when Emil reminds me Goebbels once decreed he wanted French filmmakers to make 'light, frothy films'.

I'm proud of the films we made. We gave the French people hope and helped them deal with acute hunger and fear.

I refuse to let that fear resurface.

I remind myself Herr Geller was shot with his own revolver. The Gestapo have no one to arrest.

I'm not naïve. That hasn't stopped them from executing innocent people in retaliation for the killings of German soldiers. We don't know what they're planning, but as the Allied forces make their way across France, the Resistance is becoming more active and the Germans more insane in their attempts at keeping order.

Meanwhile, I walk through a dream of motherhood and listless nights... naming my child Madeleine after Sister Vincent's given name which she shared with me years ago. I shall never forget holding my daughter for the first time... kissing her little fingers and toes, hugging her close to me and feeling her small body tremble when I cried from the joy of holding her. I sang to her to calm us both and we fell asleep on the third... or was it the fourth chorus of *Frère Jacques*?

Even in my joy, I can't forget the horrors of this war, not knowing if Jock is dead or alive. I make a trip to the closed cinema as Fantine to find out from the leader Yves if there's word about Jock. Nothing. (*Did he pick up the SOE agents near Angers?* I wonder.) Instead I hear about barricades near Notre Dame, the Resistance fighters preparing to take over French police headquarters, and talk of the Allied forces entering Paris from the south.

How every grenade is checked, how every bullet counts.

It sends chills through me.

I go back to my apartment, trying to wait it out. In a moment of vanity, I look into the mirror. My figure is still a bit thick around the middle and my face is more angular, cheekbones higher. My dimple is more pronounced when I smile. Which I do a lot when I pick up my baby and sing to her. Madeleine is two months old and getting bigger every day. I continue to breastfeed when my body's rhythms are in tune, and when I can't, I secure milk and food from the staff of the Hôtel Ritz. Like many long-term guests, Emil paid for a room I can use for a year... a room on the Rue Cambon side away from the Nazi officers who commandeered the rooms with the best views on the Vendôme side. When I keep asking for milk, it doesn't take my favorite waiter long to figure out I had a child. Whether he believes the father is Captain Lunzer and he wants to save his own skin, or he genuinely likes me, I don't know.

Paris is starving and you have to do what you can to survive.

I also have to think about Madeleine's future. And her identity card.

The American Hospital of Paris doesn't register the birth of a child, the *mairie* does. With Bertrand's help, we forge a registration from the Neuilly-sur-Seine *mairie*, city hall, with my name as the mother and the name of the baby's father left blank. I can fill it in after the war is over.

But what if something happens to me?

Madeleine will be branded as the daughter of a Nazi sympathizer. I can't let that happen. Halette volunteers to go the *mairie* and say she had a baby with a German soldier and wants an anonymous birth registration. Both parents unknown.

A common occurrence. No questions asked.

I give thanks, even when I have to bend a few rules. Like rifling through the studio wardrobe department for baby clothes and blankets. Scarfs for diapers. Yes, I can buy what I need from the black market, but I'm careful not to purchase anything that would make someone suspicious. The fewer the number of people who know I have a child, the better. Luckily for me, the wardrobe girl is used to my visits and turns a blind eye, which makes me believe she's taking leftover wardrobe for her own children.

I don't judge her.

Movie star. Wardrobe girl.

We're both mothers and our children come first.

Halette also comes to my rescue with doll clothes. I insist she remain with me at the Trocadéro apartment and together we make the trek to the deserted doll and candle shop. The Germans weren't interested in doll clothes when they ransacked the place. We have fun dressing up my baby to look like the perfect doll she is, both of us laughing and playing with *ma petite* Madeleine.

A diversion.

A way to pretend everything is all right, when it isn't.

The news I've dreaded comes in the middle of the night... and I fall to pieces.

* * *

Three a.m.

A *knock* at the door.

I grab my white silk kimono, tie it around me, and rush to open it.

Jock, I pray?

No, it's—

'Bertrand, *mon cher ami*, what's wrong?'

'Let me in, Sylvie... quick before anyone sees.'

He rushes by me, almost knocking me down, and collapses on the divan. I gasp when I see a trail of blood on the parquet floor.

'You're wounded... let me get you some towels, hot water.' His left arm hangs limp. It's then I see a gash in his shoulder where a bullet entered and made a clean exit on the other side.

'Forget me. Get dressed and take the baby and Halette to the Hôtel Ritz. You'll be safe there.'

'Why, Bertrand?' I ask, not understanding. 'What happened?'

'We were set up. That SOE agent Jock picked up in Angers... he was an Abwehr agent. He used Jock to make contact with our Resistance group. He may have followed him here at some point before we rendezvoused in the Bois.'

'Where's Jock?' I take heavy breaths, my lungs bursting. The Bois de Boulogne is less than two kilometers from here. A twenty-minute walk. I don't have a good feeling about this. *Where is he?*

His face contorts with pain, but Bertrand won't look me in the eye.

'The agent kept insisting he could supply us with weapons to launch our offensive against the Nazis. We need guns, ammo. We met him at the designated spot deep in the wooded area not far from here where the arms would be delivered. When the tarpaulin-covered truck arrived, German soldiers jumped out and opened fire.'

My hand goes to my throat. 'A trap.'

'*Oui.* Before I knew what was happening, a bullet smashed into my shoulder. The Nazi was ready to finish me off when Jock lunged at him and the bastard fired his rifle.'

'Oh, God, no...' I sink to the floor. This is a bad dream, *it has to be.*

'Jock died protecting me, Sylvie.'

'No... I don't believe it... I can't.' I choke out a sob, then a groan so deep down inside me I can't catch my breath.

'Somehow I pulled myself to safety behind some bushes then escaped. The others didn't. They mowed them down and tossed grenades into the pile of bodies to cover up their tracks.' He holds me with his good arm, grabbing my hair in his fist, the blood from his shoulder wound seeping into the silk of my white kimono and turning it red.

His blood.

My pain.

Jock, mon amour... you can't leave me. Not now.

I can't move. My arms feel leaden, my legs numb. It's only when Bertrand squeezes me so tight and I feel pain do I come alive again, his hot breath blowing in my ear as he whispers, 'Jock loved you and the baby more than anything, Sylvie.' He gives me an uneasy smile. 'I wish it had been me who took that bullet.'

'Don't talk... I'll wake Halette and we'll get your wound cleaned up.' I struggle to keep my voice calm... a choking feeling in my throat... hands trembling as I check the wound again, then my whole body trembles. He can't die... *he can't!* Not both of them. What insanity rules this world when in the cause for freedom, the most willing to die for it always do?

A damning resolution to help this man sparks my muscles to move, do what must be done. Then I shall deal with this horrible pain that's left such a gaping hole in me.

I rush upstairs, my hand covering my mouth to keep from screaming, my bare feet tapping on the winding staircase, but my heart has flown somewhere else.

Out there in the Bois with my love.

I wake the sleeping girl, tell her Bertrand is wounded and needs our help. I say nothing about Jock... I can't, not when I don't believe it myself.

'Bertrand is a good man,' she says, her pretty face going pale. He's been like a father to her since Raoul was sent to the camp. 'I'll get some towels.'

I nod. Grab soap, a basin for hot water, then I rush down the staircase.

I'm too late.

Bloodspots trail to the open back door leading to the veranda.

He's gone.

* * *

My husband is dead.

The beloved rogue in the white dinner jacket with the black bow tie I met in Monte Carlo, the downed flier turned brave Resistance fighter, the father of my baby.

Caught in a mad skirmish with the enemy saving his friend. My friend.

My breath comes in short gasps, my hands shaking. I go through the motions, doing what Bertrand asked. He wouldn't risk coming here if he didn't believe I was in danger.

I sent Halette to the Hôtel Ritz last night before curfew with two suitcases filled with extra clothes, personal items. Disguises. (*Fantine, a nurse, and a nun.*) It's best if we're not seen together. If anyone asks, she's a lady's maid, bringing her mistress a change of wardrobe. She has the key. As long as she enters the hotel on the Rue Cambon side, she'll be fine.

I'm not so fine.

I need time to myself, to think. To grieve.

Yet all I can do is think about the sweltering August heat.

Suffocating, invasive, draining me so I can no longer feel. I don't want to feel. *I want to die.* I'm no longer the actress playing a part in a movement bigger than I am. I want nothing to do with this horrible, miserable war. I want to be a wife, a mother, a lover.

I want him back.

My husband.

But he's gone. Big, ugly sobs escape my throat. I want to claim his body, hold him one last time.

I can't. I can't even give him a proper burial. Now I know how the women in the boxcar felt, women on their way to a concentration camp which meant certain death for so many. For those who do survive, no closure. No place to lay a gentle rose and touch the cold stone bearing the name of your husband that warms under your fingertips. As if his spirt knows you're there and touches you with his enduring love. Telling you to be at peace.

For me, for those women, there is no peace.

This war stole that from us. I'm angry, bitter, and want to grab a pistol and join them at the barricades. Fight till the end... I want vengeance.

Until the sound of my baby's cry reaches my ears.

Not the anxious cry when she's hungry, the irritated cry when she's wet, but a deep, penetrating wail that begs me not to be bitter, not to hate, but to remember the love Jock and I had for each other that brought her into this world.

I pick up my dearest angel and rock her back and forth, my voice a harsh whisper as I hum to her. I kiss her chubby cheeks, nestle her close to my breast so she can hear my heartbeat as I take slow, steady breaths. Soon our hearts beat as one as mine did with Jock's. A time I shall remember always when in the face of war and hate, we owned that special place lovers do, a place when a deep, tender love finds a permanent place in the heart that can never be taken away.

I listen to her tiny breaths. She sleeps so soundly.

Perhaps that's a blessing.

Mais oui, perhaps it is, I tell myself as I pack a few things, my brain swirling with questions and new fears as dawn comes and brings with it more heartbreak.

* * *

'Don't lie to me, Sylvie, I know you're working with the Resistance.'

Emil.

Using a threat that once would have caused me to panic, but that young girl of sixteen, that insecure actress, they're both gone. I've changed. I'm the widow of a Resistance fighter, stronger now because of Jock.

I'm also hiding out.

I entered the Hôtel Ritz three days ago dressed in a light summer frock with a big brim straw hat, billowy scarf flying behind me as I walked quickly through the Rue Cambon entrance, past the bar, then took the tiny, oak-paneled lift to my floor. I made a point of tossing my long scarf over my shoulder as a diversion from the oversized carrying bag I clutched in my hand, praying the whole time Madelaine wouldn't wake up from her nap.

Earlier I wrapped my child in blankets and laid my lace veil over the carryall as one would do to a pram. Keeping the baby out of sight.

The staff ignored me. I'm not naïve to believe they don't see me. It's the hotel credo to *see, hear* everything that goes on while being discreet.

Emil's appearance will be duly noted.

'What do you want, Emil?'

I push aside the peachy chiffon curtain and look out the window down at the garden below in full bloom. A good sign? I hope so.

'You've got influence with the partisans to get me out of Paris before the Allies come.'

'No gas for your Citroën?' I toss back at him.

He ignores my sarcasm. 'You know I have to bend the rules to get my pictures made... and... well, not everyone respects my talents like you do.'

I snicker. 'Who'd did you rip off this time? Phony gold watches to the SS?'

'That's not funny, Sylvie. The Nazi staff at Avenue Foch are destroying files. What if they leave a few behind? I'm ruined. Or dead. Or both.'

I turn and see a man who is nothing more than broken shell, a man who for all the years I've known him, has never shown emotional attachment to anyone, anything.

Till now.

He begs me to remember our years together, how he discovered me, the hits we made. I let him sweat, as he twists his Panama hat in his hand, then get him to admit he's been working his black market connections to line his pockets with francs and Reichsmarks. That he got involved with a gang of thugs who were part of the French Gestapo, a network supplying Germans with luxury goods. He claims he knew nothing about their involvement with the SS, giving up Jews and betraying *résistants*.

'I know you tried to help Raoul and you're hiding his daughter. You must have connections with the Underground.'

How long has he known?

Somehow he'd put the pieces together. Does he know about Bertrand? I haven't seen *mon cher ami* since that night he came here, wounded. I'm grateful Halette isn't here to witness his spewing. I let her take Madeleine to the walled garden near the dining room so they could both get some fresh air.

'Why didn't you expose me?' I ask.

'Because I've always loved you like a daughter, Sylvie,' he says, tears in his eyes.

'*Oh, really?*' I roll my eyes.

'You don't believe me, but it's true. I have to get out of Paris before my dirty laundry list of sins falls into British and Americans hands.'

'And if I don't help you?' I want to know.

He puffs out his chest. 'Then you leave me no choice. I will report you to the Gestapo as a member of the SOE.'

Every muscle in my body tightens. The sudden racing of my pulse wipes out any rational logic I had. We both know it's not too late for the Gestapo to arrest me and take my baby. With the liberation of France in the wind, the SS is seeking out and executing SOE agents.

I try a different tactic.

'I have nothing to fear. The Gestapo won't believe you.'

Herr Geller is dead. That's in my favor.

'Are you willing to take that chance?' Emil says, smug. 'Or would you prefer I buy my way out of this mess when I give you up to the Allies, tell them how you collaborated with the enemy.'

'When the Allies come,' I insist, 'they'll believe me when I tell them about my work with the Resistance.'

'Will they? You always were too trusting, Sylvie, or else you never would have allied with an old bastard like me.'

* * *

I've always believed I controlled my destiny.

Unfortunately, Emil is right. I don't. I have no choice but to get him out of Paris. But how? Our Resistance movement has joined up with a bigger movement under General de Gaulle, I discover when I become Fantine (I don't explain to Halette, she doesn't ask, and I make the daring move to leave by the Vendôme entrance of the hotel swarming with Nazis too busy to notice an old woman with a limp).

I also find out Bertrand is dead.

In spite of the sizzling undercurrent in the city, the bells in the great cathedral remain silent till the fight is won, the amassing of arms and men around her graceful Gothic curves growing. I see none of it. Despair takes root in me along with an eerie wistfulness that makes me feel as if I'm floating. A passionate longing to go back to the way things were inhabits my soul for too brief a time. Then a loud sound zaps me out of it. For I can't escape the truth. I can't rid myself of the deep chill that seeps into the marrow of my bones.

Bertrand is dead... echoes in my head.

I'm struck again by an arrow to my heart when I go to the closed cinema and find Yves a block away painting over the license plate of a vehicle they commandeered for the fighting.

He tells me Bertrand lost too much blood and the wound became infected.

He died three days later.

I'm overcome with grief for a second time. I go numb. My mind, my body can't absorb it all at once. I will be forever grateful to this giant of a man with the heart of a saint.

The sad thing is, I never would have known about Bertrand's death if I hadn't come here to the closed cinema on a mission of mercy for Emil. I owe the director something for that.

Yves takes me to a man who knows about my exploits as Fantine. If I need exit papers for a friend, he says, that's good enough. I secure a false identity card for Emil using the photo from the original one he gave me, then meet him in the bar at the Hôtel Ritz, knowing I'll never see him again.

36

SYLVIE

PARIS AND THE TRICOLOR FLOWER

Paris
1944

I shall never forget the day the Americans liberate Paris.

To celebrate, Halette and I put red, white, and blue flowers in our hair and make a floral headband for my baby daughter. I grab a pair of old sunglasses to hide behind, then with Halette's arm linked through mine, the three of us head out, down the inner hall along the Vendôme side to the bottom floor and through the glass entryway. The hotel is filled with a flurry of curious guests, though no Germans (I heard later the Nazi officers were rounded up and kept at the Hôtel Majestic and made to sit on the cold floor scrunched together like trapped rats. I wish I could have been there).

Throngs of people fill the streets, waving the French tricolors, yelling *Vive Paris!*

The three of us wave and wave and wave as tanks and jeeps filled with Allied soldiers drive by, the American army marching along the Champs-Élysées. We didn't dare leave the safety of the hotel sooner, what with small arms fire all over the city and German snipers on rooftops, some in civilian clothes, making the streets dangerous. Some

German convoys trying to escape didn't make it. Machine gun firing, grenades... everywhere.

But today the Occupation comes to an end.

'When you're older, *ma petite*, I shall tell you about this day and how your papa was a brave Resistance fighter,' I promise her, 'and how he and men like him freed France.'

She coos with delight and then sneezes, but her eyes shine as she looks at me, waving her tiny hands around. She looks so adorable, I can't help but hug her tight, a strange feeling seeing far beyond today that gives me a chill.

What's to become of me now that the Allies are here? Everyone who knew about my work as a member of the Resistance – Jock, Bertrand, Emil – gone.

No one else knew me as Fantine. I'm merely a service number among thousands to the British Foreign Office, known to a Mr Peeps by the number I memorized.

What if the record is lost?

Then I have no proof.

I'll be labeled as a Nazi collaborator.

I shudder with an unbelievable chill, my blood running cold. I must find some way to prove my innocence. That I did what I did to free France... not with bullets and bombs, but under deep cover to gather intelligence that ultimately foiled the Nazis search for ultimate power over the French people.

After taking several deep breaths, I try to find the joy in today with my baby in my arms. I wave at Halette when a handsome American GI grabs her and hoists her up into his Jeep. She's smiling so big, her dark hair curly and shiny, her eyes grateful she escaped *la rafle*, the roundup of Jews, though her heart breaks. Still no word about Raoul.

I move off to the side, duck inside a café away from the crowd, grateful no one recognizes me.

I smile. How can they?

Who'd expect to see Sylvie Martone with a baby in her arms?

* * *

'Mademoiselle Sylvie... you're in danger!' Halette bursts into my hotel room late at night and stops short. Breathing heavy, her long hair loose and hanging limp. Her eyes blazing. 'You must leave Paris immediately or you'll be arrested.'

Hugging my baby closer to my chest, I study her and we both remain silent because there's a horrifying consequence to what she said if it's true.

I lose my child.

I lose her.

I lose my life.

'Are you certain my arrest is imminent?' I beg to know, shifting Madeleine from one hip to another. That once unpredictable, overwhelming fear hits me again, not from the Gestapo, but the French police.

'Yes. All day I've walked the boulevards filled with American troops and French protestors wanting to round up every collaborator and tar and feather them. Or worse.' She sweeps her hair off her face. 'Men are taken and shot. Women... a more humiliating experience.'

I can see she's embarrassed as she tells me she was stunned to find out from Resistance friends of her father my name is on the list. She never believed I was a Nazi collaborator, then realized I had connections to the Underground when I tried to help her father and arranged for her aunt and her children to escape France.

But others do.

All they see are my photos in the newspaper with an SS officer, dining with Nazis at cafés, not to mention the 'goodwill' trip I took to Berlin at Goebbels' request. These things don't sit well with the French police.

Word is out.

They're rounding up known Nazi collaborators, including celebrities. I could mount a defense detailing my work as Fantine to escape what they're calling *épuration légale*, purge. But by the time I cut through the red tape and contact the British Foreign Office, it may be too late. They're out for blood. Meanwhile, with no one left in Paris to corroborate my story, who will believe me?

'When are they coming?' I ask, my mind spinning.

'Tomorrow morning.'

I grip her by the shoulders. 'Any word of your father?'

She shakes her head. 'No. The Allies haven't liberated the camp, but there's a rumor the Nazi sent several prisoners to Dachau.'

'Oh, my dearest child...' My heart breaks for her.

'Papa would want me to go on... and to help you. We'll go to the Faubourg apartment.'

'No, the informing is worse than during the Occupation. I walked the boulevards in disguise yesterday when you were bathing Madeleine and I saw what's happening. The people want revenge. They'll recognize me. I'll be dragged through the streets, stripped, my head shaved, and God knows what they'll do to Madeleine, an innocent baby.' I think a moment. 'I have to leave Paris.'

'Where will you go?'

'Back to where I started, *ma chère* Halette.'

'The convent?'

I nod. '*Mais oui.*'

'What if someone there betrays you?'

I shake my head. 'The sisters will keep their silence, but even a small village like Ville Canfort-Terre is filled with partisans keen on revenge. Still, I have no choice. I have no gas for the Bugatti. I'll have to walk.'

Halette's eyes widen. 'A woman traveling alone. Won't that be dangerous?

I grin. 'Not for a nun.'

* * *

'Need a lift, Sister?'

'*Merci, monsieur*, I can walk,' I keep my head low so the American

GI can't see my face. Not that he'd recognize me, but I didn't have time to apply makeup. Merely the old pair of spectacles I wore with my nurse disguise.

'Hey, you speak English,' he says, grinning. 'Please, let me help you. I'm going to get into a heap of trouble back in Wichita if my mom finds out I didn't give a nun a ride.'

'Wichita?' I repeat.

'Kansas. Wheat, corn, plenty of corn. I'm full of corn, according to my fellow war correspondents.'

He drives along beside me as I plod along with Madeleine tied to my back, my suitcase in hand. I'm not the friendliest nun the soldier will ever meet. My back is aching and my feet are so swollen they won't slide into a pair of heels for weeks. But I can't let anything stop me, even the US Army. Our lives – Madeleine's and mine – depend on us reaching the convent. I've been walking for about three hours, stopping under a shady tree to feed my baby, then drink from the flask of water I brought with me. Thank God for those fancy meals at the Hôtel Ritz. I have plenty of milk, but I have about eight hours more of walking before I reach safe refuge. I'll have to stop and rest when night falls.

The soldier behind the wheel of the American Jeep won't give up and continues to drive alongside me.

I panic. *Have they found me?*

No, I believe the American is a gift from God.

'I'm a reporter with the *Wichita Sun* here to cover the liberation of Paris. You come from there, Sister?'

'*Oui*, by way of Belgium.'

I tell him how I made my way across the border after being hunted by the Nazis for helping the Resistance, then I came upon a dying woman on a farm who just gave birth. 'I'm taking the child to the convent at Ville Canfort-Terre, a village about fifty kilometers south from here.'

'Okay by me, Sister.' He stops the Jeep. 'I can drop you off on my way to Rambouillet.' He smiles. 'I'm on a mercy mission myself. I was on the road to liberate Paris with the others when I met a kid there about twelve and her little sister. Her mom sent them there to be safe. I promised I'd come back for them. How about you and me do God's work together?'

I give him a big smile. 'How can I say no?'

I hand him Madeleine and he makes a cozy spot for her on the backseat, then helps me into the Jeep. I feel such relief at finding help, I nearly collapse and miss a step.

I stumble. Grab my heavy, black woolen skirts.

And my glasses fall off.

The American catches me in his arms, then looks into my eyes and lets out a low whistle.

'Holy mackerel, Sister, you're beautiful.' He grins wide. 'Did anyone ever tell you that you oughta be in pictures?'

37

SYLVIE

THE LONG ROAD HOME

Ville Canfort-Terre, France
Summer 1950

My GI knight-in-shining armor never figured out who I was.

Of if he did, he didn't believe it.

A soft, cleansing rain pitter patters around me as I sit under the overhang in the garden and I reminisce about those days after the liberation of Paris. For me, the war ended the day I left the city. As far as the world knows, I escaped to Switzerland in August 1944. Instead I returned here to the convent where I raised my daughter in a role that's been my most challenging – disguised as a Belgian nun.

I shall be forever grateful to the Mother Superior – though she'll always be Sister Vincent to me – for taking me in. She's the only one who knows who I am.

And a young girl named Jeanne.

She came here not too long ago, but Madeleine took to her immediately and the thirteen-year-old adores her. I found her to be a great companion for my six-year-old daughter. Jeanne believes that it's God's will she's here to take care of Madeleine. I often watch the two of them playing in the convent garden, how Jeanne never lets her out of her sight even when they play hide and seek, peeking through her fingers so she won't lose her. How they laugh making mud pies, but she always makes sure Madeleine is cleaned up and sparkling for prayers. She reads books to her, teaches her how to count. *She was born to take the veil*, according to Sister Vincent who confided to me the girl's mother told her how, toward the end of the war, Jeanne would drop to her knees and pray on her rosary every time she heard an air raid siren, trying to calm others. She was seven. So I wasn't surprised when she protected Madeleine from a nosy visitor to the convent asking about her. Jeanne swore on her rosary she was her baby sister.

I felt certain I could trust her, so I shared my secret with her.

I've never regretted my decision.

She's been a great help to me.

So much so, I showed her the photo of me from 1940 along with the heart-shaped diamond faux pin and the lace veil I intend to give to my daughter when she's older.

Dressed in my nun robes, I watch the two girls coloring in books with crayons while the Dutch doll I gave my daughter so long ago observes with her doll-sized cup of tea. Meanwhile, I finish assembling my notes, what I want to say when I make my phone call and tell the press about Fantine and the tape recordings, as well as the script for *Angeline*, the photos, newspaper clippings, and home movies I shot in Paris in 1943... I can't look at them and not shudder.

Every item is key to telling my story.

Jeanne and I placed them in the chateau dungeon where no one ever ventures these days, except for a noble lady ghost. It will give her something to guard, though I shall leave clues for Madeleine if I'm not successful in my quest and anything happens to me.

I finish my sweet lily flower tea... yes, I've remained sober, though my head aches from the pressure, the weeks it's taken me to put all this material together. But it's done. I intend to take my story to the *France-Soir* and have them publish it to gain the ear of the British government to listen to my plea.

God knows I've tried everything else.

After the war, I attempted to clear my name through the proper channels, but my letters to the SOE F (French) Section in England come back unopened. I'm reluctant to keep writing to them and reveal the service number assigned to me until I make legitimate contact with someone I can trust.

The *Mr Peeps* Jock told me about.

As a precaution, I wrote the service number down for Madeleine in a place where she'll see it.

Till then, I'm of the mind there are forces at work in London still unraveling the mounds of paperwork and classified documents from the war. I thought about going to England in person, but that would create an international incident since I'm officially wanted by the French police.

I tried to contact Jock's sister Winnie, but according to the society pages, she died in childbirth soon after the war ended. I brushed away tears when I read that, remembering the winsome young girl so full of life in Monte Carlo. And from what I understand, Jock's title has since been inherited by a male relative whose direct lineage traces back two generations.

Before I go into the village to make my long-distance phone call to the Paris newspaper (I want to tell my story without anyone at the convent overhearing me), I make one final recording.

About the film I shot that day on the train back from Berlin. About my shoes and why I never scraped off the mud. I pray in a small way, it brings peace to those who lost someone.

It's still raining when I change into a blouse, skirt, headscarf, and sunglasses so as not to attract attention dressed as a nun.

My fan club is a different story.

'You look pretty, *Maman*.'

Madeleine races up to me and shows me the pages she's colored with Jeanne behind her.

'*Merci, mon enfant*. Never forget, *ta maman* loves you.'

'I love you, too.'

She wraps her arms around me and the warmth of her fills me with courage.

'Now be a good girl and stay with Jeanne till I get back.'

Jeanne smiles at me, her soft brown hair blowing in her face. She confided to me she'll enter the religious life as a postulant when she's fifteen. She's praying to God the name she picked will be granted by the Mother Superior. When she takes the veil, Jeanne wants to be called Sister Rose-Celine. Knowing Sister Vincent, I'm sure it will.

I pray I have good news for them when I return.

I take one last look at my little girl waving at me, and then open the door to the world outside the convent to what I hope will be a new life.

Where I can once again walk the streets... tall and proud.

And tell everyone I'm Sylvie Martone.

Actress.

38

JULIANA

SEARCHING FOR BURIED TREASURE... AND INTELLIGENCE

Ville Canfort-Terre, France
Present Day

I can't stop the flow of tears, the heartbreak and all-encompassing grief that overtakes me when I hear Sylvie mention she's going into town to make a phone call to the press and tell her story.

Then I hear her take a deep breath and say she has one final message.

I turn off the tape recorder, unable to listen to any more. Not now... later. I go through the despair of not only losing my mom again, but my grandmother, too.

I try to wrap my head around this moment, tamp down my emotions before I go on a crying jag because it's up to me to finish the journey Sylvie began.

I try texting Ridge, but he's not answering me or picking up his phone.

I want to tell him everything, ask his advice. I know he's worried about me. I sounded awful the last time I called, telling him about how Jock died and pouring my heart out to him like a reality show contestant. I've never done that before. I hope nothing's wrong. I check the time. It's too early to call his office.

I'll try again later.

I'm sure he has a good reason for not picking up my calls.

With a heavy heart, I start sketching on a notepad to calm my nerves. I draw Sylvie in costume as Fantine, then as the glamorous film star in the photo. Sketching is good for my soul and my mental coping, though it would be better if Ridge were here, my anchor.

I sigh. God, I miss him.

Feeling lonely, I make myself a cup of tea, then look at the two sketches side by side.

The two sides of Sylvie Martone. Only I know the truth.

I can surmise what happened the day Sylvie was killed – though no one will ever know for sure. On a hunch, I go into the village and make a visit to the newspaper now digital. They're kind enough to allow me to go through their archives around the time Sylvie died.

I take a step back in my mind, keeping my emotions at bay when I find a small 'item' placed in the 'people about town' section that mentions how a die-hard movie fan *swore* she saw the infamous *Sylvie Martone walking through the village like she was a tourist, and how dare she.*

No one believed the woman, though she insisted she was an extra in a film Sylvie shot in Versailles and she recognized the actress wearing a headscarf and sunglasses.

I feel the panic Sylvie must have felt when the woman confronted her. The sudden fear everything she'd taken great care to conceal could be lost in a second along with her plan to clear herself. I can't forget this was 1950 and scars from the war were still fresh in people's hearts.

Driving back to the convent, I conjure up quick, animated pencil sketches in my mind, sketches showing Sylvie frightened for the safety of her child... knowing she'd lose her if they found the actress... racing back to the convent in the old motorcar the nuns used, rain pounding on the windshield. She's maddeningly fearful, upset, her hands sweaty on the wheel, vision blurring through her tears as she swerves to avoid hitting something on the wet road... then her car skids out of control and a sickening, awful smashing sound fills her ears when she crashes into the old chestnut tree, killing her instantly.

I slam on the brakes.

My heart pounds so fast, I feel faint.

Then I cry my eyes out.

* * *

'You have a visitor, *Mademoiselle* Juliana.'

Sister Rose-Celine speeds into the garden on her motorized scooter like she's fueled by rockets. She's beaming with the biggest smile on her face. I put down my notebook, curious. I've been sitting here for what seems like hours, staring at my notes, trying to get my head on.

'A visitor? Who—'

'Hey... Juliana.'

I jump up, my heart pounding when I see Ridge come out of the shadowy alcove. I've never been so happy to see him, aching to grab him and, in a moment of whimsy that surprises me, wanting him to hold me in his strong arms.

I hold back... barely. 'I've been trying to reach you.'

'My phone was on airplane mode, then when I landed in Paris, your phone was off.'

'And you couldn't use your cell while you were driving here.' I grin, then tell him I was in the village looking up info on Sylvie at the newspaper office. 'The reception was spotty so I turned it off.'

'I didn't leave you a message because I wanted to surprise you... and know you're okay.' He heaves out a heavy breath. 'After the last time we talked... well, I knew you needed me, so I booked a flight and got here as fast as I could.' Ridge looks over at Sister Rose-Celine, who is nodding her head and making the sign of a 'heart' with gnarled fingers. I try to shush her, waving my hands around. She just smiles. Does she know something I don't? 'The sister explained to me what you two have been up to. How can I help?'

'Sit down, Ridge, and have a cup of the sisters' lily flower tea while I tell you the most extraordinary story about a true daughter of France.'

* * *

Over the next two days, the three of us huddle together over Sylvie's diary, notes, photos, and recordings, like generals planning an invasion. We take pictures of everything we lay out in the convent library on two card tables and add sticky notes showing the timeline of what Sylvie did during the war.

Working with Jock and Bertrand and helping the evaders as Fantine.

Her films to boost the morale of the French people.

Saving Raoul's family and Halette.

I tell Ridge that Bertrand was her handler, how he was killed before the liberation of Paris but according to Jock, Sylvie's work in the SOE F Section was reported to a British officer known as *Mr. Peeps.*

A play on the name of the famous seventeenth-century diarist? I wonder.

Then Ridge goes into work mode and we unravel the red tape, enlisting the help of a London solicitor who contacts the British Foreign Office. The official tells us what Sylvie didn't know when she made the recordings was that many files in London SOE headquarters were being deleted. And what wasn't destroyed was highly confidential because of the extremely sensitive nature of the operations and was archived.

He asks for details of everything we know about Sylvie and then we send him the pictures of what we uncovered about her activities during the war.

Then we wait...

The Mother Superior is wonderful and so understanding, allowing Ridge to stay here at the convent with me (he charms her and every sister he sees). I show Ridge around the chateau (he loves the dungeon) with Sister Rose-Celine adding her memories of Sylvie and *Maman*. Then we share a special moment when we visit Sylvie's grave here on the grounds with Sister Rose-Celine. The headstone is blank, but decorated with a beautiful marble carving showing an angel pinching a little girl's cheek. Just like Sister Vincent said to a young Sylvie a century ago. The plot is a living garden with gorgeous flowers tended to by the nuns, including the Canfort Lily the sisters grow to make their lily flower tea. A tribute to the beautiful actress and her memory. We bow our heads, the three of us holding hands as we say a prayer.

Then we get the news we're waiting for.

* * *

Ridge and I listen to the head of the Foreign Office in London telling us on Skype how he unraveled years of red tape and found information in the file of Bertrand D'Artois verifying he recruited an agent known as 'Fantine'. A Frenchwoman who worked for the SOE F Section and together they were part of a Resistance group active in Paris from 1942 to 1944.

There's no record of Fantine's real identity.

Her personal file was lost.

I'm crushed. So is Ridge. And Sister Rose-Celine. We got so close...

'Back to the drawing board,' Ridge says, squeezing my hand. The fierce look in his eye tells me he won't give up the quest.

'Fantine *has* to be Sylvie Martone,' I plead to the British official, who looks as disappointed as we are. 'She detailed everything Fantine did, the meetings at the closed cinema, her missions, how she saved the RAF flier she names as 'Jock' from the hands of the SS.'

'I agree, Miss Chastain, but without verifiable proof, I can't sanction an official announcement Miss Martone was one of our agents.' A beat, then: 'By the way, I don't recall seeing a service number for Fantine on the records you sent. That could help locate her file since several high-profile agents were listed only by their service number.'

Service number.

The pinging that goes off in my brain is unreal. I get chills all over.

I'm merely a service number among thousands to the British Foreign Office, Sylvie said on the tape, *known to a Mr Peeps by a number I memorized.*

'Sylvie mentioned a service number on one of her tape recordings,' I manage to get the words out, 'but she never said what it was.'

'Did she say anything else?' Ridge says, his voice calm, but I can tell he's as nervous as I am.

I wrote the service number down for Madeleine in a place where she'll see it.

'Yes, she wrote it down where my mother would see it...' I close my eyes, straining my brain to work overtime. 'But my mother had nothing that belonged to Sylvie except...'

'Except what, Juliana?' Ridge asks. 'Take your time... think.'

Then it hits me.

'The black and white photo. I remember seeing numbers written on it... it can't be that simple, can it?'

It is. I grab the photo from the items we categorized and there written in white ink is her service number. The truth was there all the time, but I couldn't see it until I took the journey with Sylvie to the end.

I read the number slowly to the British official, then we wait... again.

* * *

After consuming two pots of lily flower tea to soothe our frazzled nerves, we watch the entire thing unfold over Skype when the British official opens the numbered file and shows Ridge, Sister Rose-Celine, and me the contents.

Documents, notes revealing information with the numerous missions Sylvie carried out against the Nazis and the names of the evaders (Allied pilots) she saved from capture, photos, identity cards, along with dates and places.

And a clear, typed notation stating Fantine was the code name for *Sylvie Martone, French actress.*

The information revealing her real identity lay buried in a file unopened since the war. Mr Peeps was more than one person, the official tells us, and when the war ended, the man in that position at the time shoved the file into a square box marked *Closed* because Bertrand died in Paris at the hands of the Nazis. Many of his agents, including Fantine, were thought to have met the same fate.

I can't contain myself. I jump up and down, kiss Ridge and he kisses me back, which stuns me for a moment. The look in his eyes says he's been wanting to do that for a long time. I kiss him again and he picks me up and swings me around, much to the delight of Sister Rose-Celine. She claps her hands with glee, the three of us thrilled with this new information that proves Sylvie *was* working for the Resistance. Disguised as the inimitable Fantine with her derring-do, courage, and perseverance, she was a brave fighter and helped free France from the Nazis.

The British official assures us his London department will document everything in the file and send me a copy. Along with the tapes and the diary I uncovered, the world will soon know the truth.

Sylvie Martone did *not* collaborate with the Nazis.

Any association she had with them was part of her work as an SOE agent.

'I can't believe it's over,' I tell Ridge, holding his hand in mine. 'Time for us to go home and...'

And what?

I leave the rest unsaid. I've changed since I came here to learn more about Sylvie, who she was, who she loved... I see my life differently.

I also see Ridge differently.

I spy him checking me out, a confident grin curving over his lips, his eyes deepening into a smoldering black with a twist of fire sparking in his pupils. His glance is penetrating, sensual, and he makes no attempt to hide it. Not anymore.

What's taken me so long to realize I'm in love with this man?

Because I'm like *ma grand-mère*, proud and stubborn and so set on doing things my way, I almost lost him. I spent my whole life building a career, not opening up my heart, afraid if I did so, I'd get hurt like *Maman*. Sylvie showed me that with the sacrifices she made, and though she lost Jock under the most horrible of circumstances, she never stopped loving him. What tears me apart is they died so young... Sylvie wasn't much older than I am.

My heart wrenches at the thought... then my brain puts out an alert not to waste one more moment without letting Ridge know I feel.

'Don't forget,' I tell him, testing the waters, 'we have a date.'

'There's nothing I want more, Juliana.' When did his voice get so sexy? Or have I been ignoring that because his low, gravelly tones do wonders for my lonely heart.

Then everything falls into place when his eyes hold mine with an intimacy that opens doors to a place I never would have imagined. I know what I have to do.

I swallow, then drag in a whopping breath before I change my mind.

'Okay, you big hunk of man...' I exhale, pulling up my courage. 'I've got something to say and you'd better prepare yourself.'

'I'm ready.'

'I love you... oh, not just best-friends-love, but throw-caution-to-the-wind, passionate, forever love.' I exhale, a shudder going through me. 'There. I said it.'

'And I love you, Juliana.' He pulls me into his arms. He's smiling big. 'If you didn't say it soon, I was about to carry you off to that dungeon and lock you up until you did.'

My eyes widen. 'Seriously?'

He grins. 'Seriously.'

Laughing and hugging, we kiss again (not too passionate – Sister

Rose-Celine is watching and loving every minute) before we settle into a comfortable rhythm making notes on what we're going to do to honor Sylvie. Together. I couldn't be happier. No one except Ridge has ever been here for me in so many ways I can't count them all, except the one that counts the most. He never gave up on me, believing in his heart someday this independent, perfection-driven artist would open her eyes and see what was there all along.

His love shining right at me.

Merci, Sylvie, for giving me the courage to find love. I think somehow you know... that this journey spans both the past and present with your words and recordings as a bridge for us to help each other.

To find redemption for you.

And love for me.

With Maman in the middle, holding onto both of us.

* * *

I hold his hand tight as Ridge hears Sylvie's lovely voice while we listen to my grandmother's last recorded words, his smile warm and caring as she talks about the home movie film she shot that day coming back from Berlin... how she never had it developed because she was fearful she'd put her entire operation at risk if it was discovered. Men and women would die if her cover was blown.

You may wonder why, ma petite, I never removed the mud from my black suede pumps.

I couldn't bear to tear away the human trace of survival that attached itself to me.

I found several scraps of paper that day near the boxcar. I picked them up, curious, and put them in my pocket. Later, I saw they each contained an address, a railcar number.

Pieces of hope that someone would find them and tell their loved ones where they'd gone. If you look in my black jacket pocket, you'll find the papers.

I pray I shall have the chance to clear my name and do what is right. If not, I leave it to you to deliver these messages of hope.

The world must never forget.

I hold back a tear, vowing to do as *ma grand-mère* wished, then let myself go as Ridge wraps his arms around me and I sob into his chest.

Sylvie died the day she recorded that message.

39

JULIANA
TO SYLVIE WITH LOVE

Paris, France
Present Day

After a whirlwind year of working to clear Sylvie's name and restore her reputation *and* planning our future together, it's good to be back in Paris.

The sun is shining down on the Champs-Élysées making it shimmer like a golden trail, welcoming Ridge and me. The chestnut trees are in bloom, the eternal perfume unique to the city on the Seine acting as a bridge from the past to the present. I close my eyes and when I breathe in the scent, I see the dark days of 1940 and the German soldiers goose-stepping... then August 1944... and Sylvie and her baby watching the liberation of the city with the Allied troops parading down the boulevard with free French citizens cheering them.

I swear I see my grandmother with red, white, and blue flowers in her hair waving to me.

Today is your day, Sylvie.

Ridge and I have returned here for a film festival showcasing Sylvie's films at the old Rex Theater, featuring her silent *Ninette* films along with *Angeline* and *Le Masque de Velours de Versailles*.

And the home movie film she shot that day in 1943 returning to Paris from Berlin.

I'm amazed at the reception this short film has received. The outpouring of support from the families of Holocaust survivors after the story went viral on social media when we published the messages on the scraps of paper online. So many people swear they knew someone in that boxcar filled with prisoners, a testament to the world never to forget, and a silent tribute to the friends Sylvie couldn't save... Raoul and Bertrand.

And the love of her life, Jock.

Although I found no letters between Sylvie and Jock (I assume she destroyed them during the war to protect him from scandal), we unmasked his identity through an unusual source and later confirmed it through his SOE file.

I'm related to the current Duke of Greychurch.

Me, the girl so desperate to find her roots.

Sylvie and Jock never legally married, but we unearthed his identity when we got permission to examine the personal journal Father Armand kept during the war archived with other documents in a chateau outside Paris. He was quite a prolific writer and his journal is considered an important source documenting religious life during the Occupation. We discovered a written notation about a marriage he performed in 1944 between the actress Sylvie Martone and British flier, John Lawrence Revell. I imagine the priest had a soft spot for Sylvie and wanted to keep a record for her to claim as proof after the war. Unfortunately, he died from a sniper's bullet giving last rites to a fallen Resistance fighter during the skirmishes that blasted through the city in August 1944.

Still, the handwritten record is proof enough for the duke's solicitor to arrange for an upcoming visit for Ridge and me to meet His Grace and tour Kyretree Castle.

I can't wait.

In the months following, we work with organizers in France to set up the film festival here in Paris and arrange to have special guests from British secret intelligence and the French government along with film executives to talk about what Sylvie did during the war.

The response is unbelievable.

The film festival sells out online in less than three hours.

I vow the sacrifice of my grandmother and all the brave men and women who fought against the Nazi regime will be remembered. Ridge and I start a nonprofit foundation in Sylvie's name to honor them.

Sister Rose-Celine is unable to make the trip to Paris, but she sends me a beautiful message along with a photo of her with my grandmother and *Maman*. And the Dutch doll. *Maman* had kept it for years and gave it to the sister as a parting gift. Hearing Sylvie speak about the doll jogged her memory.

I shall treasure them always.

I wish *Maman* could be here with us as we watch the beautiful Sylvie Martone bring Ninette to life on the silver screen. Her youthful joy and mischievous glint in her eye make us smile when she rescues the orphans from the devil, like she did years later when she saved Jock, Raoul's family, and Halette, and so many downed fliers from capture by the Nazis.

I feel their spirits here with us as we sit in the dark holding hands, our work done.

Then it's time for us to go back to our lives. I'm busy working on the costume designs for the second season of the flight attendant series and Ridge continues with his archival work. And driving me around the backlot on his motorcycle.

We'll always have Paris... and each other.

Ridge and I can't wait to tie the knot. I insist on wearing Sylvie's lace veil and design my white wedding dress to match the one in her photo.

And for something old, I wear the heart-shaped diamond pin fastened to my gown.

Soon after, I have to give up riding on Ridge's motorcycle when I find out I'm pregnant. We're blessed several months later with a daughter.

We name her Sylvie.

A joyous new beginning and a fitting tribute to the fabulous woman who was once a spy named Fantine. My grandmother.

Sylvie Martone, actress.

You will never be forgotten.

ACKNOWLEDGMENTS

I find writing about love and war requires not only a tugging at the heart, but a clear understanding of the events of the time. And in the case of *The Resistance Girl*, the movies.

Ever since I was a kid, the films of the Second World War held a special fascination for me. I sat mesmerized by Bogie and Ingrid in Paris, stories on the American home front, and the bravery of the women who dared to rise up against the Nazi war machine from France to Norway. Many films mirrored the events taking place. (Casablanca premiered in New York City soon after the Allies invaded North Africa in November 1942.)

But what was going on behind the scenes when these films were made? Especially in France when it was occupied by the Germans. Were the actors paid by the Nazis to make films? If so, why did they do it?

I've always wanted to write about a Parisian actress caught up in the chaos and the choices she made that put her in jeopardy when the Germans came to Paris in June 1940. Sylvie Martone, French cinema star, has been simmering in my brain for a long time, but to understand why she made those choices, I had to go back to her roots... how she started out in silent films, what sacrifices she made to get where she was in her career. So when the French film industry started up again in 1941, she had a choice to make: go along with the Nazis or fight them. Which would she choose? That's the dilemma faced by Sylvie. How she handles it is the crux of my story. I also needed a modern point of view... a young American woman who stumbles upon Sylvie's past and discovers it's linked to her own roots.

Aligning the lives of these two women was an undertaking I never could have accomplished without the excellent guidance of my editor, Nia Beynon. Her patience and enthusiasm to help me bring alive this part of history was amazing, her suggestions invaluable, and her encouragement heartfelt.

I also want to thank Dushi Horti, my hardworking copy editor who asks me the difficult questions, and Candida Bradford, my fabulous proofreader, who goes over my manuscripts with a loving hand and a sharp eye, along with the outstanding work of Becky Glibbery, my cover designer, who brought Paris during the Occupation to life with her lovely cover. And to Amanda Ridout and everyone at Team Boldwood, who make my dreams of telling my stories a reality.

To write this story, I also drew upon my experiences working in the film industry writing scripts and as a foreign tour guide for a major movie studio. And my childhood memory of a mysterious woman with dark hair and wearing a pearl necklace who gave me my first pair of tap shoes. A special thank you to my grandmother, whose glamorous life traveling the theatrical circuit as a ballroom and cabaret dancer inspired Sylvie's story.

MORE FROM JINA BACARR

We hope you enjoyed reading *The Resistance Girl*. If you did, please leave a review.

If you'd like to gift a copy, this book is also available as an ebook, digital audio download and audiobook CD.

Sign up to Jina Bacarr's mailing list for news, competitions and updates on future books.

http://bit.ly/JinaBacarrNewsletter

The Runaway Girl, another glorious historical romance from Jina Bacarr, is available to order now.

ABOUT THE AUTHOR

Jina Bacarr is a US-based historical romance author of over 10 previous books. She has been a screenwriter, journalist and news reporter, but now writes full-time and lives in LA. Jina's novels have been sold in 9 territories.

Visit Jina's website: https://jinabacarr.wordpress.com/

Follow Jina on social media:

facebook.com/JinaBacarr.author

twitter.com/JinaBacarr

instagram.com/jinabacarr

bookbub.com/authors/jina-bacarr

ABOUT BOLDWOOD BOOKS

Boldwood Books is a fiction publishing company seeking out the best stories from around the world.

Find out more at www.boldwoodbooks.com

Sign up to the Book and Tonic newsletter for news, offers and competitions from Boldwood Books!

http://www.bit.ly/bookandtonic

We'd love to hear from you, follow us on social media:

facebook.com/BookandTonic
twitter.com/BoldwoodBooks
instagram.com/BookandTonic

Made in the USA
Coppell, TX
03 January 2023

10273875R00197